Praise for Jo Spain

'An intriguing Rubik's cube of a novel. I absolutely loved it'
Liz Nugent

'Wonderfully drawn and more secrets and motives than
you can shake a stick at. Loved, loved, loved'
Caz Frear

'A book to sink into'
Dervla McTiernan

'Enthralling and razor-sharp'
JP Delaney

'A really cracking read'
B. A. Paris

'Brutal and brilliant'
Fiona Cummins

'Clever twists and cracking dialogue make
it hard to put down'
The Times

'Gives a certain Ms Christie a run for her money'
Sunday Mirror

'A brilliantly dark tale'
Mail on Sunday

'Keeps you gripped until the end'
Prima

D1589162

After the Fire

Jo Spain is a full-time writer and screenwriter. Her first novel, *With Our Blessing*, was one of seven books shortlisted in the Richard and Judy Search for a Bestseller competition and her first psychological thriller, *The Confession*, was a number one bestseller in Ireland. Jo co-wrote the ground-breaking television series *Taken Down*, which first broadcast in Ireland in 2018. She's now working on multiple European television projects. Jo lives in Dublin with her husband and their four young children.

After the Fire

JO SPAIN

Quercus

First published in Great Britain in 2020 by Quercus
This paperback edition published in 2021 by

Quercus Editions Ltd
Carmelite House
50 Victoria Embankment
London EC4Y 0DZ

An Hachette UK company

A CIP catalogue record for this book is available
from the British Library

PB ISBN 978 1 52940 031 1
EB ISBN 978 1 52940 032 8

10 9 8 7 6 5 4 3 2 1

Typeset by Jouve (UK), Milton Keynes

Printed and bound in Great Britain by Clays Ltd, Elcograf S.p.A.

Papers used by Quercus are from well-managed
forests and other responsible sources.

In memory of Larry Doyle, a true intellect and a good man

Dublin, July, 2017

FRIDAY

Nobody who sees her that morning will forget her.

Most people react as you'd expect.

Embarrassed, uncomfortable, trying not to make eye contact.

But the attractive young woman draws their gaze.

Hard not to.

She's walking down a city street, naked, on what will transpire to be the hottest day of the year.

It's barely 11 a.m., and the temperature has already hit twenty-six degrees Celsius.

The town is nowhere near its normal Friday morning shopping capacity. Most of the city's citizens are headed to the beaches, not Brown Thomas.

Every store has thrown its doors open; the whirring fans lure hardcore consumers in for temporary relief.

Some teenage boys, en route to the docks to cool off, titter amongst themselves. They hold up smartphones and capture the woman's vulnerability and their own stupidity.

The braver ones make their voices heard.

Nice rack, gorgeous.

It's just fun, for them.

Most people presume she's mentally ill. They fear if they offer help, she'll lash out, drawing them into this mortifying episode.

Her brown eyes are blank; she blinks for a little longer than normal each time, almost as if she's on the cusp of sleep. Her dark hair is tangled. Her skin is red and blotchy. Her body is filthy, not just the soles of her feet, which – in addition to the black dirt embedded on the skin – are cut and scratched, leaving minuscule traces of blood on the otherwise dry pavement behind her.

Some people turn away in an effort to protect her privacy. A handful of others, women mainly, ask if she's okay.

She keeps walking, seeing nobody, hearing nothing.

Three older women take it upon themselves to actively intervene.

Yes, the young woman might be sick in her mind.

Or somebody might have done this to her; stripped her of her clothing and dignity. Hurt her. Her husband or boyfriend, maybe. It happens.

She comes to a halt outside a pharmacy when the women block her path. A young, bulky security guard looks on. He's tired and cranky. His job is to watch the junkies when – if – they are allowed in. He has to monitor the teenagers too, especially the girls, who covet shiny lip gloss with almost the same blind desire as the drug users who plead for something to stop the itching. He was expecting today to be quiet. Fancied getting himself an ice cream by twelve, and a cool beer with lunch at two.

The security guard wants nothing to do with this. He refuses to engage with the girl's saviours, even though one of them, a tiny woman in her seventies, remonstrates with him.

'Are you going to call the guards?' she says, fanning herself with her hand. 'Do something, you great, useless lump.'

'Does he understand English?' one of the other women says, an eighty-year-old with large glasses and milky eyes.

'Do *you* speak English?' The third woman speaks directly to the naked girl, gently, coaxing. This woman is the youngest of the trio of rescuers, a sprightly sixty-year-old, but with enough life lived to know how to read a situation.

The young woman doesn't answer. The sixty-year-old takes a cardigan from a wheeled shopping bag and places it around the girl's shoulders, a small attempt to shield her.

'You poor thing,' the sixty-year-old says. 'What happened to you?'

The young woman trembles, eyelashes sweeping up, down, up, down.

The black filth on her body, the three women realise, is not ordinary dirt at all. It's soot and ash.

The young woman's skin is not red from the sun. It's been scorched, by fire.

And then the young woman looks around her; notices for the first time the street; the cardigan she's been gifted; then, finally, fixes her eyes on the face of the woman directly in front of her.

'The baby,' she says, her voice accented, but the words clear. 'I couldn't save the baby.'

CHAPTER 1

'What about the Gresham? They do a lovely steak. I quite fancy a steak.'

Tom was already mentally pairing the glass of red wine he planned to order alongside a medium-rare sirloin; he could almost smell the tang of the alcohol in his nose, taste the succulent, meaty juices on his tongue.

Most importantly, it would be cool. The Gresham's management had installed air con, bless their strategic souls.

Maria, his daughter, shook her head impatiently.

'Dad, I'm up to ninety. I told you when you said you were coming in, it's a sandwich in the canteen or nothing. You're lucky you have me at all. I'm a junior doctor and a good thirty years off leisurely lunches.'

She frowned, the tiny lines that normally appeared on her pretty face when she laughed now showing themselves as stress.

Inwardly, Tom sighed. Outwardly, he smiled benignly.

'I'm sure it will be the nicest sandwich I've ever had,' he said.

Maria strode at speed down the hospital corridor, her soft pumps making no noise on the linoleum floor, her brown ponytail swinging from side to side. Her hair was longer than she'd had it in a long time. No time to get it cut, her father guessed.

The last time she'd moved this quickly ahead of him, looking like that, was when she was five and he and Louise had brought her on her first foreign holiday. Maria had marched through the airport, ponytail swinging, announcing that they were getting the plane, that everybody needed to make way and that she'd keep her fingers crossed their planes wouldn't crash. Cute, and an indicator of the determined person she would become.

At least now, Tom was able to keep up, something he would *definitely* not relay to his wife Louise, because it would only provoke an *I told you so*. After years of threatening, she'd finally got him from the couch to 5K, and become unbearably satisfied with herself in the process.

Tom stood aside to let two hot, puffing, heavily pregnant women pass through the door which bore a handwritten sign clearly declaring it the entry point to the staff canteen.

'They going the right way?' he asked Maria.

'Diabetes tests,' she said. 'They've been fasting and drinking Lucozade all morning while their bloods were taken. We make them have tea and toast under supervision so they don't collapse on the way home.'

'As long as it's not our toast,' Tom said.

Maria laughed and Tom was happy to see her relax.

'Oh, I can treat you to more than toast,' she said.

One limp, thin ham sandwich and a lukewarm Coke later, and Tom was mentally planning a solo trip to the restaurant in the Gresham Hotel.

'Jesus, how do you stay standing?' he asked his daughter. 'The hours you work, they should have you on three-course meals for lunch and dinner.'

'Caffeine and sugar,' Maria said.

Tom watched as she offered up the evidence, emptying three

sugar sachets into a thick black coffee. She had perpetual bags under her eyes these days, but he couldn't deny she seemed content with her new, busy life, despite the stress. It might have been the doctoring route she'd taken – obstetrics. If Tom was forced to work at the coalface of medicine, he reckoned welcoming new babies into the world wasn't the worst option.

'So, Cáit is with you and Mam tonight,' Maria said, stirring her unhealthy concoction. 'Her dad will pick her up tomorrow and then I'm back on nights so I'll have her on the weekdays. You and Mam should go somewhere. I'm sure that child of mine has you run ragged.'

'Cáit's grand,' Tom said. 'We're redecorating her room at ours, I hear. A vat of pink paint is sitting on our landing, in any case.'

Maria smiled, but she was already distracted. Another medic approached. Tom guessed she was a midwife, based on the white uniform smock. She apologised for interrupting.

'I paged the consultant but he's elbow-deep in a C-section,' the midwife said. 'I think my patient's baby is just OP but if you can have a look, Dr Reynolds? She's pushed for eight hours and if she doesn't make some progress, we might need to get her to theatre.'

Tom sat back, realising it was the first time he'd heard Maria referred to as Dr Reynolds in a professional setting.

He grinned, that feeling of a job well done creeping up on him. Maria hadn't always been the easiest teen but her parents had got her over the line. Well, Louise, mainly.

As Dr Reynolds and the midwife discussed their patient, Tom's ears picked up the conversations around him. He couldn't help it; the detective in him refused to play administrator.

He'd taken the top job at the National Bureau of Crime Investigation, chief superintendent, just over two years ago and it wasn't the slightest exaggeration to say he missed his work on the ground.

His role these days consisted of fighting top brass for more resources, while trying to keep all the balls in the air as crime rates soared to his front and a continual cascade of friendly fire rained down from behind.

Paper, paper, goddamn paper. Meetings, press conferences, some more paper.

Tom wondered sometimes if being back on the beat wouldn't be preferable.

Still, he was on his holidays right now. A well-deserved and much-needed break, though it seemed he and Louise were destined for a staycation.

To his left, the two pregnant women at risk of diabetes – previously unknown to each other by the sound of things – had made fast friends. Ten more minutes, and Tom reckoned they'd be declaring as godmothers for each other's baby.

To his right, Tom picked up on a far more interesting conversation.

'. . . butt naked, smoke inhalation and something about a baby. Apparently, she was just walking down the street.'

Tom angled his head slightly, to better observe the two porters he'd tuned into.

'What did they bring her here for?' Porter One asked.

'Y'deaf? She was going on about a baby.'

'Is she a junkie? Totally naked, you say? What's the story with the baby?'

'She's not even pregnant. They have her upstairs in the emergency assessment ward. They're waiting for police or psychiatrists or something. They'll transfer her to a non-maternity hospital, I s'pose.'

'Dad.'

Tom turned back to Maria, who was already standing.

'Sorry, I have to go up and have a look at this patient. Are you okay to find the way out?'

Tom stood and let her give him a quick hug.

'I wish I could have taken you somewhere nicer,' he said.

'Next time,' she said, already out the door. 'Cocktails!'

Tom could smell the perfume in his daughter's wake as he took the stairs behind her, seconds later. Her usual Chanel scent mixed with the bitter, clean smell of hospital garb, antiseptic fluids and hand sanitiser.

Little had changed in the twenty-six years since Tom had been in the Rotunda maternity hospital as an expectant father; nor in the six years since Maria had Cáit.

The emergency assessment room was still just off the front reception area.

Tom spotted the guard standing at its door, a young woman stripped down to her short-sleeved blue shirt but still in the heavy navy uniform slacks and bulky paraphernalia. She was listening to a radio that, to the untrained ear, babbled an incoherent white noise.

'Chief Super—' he began to introduce himself.

'I know who you are,' she said, already a little dumbstruck. He could see the speedy calculations behind her eyes – this was a routine call-out, surely, even if the circumstances sounded unusual. Why was the most senior officer from the NBCI there? Her gaze flitted left and right, looking for the candid camera.

'I'm here on personal business,' Tom said. The words had barely left his mouth before he realised they only added to the officer's confused state. What possible personal business could a fifty-five-year-old man have in a maternity hospital?

'I, eh, heard a woman was brought in in some sort of distress?' he asked.

The officer nodded, on safer ground now.

'Yes, sir. She was wandering through the city centre, no clothes, with burn marks and signs of smoke inhalation. Apparently she'd said something about a baby but when we arrived, she wasn't talking. So, we brought her down here. Nearest, you know. But the docs say there is no baby. I'm just waiting for her ambulance transfer to a general hospital.'

'Have you checked with fire services? Is it possible her house has gone up and there's a baby there?'

The officer opened and closed her mouth.

'We, um, we were waiting for a psych evaluation. My partner ... um, because she was found naked and they said she wasn't pregnant, now or recently ...'

'You thought she'd concocted the burns, too?'

Tom cocked his head, while the young officer tried to hide her blushes. A good sign. She, at least, didn't think they'd made the right decision.

'He, eh, my partner is more senior.'

Ah.

'And where's your partner now?'

'He's – um – in the car.'

Feet up, air con blasting and easy-listening playing, no doubt. Tom shook his head.

'Good police work is following your gut as much as doing what you're told,' he said, smiling in a way he hoped came across as friendly and not utterly patronising. 'Can I have a chat with your – what are we calling them these days – clients?'

The officer smirked.

'Members of the public,' she said. 'Of course, but she's not saying anything. Shall I contact the fire department and see if there are any reports of a local fire? She couldn't have walked that far. Not in that state. There might not be a lot of people about the city but we'd still have had reports.'

'Sounds like an excellent idea, Guard.'

Tom slipped past her and flashed his badge at the midwife who opened the door to the assessment unit.

The young woman, who couldn't have been more than late teens, had been placed on a bed in a small cubicle at the end of the assessing ward. The nurses had done a good job of applying primary care to her burns. The midwife who'd shown Tom in explained that they weren't severe.

'It's likely her clothing caught fire but she got it off in time to avoid a total tragedy,' she told Tom. 'Which would explain the nakedness. The shock, too. We can't even get her name out of her.'

Tom looked at the young woman, now wearing a loose-fitting delivery gown, left low so it wouldn't chafe the wounds. It wouldn't have taken a medical expert to tell him she was in shock; she looked right at Tom when he approached the bed, but he knew she was barely registering his presence. She was slack-jawed, like she was still trying to absorb whatever she'd seen.

She didn't need a psych evaluation. She needed trauma care.

'My name is Tom,' he said, gently. 'I'm with the police. We're waiting for an ambulance to transfer you to another hospital, but if there's anything you need me to do for you, anybody you need to see or something you want to tell me, I'm here.'

The woman continued to stare at him.

'There was a fire,' Tom said. 'Your clothes were burned? But the nurses say you'll be okay.'

Silence, still.

Every one of Tom's detective senses tingled.

This woman had witnessed something.

A baby.

'Can you tell me your name?' he asked.

A wet sheen covered the woman's eyes, then tears, seamlessly, began to stream down the sides of her face and onto the white pillow beneath her head.

Tom resisted the very human desire to reach out and take her hand.

Her palms had sustained the worst damage.

But, in addition to that, he didn't know what she'd been through.

It was important, if a crime had been committed against her, that this young woman was treated with the utmost sensitivity.

When she spoke, he detected an accent. Eastern European. Russian, maybe. Her voice was raspy from smoke, and deep in tone anyway, but she still sounded young.

'I think they're all dead,' she whispered.

CHAPTER 2

It was incredible, how top brass had managed to make a conference about tackling serious gun crime so utterly, mind-numbingly boring.

Laura Lennon was flicking through the A4 folder of slides, which included images from actual crime scenes: a young man, his T-shirt blown clean off at the front, exposing the bullet holes in his chest; another man, the side of his face missing; yet another, slumped against the wheel of his car, window smashed, blood dripping from the back of what had been his skull.

Laura knew how important it all was and how grave and yet, she couldn't help stifle a yawn.

On the screen at the front of the room, the very same slides were on display, a senior officer reading the points aloud with as much bounce to his delivery as a priest intoning a funeral Mass.

Laura closed her eyes and allowed herself to gently doze, lulled by the heat of the hotel ballroom and the steady, monotonous clicking of the PowerPoint.

'You're a disgrace.'

Ray breathed the words into her ear and Laura smiled.

He handed her the tiny porcelain cup of coffee he'd brought back from the catering tray before taking his seat beside her.

'I had to have sex with the waiter to get you a fresh cup,' he whispered.

'The hairy young one or the older bloke?'

'The DILF,' Ray said.

'He should be so lucky,' Laura said.

Ray smiled and brushed aside one of her red curls, his thumb brushing her cheek and making her blush.

Even now, two years on from their wedding, which they had celebrated a couple of months after her promotion, she sometimes had to pinch herself to check her life was real. Ray was, without exception, the best-looking, kindest, smartest man in the room and he was her husband. And, at just thirty-five, she was one of the most senior officers there.

The power couple, she thought, then laughed a little at her ego.

Another victim flashed up on the slides as she snorted, and her neighbour to the right cast her a puzzled glance, reminding Laura that, no matter how content she might be feeling, she still had to sell that image of seniority.

She could practically read the thoughts of the officer sitting beside her.

The detective chief inspector of the murder squad was not only too young for her job, but also a borderline psychopath by the looks of it.

Laura composed her face into the grave expression she was supposed to wear, the one that these days gave her perpetual jaw ache.

Yes, she'd been promoted to a top position in her thirties but it wasn't like Tom Reynolds was known for his maverick, ill-thought-out decisions. He'd left an excellent team in his wake; Laura was buffered on all sides with support, not least from Detective Sergeant Ray Lennon.

Her promotion over him had taken everyone, especially her and Ray, a little while to get used to, but they'd soon found an easy rhythm. Laura had been moulded in Tom's image and she made sure her leadership was democratic; that she was an addition to the team, not a drag. She shared out roles, responsibilities and, most importantly, praise and rewards. Her presence at this conference today was box-ticking. They'd already agreed that Ray would be the representative for their squad on the new interdepartmental unit that had been set up to address the country's escalating number of gun-related crimes.

Laura was relieved when the event wound up and only mildly irritated that she had to hang on so Ray could do some networking with his new, temporary colleagues.

Bridget Duffy, Laura's flatmate of old and now a senior figure in the drugs squad, was there, having also been sucked into the shit-hot sub-unit. As soon as they spotted each other, even though they hadn't seen each other in a while, they slipped into the familiar chat that came easy to them.

'I bet this new bloke you've hinted at is loving all this new responsibility you have,' Laura said, an eyebrow raised. 'Like you weren't busy enough.'

Bridget shrugged, but her eyes twinkled. Laura could see how happy her friend was and she was thrilled for her.

'He's a paramedic. I took your advice and started dating within the emergency services. Jesus, Laura, you were right. It's been a revelation. Last Sunday, I phoned *him*, wondering where he was. He'd done a double shift.'

'Bloody health service,' Laura said.

'Bloody health service,' Bridget agreed. 'Anyway, this unit will keep me busy while he's out saving lives. Makes a change. You must be glad of it, too. How many of these gun deaths usually end up in your lap?'

'Thankfully, not as many as you'd think,' Laura said. 'The

locals don't call us in when they know who did it, and you know yourself, most of these hitmen aren't genius at hiding their tracks, even if we do struggle to prosecute down the line. But if the unit manages to contain the number of guns coming into the country, it should have a positive effect all round. Honestly, how did it get like this, Bridget? This is Ireland. Yet it's like the Wild West in parts of this city.'

Bridget nodded, frowning.

'That lad who was shot three days ago,' she said. 'He wasn't involved with drugs. He wasn't even in a gang. You know what happened to him? He'd chased some toe-rag who'd tried to steal his car. Turns out the little runt was a runner for a local heavy. The victim was meant to be shot in the knee as a warning. Let us steal your car, or else. They shot him three times in the chest. Twenty-one years of age.'

Laura shook her head, her blood boiling. That was quickly followed by a wave of guilt that her primary feeling for the last few hours had been boredom.

She shouldn't be at the point where she was inured to gun deaths. Ireland was still relatively gun free – even rank and file guards didn't carry arms.

But things had changed.

Laura's phone buzzed at exactly the same time Ray returned.

She would have checked it immediately, but for the look on his face.

'Seen a ghost?' Bridget said, catching it too.

'Something like that,' Ray said. 'Guess who I just met?'

Laura raised her arm and made a sweeping motion at the room, which contained over one hundred officers. Ray could have met any number of old colleagues.

'Joe fucking Kennedy,' Ray said.

'No,' Laura gasped.

'Oh yeah, he's here,' Bridget said, nodding. 'The champion of horizontal career moves.'

'I didn't spot him,' Laura said. She instinctively scanned the room.

'He's here,' Ray said. 'He was sitting up front. I was right beside him out in the hall before I noticed him. Which meant I had to talk to him.'

Laura shuddered.

'Worse,' he said. 'He's coming in to talk to you.'

'Oh, thanks,' Laura said. 'You couldn't have just denied you ever met me, no? Instead you ... Hello, Joe, I didn't know you were here.'

He'd arrived.

Laura took the outstretched hand of former chief superintendent Joe Kennedy, who'd materialised beside them with all the stealth of the creepy little shit that he was.

'Hello there,' he said. 'I had to come over. I thought, well, what could make this hot, stuffy conference even more fun? Meeting your old boss, surely.'

Kennedy was as genial as ever, and as well turned out. Tight haircut, thin-rimmed glasses, erect, tidy bearing. You'd never guess at the character behind the friendly demeanour – it had been a slow, unpleasant revelation for them all.

Five years ago, Kennedy had briefly held the top job at the NBCI after Sean McGuinness, respected and admired by all, had taken early retirement to care for his ailing wife.

His short tenure, during which he'd constantly undermined Tom's good reputation, had left a bad taste in the department. When he'd been removed for far more serious offences than being a pain in the proverbial, everybody had wished he'd just sail off into retirement himself. But he'd refused to go and so had been moved elegantly sideways by the top brass. And Sean McGuinness had returned to the top job for a short time until Tom Reynolds was ready to assume the responsibility.

'I just wanted to congratulate you on the job,' Kennedy said, shaking Laura's hand. 'I know it's been a while, but I haven't run into you since your promotion. I always knew you'd go far.'

Did you, hell, Laura thought.

'Thanks,' she said. 'It's all due to Chief Superintendent Reynolds' mentoring. What are you up to these days?'

Kennedy kept smiling.

'I'm part of this unit. Been working in white-collar crime for a while but, well, this is where the resources are being thrown now.'

'Resumption of play for the bankers, so,' Laura said.

Kennedy chuckled.

'I'll leave you to it,' he said. 'Good to see you all again. Ray, I guess I'll be seeing a bit more of you, from now on.'

He strode off, greeting all those he passed like he'd no baggage to speak of.

'Snake,' Laura hissed.

'A neck like a jockey's bollocks,' Bridget agreed.

Laura pulled out her phone to check it, frowning when she saw the message.

'Don't even say it,' Ray said, watching her. 'I'll eat your arm if we don't go somewhere that serves chicken curry, stat. I'm not filling up on biscuits and you promised you'd finish early today.'

'You'll have to get dinner on your own,' Laura said, distracted. 'A text from God.'

'Isn't he on his holliers?'

Laura made an incredulous face.

'When Tom said he and Louise were staying in the country, how did you think this fortnight was going to go?'

Ray jutted out his lower lip.

'Good point,' he said. 'What's he after?'

'Something odd,' Laura said. She was already Googling breaking news.

Twitter had news of the fire up already, but the national stations hadn't even caught the story.

House near city centre, was all the amateur reporting said.

But Tom's text said more.

CHAPTER 3

Gerry Reid had been a long time in this game.

Long enough to know that July was a quiet month for the fire brigade.

December was worse. Christmas trees, tea lights, candles, home-made wiring extensions, too much drink – too many avoidable tragedies. And you wouldn't want to get him started on Hallowe'en.

Gerry's father, brothers and cousins had all gone into building work and the Reid name was still well regarded in property circles, even after the decimation of the industry during the crash. Reid & Co hung in. There'd always be a job in construction for a Reid man.

Gerry had never wanted to work with bricks. His mother had a photograph of him, taken on Christmas morning 1973, a five-year-old Gerry dressed in the only item he'd put on his list for Santa Claus. A fireman costume. And even though he'd never grown up to be the tall, dark hero Gerry thought was part of the trade description, he'd got there. Turned out hair colour wasn't important, nor height, for that matter. There were ways of carrying people and Gerry's shoulders were broad.

His wife found him sexy in his uniform, even if nobody else did.

As he directed operations outside the still smouldering house,

Gerry reflected on how his career meant that he, just like all the Reid men, knew the exact elements and components of a building. His family erected them. Gerry watched as they came down. Then he went around the blackened shell with the fire inspectors to determine what had caused the destruction.

Right now, though, with the fire spent and the situation under control, Gerry was more concerned with containing the crowd of onlookers that had gathered once the flames had become visible. Mainly kids, some worried parents, a handful of nosy passers-by. They were from further along the docks. The old city streets up that way had once been plagued by drugs and anti-social behaviour, but in the last few years, the area had settled into something more like the community it used to be. Not necessarily because of wealth in the country – or the lack of, for a short period. The forced neighbourliness was probably more a response to the onslaught of new building along the city quays – the office blocks and apartments that meant rows of tiny houses like this one were today selling for almost half a million each because of their proximity to town. Locals were being pushed out; old houses knocked down. So, those that survived stuck together.

None of the residents of the homes to either side of number three Shipping Row had come out to see what the excitement was about. The first thing Gerry had done was send two lads up and down the street to evacuate the houses on either side of the primary fire site. Nobody was in. If you could afford a house like this – a tiny, squashed, alleged three-bed with a living room so small a large man could touch either side and a *charming* galley kitchen that facilitated cooking a bowl of cereal and not much more – then you worked all day, every day, most likely up in the financial centre, for Google or Amazon or KBC or whatever was up there now.

The police had arrived earlier, a squad car with two officers, and put themselves at Gerry's disposal. Somebody more important would be there shortly, they'd informed him, once the building could be examined. They'd push Gerry, try to get in faster than they should if they suspected something was amiss. And for the cops to arrive so quickly, something was definitely amiss.

Maybe the house was on a watch list of sorts. Maybe it hadn't been a dodgy plug or cigarette, after all. It had certainly gone up quick. Gerry had his own suspicions.

Gerry looked up at the smoke, still rising into the bright evening sky. The day had been unbearably hot. It would take significant effort to reduce the heat in the house so they could investigate, to see what had started the fire and, more importantly, if anybody had been trapped inside.

The fire station wasn't far from here; Gerry's crew had got here rapidly.

It didn't matter. If people were inside, they'd be identifying them by their teeth.

'We probably could have waited until tomorrow morning to do this,' Laura said, then gulped from a large bottle of water, her futile effort to stay cool and hydrated.

'They'll tell us something in a few minutes,' Tom said.

Laura tutted. Tom was wearing a light shirt and cotton khakis. He was dressed for the summer's day. Laura was still in her suit blouse and trousers she'd worn for the conference, her underarms drenched in sweat.

She looked back over at the house, the firefighters outside it. Its railed garden was so tiny it was almost on the street. The emergency personnel filled it and spilled out onto the pavement.

The house itself – the whole row of them – reminded Laura of old rail-worker cottages; they had probably been built to mimic the originals. Cheaper and less cosy, no doubt, but with a façade that complemented the area. They were two-storey but so lacking in height, a person could drop from the top window to the pavement below and probably not risk broken limbs in the process.

Nobody had jumped from this burning building, though. That they knew of.

It was rented. Once it hit 6 p.m. the neighbours had begun to return and the police had quickly established that the houses shared the same landlord: a solicitor who'd bought four of the properties when they were first built.

They'd got hold of him quickly and he confirmed the name on the lease of the burned dwelling – Matteo Russo, an Italian national, mid-thirties, professional. Either finance or IT.

'Her boyfriend, do you think?' Laura asked Tom, while they waited to get the nod from Gerry. Gerry was in charge, even though he'd promised to accommodate the cops to the best of his abilities. Laura had watched on, amused, as even Tom deferred to Gerry after only thirty seconds in his company. All the little boys, and plenty of the little girls, wanted to be in the fire brigade. Laura had never seen *anybody* as in charge as Gerry was.

'Maybe,' Tom said. 'You've got to imagine the demographics around here are heavy on local office workers, wouldn't you? She sounded Eastern European, but I'm working off the few words she gave me. They could have met in one of the companies that relies on translators. PayPal or something. She seemed very young, but I'm an old fogey now; what do I know?'

Laura glanced sideways at Tom. She remembered her boss

when his hair used to be almost black. Now it was pretty much grey all over, bar the odd speckled patch.

He was still a good-looking man, though. He'd never been her type, mainly because her type had always been Ray. Always. But she could see what Louise saw. Tom had that sort of face. Kind, intelligent, a smile in his eyes that said he knew everything, even what you didn't want him to know.

'Landlord didn't know of any women living here, though,' Laura said. 'She's not on the lease.'

Tom shrugged.

'Means nothing. She could have been shacked up with this Matteo Russo informally, or maybe he was subletting. The rent on this place is probably two grand a month, minimum. Hard to cover that on one salary, even if it's a big one. I'm concerned there are more inside, though. She said, *I think they're all dead.*'

'Jesus. It doesn't bear thinking about.'

Tom nodded as Laura spoke, but he kept his eyes fixed firmly on the comings and goings from the house. Gerry had gone in and still hadn't emerged.

The chief superintendent had come down here, specifically. The female guard Tom had met at the hospital had returned to canvass as many witnesses as possible to the girl's arrival on the city street earlier that day. She'd specifically questioned the trio of women who'd helped the girl, to establish exactly what had been said.

I couldn't save the baby.

Tom had to find out if there was a baby inside this house.

Gerry appeared in the frame of the front door, his head hanging.

He stood there for a moment and his stillness rippled into

the garden and on to the street, silencing the small crowd of onlookers, which had taken on almost a party atmosphere.

Gerry blessed himself.

Ah, Jesus, Tom heard somebody say.

The chief superintendent stood straighter.

Gerry met them in the garden.

'Do you know the victim?' Gerry asked.

Tom frowned.

'The man inside,' Gerry said. 'I assumed, when your officers said the big boss was coming, you were keeping an eye on the bloke. It's just the one victim. Crim, was he?'

Laura reacted immediately. In seconds, she had her phone to her ear and was already ringing the landlord again to get more information on Matteo Russo.

'No, this is all news to us,' Tom said, shaking his head. 'A woman was found wandering in the city centre earlier, scorch marks, some serious burns, in shock. I knew something wasn't right. You're sure there's nobody else inside? There aren't any . . . children?'

'Just him. In the bedroom. In bed. Like he'd been asleep.'

'In bed? What time did the fire start?'

'We got the shout about 11.15. It started downstairs, spread up. The worst of the damage is to the lower floor, which is why I can tell you it's a man in that bed. Any longer and, to be honest, I would have just said person.'

'And there's definitely no baby?'

'No baby. You're a bit obsessed with this baby.'

'Something the woman said. She also implied there were more in the house.'

'There might have been more and they got out.'

Gerry pinched the bridge of his nose. His fingers were

covered in soot but his face was still clean . . . ish. He'd been wearing a mask when he went inside but now his fingers were leaving dirty black smudges on the skin.

'There are a few bedrooms,' he continued. 'But I can't let you inside. Not tonight. We need to wait for the building to cool and settle. The damage to the supporting walls could bring the upper floor down. I'm going to get some steelwork in place quickly and then we can let your gang in and you can start forensics and move the body. Don't worry, I'll make sure it doesn't fall down in the meantime.'

'So, no ambulance needed.'

'Definitely not.' Gerry hesitated. 'Where was this girl found wandering?'

'Talbot Street. Just up there.' Tom cocked his head in the direction of town. 'It would have taken her about, what, ten minutes to walk it? She was approached around 11 a.m.'

'Which sounds about right if she came from this site,' Gerry said. 'There was nobody in on either side and the street was fairly empty when we arrived. People avoiding the heat. By the way, it looks like you have a problem on your hands.'

'Bigger than a dead man and a naked girl with burns?'

'Yup. Accelerant was used.' Gerry turned his head and looked back at the house. 'This was arson.'

Tom shook his head, his shoulders hunched.

He looked up and down the street they were standing on. No cameras.

But he knew that further up, where the Irish Financial Services Centre started and sprawled, there'd be cameras galore.

It was time to start calling in the CCTV.

CHAPTER 4

John and Orla Cusack were catching up on a series that everybody had been discussing for what seemed like an eternity but had probably only been a few weeks.

Orla and John always happened on these shows when everybody else had already seen them.

At least that's how she felt. That they were in a perpetual state of catch-up, as opposed to setting the trend.

Which was odd, because pretty much all Orla and John did was work, then come home and watch TV, dinners on their laps. The biggest treat of the week was takeaway night, when they'd deliberate for a little while whether to go for chips, Indian or Chinese, and whether to have a bottle of wine between them or if John would have a beer and Orla a G&T.

They were only in their forties.

But they were old before their time.

They were aware of it, but not inclined to do anything about it.

When they refused polite invitations to events or nights out, they usually did so with the excuse of tiredness or being busy or having something else on.

Nobody ever challenged their reasons.

Asking John and Orla was only box-ticking, in any case.

Used to be, John and Orla were the most fun couple at these

things. John used to describe Orla as his little blonde bundle of fun. Orla used to call John her Teddy Boy, because he kept his hair slick and wore drainpipe jeans before hipsters found them fashionable again.

The couple *were* tired these days. That bit wasn't strictly a lie.

John's job entailed longer hours than Orla's. He worked in the city council's sanitation department, in a sorting centre. He used to be on the bins, which he loved, because he enjoyed working with other lads. The small crew did their rounds daily, jumping on and off the truck, a workout every day and finished by noon. It was the pub for lunch more often than not, a pint and a toastie, then home to Orla with oddly fascinating stories about the contents of other people's refuse.

Now, John waded through green waste, making sure customers had only placed recyclables in their green bins and had washed out all their containers. It never ceased to amaze Orla how irate John could get about people placing their cardboard in plastic bags or not washing a soup lid properly. They were trying, weren't they? She still sneaked the odd shampoo bottle that she couldn't get the top off into the general waste bin, making sure to hide it beneath plastic and junk so John wouldn't spot it.

Orla worked three days a week; she was employed as a secretary in a local doctor's surgery, where she started at 8.30 a.m. and finished at 3 p.m. What John failed to remember, when he joked about her having an easy life, was that she had two other full-time jobs on top of her part-time paid career. One, keeping the house standing and two, searching.

Always searching.

Orla wouldn't give up, and she knew John hadn't either. He just couldn't bear to talk about it.

Tonight wasn't takeaway night. It was lamb chops and mashed

potato this evening, which Orla hated, but at least the Netflix box set was entertaining. *American Crime Story: The People v O.J. Simpson.* Cuba Gooding Jr was fantastic but Orla couldn't stop watching the on-screen Kardashian kids every time they appeared, wondering how on earth they'd ended up as they had.

Bob Laird next door had recommended it when he'd dropped in the sack of spuds earlier. He'd got them cheap in the grocery wholesalers he managed. He was a good neighbour, always leaving in trays of beans or giant packs of toilet rolls. She'd never considered it strange, but standing there this afternoon, discussing wife killers *and* Bob's latest offering, had been a weird moment. Especially when they'd moved seamlessly from the blood-stained glove to whether Orla wanted Bob to drop in some real Wexford strawberries.

Orla hadn't wanted the strawberries. They summoned memories too bittersweet to bear.

Potatoes, strawberries and murderers.

Orla was utterly spellbound by Marcia Clark's cross-examination when John sat forward suddenly, his body tense, his face frozen.

For a moment, she thought he was having a heart attack.

Don't die, she thought, and in a moment of absolute clarity she realised how much she loved and needed her husband.

'Did you hear that?' he said.

He picked up the remote and muted the telly. Orla was fleetingly irritated that he hadn't paused it. It was playing away there, and they were missing what the man on the stand was saying. They'd have to rewind and hope the box didn't freeze. It was always doing that, when they messed with the remote.

'Hear what?' she said.

Then she heard it, too.

A noise out in the kitchen.

How ridiculous would that be, Orla thought, somebody breaking into a home while the residents were obviously still up, every light blazing? Only a madman would do such a thing.

And if it was a madman, they were in danger.

'Will I phone the guards?' she whispered.

'The guards!' John snorted. 'All the use they'd be. We'd be dead and buried before they rocked up.'

'What about Bob? He can come in and—'

There was another bang in the kitchen.

John shot up and walked over to the sitting room door; Orla let him, even though she was thinking the safer option would be to climb out the sitting room window.

'Break into my fucking house, would you?' John muttered, as he threw open the door.

Orla was hot on his heels. Her husband's shoulders were curled forward, the veins in his neck throbbing, hands balled into fists.

He carried a lot of rage, these days. Orla did, too, but it was a more hopeless, powerless fury that consumed her quietly.

It was actually quite possible John could kill an intruder with his bare hands.

Her husband had been longing to strangle somebody for quite some time.

John strode directly to the kitchen, which was only really four or five steps in distance, and flung open that door, too.

She was standing there, at the cooker. A pot of water was already bubbling; a packet of curry noodles sat on the counter.

It was like she'd never left.

'Nina,' Orla choked. John, man of action, was suddenly dumbstruck.

Her daughter turned and looked at them.

Nina, like her dad, had lost weight she didn't have to lose. Her hair was long – too long. It had that ratty extension look that Orla saw on lots of the young girls who passed through the surgery. Hair that wasn't natural and needed to be untaped and stuck back in every six weeks by the hairdressers, lest it look even cheaper.

Nina's sweater was oversized and dirty, the sleeves almost covering her hands. It was too hot for that sort of clothing, even though it was evening, but their daughter had only ever worn clothes that covered her arms.

She didn't look great, but she still looked like herself. That's what Orla thought at first glance.

It was Nina's eyes, though, that made Orla realise everything she'd feared for the last two years had been justified.

Her daughter looked positively haunted.

'Mam,' she said, the little word almost breaking Orla's heart anew.

John found his tongue.

'How did you get in?' he asked, like that was important.

'The key under the flowerpot,' Nina answered her father.

John glared at Orla. She'd told him months ago that she'd moved that key.

She ignored him.

She knew they were both overwhelmed, that it was difficult to process seeing their daughter after two years.

But Orla also knew that everything rested on how they responded to Nina now. Too much gushing and they might scare her. Too many questions and she could run. Too much of their own anger and they might never see her again.

'You're hungry, Nina love,' Orla said. 'Let me make you

something proper. Why don't you have a bath and I'll heat up some potatoes and chops.'

'I hate chops,' Nina said.

'That's right, you do,' Orla said, apologetically. 'I'll do the noodles, then. Go on, go up and get clean. Everything you need is in your room.'

Nina looked back at the pot of bubbling water, then nodded. She drifted past them, not even reacting to the shock on John's face, but letting her mother touch her arm lightly.

'I'll do your favourite for afters. Strawberries and cream.'

As soon as her foot hit the first stair, John closed the kitchen door and hissed at Orla.

'How the hell are you so calm?'

Orla stood there, wondering the same.

Then she picked up the packet of noodles and tore them open.

'Remember what the counsellor told us?' Orla said. 'If she came back, when she came back, we had to be careful how we reacted. We can't suffocate her.'

'We don't know where she's been or who she's been with,' John snapped. 'She could still be using.'

Orla shook her head.

'Let's just keep our heads. Put these noodles on, will you? And then go next door and tell Bob I'll have that punnet of strawberries.'

'What are you going to do?'

'I'm going to get our daughter some fresh clothes.'

John looked like he was about to argue some more, but Orla placed her hand on his arm.

'She's still our little girl, John,' she said. 'And she's alive. Let's just . . . see, okay?'

Upstairs, Nina was already in her en suite, the door shut, the sound of water running.

Nina was their only child and when they'd bought this house, just a couple of years after she was born, John had insisted on renovating so Nina would have her own bathroom.

She'll want hours in there when she's a teenager, he'd said, smiling indulgently at their two-year-old princess.

They knew they were only going to be having the one. The emergency hysterectomy that followed Nina's horrific birth had ensured that.

They didn't need more than one. Nina was everything to them and Orla genuinely felt she would never have been able to make any more room in her heart for another child.

Orla had first found the drugs – in the cabinet under the sink in the en suite – when Nina was just sixteen.

Orla hesitated now, her hand on the bathroom door, her heart beating fast.

There was nothing in there. The bathroom hadn't been used in two years and Orla had cleaned it plenty of times since.

Nina had discarded the clothes she'd been wearing in a pile at the end of her bed.

Orla opened the top drawer of the pale wooden chest from IKEA and took out a pair of brand-new cotton pyjamas. Unbeknownst to John, Orla still shopped for Nina. She'd always known her daughter would return. Whether she'd chosen to come home or because Orla had found her.

Orla placed the T-shirt and bottoms on the bed, along with an unopened pack of Dove essentials: deodorant, body cream, face moisturiser.

Then she bent down and picked up the dirty clothes.

'Are you okay in there?' she called into the bathroom.

'Fine,' Nina answered.

'I'm just going to phone your grandparents and let them know you're home safe.'

'Okay.'

'And I'm going to let some of the people who've been helping know.'

Nina said nothing.

Orla waited, then she turned to leave.

'Who?' she heard from the other side of the door.

Orla stopped. Did her daughter care who'd been searching for her for the last two years? Or was she worried that Orla would tell everybody Nina was home, when she actually planned to leave again?

'Just, people,' Orla said. 'All our neighbours have—'

'I don't want anybody to know!'

The sound of splashing water accompanied the shout.

Orla took a step back, even though she was alone in the bedroom.

'Okay,' she said, gently.

Nina said nothing for a few seconds, but Orla was afraid to move. Then:

'You can tell Gran and Grandad.'

'Okay,' Orla said and it was almost a sob.

An odd, bitter smell filled her nostrils.

She brought her nose closer to the sweater at the top of the pile in her arms.

Smoke. It smelled of smoke.

She raised her head and looked at the closed bathroom door.

'I'll be downstairs,' Orla said. 'I'm going to put a wash on.'

Nina didn't reply.

In the bathroom, Nina sat in the tub, knees tucked up to her chest, her arms wrapped around them. She'd poured half a bottle of L'Occitane Cherry Blossom bath gel in and the white, scented bubbles covered her body as the water level rose.

Nina breathed deep, letting the steam clear the acrid taste in her mouth and the burning sensation in her lungs. Letting the water wash away the filth.

She knew her parents would want answers and she didn't know how long she could hold them off.

She just hadn't been able to think of a single other place she could go.

Her mother and father would want to talk and she would have to think of something to tell them, but all that would come. Thankfully, they hadn't reacted like she'd feared they would. They'd been calm and cautious, not angry or emotional. Not like they'd been when they did the family therapy that time.

She'd no idea why they were being kind, but she was grateful for it.

It was like she'd just come home from school or a job.

Nina placed her head on her knees and closed her eyes, letting the comfort of the warm bath soothe her.

She couldn't bear everybody knowing she was back, coming around to the house and wanting to talk to her, to ask her where she'd been. It would be bad enough to keep quiet in front of her parents.

But she had to.

She'd had a lucky escape.

She should be dead.

She couldn't think about the others. She just couldn't.

CHAPTER 5

'You're having an absolute laugh,' Louise said, when Tom joined her in their brand-new conservatory that evening.

His wife was on the two-seater, legs tucked up beneath her, her dark hair loose and draped over tanned shoulders.

It had been roasting all day but the conservatory had managed to not retain much of the day's heat. It was a recent addition to their house and, even after costing a fortune, it wasn't the most insulated of extensions. In winter, it would be hellish. But after months of battling errant builders who promised the moon and, initially at least, only delivered a crater in their back garden, the conservatory was finally up and Louise was making the most of their investment.

She'd been out there every evening for the past week. Tom had to admit, it was starting to resemble something akin to a pleasant living space. Louise had adorned the windows with tea lights that twinkled against the glass, and placed bowls of dried lavender and chamomile on the sills. The rattan garden furniture set, donated by Sean McGuinness after he downsized from the house he'd owned with his late wife June and gone travelling, was draped with large cream throws and soft cushions. And Louise had polished the floor until it shone, before covering it with a thick, comfortable rug.

Now, having made the conservatory look like part of the house, she was enjoying the room. She'd a glass of wine in one hand and her latest read in the other.

Tom had kissed his granddaughter, who for some reason was sleeping in a princess tent in the sitting room, then battled through a hall full of Cáit's toys and a kitchen cluttered with fabric samples and discarded paint tins.

Eventually, he joined Louise in her peaceful retreat.

He poured himself a glass from the open bottle of Merlot and rested his feet on the pouffe.

'I talked to Maria,' Louise said. 'You're gone all day and she said she had a ten-minute lunch with you—'

'That was not my fault,' Tom interjected.

'A ten-minute lunch and yet you've been on the missing list for four hours and you come home stinking of . . . what is that, cigarette smoke? Weren't you going to help me with the decorating this weekend?'

'You need me to mansplain painting to you?'

'I could have done with you moving the effin' bed.'

Tom smiled.

'I see the paint tins are empty and you've cracked open the vino, so it looks like you had a productive day.'

'Regardless,' Louise said, sniffing, pretending to be more irritated than she was. 'Where the hell were you? And your answer had better involve alcohol, a casino and strippers.'

'Work.'

'Tom Reynolds!'

'I know, I know. I came across something when I was in the hospital with Maria and . . .'

'Nope.' Louise cut him off. 'No rationalising, no excuses. Remember the addict's code – take responsibility for your own decisions.'

'Fair enough. I can offer no defence, m'lady.'

They sat in silence for a couple of moments, sipping the wine and enjoying the fading dusk.

'So, eh, what was it?' Louise said. 'The thing that got you so interested?'

'Hello, my name is a policeman's wife and I'm addicted to his cases,' Tom replied.

Louise laughed.

Tom took her hand and gave it a squeeze. Her skin had always been softer. Now his felt like sandpaper in comparison. All that cream she lathered on herself at night was paying off, while he felt like he was turning into an old man.

'You catch the news?' he asked.

'I caught a whole lot of *Sam and Cat* reruns. Ariana Grande's voice could cut through glass.'

'This is why I go searching for work when I'm supposed to be on holidays. A house burned down on the docks. That was how my day ended. It started with a naked woman walking through town. When I say woman – I'm being PC. She's little more than a teenager, I think. Looks like she fled the fire. And it turned out, there was a man inside who wasn't so lucky. It was arson.'

'God, that's awful.' A pause. 'Intriguing, too.'

'That's what I thought.'

'What will Commissioner Bronwyn Maher do when she finds out you've gone all Scooby Doo after being forced to take annual leave?'

'I think skin and flaying might come into it,' Tom said. 'It's nothing Sean McGuinness wouldn't have done.'

'*He's* your benchmark now, is that it?'

'You know he is.' Tom smiled.

'And what do you think your wife will do if you disappear for two weeks on a case when you've already messed up spectacularly on the holiday front this year?'

Tom threw a quick glance his wife's way to check if there was something more serious beneath the gentle teasing.

'It's not really my fault, is it?' he said.

Louise pursed her lips.

It hadn't been either of their faults, and yet, it had been down to both of them, really.

It had been the same at Christmas. They'd gone nowhere because Maria had just started in the maternity hospital and with the schools on holidays, she'd needed full-time childcare. Tom and Louise had known summer would be the same. Tom wasn't even planning to take any leave until his boss, Commissioner Maher, reminded him he wasn't on the front line any more and he was supposed to follow HR protocol.

'*Do* you want to go somewhere this fortnight?' Tom asked. 'Maria is back on nights next week, she says. Cáit's dad will have her on sleepovers and Maria says she'll sleep when Cáit is in school. We could get away for a long weekend, even?'

'You won't rest now until you find out what happened in that house,' Louise scoffed. 'Arson, you say?'

'Yep.'

'Mm-hm.' Louise nodded. 'Drink your wine. Looks like you'll have an early start in the morning. I need you to rebuild Cáit's bed before you leave.'

'You took it apart?'

'It was the only way I could move it.'

'It was easier to unscrew the whole thing than just shimmy it sideways?'

Louise shrugged.

'Made sense to me.'

Tom laughed.

'I love your mad brain,' he said.

'Ditto,' she replied. 'And, yes, I think we should squeeze in at least one or two nights away over the next fortnight. You're meant to be slowing down, Tom. We promised we wouldn't end up like Sean and June.'

Tom felt the familiar wave of sorrow flow through him. Sean had never had the retirement he'd wanted with his beloved wife. She'd been diagnosed with early-onset Alzheimer's and died soon after.

'I want no expense spared,' Louise said.

'I'll get my secretary on that, asap.'

'If you put Willie Callaghan in charge of booking a hotel, we'll never speak again.'

On the table, Tom's phone buzzed with a text. He was still smiling at the notion of his unimaginative, occasional Garda driver booking a swanky hotel as he swiped open the message.

It was from Laura.

The solicitor had broken the news to Matteo Russo's parents.

'Christ,' Tom said.

'What is it?'

'A fuck-up. The body they found in the house – the property was let to an Italian national. The bloody landlord has gone and told his folks he's dead. We don't even know if it's him who was found.'

Louise sighed.

Tom placed his phone back down on the table.

His wife might indulge him looking into this case, but it was late and, for now, the communications disaster was Laura's problem.

CHAPTER 6
Saturday

Ray was normally the one who had to be dragged out of bed on the weekend but when Laura woke, just after seven, her husband's side of the bed was already empty.

She found him downstairs, halfway through a freshly brewed pot of coffee while he perused a forest's worth of notes that he'd spread out on their small kitchen table.

'Whatcha doing?' she asked, spreading Nutella across a bagel.

'I'm trying to read up on all the latest gun cases,' Ray said. 'There were ten fatal gang-related shootings this year and thirty more attempted. But only eight cases have resulted in convictions.'

'Witness intimidation?' Laura said, taking a large bite of the meal that would probably sustain her for most of the day. The weatherman had promised today would be cooler but it was still too hot to eat properly during the day.

'Partly,' Ray said. 'You've got a few of these guys being taken out in no-go areas for the cops, so when we do go in, nobody saw anything or wants to talk and that has nothing to do with threats or cajoling. They just don't see us as anything other than the enemy. The families and friends of the victims won't have any dealings with us because they want to get their own revenge. They've no interest in the courts. And then there's the lack of physical evidence. Very few of the firearms used are ever retrieved. I swear, it's like the gangs are swapping them instead of dumping these days. And the thing is . . .'

Ray paused and rubbed under his eyes, before drinking more coffee.

'. . . for all the intelligence we're gathering, we still don't have a healthy handle on exactly how many gangs are operational and who their members are. It would nearly make you long for the days of the big crime families.'

'The Cowells?'

'Yeah. Don't judge me, but I swear, since we cut the head off that organisation, the landscape has gone to shit. There's no definable structure. That gang split into mini-gangs and now we have foreign gangs, too. I'm reading these notes in the same way I have to imagine finance journos tried to get their heads around sub-prime mortgage packages.'

Laura laughed.

'You poor thing,' she said. 'Who knew my day would look easier than yours?'

'I know, right?'

He pushed himself back from the kitchen table and patted his knee.

Laura perched on it, resting her plate on top of one of his files.

'Hello, morning glory,' she said, feeling the press of his body against hers.

He laid his head against her chest, his arms wrapped around her waist.

'What I wouldn't give to just take you upstairs and have a Saturday in bed,' he said.

'What I wouldn't give to let you,' she whispered back, kissing the top of his head.

She looked at the pages covering their kitchen table and sighed.

'You know,' she said, 'Ireland is still a very small country. The drugs squad must have loads of touts in the gangs. I mean, drugs *are* their main business, aren't they? It's not like there are gangs that need the guns for holding up banks, not when they can take the bloody ATMs out of the walls with diggers. And all they need for tiger kidnappings are knives or metal bars.'

'The guns are all for the drugs,' Ray said. 'And apparently we've plenty of touts, but they're all low-level. Nobody who can help us draw up a structure with an overhead view. We'd need somebody senior to give us an inkling of how the gangs operate these days – how the territory's divided up and so on. It really is one of the biggest challenges this new unit faces. I'm supposed to look at crime scenes and trace the weapons back to a specific gang, to see then how they're bringing them in. But I don't even know who the gangs are!'

'I bet the person who used to be at the top has an idea of who's on the playing field now.'

'What do you mean?' Ray asked. 'Patrick Cowell is locked up.'

'Yeah, but he doesn't have locked-in syndrome. He can still talk. And listen. Maybe he's mellowed after a few years inside.'

'You think I should go talk to Patrick "BLT" Cowell?'

'Why not?' Laura said. 'Are there any restrictions on you doing something like that?'

'You must be joking,' Ray said. 'I'm not sure Bronwyn Maher knows what we should or shouldn't be doing. She's just put the unit in place so the minister can say we're doing something come question time on RTÉ.'

'Then use your initiative. Start mapping out the gangs with an insider's help. He might be happy to have some company.'

Ray smiled up at her.

'Listen to you, my clever little wifey.'

'You know, it felt like you got more excited there the more I talked.' Laura laughed. 'I hope that was my brilliance turning you on and not the idea of meeting an ageing, scumbag gangster.'

'It was neither,' Ray said, and started to move aside the plate and the pages on the kitchen table. 'It was your lovely warm bum. I stopped caring about guns when you sat on mine.'

'Nope,' Laura said, jumping off his lap. 'I'm heading to the hospital. Stick an IOU on my pillow.'

She was gone before her husband could protest.

The doctors in the northside Dublin general hospital had admitted the young woman found the previous day to treat her burns and make sure there was no lasting damage from smoke inhalation. But bed pressure meant she'd probably only be in the hospital for a couple of days, and she'd also been placed on a public ward.

That meant she was part of the crowd, and this made Laura nervous.

After spending an hour with her, Laura was no closer to knowing who she was or what had happened in the burned-down house – if that was indeed where the young woman had come from.

Which meant if she wandered off, Laura wouldn't have a hope of finding her.

For all they knew, this girl – who had all the outward appearance of a victim – might have started the fire that killed a man.

Not to mention the fact Tom wanted to get to the bottom of the mystery about the baby.

Gerry Reid had told Laura and Tom that the likelihood of them being able to salvage any clues from the house about the young woman's residency or identity was slim.

She would have to tell them who she was.

Laura, sick of waiting for the lift, took the stairs back down through the hospital floors, two at a time. She had her phone to her ear and had just got hold of the State's leading criminal psychologist, Linda McCarn.

'I know this is probably far below your pay grade, Linda,' she said, 'but this woman we found, she won't talk. And I've seen the on-call psych attendant in here. He looks about twelve. If I can't get her to talk, I doubt he can.'

'Hark at you feeling all superior to a fellow youthful professional,' Linda drawled.

'My secret is I always know when to request the aid of the older, more experienced generation,' Laura retorted.

'Touché. Okey dokey, darling, you know I prefer a challenge to a pay cheque. Do you think she's guilty of something? My forte is criminality, after all.'

'We haven't a clue, Linda. If she came from the house fire we're dealing with, then she walked away from a dead man. She might have been in shock, or it might be something more sinister. Though, given how she was found . . .'

'You've got me hooked. What ward is she in?'

Laura gave Linda the details.

The inspector's next call was to the chief superintendent of the Technical Bureau, Emmet McDonagh.

As Laura baby-stepped impatiently through the hospital entrance's revolving door, she thought about how, once upon a time, she'd never have dreamed of inviting Linda onto a case that also featured the Tech Bureau chief. Their relationship had once been so fractious that their colleagues had frequently applied military-style logistical planning to avoid having Linda and Emmet in the same room, let alone on the same case.

But they'd reached some sort of détente in recent years and, in the process, had made everybody's lives a bit easier. It was another win that Laura reckoned had Tom Reynolds' finger-prints all over it.

'I'm a few months off retirement and this is what you land on me on a Saturday morning?'

Emmet answered the phone in a tone as friendly and cheer-ful as ever.

'You're on site, I take it,' Laura said, glossing over the whing-ing. She was used to it now.

'There is no other detective chief inspector I would—'

'You'd do it for Tom.'

'—do this for. You're lucky you have those gorgeous red curls of yours, not to mention those adorable little freckles.'

'You're shameless, you old lech. Tell me, are you standing over a dead body while flirting with me?'

Laura had arrived at the maze-like hospital car park. She started to look for her car as she talked, holding up the key fob and pressing it repeatedly while she walked, listening out for the beep.

In truth, Laura had been nervous about establishing her own personal relationship with the crime scene chief. Tom had an uncanny knack of being able to filter out all of Emmet's many complaints and only tune into the relevant case points. But they'd been friends, at the back of it all, so Tom could be as blunt with Emmet as he liked.

As it happened, Laura got on quite well with Emmet. He was outrageously un-PC and, in any other sphere, would absolutely have lost his job by now. Yet, forced to work with him as an equal, Laura found him an absolute pussycat. Because she too had realised that the trick was to be ruder to him than he was to anybody else.

'I'm with the body,' he said. 'Moya Chambers wants it down in the morgue. Not much I can tell you, except for the fact he's dead and he's been badly burned. You coming down here? I'm going through the rest of the house with the fire inspector in tow. He'll know better than me where this all kicked off but they won't submit their report for days. I might be able to get some clues out of him, though. He's already speculating petrol was poured around downstairs and it doesn't appear that the front door was locked – it has one of those handles that you just pull down to open; it has to be actually locked with a key to secure it.'

'So somebody could have just walked in and out?' Laura mused.

'That's exactly what could have happened, my dear.'

CHAPTER 7

By the time Tom arrived, the body discovered in the house fire had been removed, under Laura's stewardship. She was shockingly pale as she described to him how it had looked and he was doubly glad he'd missed it.

He hadn't been in a rush to get to the scene, not to mention the fact Louise wouldn't let him leave until he'd rebuilt Cáit's bed. He'd witnessed the results of all manner of deaths in his long career and death by fire was, without question, among the most distressing. Even if it was the smoke inhalation that did for the victim first, the combined effect of heat and flames left something unrecognisable in its wake and was a devastating reminder of just how fragile the human body is.

The damage to the fundamental structure of the house wasn't as bad as Gerry Reid had feared. Nevertheless, supports had been erected, and Laura reminded Tom to take his time on the stairs as he made his way up to her.

'Did you tear the landlord a new one for contacting Matteo Russo's parents?' Tom asked when they reached the small landing. 'How the hell did he even get hold of them? They're in Italy, aren't they?'

Immediately after speaking, he had to cough to clear his throat. The building was safe, but he still felt like he was inhaling smoke. It would linger for weeks. Tom pitied the poor sods who lived on either side.

'I ate him alive,' Laura said. 'It did set everything in motion, though. Moya has confirmed the body is male, possibly mid-thirties – that's all she has so far – and that does fit with Matteo Russo. But we need his dental records, so the parents had to be contacted anyway. Jesus, Tom, the image will stay with me for life. The smell . . .'

'Don't,' he said, not even bothering to pretend his stomach was made of iron.

'Anyway.' Laura shuddered and continued. 'Our colleagues in the Italian police have explained to the parents that, in all like-lihood, it is their son and that we're working closely with them. And the Russos can't get hold of Matteo. His phone is off, emails unanswered, social media untouched since earlier in the week. Emmet has a ruined smartphone in an evidence bag in the back of his van. Could be his.'

'They'll still be hoping,' Tom said. 'Right up until it's con-firmed. What possessed the landlord? Who *wants* to break that sort of news?'

'My guess,' Laura said, 'is that he's probably afraid of being sued or something and is trying to get into the good books by being all compassionate. He might think it's his fault the fire started. He offered to pay for the body to be repatriated.'

Tom shook his head, amazed.

'Wait until he finds out it was started deliberately with an accelerant and not by faulty electrics,' he said. 'We'd better hold him to that offer before he backs out. Which room?'

Multiple doorways faced them. Most of the actual doors had been destroyed, though the shells of one or two still hung in their frames.

'I know,' she said, speaking aloud his confusion. 'I thought this was a three-bed house as well.'

'If these are artificially created rooms, the landlord was sure squeezing them in,' Tom said.

'Indeed. It could have been absolute carnage if all these rooms were occupied and that fire had started at night. The walls between the rooms are only partitions. The extra bedrooms were created and not very professionally. Most of them started to collapse with the heat early in the fire. According to Gerry. The body was in here.'

She brought Tom into the room furthest away from the stairs.

It was brighter in here – mainly because the window had exploded from the fire's heat, and now the bright morning light streamed in through the empty square.

The room was recognisably a bedroom, though badly smoke-damaged. A small wardrobe, or what remained of one, was against the wall. On the other side of the room, a double bed, replete with charred mattress.

The room faced on to the street and there were still puddles from the fire brigade's hoses.

'No smoke alarm?' Tom asked.

'There was,' Laura told him. 'Batteries in it, too. We have to assume it was working until the fire got hold of it.'

'Why didn't it alert him?' Tom said. 'How could he have slept through everything?'

'What was he doing in bed at 11 a.m. on a Friday in the first place?' Laura mused. 'I'm wondering if he was out of it. On drugs, maybe.'

'Do we know where exactly Matteo worked?' Tom asked. 'What sort of professional he was?'

Tom moved aside the partially caved-in wardrobe, and ran

his gloved fingers gently through the remains inside. Suits, he guessed, from the heavy feel of some of the material.

'IT up in the financial centre, the landlord says,' Laura said. 'Which is why I'm wondering why he wasn't in work. But it's Saturday, so we're struggling to get through to his employers up there, and all the landlord could give us was the name of the bank. We'll track them down soon as, see what his boss and colleagues can tell us about him.'

Tom looked around. There was nothing in this room, nothing left anyway, to give much away.

He walked outside to the small landing and opened the other doors.

There were five bedrooms in all, the two larger rooms having been partitioned into halves.

'Laura, it was only Matteo's name on the lease, though, right?' Tom asked. 'Landlord's not spoofing?'

She'd come out into the hall behind him.

'Yup,' she said. 'He was here a year already.'

'Has the landlord said anything about these alterations?'

'He didn't mention it being a five-bed,' Laura said. 'So I asked and he certainly reacted like it was news to him.'

'So, Matteo did these?'

Laura hesitated.

'It's not like Matteo can deny it.'

'And that's handy for the landlord,' Tom said. 'Because if he made these adjustments as the property owner, and it contributed to the fire, he'll be in hot shit.'

Tom pondered it for a minute or two. The housing crisis in Dublin was at its peak. Ruthless landlords were carrying through on the old adage of need-meets-greed and exploiting people's desperation in new and shocking ways all the time. Maria had shown him an ad on a rental site for a shed out somebody's back, for which the landlord was asking in the region of 800 euro a month. She'd been lucky to be both earning relatively decent money and to have parents supporting her when she'd found her two-bed apartment. Even then, it had been a friend of a friend that had secured the lease for her. Most places, estate agents were charging a viewing fee. It was nigh on impossible to find a place so people were resorting to anything and everything. The city wasn't far off heading back to the days of the tenement buildings.

Was this what this landlord had done? Tom mused. Turned a tiny house into a much larger rent generator? Matteo Russo might have been well paid but it didn't matter how much you were on when there were no actual properties available.

'I know what you're thinking,' Laura said. 'But I'm not sure why the landlord wouldn't admit to other tenants and risk them coming forward to give us statements to the contrary. It wouldn't be unusual for one name to be on the lease and for a gang of renters to actually be living here, but the landlord is adamant he didn't have any other tenants. He assumed the woman in the hospital must have been a girlfriend, staying overnight or something like that.'

'He could still be covering his tracks,' Tom said. 'How much was the rent?'

'Three grand per month.'

'Christ. And he really assumed Russo was paying that on his own?'

'That's what he said.'

Tom stroked his jaw. He didn't believe it. What he wasn't sure of was whether the landlord was lying or whether it had been

Matteo who had decided to maximise the subletting income to cover his own rent.

'Check the other houses let out by the landlord,' Tom said. 'See if similar adaptations have been made. If he did this and it contributed to the house going up so quickly, he'll be facing an involuntary manslaughter charge.'

Emmet had joined them now, and he looked from one to the other, waiting until they'd finished. Behind him, a fireman carried a stepladder. The gang of three moved out of his way as the fireman opened the ladder on the landing and climbed up to open the attic door overhead.

'I haven't bagged everything yet,' Emmet said, 'if that's what you're about to ask. We have to be careful. Some of this stuff is just going to fall apart and there's a lot of water damage, along with the rest of the destruction. I'm concentrating on what might be of use to you.'

'What's he looking for up there?' Tom asked.

They watched the fireman's legs disappear into the hole in the ceiling.

'He's checking for damage to the neighbouring properties,' Emmet said.

'We were just discussing the fact they all belong to the same landlord,' Tom said. 'He must be shitting himself.'

'I think you have an actual aversion to landlords with multiple properties,' Emmet said. 'Haven't we had a conversation like this before?'

'I just can't understand how somebody's career can involve making money out of other people's living needs.' Tom shrugged.

'Mm-hm. I think you missed your true vocation as an agent of the state in Commie Russia.'

'We really need to figure out how many people lived here,' Laura said, ignoring them both. 'Just because we only think it was two doesn't mean there weren't more, even if there is no bloody sign of them. They could be foreign students who've outstayed their visas, anything like that. They'll have lost everything and we won't touch them for statements because they'll be afraid to come in.'

'I can already tell there were plenty of women's products in the bathroom,' Emmet said. 'Though, I know you ladies like to keep twenty-odd bottles of shampoo on the go at any given time, so it might just be one woman who lived here – your mysterious girl.'

'Talk to us about this room where the victim was found,' Tom said. 'The door and window, they weren't locked, were they?'

'No,' Emmet said. 'Fire officer got in easy, just like with the front door downstairs. The door was open, in fact, not even closed over. And no restraints on the bed, no evidence the victim was unable to move.'

Tom and Laura exchanged a glance.

'We'll just have to wait and see what Moya finds,' Tom said. 'Maybe he did have something in his system or maybe the smoke got to him when he was in a deep sleep.'

'What I did find,' Emmet said, leading them back into the room, 'was a laptop, phone and car keys.' He pointed at the bedside locker, or what remained of it. 'All look damaged, but let's see what we can do. Those SIM cards can withstand a lot but the extent of the fire wouldn't leave me hopeful.'

'No other phones?' Laura asked. 'Our girl had nothing on her when she was found. Where are her devices?'

'Not here,' Emmet said.

'Linda's going in to see her,' Laura told Tom.

'Good call,' he said. 'Don't you think so, Emmet?'

'Oh, yes. If anybody can connect with a woman found wandering around the streets butt naked and seemingly batshit crazy, it's Linda.'

Tom smiled. There was no real malice in Emmet's words. Not any more. The arrival of the couple's adopted son from a long ago affair had finally put paid to their acrimonious past. They were parents and grandparents now, and that was more important than anything else.

Emmet pulled out his phone and summoned up the photo gallery.

'This is what it looked like when we came in,' he said.

Tom zoomed in on the images.

Unless you knew what you were supposed to be looking at, it would be nigh impossible to tell that the blackened lump in the bed they were now standing beside was actually a body.

'Thank God I missed that,' Tom said.

'Indeed,' Emmet said.

'You said you saw evidence of women living here. Any signs that a baby did? A cot, steriliser, anything?' Tom asked.

'Nothing like that.' Emmet frowned. 'There could be fabric from an infant's clothing, but I'll have to check through everything again to see if I missed that. I don't think I did.'

Tom pursed his lips. Curiouser and curiouser.

'There's nothing else to be learned in here,' Laura said, and Tom got the distinct impression she was as eager to get going as he was. 'I want to pay a visit to Moya and speed her up. Tom, come with me. I mean, please. If you can. She doesn't take me seriously yet.'

'She does,' Tom said. 'She treats everybody with the same level of contempt. But I'm as impatient as you, so let's go and annoy her. Emmet, let us know when the report from the fire department is in, will you? They can liaise directly with you. Any hints so far?'

'Like they said earlier – petrol poured around the place. You can still smell it.'

Tom raised his head and sniffed. He couldn't pick up anything over the smoke, but that was why he was in his job and Emmet in his.

He looked over at the bed again, noticing Laura do the same.

'Yep,' she said, reading his mind. 'If you killed somebody and wanted to hide the evidence . . .'

'It's pretty effective,' Tom said.

They were making their way back downstairs when the shout came from above.

The fireman who'd been in the attic was back on the landing.

'Hey!' he called. 'Police. I need police up here.'

He was a young guy, maybe only early twenties. Tom hadn't noticed when he'd seen him upstairs, in his large jacket and helmet. He'd just looked like another one of the team. But Tom saw it now: the fresh-skinned cheeks and large, terrified eyes; the trembling lip. The fireman was just a kid.

Tom and Laura bounded up the stairs, Emmet hot on their heels.

'What have you found?' Laura asked.

'There's a suitcase,' the fireman said. 'I had to move it to check the side wall. It was heavy. I don't know why I opened it.'

He was in shock.

Emmet was up the ladder first.

'Just don't touch anything until I've taken photographs,' he called over his shoulder to Tom and Laura. 'And we need that lad fingerprinted to deal with contamination.'

The weight in Tom's stomach felt like lead as they took up their positions behind Emmet on the boards in the attic. The fire hadn't ravaged up here to the same extent. The roof of the house was completely intact and there were no burned belongings or beams. But the smoke had risen and, if anything, was denser up here.

Tom and Laura placed their hands over their mouths; Emmet replaced his face mask.

There were few places to stand and they had to be careful. Around the edge of the attic, a shelf-like storage space had been built. It was mainly empty bar a couple of cardboard boxes, an old chest of drawers, a few black bags.

And the suitcase.

Tom had one just like it. A large, back-breaking wheeled case, one you simultaneously looked forward to spotting on the luggage conveyor belt and dreaded because your arms risked being pulled off as you retrieved it.

'You'll need to go through all those boxes and bags,' Tom mumbled through his sleeve. 'See if there's anything belonging to the current residents.'

Laura nodded. She felt stupid. She'd assumed Emmet had checked up here but he had probably been waiting for the firemen to give him a nod.

She brought up the torch on her phone, as Emmet found his and started taking pictures.

The suitcase was closed and lying on its side. The fireman had thrown the top cover back over, once he'd seen what was inside. His instincts had kicked in, even while his brain was processing what he'd seen.

The world slowed as Emmet leaned across and lifted it off, revealing the suitcase's contents.

They'd known, when they'd seen the lad's face, what he'd found.

Tom was just praying with every fibre in his being, to a God he had an on-off relationship with at the best of times, that this wasn't the baby that had led him here by the nose in the first instance.

It wasn't.

The case contained a young black woman.

And she was very much dead.

CHAPTER 8

'I can't even fathom why you're here; shouldn't you be in Costa del something? That's where I'd be right now. Sipping a cool white, reading a book, waves lapping at my feet.'

Bronwyn Maher walked as fast as she talked. Tom and Laura were almost trotting behind the commissioner as they made their way through the Phoenix Park Garda headquarters.

'Not that it matters,' Bronwyn added. 'I'm glad you hung about, Tom. But, just so you know, don't even think about claiming you didn't take holidays. It's your choice to work through your annual leave. I have all the forms, you're on your holli-bobs, my job is done. Detective Chief Inspector, are you okay with him being here?'

Bronwyn came to an abrupt halt, heels squeaking on the par-quet floor, a few hairs breaking free of her tidy, short do as she turned. She was dressed in full uniform, a skirt rather than trousers, because Bronwyn Maher had decided early that fem-inine didn't translate as weak. And there wasn't a single person who'd describe Bronwyn with that adjective. Just last year she had become the first female commissioner of An Garda Síochána, and she hadn't got there by chance.

Laura nodded, seemingly too overwhelmed by the speed at which Bronwyn talked, walked and jumped from subject to subject to offer anything resembling words.

'As long as you are,' Bronwyn said. 'You might remember Sean McGuinness cramping your style on the odd occasion, Tom. Don't be that boss.'

'I always valued Sean's input,' Tom said, defensively.

'Ha! Right, DCI Brennan – wait, did you take your husband's name? Are you Lennon now?'

'Yes,' Laura said. 'I'm Laura Lennon now.'

'Anyone give you any flak for that?' the commissioner asked.

'A few, but they're neutered when I tell them that I also took his promotion,' Laura said. 'And I earn a lot more than him.'

Bronwyn smiled.

'Good woman. Anyway, it helps for kids' names and that, doesn't it? I can't stand double barrels. What do double-barrelled kids do when they marry? Become quadruple-barrelled? You're not, are you? Expecting?'

Laura followed Bronwyn's gaze down to her virtually flat stomach.

The three of them shared an uncomfortable silence for a moment or two, each of them considering the ramifications for the investigation of an entirely phantom pregnancy only recently invented by the commissioner.

Tom realised the utter ridiculousness of the situation and threw his hands out.

'For Christ's sake, Bronwyn, take your foot off the pedal. You're mortifying the woman.'

This was the new Bronwyn, Tom knew. She'd been a lot more relaxed when she was in the deputy top job. These days she got frazzled more, and when she was particularly stressed, and in familiar company, it came out as frantic. Understandable, when you knew she was juggling forty-seven balls with one hand tied behind her back.

'The DCI is going to need a major incident room and way more bodies,' Tom said.

'Thought you had enough bodies,' Bronwyn quipped. She crossed her arms – simultaneously relaxing into well-trodden ground and preparing for the oncoming negotiation.

'Har-de-har,' Tom responded. 'Half the force has been roped into gun crime and now we have a bog-standard possible double murder, so what are you giving us?'

'I can't give you anything,' Bronwyn said. 'You know the score, Tom. The minister says gun crime is the priority. Lennon, you'll have to work with what you've got. Who have you got?'

'Ray is working with the new unit so I've only Brian Cullinane and Michael Geoghegan,' Laura said. 'We've about five rank and file.'

'That's not enough detectives by any stretch,' Tom said, 'and she'll need at least four times the rank and file. The young female in the case was black. I hate to point it out, boss, but if we don't put resources into this, certain accusations could be levelled.'

'This organisation has done more to combat racism in investigations under my watch than in our history,' Bronwyn said, her voice loaded.

'Absolutely. I'm talking about perceptions.'

Tom met Bronwyn's eye. She knew he was right, but he felt cheap for even pointing it out. Bronwyn had enough detractors because of her gender but she also had to face down much less fair criticism arising from historical issues with the force. There were still barely a handful of New Irish members of An Garda Síochána and some of the snider commentators had barely allowed the new commissioner in the door before pointing out she'd yet to improve statistics on her watch.

'Ten uniforms and isn't it fantastic that Tom isn't somewhere foreign,' Bronwyn said.

'With all due respect, ma'am,' Laura cut in, 'three investigating detectives and the goodwill of the chief super just isn't going to cut it. There are two detectives based in the docklands station; I'd like to request their other cases be reallocated and they're seconded to my squad for the duration of this investigation.'

'Would you now?' Bronwyn said, her brusque tone unmistakably admiring. She hesitated. 'What was the story with the second body in the attic?'

'We'll be heading into Moya Chambers soon but it certainly looked like she'd been stabbed,' Laura answered.

'Hmm. Okay. Tom, you let the docklands station sergeant know the score. And talk to the press office. They're inundated with requests. The locals are talking to the media already. Have you done your door-to-door?'

'It's in train,' Laura said. 'We'll get through it quicker with fifteen uniforms.'

'Do you let up? Tom, give the DCI more overtime forms and squeeze resources from somewhere, will you? Let me have a little bit of plausible deniability when the minister asks me why I'm not putting one hundred per cent of my force into tackling the latest hot potato.'

Bronwyn started off down the hall again.

Tom waited until she was out of earshot.

'Did she just give me paperwork on my holidays?' he muttered.

'I'm fairly certain you gave it to yourself,' Laura said. 'Honestly, boss. This isn't fair. If you want to leave it, I can sort it.'

Tom thought about it, for a microsecond.

He'd become so bored of the monotony that came with his new position. An actual case, one that needed teeth, was as good as a rest. Louise was right about that.

'As long as I get a day off to whisk Louise to a spa next week, I think we can manage,' he said. 'And well done on standing up to the dragon, by the way.'

'I've been doing that for years,' Laura said, squinting at Tom in a way that left him under no illusions it was him she meant.

CHAPTER 9

Linda would have been happy to sit quietly all afternoon with the young burns victim with no name.

But Laura Lennon was desperate for progress, so that wasn't an option.

For a little while, though, Linda enjoyed people-watching, leaving the young woman to lie there, silent, motionless.

The ward felt fresh. The nurses had thrown open the windows and the flowers brought by visitors managed to spread their fragrance, even over the clinical smell. The space was also bursting with fascinating characters. Across the way, a woman was reading celebrity magazines and every time she stumbled upon something she thought her co-patients should know, she practically roared the nugget.

'He was only shagging his brother's wife!' she exclaimed now, waving a picture of some guilty-looking footballer so Linda, the only person paying attention, could see it. 'Dirty bastard! All that money and flash and they're still filthy little boys underneath it all.'

Next to the nameless woman was an elderly patient who had been admitted suffering with severe constipation. She'd kept the entire floor entertained when the nurses arrived to give her an enema.

'That's the wrong hole, as I said to my husband,' she chuckled, causing the youngest nurse to shriek with laughter.

Linda nearly choked on her tea. Even the mute woman in the bed beside the psychologist widened her eyes a little, disrupted from her reverie.

Linda observed the young woman's changing facial expressions with interest. Though she knew Laura Lennon wasn't happy about it, Linda reckoned the best thing the hospital could have done was put the woman on a normal ward. If they'd left her in isolation, she could have continued staring straight ahead, her thoughts turned inwards on whatever she'd been through before she'd arrived here. But it was difficult to ignore enema-woman, no matter how much PTSD you were suffering.

And it was PTSD. Linda had recognised that straight away.

So, once the grunting and giggling behind the curtains beside them started to subside, Linda began to talk quietly to the young woman in the bed, coaxing, encouraging, reassuring.

The young woman was safe, everybody was here to support her, she could talk to Linda.

Slowly, the words started to seep through.

The girl's shoulders started to relax. Girl. Oh, Linda knew she shouldn't think of her as such, that over eighteen was technically a woman. But, fast approaching sixty-five, Linda was mature enough to admit that she often longed for the years when people referred to her as a girl.

Becoming a woman, for Linda, had meant nothing but restrictions and responsibilities and expectations.

She blinked.

She was wont to do that these days, drift off on tangents in her mind. It had been happening ever since her son had returned. She spent more and more time thinking of the past, what could have been.

'You seem to have no name,' Linda said, gently, her focus back on her patient. 'Everybody has a name. Some have multiple names. I'm Linda, but most people who know me call me crazy old bat. Partly because of my lack of fashion sense, mainly because I talk nonsense most of the time.'

A ghost of a smile, maybe?

'I'm not crazy, really. It just helps, when you want to put other people on edge. Are you afraid to tell us your name? Sometimes, people are told they mustn't give their real name. Especially if they are not supposed to be somewhere, or they're travelling with different identities. That can happen and it's understandable.'

A little quiver in the lips.

'I don't think anybody would mind if you wanted to give a different name. But we have to call you something and if you tell us who you are, we might be able to start helping. I promise, we only want to help.'

A frown. Some consideration was going on there, intense, laboured. Then a decision.

'Tyanna,' the girl whispered.

'Tyanna is your name?' Linda said.

The girl nodded.

'Tyanna Volkov.'

Linda smiled, cautiously.

'It's a very beautiful name. How old are you, Tyanna?'

'Eighteen.'

'Eighteen. So you are . . . well, you make me feel very old. I was just thinking how quickly we're supposed to be in charge of ourselves. You're only a child, though, really. I remember eighteen. I remember pretending I knew everything but it was a lie. Even then, I realised other people were in control of my life. They always would be. That happens, from time to time. And especially to girls. People take over. We have to run away sometimes, just to be ourselves.'

Linda, very softly, brushed a wisp of dark brown hair from the girl's forehead. Tyanna didn't even flinch.

Unusual, that. Most people reacted to a stranger's touch.

'Do you have any children?' Linda asked. She'd been briefed by Laura; she knew she had to get to the bottom of the baby statement.

The shaking started in Tyanna's hands and slowly travelled up her arm until her whole body was trembling.

Linda sat back, alarmed.

'No,' Tyanna said. 'No, no, no. No baby. I do not want to talk about the baby.'

Linda frowned, confused.

The girl turned her head away and started to cry.

CHAPTER 10

Tom and Laura found Moya Chambers smoking prodigiously in the small garden for staff at the hospital that housed the state pathologist's teaching lab.

The garden was pretty, a quiet enclave of greenery and summer blooms, roses and gardenias.

An oasis.

Moya was using her cigarette-free hand to pick at her nails. Her tight blonde curls were clipped up and off her face, and she was entirely focused on the nicotine she was inhaling.

A tidy pile of butts was collecting at Moya's feet and she was sucking on the latest cigarette at a speed of knots when they sat down beside her.

'I'll pick them up,' she said, glaring at the two officers and what she perceived as their judgemental expressions.

'You realise Laura's case involves a fire, don't you?' Tom said, batting away the cigarette smoke.

'Is that a real question?' Moya said. 'I'm the one with a charred corpse on my dissection table.'

Tom noticed Laura flinch. He was well used to Moya and her anarchic approach to the dead, but it could come across as brutally insensitive to the unseasoned.

'I'd have thought,' Tom said, leaning across and seizing the cigarette from her lips, 'you'd be well aware of what these little bastards do to your lungs.'

Moya scrunched up her tiny features in annoyance.

'I'm aware of what a car can do to your internal organs, Tom. I'm aware of what a burst heart valve can do to your chest cavity. I'm aware of what a small clot can do to your brain. I know the damage that can be caused by one well-aimed kick to the back of the head. We're all going to fucking die, Tom. Choose your poison.'

Tom also knew that the blunter and more undiplomatic Moya was, the more affected she had been by the victim she'd just cut open.

'Well, you're a cheery little bunny this afternoon, aren't you?' Tom said.

'Yep,' Moya said. 'I'm happy as hell and right now, my lab looks like Dante's Inferno. Two PMs done.'

She took the cigarette back from Tom and inhaled again.

'You've done them both already?' Laura asked, surprised.

'You'll have the report on your desk imminently. Once I'd started, I had to do them both. I had help. It was a good teaching case. They both were.'

'Can you give us a verbal rundown?' Laura asked. 'I've to do a press conference later.'

Moya took one last drag and threw the butt onto the pile with the rest. She stared straight ahead.

'This fucking job,' she said. 'Both your victims were dead when the fire started. There's trace smoke in the male's lungs, but it wasn't inhaled, it was absorbed. I've started a tox screen like you asked, but you know now the reason the fire didn't wake him. He might still have been drugged, but the girl's lungs are clean. External smoke damage but nothing internal.'

Tom and Laura caught each other's eyes.

It was as they expected. A double murder and the fire to get rid of the evidence.

'They were *both* stabbed to death,' Moya said. 'It was difficult to establish in the male but once it had been confirmed for the female, we gave it closer attention. There are incisions in the torso consistent with a knife attack. He's not giving up much else, but the female's wounds tell me it was an ordinary knife – something domestic, most likely. She was stabbed seven times. I can identify only a couple of wounds to the male but the deterioration of the body means there might have been more that I can't see. And I can't accurately give you depth or tell you which wound bled the most or caused the most damage.'

'So it could have been the same knife for both victims?' Laura said.

Moya nodded.

Tom knew Laura was already making a note to have Emmet search for the possible weapon at the fire site. It didn't matter. The fire would have destroyed all forensic evidence. It would nearly be better if the weapon wasn't still at the premises.

'I've a dental expert working on the teeth from the male but it's already looking like a match for the records that arrived from Italy. Impacted wisdom teeth and plenty of orthodontic work. We got them fast, by the way. The parents must have influence to turn that around on a weekend. No idea how you'll identify the female but we can get a photofit done up from the corpse. She's probably sixteen, going by the skull measurements, but I'll carbon-date the eyes to confirm it.'

'Sixteen?' Tom and Laura both spoke at once.

Tom had guessed she was young but he was conscious that, to him, young was anybody from their early thirties down. Sixteen was no age.

Moya took a deep breath.

'Yep. And she'd just had a baby.'

Laura brought her hand to her mouth, quickly.

Tom felt his throat constrict.

'When?' Laura asked.

'I'd estimate she was four to five weeks postpartum,' Moya said. 'The womb had fully contracted but the pregnancy hormones were still high, the stomach still loose. Vaginal delivery, no sign of surgical intervention.'

'Jesus Christ.' The swear left Tom's mouth before he'd even taken a breath.

They'd found the 'baby'.

But where the hell was it?

What in God's name had the girl from the street witnessed before she'd been brought to hospital?

What had she taken part in?

'Time of death?' Laura asked.

'An absolute nightmare to determine in the male victim's case, given the damage sustained. Most likely in the twenty-four hours before he was discovered. He has traces of undigested foodstuff in his system. Steak. Harder for the body to process. The female's time of death is approximately the same. It's possible they were killed together or within a short period of each other.'

Moya stood up.

'Any ideas about the girl?' she asked, looking back at Tom and Laura.

'We don't know who she is,' Tom said. 'We don't know what

happened in that house and our only possible witness won't talk to us. We'll have to go through all the hospitals, try to match up a recent delivery with her description if we can't get a name. It will be a nightmare.'

'Find out who she was,' Moya said. 'Please.' Then she walked away.

Tom sighed. He bent down and began to sweep up the butts with his hands.

'Where's her baby?' Laura asked.

'I have no idea. But that woman in the hospital is going to have to tell us.'

'Why was she hidden upstairs, but he was just left out like that?' Laura asked.

Tom sat back on his hunkers.

'I have no idea, Laura. Maybe she tried to hide. Maybe her killer wanted her hidden from others in the house.'

Laura took her phone from her pocket.

'Linda has just texted,' Laura said. 'We have a name for our burns victim. Tyanna Volkov. And she says she's eighteen.'

Tom looked around for a bin. He found one and threw Moya's waste inside.

'Of the wolf,' he said.

'What?'

'Volkov. It's Russian, I think.'

'Do you think she might have . . .'

'Been involved?' Tom completed the sentence. 'Everything's a possibility. But my gut says she didn't look like somebody who'd just committed a double murder. Did the thought cross your mind?'

'No. Definitely not. She's only a slip of a thing. And she could have died in that fire.'

'Most likely, she was meant to,' Tom said. 'The fire was started downstairs, yeah? Maybe she was upstairs and meant to stay there. But we need her to talk and tell us where she was and what happened in that house.'

'We need to give it a little time, though,' Laura said. 'Linda says she's got proper PTSD. She'll work with her for a bit. She's already getting somewhere. If we rush in, we could get nothing and she might just put up a wall.'

'I appreciate that.' Tom sighed. 'But it's bloody frustrating. It's not just her feelings we have to consider. We need to find that baby.'

'It's not about her feelings, though. It's her capacity to speak to us. We need to go slow, *because* we need to find out where the baby is.'

'God damn it, it's like listening to myself,' Tom said.

Laura hesitated.

'Should we be reading something into this?' she said. 'A black girl, a Russian and an Italian sharing a house?'

'The apartments and houses around the IFSC have the most cosmopolitan demographic in the city, I'd guess,' Tom said. 'But Matteo was early thirties, right? I'm starting to wonder if he was subletting or if there was something more sinister going on.'

'Me too,' Laura said.

CHAPTER 11

Tyanna knew that the noise of the other women on the ward served as a distraction.

But part of her just wanted them all to be quiet. To stop. To let her process her thoughts, as jumbled and distressing as they were.

The doctor woman – Linda – the skinny one with the wild red hair and strange, rambling way of talking – had gone. She'd promised she'd come back but Tyanna didn't know if she meant in a few hours or days. She liked her. There was something in the woman's face, a kindness. Tyanna wanted to trust her but she knew she shouldn't talk to anybody.

But now she had given her name. Her real name, too, not the one she knew she was supposed to use if anybody asked her any questions.

Time was going both too fast and too slow. The nurses had given her pain relief and some other medicine, which made her brain feel sluggish. She didn't mind that. It also made her feel calm. But Tyanna had no time to feel calm. She couldn't just lie here, waiting.

It wasn't safe. She wouldn't feel safe until she'd found somewhere to go. To hide.

Why had she mentioned the baby to those women on the street? If she had said nothing, maybe they would have just mistaken her for a crazy person. They might have just brought her to a hospital for the insane, like the ones they had at home.

She would have been better off there.

Not here, in this hospital which seemed so public, where people could just walk in and out.

The curtain had barely moved.

Tyanna almost missed him, her eyes flickered so slowly in his direction.

But she'd felt the weight on the side of the bed – the sudden depression and then the rise.

He'd left her a small parting gift.

It had only taken seconds.

CHAPTER 12

Nina Cusack hadn't budged from her room since she'd arrived home the night previous.

She could hear her parents downstairs, the urgent whispers – her dad's angry, her mother's soothing.

Her dad wanted to come up and start the interrogation, Nina knew that. But her mother seemed to be holding the ship steady, for now.

She knew that what she was doing to them was cruel.

It wasn't that Nina didn't want to tell her mother and father where she'd been for the last two years. She would like more than anything to let all the words spill out, to vomit the whole sorry mess into somebody else's head and remove it from hers.

But she couldn't.

Nina turned over to lie on her side.

Her pillow was scented with lavender. The duvet smelled of fabric softener. The dressing table across from her still had all her old bottles of perfume and creams, but they weren't old at all – they were just familiar makes and they'd all been bought brand new.

Nina's mother had kept her daughter's room fresh and welcoming for each of the twenty-four months that Nina had been gone.

It had been like this the first time she came home from the rehab clinic.

Sixteen, and she'd already had to go through detox.

She knew her parents couldn't understand where they'd gone wrong.

It hadn't been their fault.

It was Nina that had gone wrong, that was the truth of it.

There was a reason for it, of course. She could pinpoint the exact moment she'd decided to take drugs.

But it had been her choice, in the end. That was the one thing the counselling had taught her. Accept responsibility.

When she'd started using again, she'd kept it to herself and she'd never gone back on the really hard gear.

But she'd still managed to fuck everything up.

Nina closed her eyes and her head filled with images.

Nasty, dirty, repulsive images.

She opened her eyes again.

The handbag she'd brought back with her was vibrating on the floor.

Nina reached for it and took out the cheap phone inside.

Where are you?

Nina read the message, sent from an unknown number.

She flung the phone on the floor and pulled the duvet over her head.

The smell of roasting chicken travelled upstairs and began to fill the room.

Nina felt like throwing up.

Matteo had had no idea how dangerous their world was.

Now they were all paying for it.

CHAPTER 13

The Skype call was as clear as day and Laura thanked God for the quality of the Russos' broadband. There was little more distressing than speaking to bereaved parents and having to repeat the same questions through a glitchy connection, only to see their faces frozen in pain on a paralysed screen.

Outside, dusk fell. The incident room was more or less empty. The street teams had been operational since that morning, going house to house, trying to establish if anybody knew anything about Matteo Russo and the women who lived in three Shipping Row.

On the screen in front of her, Matteo's mother was holding a photograph of Matteo up to the monitor so Laura could take a screenshot. Mrs Russo had promised to email it through also, but Laura was hungry for as much information as she could lay her hands on; she didn't want to risk hanging up and then waiting for an email that the mother was suddenly too grief-stricken to send.

The dental records had confirmed that the fire victim was the Russos' son.

But Laura had had no idea what he even looked like until now.

'This is my favourite photo,' Mrs Russo said. 'It is a few years old but he did not change much, my boy. Always a handsome man.'

Matteo's mother was a stunningly beautiful woman, even in

her fifties. Long, thick black hair, an elegant bone structure, expensive clothes that hugged a trim figure. Her husband sat beside her, barely taking his head out of his hands, but the glimpse Laura had caught revealed an attractive, kind-faced man, who also appeared utterly heartbroken.

From the photograph, it was easy to see that their son Matteo had inherited the best of both of them. Dark, glossy hair; brooding brown eyes; cheekbones you could cut diamonds on; and a well-defined, muscular figure.

The photograph had been taken on a family holiday at Lake Como. Matteo smiled for the camera as he sat on the edge of a pier, topless, in a pair of swim trunks. One leg dangled into the water, the other rested on the deck, an arm slung across his knee.

Calvin Klein model, Laura thought.

The Russos were wealthy. The Irish embassy contact had informed the DCI of that before the call was set up. Mr Russo worked in television – was a board member, in fact, of one of Italy's top channels. His wife was a former beauty model; of course she was. Laura couldn't take her eyes off Mrs Russo, except to look at the picture of their gorgeous son. She was exceptionally grateful the decision had been made not to allow the parents to see their son's body. For their part, the Russos hadn't asked if it was possible. It had been explained to them that an eyewitness ID wasn't necessary or possible. The Russos had understood and not pressed the matter.

Sadly, Laura knew, that decision would ultimately haunt them. Right now, dealing with the police and the authorities, the Russos were outwardly accepting of the facts. A degree of pragmatism had kicked in. Their son had died in a strange country and it was time to go through all the steps necessary to ensure they could get him home. But in time, without having seen the body, they would struggle to come to terms with their loss. Especially as the parents were used to Matteo living abroad and not having him in their lives every day.

'I have it,' Laura said, saving the screenshot. She'd get the press office to zoom in on his face and cut out the torso for the photo release. It was a lovely picture but Laura didn't want to issue an image of a murder victim that looked like it had been cut out of a magazine.

'So, Matteo had been living here for four years,' Laura said. 'And he was thirty-four years of age?'

Mrs Russo nodded. She began to talk again, in a sing-song accent that made the devastating content of the conversation almost sound cheery.

'He loved Ireland. He was a good boy, clever. Always wanting to travel, yes? He visit all of Europe, but it is not far enough. So he go to England for a year or two, and he like it there but it's expensive. In Ireland, he earns a lot of money and it's nice place. The money, the beer, the girls.'

Laura's senses prickled.

'Did he have a girlfriend?'

'My Matteo had many girlfriends.' Mrs Russo looked down at the photo in her hand. She stroked her son's cheek, lip quivering. Just outside of shot, an arm leaned across and placed a glass of water in front of her. Laura's Italian counterpart was in the room, an inspector who'd agreed to sit with the family for the duration of the call.

'He was not a . . . I do not mean he was not respectful to women,' Mrs Russo said, looking up hastily. 'He was just a good-looking boy, and the girls, they liked him. Always did. I wanted him to settle down and have children but that is every mother's wish. He had much more living to do. He . . .'

Her voice broke and she turned away from the camera.

Mr Russo lifted his head and placed his arm around his wife. He looked straight into the screen and at Laura.

'How did this happen? Matteo said he lived in a nice house, near the city centre. Expensive. Why did the fire start? Was it an accident?'

Laura winced. The full details had yet to be communicated to Matteo's parents and she'd drawn the short straw. But she knew that once she'd lobbed that grenade, she wouldn't get more information out of them. They'd be destroyed when she revealed their son hadn't just died in an accidental house fire; that he had, in fact, been murdered.

'Had you ever visited your son here?' she asked. 'Had you seen the house he lived in recently, or met any housemates?'

'No.' Mr Russo shook his head. 'Matteo came home a lot. We visited Ireland a couple of years ago and saw the apartment he had at the time, but he put us up in one of your nice hotels. The Westbury? His apartment then was small. He moved to this house because it was larger, he said. But then he got some students in to help pay the rent so there still would not have been room for us. It was easier for him to come here.'

'He told you he sublet to students?' Laura asked.

Mr Russo hesitated.

'I'm not worried about the terms of his lease,' Laura said, quickly. 'There was a female victim in the house, also, and we haven't identified her yet.'

'Her poor parents,' Mrs Russo cried.

Mr Russo shook his head, appalled.

'Yes,' he said. 'Matteo said he had let out rooms to a few girls. But I do not know their names.'

'Is it possible he was seeing one of them?'

Mr Russo shrugged.

'I do not think so. He said they were young. He said the rent in Dublin is high and students struggle to get anywhere but he did not mind sharing. It pays for him, too.'

'Why are you asking about girlfriends?' his mother asked suddenly, looking up. 'Was he found with the girl? Did they die together? I would like to know if somebody was there. I do not want to think of him alone.'

Laura took a deep breath.

It was time.

Tom had turned up to help Laura coordinate the results from the door-to-doors. One of the reassigned detectives from the docklands had been put on the team overseeing the hospital contacts but he had little or nothing to go on. The fact the victim from the suitcase was black and sixteen worked a little in their favour in terms of statistics, but that only worked on the assumption she'd had the baby in a hospital to begin with. But there was an energy in the team – trying to solve a murder or multiple murder was one thing; actively searching for a live victim was quite another. Nobody cared they were working late. Nobody was worried what time they got home.

With one exception.

Detective Michael Geoghegan had been overseeing the door-knocking, but he and his wife Anne had a joint birthday party planned that Saturday night and Laura already felt bad enough that none of his immediate work colleagues would be able to attend. She sent him home with a bottle of champagne and a massive apology on behalf of the squad.

She hoped the night went well for the Geoghegans. They'd had a difficult time a couple of years back – Anne had turned down a fantastic job offer because Michael refused to cut back on his hours, and Laura was almost positive they'd ended up in marriage counselling. Anne was back working now that their two children were in school, and they'd found a good au pair to pick up the slack, but Laura got the impression that a bad taste had been left after Michael's refusal to compromise.

Maybe things would get easier for them both in the time ahead, but Laura certainly wasn't going to add to their problems by making Michael miss the birthday celebrations.

'It doesn't sound like Matteo Russo was up to anything dodgy,' Laura told Tom, as they walked the small residential cul-de-sacs off Shipping Row. In the gardens they passed, police officers filled the porches. Most nights round here, Laura suspected, people wouldn't have bothered opening their doors to a stranger's knock, even in summer. But everybody was aware the police were doing their rounds. The public were as curious as the guards about what had happened in the burned-out house. Everybody wanted their tuppence-worth.

'He was an A-student in school and college,' Laura continued. 'Really steady home life, plenty of money. Only child, very loved. I mean, there may be dark family secrets there, but they certainly weren't coming across in the interview with the parents. He wasn't perfect, by any stretch. Definitely a little greedy, if the subletting – if that's what it was – is anything to go by, and maybe a bit of a womaniser. Most blokes in their early thirties, regardless of their fantasies, would rent with other men, just so they could get away with leaving dirty dishes in the sink and have the footie on every night. But it sounds like Matteo had stacked the house with young, pretty females. He mightn't have known that girl was sixteen, or pregnant. He could have got caught up in something he was entirely ignorant of.'

'That's a pretty mind-blowing wrong place, wrong time,' Tom said. 'So they'd no suspicions he had any enemies, anyone who might have attacked him?'

'None. And clichéd and all as it sounds, I didn't get the impression they're Mafia, despite the Berlusconi-like career choices. TV and modelling. What a pair.'

Tom snorted, then frowned.

'What do you think happened, then?' he said. 'If Matteo wasn't the target? Did he stumble upon somebody attacking the girl and the attacker turned on Matteo? Or was Matteo being attacked and the girl happened upon it?'

'I don't know. Where was the baby while this was going on? I'm sure if it was there, the mother would have tried to save her child. Isn't that what Tyanna claims she too was trying to do?'

Tom frowned and Laura knew he wasn't buying it. It was too much speculation.

'Have you definitely linked Tyanna Volkov to this house?' Tom said. 'Any addresses coming up on her background check?'

Laura shook her head.

'Nothing from the background check at all yet. She hasn't given us anything but her name, though Linda is going to talk to her again. There're CCTV cameras at the end of the road where the Financial Services Centre starts. The first one, which has a camera pointing right at the top of Shipping Row, is outside a Spar shop. We're hoping to pick Tyanna up on it around the time of the fire, so then we'll know for sure. There's plenty more CCTV in the direction of town, so once we find her we can start charting her progress.'

'Boss!' Detective Brian Cullinane was standing at the bottom of one of the gardens. 'Can you come here for a moment?'

Laura and Tom walked past a couple of gates to join the

detective in the small garden of the end house. Brian stood waiting, sweating a little from his bald pate, even though most of the day's strong heat had faded.

As a colleague, Laura hadn't spent that much time working with Brian and had found him quiet, maybe even a little aloof. A couple of years ago, though, after he'd started bringing his boyfriend on nights out, Laura had realised it wasn't that Brian was shy – he just kept to himself, choosing to keep certain aspects of his life private. Being gay in an organisation traditionally known for its toxic masculinity was a challenge. Brian, however, had coped admirably. He was married now, and the whole team had been at the wedding, filling the void left by Brian's parents, who'd refused to attend.

With Ray reassigned, Laura had found herself leaning on Brian more and she'd realised he was a really good detective.

'I've been getting a sense of something as we've gone through the neighbours today,' he told them, 'but this is the first resident to actually say it, eh, bluntly. Thought you might want to hear.'

He gestured them up the short pathway towards the open front door.

The homeowner stood in its frame, arms crossed, leaning against one side. He was in his sixties, hair brushed into an old-fashioned comb-over, and his bearing indicated a man who took himself and his opinions very seriously.

'This is Mr Carroll,' Brian said, introducing them. 'He's a taxi driver and he mainly works nights.'

'Which means I'm here during the day,' Mr Carroll cut in. 'I get in about nine, stick the breakfast on, get a few hours' kip, then I go out again in the evening about five.'

Laura mentally calculated the hours and judged instantly

that she never wanted to meet Mr Carroll on the road late at night, when he was struggling to keep his eyes open. Not the smartest either, considering he'd just told serving officers of the law that he broke it routinely.

She bit down on her instinctual dislike and smiled pleasantly at the man. Brian wouldn't have brought them here unless there was a point.

'And so you've noticed something about number three during the day?' she said.

'Yep. You see a lot in my game. You know what I'm saying? The taxi man is like a priest. I'm telling you now, what goes on in this country would make you blush.'

Sure, what would they, the police, know about shameful goings-on? Laura glanced sideways at Tom, who was smiling and nodding away like this was the most fascinating conversation he'd ever had.

Mr Carroll noticed it, too. He adjusted his body language, not so subtly, so he was facing Tom and directing his nuggets of wisdom where they'd be properly welcomed. Man to man.

Laura tried to not let it bother her.

'I've solved some of my toughest cases with the help of taxi drivers,' Tom said, and Mr Carroll grew a few inches taller.

Laura's jaw was aching. She let the smile slip off and instead pulled out a notepad that she never used and pretended to write.

'What drew your attention to number three?' Tom asked.

'The amount of people going in and out,' Mr Carroll said. 'These are small houses. I'm here on my own. Turned the second room into a bit of a man cave, you know yourself.'

Why on earth would you need a man cave when you live on your own, Laura wondered. She gripped her pen harder, all the better to not poke Mr Carroll in the eye.

'Well, we believe the lessee may have been subletting,' Tom explained. 'He had a number of tenants in there with him. Young women. Did you know any of them?'

'Tenants?' Mr Carroll snorted. 'If they were tenants, I'm the next manager of the national soccer team. There was a stream of men in and out of that place all day long. And anyone will tell you, brothels are always busier during the day. People think it's at night. Lads rocking into these places after a club, that sort of thing. You'd be surprised. It ain't stag parties that keep brothels in business. It's regular punters. And you know where those punters are at 3 a.m.? In bed with their wives. They pop around to get their ends away during lunch hour.'

Laura had driven a hole through her notepad onto the next page.

'You believe a brothel was operating in number three?' she said.

'I'm positive there was.'

'How are you *positive*?' Laura made a point of looking around her. 'You can't actually see number three from here. The only way you could be so familiar with the goings-on is if you were actually keeping an eye. Had you been in the house? Did you *use* it?'

Mr Carroll blinked rapidly.

Of course he had.

'No, I didn't!' he roared. 'The nerve of you, insinuating something like that.' He looked to Tom. 'Rein her in, would you?'

'She's the boss,' Tom said, raising his eyebrows and clicking his tongue in a *what can you do?* fashion.

'Well, she shouldn't be allowed to speak to witnesses like that. And me only trying to help. That'll teach me. I walk around the area a bit; I see stuff when I'm driving home. That's all.'

Mr Carroll made as if he was about to close the front door.

Brian placed his foot in the gap, so the taxi driver was forced to keep it open.

'I want to show you a photograph of a girl,' Laura said.

She took her phone out and pulled up a photograph of Tyanna she'd taken that morning.

'Do you recognise her?' Laura asked.

The taxi driver stared at it.

'Yeah,' he said, begrudgingly. 'She'd normally have a load of make-up on, but she lived in there.'

'You seem sure of that, too,' Laura said.

'What does that mean?'

'Most men wouldn't recognise a young woman they'd only seen a handful of times, especially if she was normally done up to the nines. Your powers of observation are superb.'

Mr Carroll's face contorted as he tried to figure out if Laura's comment was entirely or just partially insulting.

'Did you ever see signs of a baby in the house?' Tom asked. 'Ever see any of the women coming out with a child, or walk past and hear crying, anything like that?'

'A baby? Hell, no. What would a baby be doing in there?'

'Once again, can you confirm if you were ever inside the house?' Laura asked.

'If that's everything, I need to get ready for work,' Mr Carroll snapped. 'I'd be out by now only I hung on to see if I could be of assistance.'

'It is for now,' Laura said. 'We'll speak again, I'm sure.'

'I'll tell you something, Laura,' Tom said, as the detectives headed in the direction of their cars. 'The chances of Mr Carroll stopping for you on a rainy night just plummeted. You'd better hope he doesn't spread it around his taxi friends.'

'I don't think Mr Carroll has many friends,' Brian said. 'But I think he's onto something about the house. Most of the people around here work – out at the crack of dawn, back late in the evening. They can barely describe their immediate neighbours, let alone know their names or their business. But several of them still managed to pick up on the vibe that there was something amiss in number three. Blinds down all the time, bins left out on the wrong days, strange cars parked up on the footpath, that kind of thing. Lots of sightings of girls, mainly young, mainly foreign. And, as our helpful witness put it, a stream of men.

'Plus,' he continued. 'We looked in the neighbours' houses on either side of number three. There haven't been any adaptations upstairs, no extra bedrooms. So, the landlord may be telling the truth about not being responsible for the partitions. I guess Matteo Russo made his own adjustments. More rooms, more girls.'

'I thought we'd called it wrong,' Laura said, despondently. 'We know Matteo Russo had a good job and wasn't in need of money. He comes from a good family. Why do this? Was he just letting the girls work out of the place or was he actively running it? It just doesn't add up.'

Tom shrugged.

'Half the serious criminals we deal with make their money early, Laura, and they keep going anyway, despite the risk. You and I will never understand it. But at least now things are slotting into place about that house. If Matteo was in the brothel game, he could have easily made enemies. Especially if he was trying to run an independent operation. We all know most of these places are connected to bigger gangs.'

'Will I round up the troops for the evening?' Brian asked. 'It's half seven now, there's a match on the telly tonight and, with it being Saturday and all, I don't think we're going to get as many doors answered. We got the bulk of them during the day, anyhow.'

'Yeah, call a halt,' Laura said. 'If any of you can, try to head over to Michael's birthday party, will you? I feel bad for missing it. And I bet he's orchestrated it so the match will be on.'

Brian signalled he would with a salute, then headed off to gather up the team.

'What now?' Laura said, opening the car door.

'You tell me,' Tom said, with a hint of a smile.

'Vice,' Laura said. 'See if this place, or Russo, is known to them. And we're going to have to try to make some progress with Tyanna Volkov. Linda's speaking to her again this evening. Let's head in, see whether she's ready to open up.'

'As I suggested,' Tom said.

'Nobody likes an I-told-you-so,' Laura snipped.

'What about a talking reminder? You're forgetting one other thing you have to do before beddy-byes.'

'What?' Laura said, momentarily panicked.

'You've to give a press conference in time for the nine o'clock news. Happy days.'

Tom got into the car, so he missed the evil look Laura threw his way.

He was enjoying this delegation of responsibility a little bit too much, in her opinion.

CHAPTER 14

Linda returned to Tyanna's bedside later that evening.

The young woman seemed even more agitated, which was unusual because Linda knew the medical staff had administered a mild sedative.

Linda took the opportunity when Tyanna went to the toilet to read her chart, which hung on the rail at the end of the bed. There it was – a dose that at least should have calmed, if not completely sedated, the girl.

The fact that Tyanna had barely responded to it made Linda concerned.

It was entirely possible that she was used to being drugged with much higher doses.

The ward was quieter this evening. It was after hours for visitors – Linda had received a special dispensation because of the patient and Linda's own status.

Most of the other women on the ward were watching the television hung on the wall down the far end. Some reality show was providing the night's entertainment.

'Have you been able to eat something?' Linda asked, when Tyanna shuffled back and climbed gingerly into the bed.

The girl shook her head.

Linda reached into the bag she'd brought with her.

'I got you some bits from M&S,' she said. 'The last time I was in a public hospital – and I only consented to it, darling, because the private one I normally attend couldn't perform the procedure I needed – anyhow, the last time, the victuals they presented me with looked like they had been regurgitated.'

Linda began to arrange the food she'd purchased on the table in front of Tyanna. Sushi and salads and chopped fruit.

'I'd have brought you in some vino but we mustn't mix it with the meds, darling.'

Tyanna stared at Linda.

'And I got you some jim-jams. Can't have you in that awful scratchy gown-thing they've given you.' Linda placed an expensive brushed-cotton T-shirt and leggings on the bed. 'Now, just get the nurse to help you into those. We don't want to upset your dressings. I thought you'd prefer this to silk; it's a little softer.'

'Why you do all this for me?' Tyanna asked, suspiciously.

Linda placed the final items from her bag onto the table. Some magazines and a box of chocolate truffles.

She scrunched up the plastic bag and placed it in the bedside locker.

'I've spoken to my colleagues,' she said. 'There was a fire in a house, not far from where you were found wandering. Number three Shipping Row? We believe that's where you were running from. Are we right, Tyanna?'

The girl looked down at the array of gifts on the bed in front of her.

Linda swallowed back the guilt. She'd have brought something in for the girl, in any case. Tyanna, quite literally, didn't even have clothes on her back. She had nothing to her name and didn't seem to want to contact anybody to bring anything in.

But Linda saw how it looked. Tit for tat. Here's some chopped pineapple and a copy of *Hello!*, now tell me what you know.

It wasn't fair, especially if the girl was used to being bought.

However, Chief Superintendent Reynolds and DCI Lennon were downstairs and they were itching to talk to Tyanna. They didn't have the luxury of time; there was a baby involved. Linda had asked for days; they'd given her hours. This was her last-ditch attempt at extracting some information from the girl before the badges intervened and risked her shutting down completely.

The girl nodded her head, slowly. Her eyes narrowed, more cautious now she knew the parameters of the exchange.

'Two people were discovered dead in the house, Tyanna,' Linda said. 'A man, Matteo Russo. And another girl. Around the same age as you, I think? A little younger. You had a lucky escape, by the sounds of things.'

Tyanna blinked away tears.

'The girl who died,' Linda continued. 'Did you know her?'

'Lola.' Tyanna sighed. 'Her name was Lola.'

'Do you know her surname?'

A shake of the head.

'You were friends?' Linda asked. 'Or you just ... worked together?'

'We – uh – we work together,' Tyanna said. She sighed again, a tiny catch of a sob. 'And we were friends.'

'What kind of work was it, Tyanna?'

Tyanna looked away, heat in her cheeks.

'Do you know who started the fire?' Linda asked.

'No.'

'Do you know who might have wanted to hurt Lola and Matteo?'

'No.'

'Do you know where the baby is?'

Tyanna's breath quickened.

Linda, for her part, tried not to breathe at all.

On the other side of the curtain, over on the TV, an argument had started on the reality show. Somebody had cheated on somebody.

'Your work,' Linda said, gingerly. 'Did it involve many men coming to the house? I'm not here to judge you, Tyanna. You're not in any trouble. We just want to know what you know.'

Tyanna blinked rapidly. Then she nodded.

'Yes. Many men.'

'Okay,' Linda said. 'And did any of these men – did you or Lola feel threatened by any of them?'

Tyanna hesitated.

'There were many people who would hurt us,' she whispered. 'Matteo, he . . .'

She trailed off. Linda sat back, considered her next question.

'Who was Matteo to you? Did he take care of you or was he – was he a bad man?'

'No. Not a bad man.'

Tyanna sounded certain for the first time.

Linda tugged at her bottom lip. The girl was opening up. She had to get the real detectives up here now, as quickly as possible.

'Tyanna, my colleagues are downstairs. The two police officers – I believe you've met them both already? They really need to talk to you. I can vouch for both of them and I can stay here with you, if you like. Are you okay with me asking them to join us?'

The girl looked away, then reluctantly nodded.

Linda was about to stand up when Tyanna grabbed her hand.

'Did people take pictures?' she asked.

'Pictures of what?' Linda said, confused.

'Pictures of . . . of me. With no clothes on?'

Linda opened and closed her mouth, kicking herself for not having thought of an answer for this most obvious question.

'The house was on fire,' Tyanna said, her eyes clouding with the memory of the pain. 'My dress. It was some stupid material. I had to pull it off. It was burning me.'

Linda shook her head.

'I haven't seen any pictures,' she said.

That was true. She hadn't. But only because she hadn't looked.

#DublinUnwrapped had been trending on Twitter since yesterday.

CHAPTER 15

While Laura was gearing up to interview the seemingly sole living witness to the murders on Shipping Row, Ray was preparing to talk to one of Ireland's most notorious former gangsters.

The recurring trait Ray had heard ascribed to Patrick 'BLT' Cowell was friendly.

Cowell was allegedly cheery, chipper and generous – the pictures of him leaving the courthouse after being sentenced to life imprisonment showed a smiling, happy-go-lucky bloke with a dapper dress sense and a greeting for everybody.

Apparently, what made it so much worse for the people who got on the wrong side of Cowell was the knowledge that they'd let down a man who acted like you could have been his best friend if you'd only tried harder.

But you'd messed up and there he was, beating the living daylights out of you – and your overriding feeling was that you'd been a disappointment.

The papers had a habit of nicknaming Irish gangsters, often with the wittiest of monikers.

They had a field day when they discovered Cowell had his own pet name. BLT.

At first, people on the outside assumed the man had a love of the sandwich. Why wouldn't they? He seemed exactly the sort of fellow who'd down tools on a torture victim and order in a sub.

But BLT wasn't Patrick's sandwich preference.

It was his favourite method of torture.

Balls. Legs. Teeth.

Patrick 'BLT' Cowell was one of the most vicious gang leaders in the country.

Every police officer, the public, most of his own gang and probably several of his own family members had breathed a sigh of relief when his sentence was handed down several years ago.

The legend of his kindness was something propagated and maintained by people who'd never had cause to fall foul of him. And they were mostly people who hadn't met him.

But the first thing Cowell did when Ray arrived was fetch the detective sergeant tea.

'Sorry, it's just from the machine,' Cowell called over his shoulder, as Ray watched on. 'It's not too bad, mind. Nor is the rest of the grub. It's a myth, that they feed you slop when you're banged up. Every year, we actually look forward to Christmas Day. They do a great feast for that. Jesus, better than my wife's turkey ever tasted. Course, she'd a habit of cooking it the night before and recooking it the morning of.'

He came back with the tea and placed it in front of Ray.

'It's all right,' Cowell said, laughing. 'I haven't stuck glass in it.'

Ray frowned. He hadn't considered for a moment there'd be anything in the tea to harm him.

Now he was wondering.

'It's the least I can do to thank you for rescuing me from Saturday night television,' Cowell said. 'The one downside of being in here. Even talking to an officer of the law is better than bloody *Love Island*. Later, now, I think there's a movie on. *Jaws*. Never gets old.'

'One of my favourites,' Ray said.

Cowell nodded at him, pleased.

'You're on this new unit, then,' Cowell said.

Ray tried not to let the surprise show on his face.

'I watch the news, lad. It's all over it. Minister cracking down. About time. The country's lawless. I'm not being funny, pal. I know what I did. Serving my time for it and all. But there was a code, you know. In my day.'

'You weren't operating in the sixties,' Ray jibed. 'What was your code when you were pulling somebody's teeth out? Did you give them a safeword?'

Cowell's face froze for a moment. Then he guffawed loudly.

'Fair enough,' he said. 'Maybe not a code so much as an order to things. You lot knew what you were dealing with. Now? You've every little runt who can drive a stolen car. You've the foreign ones. Albanians, Romanians, Nigerians, Brazilians, Russians. The only foreigners I used to worry about were the Chinks. You couldn't trust those little Triad shits. But mad into their gambling, they were. Smoking and gambling. Used to wish they'd stick to the Jaysus curry vans. *You wan sore finger with that?*'

'Nice bit of racial profiling there,' Ray said, laughing.

'I'm no racist, pal. Some of my worst fucking enemies are foreigners. Not to mention I always dreamed of retiring to the Costa del Sol.'

Ray couldn't help but smile.

Costa del Crim was the nickname Ray and his colleagues usually applied.

'So what do you want from me, eh?' Patrick asked. 'You need me to join your task force, is it? I'll be wanting a room with a view of the sea, access to art materials, classical music and a nice Chianti. Like all the best cons. Do you get that reference, wha'? *Silence of the Lambs*. Chianti. Great flick.'

'I get it,' Ray said. 'But I don't think I can match Jodie Foster's offer. You *could* talk me through a few things, give me the lay of the land as you see it now, and I could talk to them in here about some perks on site. Not sure I can get you a room with a view of the sea in Mountjoy, though.'

'Perks!' Cowell scoffed. 'You haven't a clue, son. I don't need you to sort me with perks. Didn't I tell you? I live like a king in here. And don't think you can try the stick over the carrot, either. The screws in here know how to run things and it's not by upsetting somebody like me.'

'Then just talk to me because you're interested,' Ray said. 'Because I'm asking.'

Cowell sat back.

'You're brave, coming in for a little chat,' he said. 'I'll give you that. But what would I know? I'm in here a good few years. A lot changes in my world when you're out of it. I only know what I hear on the news.'

'I doubt that's true,' Ray said. 'In my experience, if you want a crime solved, half the time you could hang out in the canteen here and get the low-down on every detail.'

Cowell shrugged.

Ray took a sip of the tea. The man across from him smiled approvingly.

They were friends now. A drink had been taken.

'Look, I'm going to level with you,' Ray said. 'There are more guns than ever coming into the country and we have to get a handle on who's importing them. For everyone's sake. You have family and friends out there yourself, Patrick. There's no controlling what goes on, not unless we start arming every guard on the street, and if we go that way, it's just a vicious circle. Everybody's at risk.'

'Bollocks,' Cowell interrupted.

'It's not an exaggeration—'

'It is. Gun deaths are going up but it's the ones living in piss-poor estates that are caught in the crossfire. Not the nice, safe middle-class households you're meant to serve and protect. You and your lot don't give a toss about the people who are suffering because of crime. The government, the police, what you're all involved in is what I like to call a cosmetic exercise. A sticking plaster. Things will quieten for a while, because there's a bit of heat, and then play will continue as normal. Because none of you care to fuck what happens to the lads and lassies growing up in those shitholes. You don't care that they have no options. If you wanted to tackle crime properly, you'd be pouring money into those estates. Not coming at the problem from the arse-end.'

'I get the impression you see yourself as a bleeding-heart Robin Hood,' Ray said. 'I'm from one of those estates, Patrick. And I know for a fact you and your kind are only too happy to exploit those kids you're speaking about so passionately. If the government built a community centre for them and filled it with Xboxes, you lot would still be hanging around outside waiting to swoop when the lads came out. Children make easy targets.'

Cowell's face turned blank.

Ray could have sworn his pupils grew smaller.

The detective had crossed whatever line Cowell had set.

Well, how did the gangster think this was going to go?

Maybe he shouldn't have been quite so blunt, though. Cowell had probably invented a whole new revisionist narrative for himself while he'd been in here.

'I don't want shitloads of guns coming in any more than you do,' Cowell said, his voice low, dangerous. 'The problem with everybody having a loaded weapon is it's a zero-sum game. If I could cut down on the volume, I would. And if your fucking force was in any way inclined to sort this shit out, you would do what you have to. It takes a bit of willpower on all sides. That's all I'm saying.'

Ray stared at Cowell. That was obviously all he was going to get and, in truth, the detective sergeant was wondering if the old gangster had anything more to give.

'Right, well,' Ray said. 'I didn't come here to spar with you. Just to see if you knew anything that could be of help. You don't know anything. That's grand.'

He stood up.

'I'll let you get back to *Love Island*.'

Cowell stayed sitting.

He started to laugh.

'I know everything, son,' he said. 'It's you who knows nothing. You haven't a clue, have you? You really don't have a clue.'

'A clue about what?'

Cowell seemed to find that even funnier. He slapped his hand on the table, laughing so hard tears welled in his eyes.

Ray was confused.

'Man, you lot haven't a hope against the new generation,' Cowell said. 'Not a hope. Who sent you in here? Your boss, was it? Send the organ grinder next time. I only talk to the higher-ups, the ones who can get things done. And here I was thinking you were going to offer me something. But you really thought I'd do this out of the goodness of my heart.'

Ray walked to the door of the visitors' room.

What a waste of time.

The prison officer there walked him down to the sign-out desk.

Behind the hatch, another officer waited while Ray filled in the exit time beside his name.

'You get what you were looking for?' the prison officer behind the desk asked.

Ray shook his head.

'You didn't drink the tea, did you?'

Ray frowned.

'Why?' he asked.

'He spits in the tea.' The officer shrugged.

Ray's stomach churned.

The absolute fucker.

CHAPTER 16

Linda had managed to cajole Tyanna into talking to them but it was still like drawing blood from a stone and time was ticking on.

The nurses had given Tom and Laura several pointed looks as 9.30 p.m. came and went. If they'd arrived a little earlier it wouldn't have been so bad but they'd been delayed by the piece to camera Laura had had to do for the media and it was past visiting hours before they even got onto the ward.

Eventually, one of the nurses was brave enough to come over and explain that it would be lights out shortly.

'These ladies need their rest,' she explained to Tom, who nodded understandingly.

He didn't understand, though. He never could get his head around hospital routines, where they expected you to go to sleep at half nine and be ready for your breakfast at six. It was like a whole system predicated on the days before electricity.

'We'll be out of your hair very shortly.' Tom gave the nurse his most charming smile.

Tyanna was tiring in any case. She hadn't been able to tell them how or when the fire started. She'd no recollection of Matteo and Lola being attacked. She couldn't tell them who'd been in the house when it was set alight. And, more importantly, she'd given them nothing on the baby.

While they'd been waiting downstairs, Laura had received a call from HQ. The admin support team had discovered a record of Tyanna entering Ireland on a student visa the previous year.

She was allegedly attending an English language school and the visa allowed her to work part-time hours to fund her living costs while she undertook her studies.

Tom doubted she'd ever seen the inside of said language school, especially as it had gone out of business eleven months ago.

But he still clung to the hope that the girl would talk. She'd started and the road was bumpy, but they'd get there. They just needed to ask the right question to trigger a response.

'You knew, didn't you, that Lola was still in the house when it went on fire,' Tom said. 'When you were admitted to hospital, you were talking about not being able to save the baby. You knew Lola was dead.'

'I did not know,' Tyanna said. 'I remember the fire. I remember running from the house and I did not look for her. She had to have been inside. And I feel so bad.'

'Who was inside? Was the baby inside?' Tom persisted.

'I don't know.'

'What was Lola's baby? A boy or a girl?'

'I don't know.'

Tom flinched, his patience starting to fray.

'Tyanna, you must have known,' Laura insisted, gentle but firm.

'I think a girl.'

At last. Progress.

'And where did she have the baby? What hospital?'

Tyanna shrugged. She began to cry, quietly.

'There was no baby in the house,' Tom interjected. 'Where's the baby?'

'I don't know! I don't know!'

Tom sat back. Laura caught his eye. They both knew what the other was thinking. Much harder and they'd get nothing. The girl was traumatised enough.

'Do you remember what happened in the house before the fire?' Laura asked, softly. 'Do you remember any arguments? Anybody being violent with Matteo and Lola?'

'I keep trying to remember exactly what happened,' Tyanna sobbed. 'It is like my head cannot work. I only remember running and pulling my clothes off and then I was walking and I did not know where to go. I didn't save anybody.'

'Were there other girls in the house before the fire started?' Tom said. 'Who lived there with you usually?'

'I do not know. Sometimes girls come and go. I do not know who was there when the fire came.'

Tom and Laura glanced at each other. They were getting nowhere.

'Tyanna, you told our colleague Linda that many men came to the house. Before the fire, before all this happened, was there any one person who stands out in your mind as somebody we should talk to? Anybody who was there recently and caused trouble – somebody who might have threatened Matteo or Lola or you?'

Tyanna started to shake her head.

'If there's somebody out there who might be dangerous, I really want to talk to him,' Tom said. 'So I can make sure he doesn't harm anybody again.'

Tyanna bristled.

'There was a man,' she said, her voice clipped, uncertain. 'He come to the house. He is not good to the girls.'

'Did the man come for sex?' Laura asked.

Tyanna winced. Her silence spoke volumes.

'Were you ever with him?' Laura said.

Tyanna shook her head.

'No. He liked the . . . the black girls. He would . . .'

She lifted her hand, mimed a hitting action.

'Not nice,' she said. 'Matteo, he didn't like it. He angry with him. Told him he couldn't come back. Matteo said real man, he does not hit a girl.'

'Did Matteo take care of you?' Tom said. 'Was he good to you?'

Tyanna closed her eyes, pain all over her face.

'Matteo was good,' she said. 'His job was to protect us. That's what he said.'

'Okay,' Tom said. Now they were getting somewhere. 'So, did Matteo organise the men coming to the house or did you work for yourselves? Did Matteo take the money?'

Tyanna looked away.

Tom bit back his frustration.

'This man who was violent,' he said. 'The man Matteo fought with. Can you describe him to me?'

'Respectable man,' Tyanna said. 'Money. Nice car. Nice voice. He had a tattoo on his arm. I remember. It look wrong, do you know? Because he has nice job.'

'What was the tattoo?' Laura asked. 'Where on his arm?'

Tyanna pointed at Laura's forearm.

'There. Writing. A sentence. I don't know what it said. Lola, she said it was a . . . book quote?'

Tom and Laura looked at each other. It didn't give them much.

'You don't remember the make of his car?' Tom asked.

'I don't know cars,' Tyanna said. 'Big. Black. Something on the front.'

'A hood ornament?' Tom asked. 'Like a Mercedes?'

Tyanna shook her head.

'Flat. Not sticking up.'

'Okay,' Laura said. 'Thank you, Tyanna. You need to get some sleep now, okay? We'll come back tomorrow.'

The two police officers left the ward. The lights went out behind them almost as soon as their feet hit the main corridor.

'We're looking for a man with a tattoo and a nice car,' Laura said. 'What do we do – go around middle-class estates asking blokes to pull up their shirt sleeves?'

'I'm trying to figure out the make of car,' Tom said. 'Could be a Beamer. Or an Audi. You know who'd have probably clocked it?'

'Our local, friendly taxi driver?' Laura suggested, pulling her phone out of her pocket.

'In one,' Tom said. 'Who's that texting?'

'Ray,' she said, her face scrunched in puzzlement. ' "The bollix spat in my tea." What do you think that means?'

'Haven't a clue.'

'Oh, that reminds me.'

They stopped by the lift.

'You know who's on that new unit Ray's been assigned to?'

Tom shook his head.

'Joe Kennedy.'

Tom tried not to let the dismay show on his face.

He knew Kennedy had been moved somewhere within the force. He'd inquired once as to where and Bronwyn Maher told him not to worry about it. So Tom reckoned the little shit was serving out his time in a country station somewhere, or sitting in a dark office performing admin tasks. It was some drop – from chief superintendent to foot soldier – but Kennedy would have known his big fat pension would remain intact if he just kept his head down.

'He's on the new unit?' Tom repeated. 'To tackle gun crime?'

'I know,' Laura said, eyebrows raised. 'I thought you might know something about it.'

'No,' Tom said, his features darkening. 'Nobody told me anything.'

He was fuming.

Where Kennedy went, there was always trouble.

Laura's phone buzzed again. This time, it was ringing.

'You're popular,' Tom said.

They got into the lift. Laura answered and Tom could hear the noise of a party in the background.

'Brian?' Laura said.

Ah. The Geoghegans' joint birthday party.

'BOSS!' Brian roared.

Laura removed the phone from her ear. She and Tom exchanged a glance. Neither was sorry to be missing the night out now they could hear how noisy it was.

'I can hear you,' Laura said. 'What's up?'

'Just got hold of a manager from the bank Matteo Russo worked in!'

Tom's ears perked up.

'And?' Laura asked.

The phone was silent.

'Bloody reception,' Laura hissed.

They waited until the lift reached their floor and the doors opened. As soon as they got out, Laura dialled Brian back, while standing in front of a No Mobiles sign.

Out here, on the marginally noisier corridor, Tom couldn't hear exactly what Brian was saying, but he guessed from the expression on Laura's face.

She thanked Brian, then hung up.

'Matteo Russo hasn't worked in the IFSC in two years, and when he did, he wasn't a hot-shit IT guy,' she said. 'He was in admin, part-time.'

'He lied on the lease,' Tom said.

'He lied,' Laura agreed. 'And we know how he was paying the rent. He didn't need a full-time job.'

'Wait until his parents find out,' Tom mused.

Laura's face fell.

CHAPTER 17

Viggo had no interest in being out this late.

Viggo had a wife and child that needed to be taken care of.

But Viggo also had a job.

And bosses.

One job.

Many bosses.

So Viggo was out, working, trying to fix the absolute shitstorm that was number three Shipping Row.

He caught sight of his face in the rearview mirror.

Stocky, strong, not particularly good-looking or smart, but Viggo had always managed to land on his feet.

Matteo Russo had everything going for him.

Except brains.

Matteo was sadly lacking in the brains department.

But that didn't matter any more because Matteo was dead.

Unfortunately, so was the girl – and several more were about to be, if one of Viggo's bosses had anything to do with it.

The problem was, the other boss wanted the girls alive.

And they also wanted the baby found. Alive.

Viggo was in panic mode. Because he knew they'd never find that baby.

The traffic lights turned green.

Viggo put the car in gear and left the hospital car park.

He'd be back to check on Tyanna tomorrow.

He had to keep an eye on her while he decided which boss to obey.

The Albanians were family but Ireland was where he lived.

Tough choice.

CHAPTER 18
Sunday

'I know you said you owed me a meal, but this is above and beyond.'

Natasha McCarthy, head of sexual crimes, unwrapped her breakfast roll as she walked with Tom through the headquarters car park.

'Sometimes I try to describe the cuisine in Ireland to my aunties in Mali but I can never quite do it justice,' Natasha said. 'You have to grow up with it to appreciate just how godawful some of the concoctions we've created are.'

'You're welcome,' Tom said. 'That's a garage deli special, by the way. I believe they're award-winning. You're worth it. How many meals did you buy me in thanks for Daniel?'

Just over two years ago, Tom had helped get Natasha's nephew off a wrongful murder charge. She'd been so grateful, she'd gone overboard, initially taking Louise and Tom out for an incredibly expensive dinner and then making sure she got Tom's lunch any time they met up, until he'd put his foot down and insisted the next one was on him.

Time had got away from him but when he asked Natasha to meet himself and Laura in HQ early on a Sunday morning, he knew he couldn't turn up without some sort of offering.

He was already in the car when he remembered, though, so two sausages, bacon and a runny egg, crammed in a crusty roll with a dollop of ketchup, was all he could come up with.

'This cancels out all the meals I bought you,' Natasha said. 'No, really. Please don't buy me any more food. We're even.'

Tom laughed.

'Okay,' he said. 'Your arteries are safe. I just didn't want to land a favour request on your lap without paying my dues. Here's Laura now.'

They waited for Laura by the front door until she caught up with them.

'How do you keep so skinny and gorgeous when that's your breakfast of choice?' Laura asked, eyeing the large roll in Natasha's hand.

'Strategic dressing,' Natasha answered.

Tom knew it wasn't true. Natasha had lost weight around the time of her nephew's case and she'd never put it back on. But Louise always said it didn't matter with a woman like Natasha, that she had class oozing out of her veins and would always look well.

Natasha gave Laura a one-armed hug and the three officers made their way into a building that was already hotter than outdoors, despite the fact it wasn't yet noon.

'Do they actively heat this place in summer?' Laura asked.

'No, they just don't air-con it,' Tom said. 'It's the same thing. Do you remember a few years ago when we had to have the fans going full-time during the . . .'

Tom trailed off.

'Sleeping Beauties case,' Laura said. 'I remember.'

None of them said anything, but Natasha gave Laura's arm a little squeeze. That case had been traumatic for Laura but she'd survived it.

Come out stronger, if you asked Tom.

They sweated all the way up the stairs to the top floor and Natasha's office.

She'd left her windows open, meaning the room was a little cooler than the narrow, hot staircase.

'So,' Natasha said, switching on her computer. 'Talk to me.'

'Matteo Russo,' Tom said. 'Stabbed in a house we believe was being used as a brothel, along with another victim, a young woman we only know by the name of Lola. She'd recently given birth. The baby is missing.'

Natasha made a sharp intake of breath.

'Matteo held the lease to the house,' Tom continued. 'The building was set alight following the murders, removing any hope of forensics. We've a witness who's talking a little, Tyanna Volkov. Only to tell us she lived there, she was selling herself and Matteo was *taking care* of her and the other girl. She claims he was a good man, if that's not too much of an oxymoron for a pimp. You heard of him? Number three Shipping Row, just down from the IFSC beside the docks.'

Natasha pursed her lips as she typed in the details.

She scanned the results on her screen.

'He's not coming up in my files, Tom. We weren't aware of him. Unless one of my team was keeping a quiet eye.'

'A quiet eye?'

'A soft watch,' Natasha said. 'We've adapted our work practices to suit our resources. Where we know a violent pimp is operating, we make that a priority case. If there's a brothel running and we haven't had reports of abuse or the girls being under age, we keep a soft watch on it, just in case. Then there's the rake of them not on our radar. The new law means it's a crime to solicit sex, and also to organise the selling of somebody else for sex, i.e. pimping. But sex work or living together in a brothel isn't illegal, so we're not raiding them to the same extent any more.'

Laura frowned.

'But how do you know if the girls are happy in a place? How do you know if a pimp is being violent or not, if you don't raid and bring the girls in?'

'Sadly, that's where we're at,' Natasha said. 'The standard of proof for determining if somebody is a brothel owner and securing a successful prosecution against that person is unbearably high. When we put a shop under surveillance, it can take weeks of collating evidence before we can raid and arrest the pimps. The girls never talk. We have to target efficiently and make sure we've done our homework.'

Natasha shrugged, not happy, but too pragmatic to be defensive about how the practice sounded. It was just the way things were.

'Leave this name with me,' she said, a consolation prize. 'I can ask around, see if anybody is willing to talk about him. Was he there long or was it a pop-up?'

'A pop-up being . . .?' Tom prompted. A bird had landed on the windowsill outside. Tom glanced at it, squinting against the sun streaming through. Here they were discussing murder and prostitution while the park outside was filling with families ready for a Sunday out.

Almost as if he'd willed it, a cloud passed over the sun and the day was shadowed.

Jesus, I'm getting very philosophical and fanciful, he thought.

'A pop-up is a short-term lease,' Natasha said. 'They move around a lot these days. The bookings are all online through allegedly legal escort and massage sites, so the pimps don't need a permanent address. Often the girls work from their own apartments, but where there's a shop, it can move from house to house. They use hotel rooms sometimes, the cheaper ones, rented out for weeks at a time. Airbnbs are great for it.

One man was using several mobile homes in a caravan park in North County Dublin.'

'In this rental climate?' Tom said. 'I'm amazed they can move with such ease.'

'They don't quibble on rent,' Natasha said. 'It might be bleeding the rest of us mere mortals dry, but it's quite a small overhead compared to what the girls make and it's barely a pebble drop for pimps running multiple girls in the one operation.'

'Well, this guy didn't move around much, anyway,' Tom said. 'He's held the lease for the place for a while.'

Natasha jutted out her lower lip.

'Hmm. I'm surprised he hasn't come to our attention, so. Normally, somewhere that's constant like that, residents would have phoned in. People would be talking, you know.'

'It's one of those new builds near the financial centre,' Tom said. 'Young professionals, nobody talks to each other. Easy to be invisible when nobody's looking at you.'

Natasha picked up her breakfast roll and took a large bite.

Her face said it all. Clearly, it was delicious.

'Russo,' Natasha mused through a mouthful of grease. 'Italian?'

'Tuscany,' Laura said. 'Good family, plenty of money. The mind boggles.'

'Might have a sense of entitlement,' Natasha said. 'Good-looking?'

'Very,' Laura answered. 'Before he was burned to a crisp, anyway. He'd been lying about his job. Claimed he worked in the IFSC but he'd only been there for a little while, part-time, in a desk job.'

'He's had women flocking to him all his life,' Natasha said. 'He's working in the IFSC job, either realises it's crap or it's been a front for him to begin with. Something to help him get into the housing market, where landlords are looking for professionals. But he knows running girls is a really easy way to make money. He has the lease, he offers the girls a room in the house. He provides a bit of muscle, they have to pay over a percentage. If that's how he was operating.'

'If?' Tom asked.

'If there wasn't something more sinister at play. You're positive he was Italian? Not posing as one? Sometimes the Romanians or Albanians . . .'

'He was definitely Italian,' Laura said. 'I spoke to his parents and the Italian authorities put us in touch. Why do you ask?'

Natasha tapped the desk with a pen thoughtfully.

'The girls could be trafficked,' she said. 'The Romanians and Albanians are the worst for it – over here, anyway. Them and the Nigerians. Sometimes they use nice-looking lads to lure the girls in. How did – Tyanna, is it? How did she come into the country?'

'Student visa for a language college,' Laura said.

'What age is she?'

'Eighteen.'

'Hmm. Well, like I said, let me ask around. Did she say anything of use at all?'

'Yeah, that's the other thing we wanted to ask you about,' Laura said. 'She said they had one client in particular who was rough. It was the only real lead she'd give us. She said he preferred black girls and that he was known to hit them. Apparently he fell out with Matteo after the guy hurt one of the girls. The dead girl, Lola, was black. Tyanna didn't have a name for this guy but she said he seemed respectable. Had a nice motor, too. What were you guessing, Tom?'

'Might be a Beamer,' he said. 'I contacted a local this morning, a taxi driver who curtain-twitches. He said he'd seen one parked up the street a couple of times but had never seen anybody getting in or out of it. You come across anybody like that?'

'It's not setting off any alarm bells,' Natasha said. 'As in, I don't have an outstanding case where we're searching for a respectable man with a nice car who beats up black girls. But what I can tell you is that being respectable and having a nice car will not make him stand out. It's the very definition of half the customer base. These girls cost money – they're not surviving on horny stag parties. They have regular clients, well-paying regular clients.'

'I'd a notion you were going to say that,' Tom said. 'The taxi driver did, too. Not that it helps us.'

'Do you want me to send in specialists to talk to Tyanna, or do you think she'll open up to you?' Natasha said. 'She has to be treated sensitively. No offence to the murder squad, Laura.'

'None taken,' Laura said. 'Know your roles, I always say. But we didn't wade in, size fives first. We didn't know it was a brothel, but we sent in Linda McCarn, so at least there'd be somebody there with a bit of cop-on. They seem to have made a bit of a connection. But she wouldn't give us much and we need more information on this baby. Emmet hasn't turned up anything at the house. Tyanna needs to tell us more.'

'So, it's over to me,' Natasha said. 'I get you. Will we see if there's anybody in the canteen? I need some coffee to wash down this delightful breakfast you got me.'

'I'd murder a coffee,' he said. 'Oh – sorry, our guy, he had a tattoo as well. Tyanna thought that was incongruous. It ran along his arm. Does that help?'

'It will if you find him,' Natasha said. 'I'm sure there's more than one well-to-do man with a tattoo on his arm.'

'It was a quote,' Tom said. 'Something literary.'

Natasha had stood up from her desk, her hand reaching towards the keyboard to log out of her computer. It stayed hovering there, her body prone, as the calculations ran behind her eyes.

Tom sat forward.

'I'm sorry,' Natasha said. 'Middle-class, drives a BMW and a literary quote on his arm?'

'You know him?' Laura said, eagerly.

'Yes,' Natasha said. 'I actually think I do. But not from anything to do with frequenting prostitutes.'

CHAPTER 19

Nina Cusack's father liked to consider himself a mild-mannered man. A considerate, thoughtful man. John had never wanted much from life and he never felt the need to argue for more than he had. So, he took his time in all things. He deliberated before he gave his opinion, especially if it was contentious. He wasn't a pushover, not by any stretch, but neither was he a loose cannon. He didn't get riled up like other men. John Cusack had always been able to control his temper.

Which meant when he did explode, it was only ever because something really bad had happened or somebody had really upset him.

Like that time he punched the driver of his bin lorry in the face.

His bosses had known immediately that John had to have been provoked.

Orla didn't know the full story of why John had been transferred to the sorting centre. He'd sold it to her as something like a promotion, even though she knew he preferred to be in company and liked the outdoor nature of the lorry collections, not to mention the hours.

He'd never minded the smell of other people's refuse. You got used to it, after a very short time. It was humanity in a bag, that's what it was.

And the lads were great craic. All working-class blokes like John, no airs and graces, just normal, likeable Dubs – even the flawed ones like Robby, who, if he told you a story once, told you it a hundred times before the week was out; or Andy, who made them laugh with his tales of womanising, but also made most of the lads cringe with his absolute misogyny.

You were meant to challenge that sort of thing nowadays, John knew. He had a daughter and a wife. He had a mother and sisters. He shouldn't have laughed when Andy talked about shagging a girl then riding her sister. He shouldn't have grinned when Andy said he'd had unprotected sex with a woman but had sworn blind to her that he had worn a condom because he knew she was too drunk to check.

But John got his karma for not challenging Andy.

And it was Andy that John had attacked.

John had arrived into work eighteen months ago to find some of his workmates sniggering at pictures Andy was showing them on his phone.

John was having a hard time of it. His daughter had gone missing six months previously and he and Orla knew she was back on the drugs. The police weren't seriously helping. Nina had form – this wasn't a case of some fourteen-year-old unexpectedly vanishing from her home. Even though Nina was only seventeen when she first left, she had already been to rehab.

John had no idea what he'd done wrong. When Nina had been a little girl, he'd read her stories every night at bedtime. He'd helped decorate plastic horses with glitter and bows, so they were transformed into unicorns. He'd painted a whole bedroom pink, even though it practically made his eyes bleed.

Orla was the same. Special breakfasts of chocolate pancakes

on cold mornings, mother-and-daughter shopping trips, saving all year for Christmas presents, holidays designed around Nina.

They hadn't spoiled her. They'd just doted on her.

And still, they'd failed.

When John approached the group of laughing men at work that morning, he already wasn't in the form for whatever they were looking at on Andy's phone. It had been getting worse as the months wore on and there was still no sign of his daughter.

John's worst nightmares imagined Nina being used and abused by some bastard like Andy so she could fund her habit.

He often thought that it was the one decent thing she'd done – running. She hadn't wanted to be a burden on them. That's what John told Orla. Nina didn't want to be that daughter who stole from her parents, who hurt them twice over. She'd saved them that.

But how is she getting the money for the drugs, Orla would ask, and John couldn't bear to go there.

At work that morning, the group had dispersed as John approached, guilty looks on their faces. Something in John's demeanour had brought them back to civilisation, had reminded them that it probably wasn't okay to be laughing at some poor girl's embarrassment on Andy's phone, not when John was worrying about his own daughter day and night.

Andy had no sense.

'Here, mate,' he said. 'Look at this. Some girl I was with last night. She wanted me to pay for it after. The state of that. I took a pic and told her I'd send it to all her phone contacts if she went down that route.'

Nina looked skinny in the photograph, her arms thrown helplessly across her bare chest, her eyes filled with despair and humiliation and shock.

If the other lads hadn't been there to drag John off Andy, Andy would have died, right then, at the side of the bin lorry.

The bosses accepted Andy's defence that he'd had no idea that the girl was John's daughter.

But, to their credit, they'd also accepted the basic code of honour that said John was entitled to beat the crap out of Andy for what he'd said and done.

John sat in his sitting room now with a recording of the news from last night playing on the TV in front of him. Nina was upstairs, hiding in her bedroom, while her mother hovered on the landing, pretending to fold towels in the hot press. She was afraid to let the girl out of their sight.

He was meant to be thanking Bob Laird for the presents he'd dropped in for Nina. It was Nina's birthday next week. Bob remembered, like he'd remembered the last two years.

John had no interest in talking to anybody.

Orla still didn't know what John knew, what their daughter had been doing when she was gone.

He hadn't the heart to tell her. He'd assured her Nina was alive – they'd have known if she had died. But he couldn't tell Orla what Nina had been doing.

Even John didn't want to know.

He just wanted to find out why she'd come back and if she'd be staying.

The door to the sitting room opened and Orla slipped in.

'Did you call in to Bob to say thanks?' Orla asked. 'He said a few more neighbours have done a whip-round for a bunch of flowers, but it might be a bit much for her.'

Orla glanced over at the pile of gifts in the armchair in front of the window.

John grunted.

He was with his daughter on this one. He didn't want to see people; he didn't want them feeling sorry for the family. Bob and the rest could keep their bloody presents and sympathy.

Orla, gauging his mood, sat beside him wordlessly, and they watched the news together.

A police inspector, a youngish-looking woman, was making an appeal about a house fire that had taken place on Friday, in which two people had been found deceased. She was asking for witnesses to come forward, particularly people who had lived in or visited the house in the run-up to the blaze.

'Is this today's news?' Orla asked.

'Yesterday's. The telly recorded some of it before that film I wanted to see last night.'

Orla sat forward on the couch.

'Turn it up,' she said.

John frowned, but he did as he was asked.

He listened as a DCI Lennon appealed again for anybody who had witnessed anything suspicious near the house in Shipping Row, or had seen a distressed young woman near the vicinity of the fire, to come forward.

'Must have been arson,' John said.

'Shh,' Orla hissed.

'What?'

Orla took the remote control out of his hand and paused the TV. She turned and looked at her husband.

'I think Nina might have been in that house,' she said.

CHAPTER 20

The solicitor Natasha had directed them to occupied an office barely worthy of its city centre address, located as it was on the outskirts of the centre, but its owner had clearly decided to play up the D1 postcode and was paying top rent for the privilege.

On his website, Hugo de Burgh had placed the office logo, simply *de Burgh & Co.*, against a mocked-up background image of the famous Ha'penny Bridge, which had been similarly geographically altered to now appear as though it sat in front of Trinity College.

'Who's *& Co.*?' Tom asked, as he and Laura strode down Infirmary Road, away from the Phoenix Park and Garda headquarters and towards Collins Barracks. De Burgh's office was only a ten-minute walk from theirs, much closer than either the Ha'penny Bridge or Trinity College.

Tom had suggested the stroll. He fancied the exercise after the indecently unhealthy meal he'd consumed that morning. The breakfast rolls had been a two-for-one offer. He was regretting it.

The day had turned overcast and muggy. Oppressive, even. Tom was longing for the sun again, after only a few hours of clouds.

'Natasha doesn't think *Co.* exists,' Laura said. 'It's just one of those solicitor things. Do you think it's a good or a bad thing, him being willing to come into his office on a Sunday to speak to us? And the way he responded so fast?'

'I'd hazard a guess he doesn't want us near his family home,' Tom said. 'And that he'll want to get rid of us quickly.'

'Could this be the same man? Natasha didn't sound convinced.'

'She didn't sound unconvinced, either. She says he has a Beamer, he has a literary tattoo, he's defended several pimps and that she's always felt there was something off about him . . .'

'She's just speculating, though. He has no priors and he's a bloody solicitor, after all.'

Tom shrugged. 'Yes, but Natasha has good instincts, you know.

'I doubt he'll lie to us, anyway. *Because* he's a solicitor. He'll understand the damage he'll do to himself if he starts off with us on the wrong foot. If he was at Shipping Row and he knows somebody can ID him, he can only be honest.'

'Hmm.' Laura grew quiet.

'What's on your mind? Ah, hang on. Is that rain?'

Tom held out his hand, felt the first cold drops. They started to speed up.

'I know far more people visit sex workers than I'd ever imagine, but I still struggle to get my head around it,' Laura said. 'This man is a successful professional; he's married, has children. What sends him into a brothel and makes him slap women around? Why take that risk?'

'It's a calculated risk,' Tom said. 'Who better than a solicitor would know how few prosecutions are taken against men who assault sex workers? He knows what he's doing. If it's him.'

It was pelting down now and the trees that stretched over the park's boundary walls were doing nothing to protect Tom and Laura from the deluge.

By the time they arrived at de Burgh's office, the sun had re-emerged and the two officers were saturated. They stood there for a moment, trying to wring themselves out. Laura had the good grace not to point out that the walk had been Tom's idea.

The door was locked when they knocked, but they knew from the black BMW parked up on the pavement that the solicitor was inside.

Within seconds, a man appeared in the narrow hallway and opened the door for them.

De Burgh was fairly nondescript in appearance. Average height, average looks – mousy brown hair and nice eyes, but a weak chin. He would have made even less of an impact but for the expensive cut of his suit and his bearing, which was confident with good posture.

'That's one way of cooling down,' he said, taking in the pair of them.

'Sudden weather event,' Tom said. 'Sent by the gods to teach me to be grateful for sunny days.'

De Burgh smiled and ushered them in.

'Let me stick the coffee machine on,' he said.

'Thank you,' Tom said. 'And thanks for seeing us. How do you know Natasha McCarthy, by the way?'

Tom knew how they knew each other. He just wanted to know how de Burgh would present himself.

'I've done a little pro bono work for women in bad situations. Domestic violence, rape, that sort of thing. All solicitors take on a couple of those cases or similar; I'm not bigging myself up.'

So far, so humble. Natasha had told them she had thought it strange that de Burgh took such a large share of pro bono cases when his practice was dedicated to defending the worst sorts of men.

That in itself was not proof of anything; maybe he was trying to redress the balance, but it was another little contradiction worth noting.

'It's a quote from Oscar Wilde on his arm, from what I remember,' Natasha had told them. ' "Every sinner has a future." '

' "Every saint has a past," ' Tom had said, smiling thinly at the irony.

'And yet, there's just something about him,' Natasha added, 'that's always made my skin crawl. He's so pally with those pimps in court and then he's Jesus reincarnated with battered women. It's . . . off.'

'What's your normal practice work?' Tom asked de Burgh now.

'Mainly defending the indefensible, to be fair,' de Burgh said. 'Criminal law; we're not usually on the side of the angels. Might be why I prefer the pro bono work. At least it means I'm not always sitting on the wrong side of the courtroom to yourselves.'

He led them into a small kitchen area, offered them comfortable chairs and began to fuss over a complicated, expensive coffee machine.

The whole area looked brand new and smelled of paint.

'Sorry, I'll get the hang of this in a sec,' he apologised. 'Normally my secretary does it. That would make me sound completely antiquated, but my secretary is a man. We've had the whole place redecorated recently and got all this new . . . ah. There we go. That should heat up in a few minutes.'

De Burgh took the third seat at the table and extended his hands to the two police officers in a gesture that offered his services.

Tom shifted awkwardly, well aware his discomfort wasn't just down to his wet clothes. He silently threw the baton to Laura. It was her case, after all.

'Mr de Burgh—'

'Hugo.'

'Um, Hugo. You may have heard about the fire on the other side of town that occurred this Friday just gone? Two people were found dead inside the house.'

'I did. Very sad.'

'Would you have – were you ever a visitor to that house?'

De Burgh looked from one to the other of them.

'Has somebody said I was?'

And in that instant, Tom knew de Burgh was their man. It was a solicitor's answer. A defensive, strategic reaction.

He couldn't help but feel a little disappointed.

'Well, we're here,' Tom said.

'Ah.' The solicitor sat back and stroked his chin. It looked like a repeated gesture, an attempt to put some definition on it, established over a lifetime.

'I see my sins have come back to haunt me,' de Burgh said, with the good grace to blush as he did.

'Your sins being . . .?' Tom said.

'I'm a happily married man. A father to two brilliant sons. I'm thriving in my career. And, yes, I visit, eh, working girls.'

De Burgh hung his head. He said nothing for a moment or two. Then he looked up. A quick glance at Laura, but then straight to Tom.

'I'm in this game long enough. I know how it goes. Something happens in one of these places and everybody who thought that their proclivities were top secret gets a very sudden and nasty surprise. I suppose you're visiting all the regulars, asking questions.'

'Of course,' Laura said smoothly, and Tom knew she'd instantly noted 'regulars'. 'But your name did come up in a very particular fashion.'

'Oh?' de Burgh looked taken aback.

'Do your, eh, proclivities, involve girls of colour?'

De Burgh blinked rapidly.

'Well,' he said, coughing a little. 'This is as humiliating as it gets. Yes. I'm afraid I am as base as you imagine me to be. In my defence, at least I wasn't looking for women who look like my wife. A lot of men do, you know. Or worse, they go for very young girls. My tastes are just . . . exotic, I guess you'd call them.'

'You were with one of the young women in the house – Lola?'

'I don't really – yes, that might have been her name.'

'Were you violent towards her?'

Laura asked the questions as matter-of-factly as de Burgh answered them.

But the solicitor was starting to give a little more away.

Tom observed the tension that had begun to register in the man's shoulders, the hardening in his eyes, even while his face was still open and cooperative.

'No, of course not,' he answered. 'If you'll excuse my crassness, I was only after vanilla sex. I'm not a beast.'

'You say some men go after young girls. Do you know how old Lola was?'

'I have a really bad feeling you're going to tell me younger than I think. I would have thought she was early twenties. I know that makes me seem lecherous but it's not as though it's a career awash with middle-aged women.'

'We estimate her age at sixteen.'

'Oh, God.' De Burgh paled. 'She never said. He – her pimp – he never let on she was that young. I just asked to see the African girls . . .'

'When was the last time you were with her?'

De Burgh hesitated.

'I don't know. A few months?'

'A few?' Laura repeated. 'Three, four? And before that? We're going to need you to be accurate.'

'I genuinely can't remember. I'll have to look at my diary. Why is this relevant?'

'Why do you think we're here, Hugo?' Tom asked.

De Burgh looked across at Tom.

'A brothel went on fire,' he said. 'You're asking people to come forward with information. I'm assuming you're looking into whether some angry customer got annoyed about the price or was being blackmailed or something, and lost his mind. But I can categorically tell you I wasn't anywhere near that place when it went on fire, or in the lead-up. I haven't been there in ages. So, I don't know why you want to know the exact time I was last there, when it can have no relevance to your current investigation.'

'Maybe it's not relevant,' Laura said. 'But we're wondering if you noticed the sixteen-year-old girl you were paying to have sex with had just had a baby? Or was pregnant when you were having sex with her?'

'No! Christ, of course she wasn't. Was she? I'd have noticed something like that. What is this – what's really going on here? A baby? Is she saying it's mine?'

'It was Lola who was found dead in the house,' Tom said. 'She and another victim – the brothel manager, Matteo Russo. And it wasn't the fire that killed them. They were stabbed to death, then the house was set alight.'

De Burgh's face drained of colour. He looked at Tom, and back to Laura, then back to Tom again.

'I'm sorry,' he said. 'This is way beyond me. I'm a stupid man who uses prostitutes. I've never committed an act of violence in my life. I never saw Lola with any baby and she may have been pregnant when I was with her the time before that but how would I have known if she didn't tell me? She was always on the heavy side.'

Tom winced at de Burgh's insensitivity.

'You didn't fall out with Matteo Russo, the pimp?' he asked.

'No. Not fall out, fall out. I mean, we had words once or twice.'

'Over what?'

'He kept hiking up the rates and he wasn't passing on the increase to the girls.'

'So, it wasn't because he thought you were a danger to his assets? Did you hit Lola?'

'Never.'

'And you fought with Matteo because you were advocating for the girls? Did that fight get physical?'

De Burgh shook his head angrily.

'Look, I think you might be mixing me up with somebody else. I'm guilty of nothing more than visiting the place. I'm being as upfront as I can possibly be. Given we're all in the same business, I'm going to skip the small talk and suggest I do what I know you need me to do.'

'Which is?' Tom asked.

'Give you a solid alibi for that fire and the time period leading up to it. And I'll check my diary to see when I last visited. I think if you want to have any further discussions with me outside of that, I might need to secure representation.'

Tom studied the solicitor shrewdly.

This little shit was going to run rings around them.

Outside, the sun shone. The city was full of people walking around in shorts and vests.

Tom and Laura walked miserably back towards headquarters, still dripping.

'It's all an act,' Laura said. 'The cooperation, the falling on his own sword. He's helping because he can give us an alibi for where he was when the fire started.'

'And I bet it will be cast-iron,' Tom said. 'He's giving us his version of events knowing that nobody living can contradict them.'

'Unless Tyanna Volkov does. What if she was supposed to have been in that house when it was burned down? What if she wasn't supposed to get out, even if she hadn't been stabbed? She's what led us to him. And where are the other girls? There had to have been more, surely?'

Laura stopped. Tom did the same, each of them looking at the other, their clothes practically steaming in the hot sun.

'Hugo de Burgh is a man who needs to keep his secrets hidden from those who know him in real life,' she said. 'He can't have people knowing he beats up working girls and fights with their pimps. Maybe he was the one who got Lola pregnant and when he wanted her to get rid of it, she wouldn't. Maybe he didn't see her for a while and then when he did, he discovered she'd had the baby. She could have asked for money. Put his whole lifestyle at risk. So Hugo took matters into his own hands.'

'That's an – eh, interesting reaction,' Tom said.

Laura frowned.

'Let me think about it,' Tom said.

They started to walk again, slowly, processing the theory.

'After hearing him, I'm pretty sure he didn't give a toss about Lola and could easily be the sort to have hit her,' Tom said, 'but there's a long way between visiting sex workers and getting a little rough and actually murdering two people. That said, look at what he does for a living. He encounters people much more violent than him all the time. So, what if what you say is true, and he pays somebody to take care of his problem?'

'Like hires a hitman?' Laura said. 'Plausible, I guess. Is he our man, then?'

'Maybe,' Tom said. 'The problem for you is going to be prosecuting him. His tracks will be better covered than the train line running under this park.'

They'd just turned in the gate for headquarters.

'Is there a rail line under here?' Laura asked, taking the bait.

'Exactly,' Tom said. 'But where's the baby in all this?'

'I've been thinking about that. What if the hitman took the baby? Or one of the other girls who lived there? It has to be somewhere.'

'If it's alive,' Tom said, grimly.

Laura pursed her lips. They continued walking in silence across the carpark.

'Anything from the maternity hospitals? I could ask Maria to inquire in the Rotunda if we want to speed things up.'

'They're being really helpful, actually. Michael is helping out our on-loan guy. The hospitals are obviously concerned about an infant that young so they've all gone through their records quickly. We have a small number of potentials – black girls in the fifteen-to-eighteen category who gave birth in the last couple of months. We widened the age group and time span, just to be on the safe side, but it's still not so many that the numbers weren't easy to collate. The lads are contacting them all. None named Lola; we know that already, anyhow.'

Tom didn't respond. Laura had said something that pinged in his brain but he couldn't reach it. Bloody hell. This paperwork job was slowing him right down.

'What will I do about Tyanna?' Laura asked.

'Position a uniform on her ward,' he answered. 'If what you suspect about the fire is correct – that she was meant to die in it, too – then she's at risk.'

'I don't have personnel coming out of my backside,' Laura said. 'As you well know. Do you really think de Burgh could be that dangerous that he'll tie up loose ends?'

'He wouldn't be tying them up,' Tom said. 'He'd be paying somebody else to do it. When you fork over big money, you expect the job to be done right, don't you?'

'I hope you're wrong, Tom. I'll see if I can get somebody for the hospital. I was worried about her doing a flit, so I can't say I wasn't considering sticking somebody on anyway. Now this. So, you do think it's him, then?'

Tom hesitated.

'To be honest, it seems a little too handy,' he said. 'Sorry, Laura. This case has messy written all over it. Seems to me, if you've found your man – or at least your instigator – within two days, then you've had an incredible stroke of luck. And it doesn't happen like that. Not in real life.'

CHAPTER 21

Nina knew she had no right to ask anything of her parents.

If she had the right words, she'd say: *It's not fair of me to ask you to trust me on this, but please, trust me.*

In the absence of the right words, she could only be silent.

'Nina, the police aren't going to be after you for drugs,' her mother said, for what must have been the tenth time. 'They aren't going to be *after you* for anything. But something awful happened in that fire, you can tell from the news. Were you there, love? You really need to tell us if you were.'

Nina looked away from her mother. Her father was standing in the door frame. He hadn't said much when he'd come up the stairs behind Orla. He was just looking at Nina and she could see he was thinking something; but whatever it was, Nina wasn't entirely sure it had anything to do with a house fire.

'Your clothes,' her mother said. 'I smelled them when you took them off. They smelled of smoke. And your face – it was dirty.'

'Right, so I must have been in a house fire.'

'Nina, we're not stupid,' Orla snapped. It was as fierce as her mother had sounded. 'You walk back into your home the same day as that house in Shipping Row went on fire and another girl your age is seen running from it. They're saying two people died in it! Were you living there? Is that where you were? Was it a drug den?'

'Mam, enough!' Nina didn't shout, but her voice was firm, angry. 'Why do you need to know where I was? Can't it be enough that I'm here? That I'm home? I'm not on drugs. I haven't been for months. I'm fine.'

'You're not fine, Nina. I haven't asked you anything because I don't want to pressure you but you're home two days now and you've barely eaten, you haven't told us anything and look at you – you look ill. You look . . . terrified.'

Nina glanced over at her father again. What was going on in his head? Why wasn't he leading the interrogation? That's what she would have expected.

'You don't understand,' Nina said. 'I can't . . .'

Did her father know? Did he know what she'd been doing? What she'd been forced to do?

'I can't talk about it,' she said, with as much finality as she could muster. 'I don't want to talk about it. Especially to the police.' She met her father's eye.

'And if you try to make me, I'll leave again.'

It had the effect she wanted on her mother.

Orla's hand flew to her mouth; absolute panic filled her eyes.

Nina felt so guilty.

It might be easier if she could tell them that not talking about what had happened was not just to protect her. That it was to protect them, too.

But she didn't want to scare them.

She looked up at her dad again.

He hadn't reacted like her mother. John was eyeing her strangely, in a way that Nina almost couldn't bear.

Like he could see through her.

'No,' he said.

'No, what?' Nina said, even though she was afraid to ask.

Her dad kept his gaze fixed on her.

'You won't be running anywhere,' he said.

And Nina didn't know if that meant he wouldn't let her, or if he knew that her threats were empty.

She couldn't leave.

This was the only place she was safe.

CHAPTER 22

When Ray and Laura had settled into a steady relationship, Laura witnessed a softening in her father towards her boyfriend, from *No man will ever be good enough for my daughter* to *You might just do*. Once they'd married and the Brennans realised that Ray was in it for the long haul, Jim had been won over completely. Now Ray was just one of the gang.

Which was probably why, when they arrived that Sunday evening late for dinner, nobody had thought to save them any and didn't even consider that either of them would be offended.

'I suppose I could peel more potatoes,' Laura's mother Kaye said, reluctantly, as she fanned herself at the open kitchen window. Even in the height of summer, Kaye liked to do a full Sunday roast. Neither Ray nor Laura would conceive of putting her through cooking a second one in the same day. Kaye was feeling her age; she'd been in steady decline since Laura had discovered the horrors her Auntie Peggy, Kaye's sister, had endured when she'd been forcibly held in a Magdalene Laundry. These days, Laura went out of her way to help her mother work less, including making one or all of her shit-for-brains four siblings do their share.

'Mam, send one of the twins around for chips,' Laura said. 'We're only here to see you, anyway.'

'It's disgraceful,' her mother tutted, for form's sake. 'I made a dinner big enough to feed an army. It's like the hordes coming through this kitchen when they get started. And, God forgive me, but all the boyfriends and girlfriends turn up these days, too. I mean, don't their own mothers feed them? Why won't they move out, Jim? You're such a good girl, Laura. All set up on your own.'

'Tea, Mam?' Laura interrupted.

She got the kettle on while Kaye went up for a nap.

Ray settled into the corner of the kitchen with Jim. The back door was wide open and Laura's siblings were down the back garden, kicking a ball about.

Laura actually felt sorry for her brothers and sisters being stuck at home, even if they were pretty useless. She and Ray could afford to rent but most people Laura's age were stuck at home and it was looking bleak for singletons the land over.

By the time she joined the two men, they were deep in conversation about the growth in gun crime.

'I thought it was no shop talk at the dinner table,' Laura said. 'You always used that excuse when we were growing up and I was desperate to know what you'd done in work that day.'

Laura's father had also been a guard, though he liked to tell her, often and proudly, that he could never have dreamed of rising to the dizzy heights Laura had already achieved.

Ray had a small tumbler of whiskey and water in his hand – her father's drink, and now his favoured son-in-law's.

Laura was sticking to tea. She knew the week ahead would be hellish; she'd no plans to start it with a hangover.

'The IRA buried a cache of arms down in Kerry sometime after the Civil War,' Jim said, ignoring Laura's chiding. 'And some feckin' eejit stumbled upon them and sold them into dodgy hands. I remember they turned up in the seventies. Jesus knows how they still worked, but suddenly there was a flood of pistols and rifles – German Mausers and Austrian Steyr Mannlichers – down in that part of the country. We didn't know what to do; we weren't used to dealing with armed robbers, not to that extent. You had guns in the country, sure, but they were rare. Now they're bloody everywhere. You can cause a lot more damage with a gun than a knife.'

'They're using knives too, Dad,' Laura said.

'They'll use anything,' her father agreed. 'No value in human life at all these days.'

Laura's brother Daithí arrived, depositing a brown paper bag of fish and chips on the kitchen table.

'What, not like in the old days, Da?' Daithí said. 'When people all looked out for each other? Like in World War Two, that sort of era? It's like fucking *Call the Midwife* in here. All nostalgia, no sense.'

'Get plates, you cheeky git,' Laura said. 'I'm not in the mood.'

'You seem stressed,' Ray said to her, softly. 'What's on your mind?'

Laura emptied the chips onto two plates provided by Daithí and drowned hers in vinegar.

She'd had to shower when she'd gotten home and Ray had been working anyhow, so by the time they got on the road they were already late for her parents'. They hadn't discussed how their respective afternoons had gone – at least, not hers. Ray was still bitching and moaning about Patrick 'BLT' Cowell spitting in his tea.

'The house fire deaths,' she said. 'Tom and I have someone in our sights but he's a slippery one and we're worried about the safety of our surviving witness, on top of that. I've managed to get a uniform on the hospital corridor but if this guy is using professionals, they'll get to her eventually. We don't have the personnel to protect a witness properly unless it's high priority.'

'*If* your guy is using professionals?' Ray repeated. 'Who is he? A gang member?'

'No. He's a solicitor. We don't suspect he's in a gang but he could have accessed gang members to do a job for him.'

'You're joking,' Jim said. 'Gone rogue, has he?'

'It certainly seems so. He's very middle-class. But he's a defence solicitor and he said himself he works with a lot of undesirables. He may have tapped his contacts.'

'What's his name?' Ray asked.

'Hugo de Burgh. Has he come up at your end? He could easily have got somebody off a firearms charge in the past. That's half the cases in front of the courts these days, isn't it?'

'I've only started reading up on everything this weekend,' Ray said. 'But I'll keep an eye out for the name.'

'He must have done something terrible, if he'd go down the route of murder to cover it up,' Jim said.

'What do you mean, Dad?'

'Well, look. A solicitor knows how things work. They know how hard it is to get away with anything and what we're like once we sense a pebble in our shoe. They've also seen enough of the world to know that blackmail can be overcome and that threats can be dealt with.'

'Yeah, but not everybody thinks as logically as that,' Laura said. 'Our hypothesis at the moment is that he may have been violent with an underage girl in a brothel and might have got her pregnant. She and/or her pimp may have been threatening to bring his world down. And he might be using his knowledge of the legal system to ensure he's at enough of a remove that we can't pin it on him.'

'Not heard of anything like that before,' her father said. 'A normal, law-abiding, law-enforcing citizen becoming an accessory in a double murder to save his good name. How good is his name, anyway? If he's defending scumbags, surely being caught out by a pregnant working girl is not exactly the end of the world?'

'There might be family implications,' Ray said, throwing Laura a lifebuoy. 'De Burgh is one of those names, isn't it? He probably has shedloads of old money and a reputation to protect.'

'Well, we're just looking into him for the moment,' Laura said bluntly. She was starting to see the allure of no shop talk over food. She wanted to enjoy these chips but her stomach was tensing.

What her father said had a ring of truth to it and it chimed with the doubts Tom Reynolds obviously had — that finding de Burgh this early was just too easy.

Laura felt a prickle of panic.

Everything about this case unsettled her. A nice straightforward motive that could clear it up quickly was the best outcome she could hope for.

But if de Burgh wasn't their man, then who the hell was?

CHAPTER 23

Natasha suspected that Tom's latest case would always have garnered her attention.

Laura's case, Natasha corrected herself. Of course, the murder squad was in Laura's capable hands now and Tom was in charge of the entire Bureau of Criminal Investigation. But for whatever reason, Tom had decided to involve himself in this one and because he had, Natasha couldn't deny she was now paying it special attention.

Tom had never allowed her to properly thank him for what he'd done for her family two years ago. Not that she could even begin to find a way to express how grateful she was. The odd dinner or lunch just didn't come close. Tom had not only proved Natasha's nephew Daniel's innocence, he'd quite possibly saved the kid's life. Daniel, for all his bravado at the time, was a gay black kid who'd just lost the love of his life and was heading to prison for the rape and murder of a white teen from a well-to-do family. Daniel had no gang affiliation, no experience at all of having to defend himself, not properly. He would quite possibly have died inside, or ended up so damaged he'd have killed himself or got himself killed on the outside when he emerged.

Every time Natasha thought about it, she shuddered.

So, whatever she could do for Tom Reynolds, or any member of his family, she knew she would do it.

This evening, that meant visiting Tyanna Volkov and taking over from Linda McCarn, who'd done quite a decent job of getting the girl to start talking.

Natasha was hoping she could maintain the progress.

'What part of Russia are you from?' Natasha asked Tyanna, gently. She kept her voice low. The curtains were pulled around the cubicle and the other women on the ward were chatting softly, but Natasha still wanted to protect the girl's privacy.

'You would not know it,' Tyanna said.

Natasha shrugged.

'My father is from a township called Kati in Mali and my mother is from a village called Wallintown in Westmeath. Have you heard of either of those places?'

A faint hint of a smile played on Tyanna's lips.

She was still so very young, Natasha thought. Even her eyes, though reflecting trauma, didn't bear the scars Natasha often saw on girls who'd ended up in this life.

Tyanna didn't seem to have drug issues, either, if the medical staff were to be believed. She was a little resistant to the sedatives, something Linda had noticed, which indicated she probably had been drugged in the past, but there wasn't any organ deterioration or other long-term-use indicators – she wasn't an addict.

Tyanna was beautiful and, perhaps, not as damaged as she could have been.

There might be hope for her.

'I am from Kurgan,' Tyanna said. 'It is in the south of Russia. You know the Urals?'

'Only from watching *Pointless*.' Natasha smiled. 'Russia isn't a big study in geography in Irish schools. Is it big – Kurgan?'

'It's not big city, no. Big for Ireland. For Russia, three hundred thousand population, maybe?'

'Very big, for Ireland,' Natasha said. 'What was your life like there?'

'Poor,' Tyanna said, matter-of-factly.

'Do you have a big family?'

'No. No family. Not any more.'

'No reason to stay,' Natasha said, her head cocked sideways. Tyanna had yet to fully open up but, sadly, Natasha felt she already knew this story. It was as old as time. A woman travelling to a capital city or another, wealthier country, assuming opportunity would present itself, willing to work hard. Never understanding the statistics stacked against them as single, vulnerable women. Thinking they were the centre of the universe when, really, there were many in the universe who saw young women as disposable.

'When you came to Ireland,' Natasha asked, 'did you intend to study or did you know you would be doing something else?'

This was the heart of what Natasha wanted to get to. Had Tyanna come voluntarily and decided there was only one way she could earn money when she was here, or had she been coerced to travel and tricked into the business? How willing was her participation?

It was important, because if Tyanna had been trafficked, then Lola might have been trafficked. And if traffickers were involved . . .

Natasha hadn't said anything to alarm Tom and Laura. Not yet. But she knew, more than most, that to traffickers humans were a commodity.

And babies were a very valuable commodity indeed.

Red blotches broke out on Tyanna's pale, clear skin. Her eyes flitted left and right; Natasha could tell she was checking if anybody was listening in on the conversation beyond the curtains.

'Is there still the policeman?' Tyanna asked. 'The one they put on the end of the corridor? I see him, when I go to the toilet.'

'Yes, he's still there,' Natasha said. 'He's only here to protect you. He's not listening.'

'How do you know he will protect me?'

'I know. This is not Russia, Tyanna. There are bad people everywhere, but in the Irish police, it is not the same. Whatever you have been told.'

Her senses prickled. This girl was talking, but she was scared. Very.

Tyanna opened and closed her mouth.

Retreat, Natasha told herself. Back off a little bit.

'The girls you worked with over here, were they nice?'

Tyanna nodded.

'Were they like you? From Russia?'

Often, Natasha knew, the girls would find each other. Sex work could be hellish but at least if the girls were living through it with other women from similar backgrounds, who had the same homesickness, the same fears – and importantly, the same language – it was a little more bearable.

'Lola was . . .' Tyanna considered. 'She was like you. Black. But I don't know where from. Somewhere in Africa. I never ask.'

'You think it was Africa, though? She wasn't from France or Italy or . . .'

'No. Her accent was – I don't know how to say it. She had funny English. Like, she spoke English at home but it was not to my ears English?'

'Pidgin English?' Natasha suggested.

Tyanna shrugged. She didn't understand the concept. But Natasha logged it away in her brain. Lola could be from Nigeria.

Which was also the originating point for many women trafficked through the African continent. Benin City, especially, was notorious. Create a trade route, anywhere, and it became easy to keep flowing goods through it, as opposed to sourcing other options. And Benin City was the starting point of many exports in the human-trafficking market.

Natasha was starting to feel uneasy.

There wasn't a huge amount of trafficking cases in Ireland. And where it happened, it was predominantly into the labour market, the higher of the trafficking statistics. But the numbers were growing across all the sectors.

And her department knew that whatever empirical stats they had, the prevalence tests meant the number of trafficking victims was probably at least fifty per cent higher in real life.

'The other girls in the house?' Natasha prompted. 'Were there many?'

'They come and go. A girl leave last month. She was Russian, too. Moscow.'

Tyanna pronounced it *Moskva*.

'One more girl go with a man a while ago. She is . . . Poland?'

If it was trafficking, Natasha thought, this was an international smorgasbord of exploitation. That was a little unusual. The Nigerians tended to stick to their own girls. The Brazilians the same. The Albanians often took whoever they could, but they were mainly from across Eastern Europe and Russia; they wouldn't have as much access to Nigerian girls.

'So, was it only yourself and Lola living with Matteo?'

Tyanna's face froze.

She wasn't a good liar, Natasha realised. Tyanna's response when they veered into uncomfortable territory was to say nothing.

Natasha considered her next question carefully.

'Are you frightened, Tyanna?' she said.

Tyanna shook her head quickly. Too quickly.

'You're safe here,' Natasha said. 'But if you are worried that somebody might be coming for you – if somebody has told you you owe them money – it will help us if you tell us. We can protect you better. Do you understand? We can keep them away from you. They might not have told you the truth.'

'Nobody is coming for me,' Tyanna said, and Natasha wasn't sure who she was trying to convince.

Tyanna looked down at her bandaged hands. Natasha followed her gaze.

'They will get better,' she said. 'Your hands. All your burns, they'll heal. The doctors have told you, haven't they?'

Tyanna nodded.

'I pay all my debts,' she said, so softly that Natasha barely heard her.

'Who were you in debt to?' Natasha asked, scarcely breathing.

'The men who get my visa. I pay them. I am safe now?'

She said it like a question, and looked up at Natasha as she did so.

Natasha opened her mouth a little, but she said nothing, at first.

Paying for visas was just one of the many tools the traffickers used against the girls. Usually it was a fraudulent debt, or at the very least, extortionately overpriced.

Natasha sighed heavily.

'We will keep you safe,' she said. 'Tyanna, it's really important that we know that Lola's baby is safe, also. Do you know where she is? Was she taken from the house?'

'I don't know,' Tyanna said, her face filled with despair.

A phone began to ring. Natasha almost reached into her handbag before she realised it wasn't hers – the ringtone was old, no longer familiar.

The phone continued ringing.

Natasha looked around, puzzled.

Tyanna flushed bright red.

It hit Natasha after a few seconds.

'Tyanna, do you have a phone?'

The girl shook her head.

Not a good liar at all.

Natasha stood up and walked around to the other side of the bed.

The bedside locker had an M&S bag stuffed into it. Linda McCarn had brought the girl pyjamas and a few bits, Natasha knew that.

The ringing was coming from behind the bag.

Natasha reached in and withdrew the phone. An old Nokia.

Unknown flashed on the screen.

Tyanna looked at the phone like it was the first time she was seeing it.

'Who gave you this?' Natasha said.

'Nobody.'

'Tyanna, you need to tell me the truth. Who gave you the phone?'

Still, the girl said nothing.

Natasha pressed the answer button and put the phone to her ear.

There was silence on the other end.
Natasha waited a few seconds, then she spoke.
'Who is this?' she said.
The line went dead.

CHAPTER 24

Monday

'God, Monday mornings,' Tom said, as he and Laura made their way through the incident room, checking progress at each of the desks as they went along.

The CCTV coverage had started to pour in from the areas surrounding Shipping Row and most of the guards present were going through it, slowly and painfully. The entirety of the IFSC had to be covered and then the route into the city centre proper. The sheer volume of footage practically made it useless, but they still needed to examine it, especially the Spar camera closest to Shipping Row, to try to gauge a pattern of toing and froing – of local residents and of Tyanna, Matteo and Lola. So far, they had managed to spot a naked Tyanna passing on Friday morning, not long before she was approached on the street.

The zoomed-in graphics showed the abject shock on Tyanna's face.

'The Boomtown Rats,' Laura said.

'What?'

'You said something about Monday mornings. I thought we were doing song titles.'

Tom frowned.

'It's "I Don't Like Mondays". And that's not what we're doing.'

'Oh,' Laura said. 'You're just moaning, are you?'

They'd stopped at Brian Cullinane's desk but he was nowhere to be seen.

'You're getting fierce grumpy in your old age,' Tom said.

'You're the one about to launch into a tirade about having to get up early after the weekend, and traffic, and the start of a long week, and traffic, and blah de blah blah.'

'Fine, then,' Tom said, petulantly.

'Has anybody seen Brian?' Laura called out.

'Jacks,' somebody yelled back.

'This team has too many men in it with prostate problems,' Laura said. 'Every time I look for somebody, they're in the loo. I'm going to organise a full-sweep health check. Only the women will be left standing.'

'Give the man a break; there he is, look.' Tom nodded at Brian who was trotting across the office towards them.

'Sorry,' Brian said. 'I was actually looking for you. I've a message here. Somebody rang the public line we gave out at the press conference.'

Laura turned back to Tom while Brian searched for the typed transcript.

'Who do you think gave Tyanna that phone?' she asked.

Tom rubbed his jaw.

'This is the problem with having her on a public ward,' he said. 'The guard on duty is expecting members of the public to be visiting; we can't shut it down. There was nobody suspicious in with her that we know of, but she has those curtains pulled all the time and if the other patients had visitors, they wouldn't have noticed somebody pop in to her. They only had to be there for a few seconds to drop the phone. Or . . .'

'Or?'

'Or whoever wanted her to have it could have paid somebody visiting a relative to drop it in.'

'How do they know she's in that hospital?' Brian asked, looking up.

'"#DublinUnwrapped" is still trending on Twitter,' Laura said. 'And Tyanna is not in witness protection; it would be easy to find out where she is.'

'I suppose,' Brian said. 'Did we get a trace on the phone, see who it belongs to?'

'Pay-as-you-go,' Tom said. 'And only an unknown number dialling in. No numbers saved and the unknown number is not answering when we dial it.'

'We still gave it to IT,' Laura said. 'If Tyanna rang anybody or sent messages, we should be able to retrieve them, even if she erased the records.'

'Natasha McCarthy believes we're dealing with a potential trafficking situation,' Tom said. 'Which means that if somebody is putting a phone in Tyanna's hand, it is less likely to be somebody trying to help her and more likely somebody under the impression they own her. That worries me. Not least because it poses a terrifying prospect for that missing baby.'

'Better missing and trafficked, or missing and dead?' Laura asked, gloomily.

'Here it is,' Brian said, pulling out a piece of paper. 'A man rang in, said he might have information on the fire.'

'Along with the hundreds of other callers who may or may not enjoy phoning police helplines and wasting our precious time,' Laura said.

'Oh no, wait,' Brian said. 'He said his daughter may have information.'

'Why are we deeming him legit out of the legions of callers?' Tom asked.

'The guard manning the line has a note here.' Brian squinted and brought the page closer.

'*Decent guy, not a nut job,*' Brian read. 'That's what he's actually written.'

Tom and Laura looked at each other.

'I know,' Brian said. 'Thin. But he says here his daughter was missing for two years and came back on Friday night. Apparently her clothes smelled of smoke and she won't say where she was. She had a drugs problem but he thinks she may have been involved in something more unsavoury.'

'Ah,' Tom said. 'Now I can see why it stood out. Might still be nothing, though.'

Laura nodded in agreement.

'You wanna call out to their house?' she asked Tom.

The ping Tom had heard in his head when he was with Laura yesterday suddenly made sense.

He looked down at the address.

'They're on the south side,' he said. 'Lots of fancy restaurants over there for lunch.'

Laura squinted, waiting for more.

'If it was one of the girls who took Lola's baby – well, that's a slightly less horrific prospect, isn't it?'

'How's the CCTV going, by the way?' Brian asked. He'd been saved the job because of medical issues. He'd had laser eye surgery the year before and suffered recurring migraines.

Tom looked around the office and guessed that right now, half the people there were considering laser eye surgery to liberate themselves from the screens.

'Not very productively,' Laura told Brian.

'What are we looking for, anyway?' he asked. 'Somebody creeping towards Shipping Row with a can of petrol marked "fire starter"?'

'CCTV could pick up Tyanna or Matteo or Lola in company going to or from the street in the lead-up,' Laura said. 'And it will give us an indication of when they were last seen. For all we know, they brought their killer back to the house with them. Unless one of the neighbours fesses up to taking a sick day and seeing more, CCTV is all we have to go on.'

Brian shrugged in begrudging agreement.

Every guard hated CCTV, none more than Tom. Sadly, unlike in the books and films, it was camera footage and mobile phone triangulation that solved most crimes these days.

Not clever guys like Tom.

The Cusacks lived in a little cul-de-sac on Dublin's south side. The area was gentrified working-class – each of the houses was originally council built, but had typically been bought out by its inhabitants and then later put on the property market at a disproportionately high price.

John and Orla lived in the end house, a rare detached property with a gate to one side and a disused alley to the other. Their bins were positioned in the alleyway and Tom could see a bike on the other side of the gate, resting against the back garden wall.

The house was well kept – the white paintwork on the masonry and window ledges was fresh, probably applied for the summer. Immaculate net curtains hung in the windows, and a small vase of flowers was positioned on each internal sill.

A tidy, modest home, owned by good, honest people. That was

the impression Tom had walking up the short drive, an opinion compounded when John Cusack opened the door.

He'd obviously been watching out the window for their arrival, if the speed of the door opening was anything to go by. So had the next-door neighbour, the second-to-last house, if the twitching curtain in the sitting room was to be believed.

Laura reached for her identity card but John was already ushering them into the front room, not even asking who they were or why they were there. He'd guessed.

Inside, a woman was perched nervously on the edge of an armchair, legs crossed at the ankles, two hands resting in her lap. She was pretty in a well-maintained way. Blonde hair swept into a neat bun, full make-up and a cardigan-vest twinset that looked more Debenhams than Dunnes.

Orla Cusack, Tom presumed.

She was knotting and unknotting her fingers and as soon as Tom and Laura were in the room proper, she motioned to her husband to shut the sitting room door.

'Sorry for the subterfuge,' John said. 'Nina's upstairs and we haven't told her we rang you.'

'You rang them,' Orla snapped.

John looked pained for a moment.

Then, politely, conscious of the police, Orla spoke again.

'I'm sorry. It's just – it was my husband's idea to contact you. I . . . Well, I'm just so glad to have her back, I don't want to . . . risk anything.'

'Of course,' Tom said.

He and Laura had quickly familiarised themselves with Nina Cusack's missing persons' file en route to her parents' home. The detective who'd opened the file following the report two years ago had taken care to point out that Nina's history was troubled and there had been a couple of convincing sightings, so her case – even though she'd only been seventeen when she'd first disappeared – had very quickly been relegated to non-priority.

Tom looked at her parents now and imagined how hard that must have been for them.

And he also knew why they wouldn't have a great deal of faith in the police.

And yet the father had called them, even while the mother resisted.

'Orla's terrified she'll run again,' John said. 'But honestly, I don't think she can. The first time, it came as a bit of a shock. She'd never pushed us for money or anything like that. It wasn't building up to some big argument where she threatened to leave or we threatened to throw her out. She just vanished. I thought, later, it was because she was ashamed. She didn't want us to see her the way she was. Especially because we'd all worked so hard on her rehabilitation the year before. For her to come back here now . . . I think there's more to it. I think she needs us.'

'You're worried she's in danger,' Laura said.

'Yes,' John said. 'I am. She came back here with only a little handbag, not even a set of clothes to her name. She's been gone two years and she's ended up with nothing and nobody. And whatever the counsellor says, I'm not sure going easy on her is the best route.'

He looked across at his wife.

She sighed, but she didn't argue with him.

'You did the right thing, Mr Cusack,' Tom said.

'Please, John is fine.'

'How do you want to play this, John? Would you like us to speak with her alone or with you?' Tom asked.

'Alone is best,' John said. 'There are things . . .' He glanced at his wife, who was eyeing him curiously. 'I think she'll be more open with you if we're not there.'

'That's fairly common,' Tom said, helping the man out. He was obviously much more in tune with what his daughter's life must have been like for the past two years than his wife was. Or at least, not in as much denial.

'She'll be angry,' Orla said, a pleading note in her voice. 'I think we should—'

'Honestly, we're used to this,' Tom said. 'If you two could give us a little space – maybe make us all a cup of tea – I promise, this will be as relaxed as possible. Nina might not have even been in the house we're investigating.'

John nodded.

'I'll get her,' he said.

Orla looked from Tom to Laura when her husband had left the room.

'You were the one at the press conference,' she said to Laura.

Laura nodded.

'So – you must have taken him seriously. John, I mean. To come all the way out here when you're in charge.'

'We're taking all leads seriously,' Laura said.

'Are you another inspector?' Orla asked Tom.

'I'm a chief superintendent.'

Orla's eyes widened in alarm.

'Was there anything else about Nina's arrival home that you think might be of use to us?' Laura asked, winning Orla's attention. 'Did she mention anything at all about where she'd been, or who she'd been with?'

'She's barely spoken. The people who died in the fire, were they – were they other drug users? She says she's clean and she doesn't seem to be taking anything. She hasn't left the house and I've been through her things . . .'

There was the sound of shouting upstairs.

'Oh, God,' Orla said. She jumped up, ran out of the room and into the hall.

A young woman appeared at the top of the stairs, John right behind her.

'Are you fucking joking me – they're actually here?'

Nina, even wild-eyed and furious, was a carbon copy of her mother, or how Tom would imagine Orla had looked in her younger days.

The nineteen-year-old at the top of the stairs was skinnier. The leggings and baggy long-sleeved T-shirt she wore did little to hide the gaunt, angular figure beneath.

She was too young to be already so shaped by her habit.

She'd started using drugs before she'd even finished developing, Tom realised.

'You can fuck right off,' Nina said, looking at Tom and then to her father. 'I'm not talking to them. I told you. Do you know what you've done? Have you any fucking idea? This is why I can't tell you anything. You're useless. Fucking useless.'

John stared down at the multicoloured carpet, his whole body sagging under the weight of his family's problems.

'You are going to speak to them,' he said, quietly. 'You will tell them where you've been for the last two years and you will tell them if you know anything about that fire and those people dying. Or you will be put out of this house.'

'John!' Orla gasped.

His daughter gaped at him.

Silence fell.

The tension was broken by Tom, who knew he had to step in

before father or daughter, or both, cut off their own noses to spite their faces.

'Nina, we're only here for a friendly chat. No pressure, no recording devices, we won't push you to tell us anything you're not comfortable with.'

Nina stared down at Tom like she was seeing him for the first time. The battle raged on her face – frying pan or fire, which would she choose?

'Fucking fine,' she said.

'We'll make the tea, so,' John said, ushering her down the stairs. 'You can sit in the living room. Orla.'

At the foot of the stairs, John indicated to his wife to follow him into the kitchen at the rear of the house. She did so, reluctantly, glancing piteously at her daughter and then glaring at her husband.

Tom stood aside for Nina to enter the living room.

Unconsciously, he was already blocking the way to the front door, in case she changed her mind.

When they were all sitting on Orla's comfortable couch and armchairs – and Tom could tell from the beige-striped upholstery and red-lace-covered cushions that the couch had been Orla's pick – he held out his hands in an appeasing gesture.

'Your parents only want to protect you,' he said. 'I've a daughter in her twenties. I understand where they're coming from.'

Nina couldn't sit still. She shook her head slightly at Tom's words, then went back to crossing and uncrossing her legs. She began to chew on her nails, while glancing at the door and window.

'Are those presents for you?' Laura said, following her eye and spotting the small pile on the armchair. 'Everyone must be thrilled to have you back.'

Nina said nothing but Tom thought he could see her shudder. She wasn't comfortable in the house, even if she had to be there. That much was apparent.

She looked at the phone in her hand – she hadn't let it go since coming downstairs.

'Are you expecting a call from somebody?' Tom asked.

Nina shook her head.

Tom and Laura exchanged a look.

'Okay,' Laura said. 'We don't have a whole lot of time here, Nina. Your parents say you came home on Friday and your clothes smelled of smoke . . .'

'Yeah, well, I smoke,' Nina said. 'What they're doing smelling my clothes, I can't explain. You'll need to ask them that. And I didn't ask her to start doing my laundry.'

'Were you living at an address on Shipping Row prior to this weekend?' Laura asked. 'Specifically number three, the house that went on fire?'

'No.'

'Were you in the vicinity?'

'No.'

She wouldn't even look at them.

It wasn't hard to tell Nina was lying.

'I'm going to be straight with you, Nina,' Tom said. 'We're in the process of going through all the CCTV surrounding the house on Shipping Row. On one of those tapes, we've already found a resident from the house fleeing the scene. She wasn't hard to spot. She had no clothes on. It might be harder to identify you but if you've been to that house in the recent past, we *will* find out. If you talk to us now, it stays relaxed like this. Friendly. We can help you. But if you don't talk to us and we spot you on the CCTV, then we have a problem.'

Nina glared at Tom.

'I know your sort,' she said.

'No, you don't.'

'Trust me. I do. You want to *help* me, do you? Yeah. I've heard that before.'

She stared at him for a few seconds more. Tom expected it to roll off his back, but something in her eyes surprised him. He felt . . . embarrassed.

Maybe she didn't know him. But that look said she knew *men.*

And Tom, in that instant, felt ashamed of whatever she'd endured at the hands of fellow members of his sex.

'Whatever you've been through, we can help,' he said. 'We can get you the right people to talk to, we can get the best medical and legal aid you need.' He knew the words were ineffectual, that if the girl had been forced to live as a sex worker for the last two years, there were scars she'd always bear.

'Oh, for fuck's sake, yes, I was living there.' She cut him off, impatience oozing. 'In Shipping Row. But I wasn't there when the fire started. You'll see that – if you *spot* me on the CCTV. I was on my way back there and I saw it. It was already on fire. I could see smoke in the sitting room window. I went up to the front door; I didn't realise how bad it was and I was going to go in. Get my things. But as soon as I opened the door, smoke started coming out. I ran.'

Nina stopped. She stared across at Tom, almost daring him to contradict her.

'Okay,' Laura said. 'Why wouldn't you tell your parents that?'

Nina threw her eyes up to heaven, then looked at Laura like she was thick.

'What does it have to do with them? I was embarrassed. I didn't call the fire brigade, okay? I just legged it. I didn't want to be caught up in whatever had happened there.'

'What were you doing there?' Laura asked. 'We have our suspicions about what was going on in the house, but why don't you tell us?'

Nina glanced at the closed living room door.

'If you know what I was doing there, why do I have to tell you anything?'

'Because it will help us.'

'It won't help me!'

Laura pursed her lips. She looked over to Tom.

'How did you end up there?' he asked. 'How did you meet Matteo? Did he bring you into it or was it somebody else?'

'I was doing it anyway,' Nina said, shrugging like it meant nothing. But her face was roaring red and the fidgeting had increased in pace. 'I needed the money. Matteo had a house and it was safer to just do it there.'

'Are you saying you were there voluntarily?' Tom asked. 'Did anybody force you to stay there? Or could you leave if you wanted to?'

'I. Was. Already. Doing. It.' Nina stared at them like they were idiots.

Tom took a deep breath. The young woman didn't understand that it didn't matter if she'd been selling sex before. If they'd kept her in that house against her will, that was exploitation. The sad thing was, this was how the traffickers normally operated. Take those with the least self-worth or the most vulnerable to begin with, and then make it worse.

'When did you start?' Laura asked.

Nina blinked rapidly and looked away.

Too young to say, Tom realised. Probably too young to even

decide. Had she approached the first man who'd used her, or had he approached her?

'How did you meet Matteo?' he asked.

'I . . . I can't remember.'

Tom bit his lip. She was becoming less defensive but also less talkative. They couldn't risk her shutting down completely.

'Nina,' Laura said. 'One of the other girls in the house – Tyanna – she got away. She's a little burned but she'll be okay. Matteo and Lola weren't so lucky. They were dead, even before the fire.'

Nina looked away.

'Do you . . . could you tell us Lola's full name?' Laura asked.

Nina's face lost its colour. Even from across the sitting room, Tom saw her eyes water.

Who was she upset for? Matteo? Lola? Or both?

'I don't . . . it might have been Lowel? Lowal? Something like that. She was from Nigeria.'

'Right,' Tom said gently. 'And was she there voluntarily as well?'

'She was there,' Nina said. 'That's all that matters.'

'It matters to us if there were girls trafficked to work in that house,' Laura said. 'If you were trafficked. Just because you're from this city, that doesn't mean that word doesn't apply to you, Nina. Trafficking doesn't mean sending people from one country to another. It means forcing a person into a position or work. They haven't given consent, they're probably not even being paid. Tyanna is not telling us much. She seems extraordinarily frightened. Are you scared, Nina?'

It took barely a second, but Nina glanced down at the phone in her hand.

It was a cheap smartphone. Not a Nokia, not like Tyanna's.

But Tom wondered if it was just as problematic. Was somebody in contact with Nina who shouldn't be?

'Where did you get the phone?' he asked her.

'It's mine.'

Nina shoved it into her pocket.

Tom clenched his jaw. They couldn't take that phone into evidence without a warrant. They could ask Nina to voluntarily hand it over, as they had with Tyanna, but they couldn't seize it and Tom instinctively knew Nina would not comply as Tyanna had.

'Matteo and Lola had been murdered,' he said. 'Stabbed to death.'

As he said it, Nina clutched her stomach. She looked like she might vomit. Both Laura and Tom half stood, ready to run for a bowl, or tissues, whatever was needed.

Nina began to breathe faster, her shoulders shuddering with each gasp.

'I can't . . .' she said. 'Please, stop talking about it. I don't want to hear.'

The tears that had been threatening spilled onto her cheeks.

'Nobody wants it to be true, but it is,' Tom said. 'When you were last in the house – did you see anything?'

'No.' An adamant shake of the head. 'I went with a customer, a couple of nights before. I was just coming home that morning.'

'What customer?'

'You think I know his real name?' Nina scoffed. 'I can't even remember his address.'

Tom didn't believe for a second she couldn't remember his address.

'And what time did you arrive back at the house?' Laura asked. 'Didn't the customer drop you back? Did you have to walk?'

'I walked. It was about, I don't know, half ten?'

'So, two nights before,' Tom said. 'Did you see Matteo and Lola then?'

'Yeah. Matteo sent me with the customer. He was fine. They were all fine.'

'Where was Lola's baby?' Laura asked.

Nina cried harder.

'Gone.'

'Gone where?' Tom sat forward, all ears.

'I don't know. One day Lola had the baby, the next it was gone.'

'Who took it?' Tom asked. 'How did Lola feel about that?'

'I don't know who took it.' Nina's eyes went sideways again. 'Lola – she didn't want the baby. She couldn't take care of it.'

She was lying. Tom knew it. He could see by the look on Laura's face that she knew it, too.

If the baby hadn't been in the house when the fire started, that was a good thing. But if it had been taken forcibly from Lola, then Tom couldn't imagine what the girl had been through.

'You didn't – did you take the baby from the house, Nina? Did you give it to somebody?'

'To who?' Nina cried, anguished. 'One of the clients? What the fuck are you talking about?'

Tom shook his head softly. He'd wondered if another girl had fled the fire, like Tyanna, but had actually rescued the baby. Now they'd found another girl who'd fled, but it was obvious she hadn't taken the baby with her.

'Who else had been living in the house?' Laura asked.

'Matteo, Tyanna, Lola,' Nina said. 'There was another girl there recently but she's been gone a couple of months. Wendy, but that wasn't her real name. She was really fair, very pale skin, I think she was Polish or something. And sometimes girls would come for a few nights but they'd go again. A girl from Russia was there; she and Tyanna were friends. She left as well. I was the only Irish girl.'

'Okay,' Tom said. They had to slow it down. Nina was getting too upset; she was shaking violently now. They needed to bring in specialists to talk to her. Natasha would have her hands full by the time this week was out.

'Nina,' he said, 'Tyanna gave us what might be a lead. She mentioned a . . . customer, who'd been violent towards Lola and fought with Matteo.'

Nina's face filled with confusion.

'Do you know who she's talking about?'

'I don't know. There were a few . . . there was more than one client who got . . .'

She bit on her lip, unable to finish the sentence.

Tom pulled out his phone. He opened Google and pulled up an image of Hugo de Burgh from his search history of the solicitor's firm.

They'd yet to show the photograph to Tyanna, and Tom had a suspicion Natasha would make him wait a while before he did. He knew it was probably wrong to ask Nina to look at it but the girl, for all her distress, didn't strike him as being as fragile as Tyanna. He couldn't put his finger on why that was the case; it was just something he felt, innately.

He stood and crossed the living room, dropping to his hunkers in front of the girl.

'Do you recognise this man?' he asked.

Nina stared at the picture through watery eyes.

'No,' she said, when she looked back at Tom.

CHAPTER 25

The anti-gun crime unit had taken over an entire floor of Garda headquarters.

Ray watched the rolling news bar running under the RTÉ news piece, filmed at the scene he'd just left. The victim, twenty-one years of age, had been 'known' to the guards. It was a euphemism the media used when the dead person was somebody who'd appeared on the police's radar in relation to a crime or gang affiliation. The ticker-tape also said that Garda sources remained tight-lipped about the details of the incident.

Ray snorted. For tight-lipped, read clueless.

He knew that the victim had just become a father. He'd been working that Monday morning when he'd stopped at a red light. A motorcycle had pulled up alongside the white van and the pillion passenger fired six shots into the driver's side.

The victim had bled out at the scene.

The unit's specific role wasn't to investigate who had committed the murder, though finding who would lead them to how. Their actual job, as loosely defined by the head of their unit, was to follow the guns and try to curtail the supply into the country. Fewer guns, fewer shootings.

In the long run.

But in the very immediate term, it looked bloody awful to

have people shot in the streets when the Minister for Justice had just pledged to target gun crime.

Ray had spent the last hour looking through the victim's background – previous offences, known associates, people he may have encountered in the neighbourhood where he lived, the pub he drank in. Then he'd examined his Facebook page. The latest bunch of photographs were taken at the man's niece's communion party. A large extended family on a very happy day. The victim posed contentedly with a pint of Guinness and an arm around his small niece.

The detective squad in charge was feeding the information in as quick as it could be collated, in the hope that somebody would help them identify who'd taken out the contract on the man's life. The current lack of intelligence about Dublin's crime gangs meant everybody was relying on everybody else for information, and even within the force, the anti-gun crime unit was fast being seen as the answer to everybody's prayers.

If the cops were lucky, somebody would leak who had decided to kill the latest shooting victim.

The information coming in had started to slow, so Ray took the opportunity to grab a salad and a Coke. Now, back at his desk, he pulled up the online profile of Hugo de Burgh. A break was as good as a rest.

Ray was making his way through some news articles on the man, former cases he'd been loosely involved in, when he heard a familiar voice.

'Hugo de Burgh? How has he come to your attention?'

Joe Kennedy.

Ray spun his chair around.

Kennedy was perched on the desk behind him, peering over Ray's shoulder.

'You know him?' Ray asked.

'Absolutely I do,' Kennedy said.

He grabbed one of the chairs and wheeled it over beside Ray's desk. He unbuttoned his suit jacket as he sat down, about as relaxed as Kennedy got.

'You're going to struggle to get the full story on him online,' he said, nodding at the screen. 'He's not a barrister – he's not the one doing the press interviews after the court sessions. He's just the man in the background, bringing in the cases, lining up the grubby money.'

'I don't follow,' Ray said.

Kennedy pushed his glasses up his nose.

'Well, you're looking at him in relation to the gangs, aren't you?'

Ray shook his head, puzzled, but starting to catch on.

'No,' he said. 'I'm not. I'm just looking out of interest. He cropped up in somebody else's case. I know he's a defence solicitor, but – are you saying he's tied into gangland?'

Kennedy sat back, arms folded, and studied Ray.

'Hugo de Burgh is the go-to man for half of the gangsters in Dublin,' he said. 'It's a running joke down in the Law Society – the fact he hasn't been taken out yet. It's not that the scum of our earth don't deserve representation and all that PC blah blah, but de Burgh is a greedy fool. He'll take on a case for a gang member in one part of the city and the next day, he'll take on a case for a rival gangster in another. It's amazing there hasn't been an accidental meeting outside his offices. Lucky, I guess. So, how has he cropped up on your scum-dar?'

Ray inhaled deeply. Laura was not a fan of Joe Kennedy, but it looked like Kennedy had more insight into Hugo de Burgh than Ray could give her. This was exactly what she was looking for.

Hopefully, she'd bear that in mind when Ray sprang it on her.

CHAPTER 26

They hadn't told Tyanna how much her burns would itch as they slowly recovered.

She was lucky, they said. She'd only been scorched, not properly scarred. Except for her hands, which had pulled the burning dress off. They might require some skin grafts, if the scarring was too bad. Ironically, the tips of her fingers were fine. It was her palms that hurt the most.

She'd had nothing on under the dress. If she'd been wearing underwear, they still would have taken photographs of her on the street. But at least she wouldn't have been naked.

Tyanna didn't understand why she'd started walking. The police, the doctors, they all said it was shock. Tyanna was shocked she'd left herself that exposed.

She didn't really care what her hands ended up like. She might in the future. Her looks were the only thing she'd ever had going for her.

She certainly wasn't clever. Her mother had beaten that into her mind and flesh.

Stupid, stupid girl.

Maybe one day, Tyanna would feel sad about the lingering scars.

But for today, she was telling herself she should feel happy to be alive.

If she could stay that way.

Lola hadn't been so lucky. Lola hadn't been lucky at all.

The nurses were happy to let Tyanna go to the toilet by herself, as long as she wiped herself gently with the hand that wasn't as badly damaged and didn't get the bandages wet when she ran the tips of her fingers under the tap.

She did that now, then looked up at her reflection.

Her face was paler than she'd ever seen it, her skin almost grey in the harsh, bluish overhead light. Her hair was flat, lips chapped, eyelids heavy.

Tyanna looked ugly.

Stupid and ugly.

It hurt Tyanna to use even the less wounded hand but anything was better than the indignity of asking the nurse for the pot when she needed to defecate. Tyanna had listened enough to the lady in the next bed deal with the result of whatever they'd given her to address her constipation.

Yet, of all of them on the ward, Tyanna had the most to feel ashamed about.

The things she'd done.

The things that had been done to her.

Tyanna had thought, when it began, that she would never stop feeling sick at the path her life had taken.

Every time a new man was brought in, she fought. She wanted people to know that. She hadn't just accepted what was being done to her.

She'd fought until she was subdued. She'd fought until they broke her.

They hadn't needed drugs to keep Tyanna in check. A lot of the girls were forced to take whatever was given to them; some asked for pills, anything to take the edge off what was happening to them.

With Tyanna, they had threatened what was left of her family. Her younger siblings.

Tyanna really *was* stupid to have ended up in her situation. She knew this happened to girls, especially girls who came from the poverty she did. She had heard the rumours – the ones who went to *work* in a city and sent home a lot of money but never returned, their families happy to take the cash but unwilling to speak about their daughters again.

Tyanna knew it happened. She just didn't think it would happen to her.

She had utterly loved the boy who brought her to Ireland. She'd have done anything for him and he'd been, she'd believed, very honest. He'd told her they would struggle and they might have to do things neither of them liked.

It wasn't that Tyanna had been an angel. She'd skipped school, she'd shoplifted, she'd burgled the home of one of her elderly neighbours when she knew the woman was staying in hospital with her sick husband.

And Tyanna *had* slept with men for money before. She was no angel, no virgin.

She hadn't considered it prostitution. Not then. Meeting a man in a bar and letting him buy her drinks, and maybe loan her some money for going out, in exchange for sex, that didn't seem a bad thing. Tyanna was young, she was sexy, beautiful, she would be having sex with boys anyway, so why not sleep with men and make some money from it? It was nothing her mother hadn't done, before her. Tyanna knew, because she and her two sisters had been the products of three different one-night stands.

Tyanna would have slept with Irish men for money. Men she chose, men she could manipulate, men she could stomach being with. She might have even married an Irish man, for a while, before she could leave and be with the boy she truly loved, but now with a residence visa and security.

Tyanna hadn't thought she was naïve.

But she was.

Because, when she'd arrived in Ireland, that wasn't what happened.

It wasn't her and her boyfriend in it together. He hadn't brought her there so they could live happily ever after.

There'd been a room.

There'd been a bed.

There'd been customer after customer after customer, a collage of men hovering over her, until she ached and her body felt hollowed out and no longer her own.

There'd been no money.

And the boy who'd brought her here had disappeared.

He'd sold her, and whatever money he'd got for her, Tyanna never saw. She was told she owed money, in fact, that she had to pay back whatever they had paid for her visa and travel and to the guards to stay away, and more. At no point along the line did Tyanna benefit from what she was expected to do, even though she'd calculated that she'd earned way more than she had to repay.

But at least Tyanna was alive.

The phone in the pocket of her pyjama bottoms buzzed.

The police had taken the first one. It had been replaced, quickly.

They would never let Tyanna go.

She took it out and looked at the message.

It told her to stop talking to the police.

She gasped. She hadn't even told the police anything. She'd

said nothing about Lola's baby, even though they kept asking. She'd given no names, not even for the man who had beaten Lola.

She would see what would happen, the message said.

She would see.

CHAPTER 27

When their starters arrived, Tom remembered why he generally avoided restaurants like the extremely fancy one they'd booked for lunch.

The menu had proudly declared approximately fifteen components of the dish.

All Tom could see was a tiny morsel of food and what appeared to be minuscule, dust-sized dressing elements dashed around the sides.

'Jesus,' he said. 'We should have ordered sides with the main.'

'You'll eat it and you'll enjoy it,' Laura retorted. She'd been in a bad mood since spotting the cost of the three-course lunch, hidden at the end of the menu in infinitesimal print.

At least the surroundings were pretty. They sat outside, under an awning of scented night-blooming jasmine, with the Royal Dublin Society complex on their left and a view of the River Dodder. It was warm, but not stifling. A pleasant afternoon for anybody lucky enough not to be working a double murder.

Tom swallowed his starter in pretty much one gulp, and with nothing but work left to chew on, asked Laura what she'd made of Nina Cusack.

Laura considered for a few seconds.

'Terrified,' she said. 'That petulant wagon thing with the

parents is a front. And I'm positive she recognised Hugo de Burgh. She's not a good liar. Lucky for us.'

Tom nodded.

'Why deny it, then?' he said. 'Is she on the receiving end of calls and texts, too?'

'Without a doubt.' Laura nodded in agreement. 'She kept checking that phone like it was bugged. But we can't take it off her. She's an adult, in a safe place. This isn't a vulnerable situation, not like Tyanna in that hospital.'

'My thoughts exactly,' Tom said. 'She said she lived in the house, and that's cooperating. But so far we don't have proof she was there when the fire started or had any connection to it. So we can't compel anything from her. Though she may be witness to the kidnapping of an infant.'

'Agreed,' Laura said. 'The whole "Lola didn't want the baby" thing sounded unconvincing. And now we might have the motive for the deaths. Somebody wanted the baby and Lola wasn't giving it up without a fight.'

'Is Matteo a hero of the piece, then?' Tom probed.

'Well, neither Nina nor Tyanna have anything bad to say about him so he may have been trying to help Lola. Which brings us back to a third player, one we don't know about. Either Hugo de Burgh or someone Matteo got involved with and couldn't extricate himself from. Remember what Natasha said? That some of the trafficking gangs use pretty boys to lure the girls in? What if Matteo was working for somebody? Someone Tyanna and Nina are too afraid to mention.'

A waiter appeared, hovering at Tom's shoulder.

'Did you enjoy your starter?' he asked.

'I think I did,' Tom said. 'It was gone so fast, I'm not sure it actually happened.'

The waiter laughed awkwardly, while Laura blushed bright red.

'Can I bring you anything while you wait for your main? A glass of wine, perhaps?'

Tom discussed the various house reds, before settling on a glass of Chateau Musar. This despite the waiter trying to nudge him in the direction of a cool white, to complement the warm weather.

'What?' he said, catching Laura's horrified expression when the waiter had left. 'We are sitting outside a lovely restaurant on a beautiful summer's day. It's one glass. I'm not driving and technically, I'm not even supposed to be working.'

'You didn't ask how much it cost!' Laura said.

'I'm not really expecting you to shout me lunch,' Tom said. 'Anyway, you should be more concerned that I'm drinking on an empty stomach . . . practically. Do you need to get that?'

Laura's phone was buzzing incessantly in her bag. She reached down and rooted it out, sighing at the interruption. Tom could tell that, even though protesting the sit-down fancy meal, she too had needed a break.

'Ray,' she said. She opened her texts. 'He wants to know where I am. Will I tell him to come meet us?'

Tom shrugged.

'The old gang's getting back together,' he said.

Laura typed in their location and sent a text.

'Do you believe Nina wasn't around in the lead-up to the fire?' Tom asked, when she'd put her phone down. 'That she was out with a customer?'

'CCTV might help us there,' Laura answered. 'If she went in the direction of the city centre with her client and not the other way, further down the docks. We've nothing down that end, camera-wise. It's not as developed. What makes you think she's lying?'

'Why go *anywhere* with a customer?' Tom said. 'The very purpose of that house, the partitioning of the rooms, was so each of the girls could have their own space. Why go out?'

'We'll need Natasha McCarthy more actively involved in these interviews,' Laura said. 'We need to find out more about Lola . . . Lowal? And we have to bear in mind these girls are victims, first and foremost. We can't just treat them as witnesses. I don't think Natasha would be impressed with us showing Nina that picture of de Burgh. It probably risked a trauma response.'

'I appreciate that,' Tom said. 'But we also can't go as gently as we'd like. That would take time. And we mightn't have time. Not just because we want to find the baby. If somebody is trying to keep those girls quiet, they're at risk. I think Tyanna knows that. It might be why she hasn't told us the full story of what happened in the house.'

'You don't believe she didn't see anything,' Laura said – a statement, not a question.

Tom shook his head.

'No,' he said. 'I think she knows who killed Matteo and Lola but she's either so traumatised that she's blocking it out or she's staying quiet because she's scared.'

They'd finished their tiny mains and were on to the Lilliputian desserts when Ray turned up.

With Joe Kennedy.

Tom nearly choked when he spotted the two of them walking along the riverside in their direction.

'What the actual?' Laura hissed. 'He's brought *him* here?'

Tom knew exactly what she meant.

He'd have happily gone about his life avoiding Joe Kennedy in general, but if he'd known he was to meet him at some point, he wouldn't have chosen for Kennedy to catch him on an extended lunch break in a five-star restaurant when he was channelling Lord Muck.

Why he was bothered by what the man thought was beyond him. Bronwyn Maher and Sean McGuinness had prevented him having a final showdown with Kennedy when the latter had been removed from his job as chief super. When Tom had discovered it was Kennedy who had leaked his home address to the newspapers, he'd been prepared to do violence to the man. He'd endured plenty with Kennedy as his boss, but that had been beyond the pale, especially as the man had espoused unity in the force over all else.

And now, here he was, pulling up a chair at the table and ordering coffee.

It was Ray who landed the first blow, though.

'Jesus, you never brought me anywhere like this for lunch when you were my boss, Chief,' he said, eyeing the prices on the dessert menu.

'The witness we went to see lives near here,' Laura said, defensively.

Leave it, Tom said in his head. *Explaining is losing.*

'I've never gone in for the whole depriving yourself of sustenance on the job mentality,' Kennedy said. 'You can't think if you haven't eaten and snacking at your desk isn't healthy for the brain, either.'

He smiled at Laura.

And that was how Kennedy operated, Tom remembered. So amiable, so on your side. Until he wasn't.

Kennedy still hadn't made proper eye contact with Tom.

Tom had seen through him, Kennedy knew that. He couldn't play any of his tricks with Tom.

Yet he'd turned up here, bold as brass.

On cue, he turned to Tom and smiled broadly.

'Fair play to you, Chief Superintendent. You're meant to be off and you're still working. Congratulations, by the way. On the promotion. I emailed at the time, but I don't know if you received it?'

Tom hadn't. Either Kennedy was lying or somebody in the know had protected the chief super from the unwelcome contact. It was vintage Kennedy, though. As passive-aggressive as it got. Now Tom was the baddie for not responding to an email he'd never received and hadn't wanted.

He knew how to manage the man now, though.

'I did get it, thanks,' Tom said, sounding puzzled. 'I replied. Did you not get that?'

Kennedy's mouth formed a silent *Ah*, and a hint of a smile ghosted his eyes.

'What's so urgent?' Laura spoke directly to Ray, and Tom almost felt sorry for him, knowing the ear-bashing his former deputy was going to get at home later.

'Hugo de Burgh,' Ray said, flinging his ace card on the table. 'Joe here is a fount of knowledge on him.'

The look Laura gave her husband asked, wonderful and all as that was, couldn't Ray have extracted that knowledge from Kennedy himself and saved them all this excruciating get-together?

Tom had worked with Ray for so long, however, that he could see on Ray's face that he hadn't realised Laura was with him.

All is forgiven, Tom thought, and smiled thinly at Ray so he'd get it.

He turned to Kennedy.

'So, what's de Burgh been up to?'

Kennedy sat back, ostensibly to let the waiter place the extra coffees on the table, but also because he was obviously enjoying being needed.

'Ray's role in the new unit is to look at the victims of the gun shootings and trace the contracts on them,' Kennedy said. 'I've been tasked with examining those professional people who protect the top tier. The solicitors, the barristers, the accountants, etc. When we move on the guns, we need to make sure there isn't a line of defence standing in the way of our search warrants and seizures. De Burgh has his own file but I've encountered him before. It started small, from what I gather. Rob Cowell's sister – you know Rob?'

Tom nodded. Rob, a member of the notorious family gang, was a long-time drug dealer on the north side of the city. Like his uncle Patrick, he'd spent more time in prison than out on the streets but had still managed to help build the Cowell empire in his home estate and the surrounding areas.

'Well,' Kennedy continued, 'Rob's sister had an acrimonious break-up with her husband – she, and he, weren't gang members. She put her foot down, said it was none of Rob's business and he wasn't to go getting involved, especially in the way he usually would. But the husband, thinking he was getting off light, got cocky and stopped paying child support for the kids. So the sister went to Rob. All she asked was that he help her get a good solicitor so she could take the ex to court and get him to pay what was owed.'

Kennedy sat back, relishing the fact he had the table in thrall.

Tom really wished he could order more wine to numb the

allergic reaction he couldn't help having to the man, even when what he was saying was of interest.

'Anyhow, de Burgh had a good reputation for standing up for women and not being afraid to play a bit dirty on their behalf. So Rob put him on retainer, but not just to get the maintenance payments resumed. Rob saw the ex-brother-in-law's actions as a slight on him, so he had de Burgh go to town. By the time they were finished with him, the Revenue had been all over the ex, his employer let him go and our lot were watching him because of suspect material on his computer. He ended up bankrupt.'

'How did she get her child support, then?' Laura asked.

'She didn't,' Kennedy said. 'The ex was ruined. Rob sorted her out with money. Until he ended up in jail, of course.'

'Bet Rob's sister wasn't too pleased at that outcome.'

'Nope. I only found out about all this because the ex ended up hanging himself a few months later and it looked like it might not have been his own choice. I was working in headquarters at the time but never got to look into it properly. Got moved.'

Tom knew he wasn't the only one internally bristling at that little dig.

Kennedy smiled, like it was all water under the bridge, when he was the one who'd opened the floodgates to begin with.

'Anyway, de Burgh had made such an impression on Rob that he started using him more,' he said. 'But de Burgh had one stipulation. He wasn't going to be an in-house solicitor. He convinced Rob that he would be far more use if he was considered an honest Joe, a practising solicitor who sometimes represented high-profile clients but wasn't working for any one person in particular. De Burgh is obviously a strategic fellow, because what actually happened is he built a reputation as a reliable representative for all sorts of shady characters who could pay well. He's now the go-to brief for half the gangs we're looking at in the new unit.'

'We thought he might have encountered some gang members, given he's helped out with a few defence cases,' Laura said. 'We were looking for a link. We didn't realise there'd be several.'

'You name a top man and de Burgh has worked with him at some point,' Kennedy said. 'Most of the Cowells and then the gangs that split from that organisation. I hear he's even branching out to work for some of the foreign mobs.'

'Wonderful.' Laura shook her head. This was disastrous for them, Tom knew. It looked like de Burgh would have any amount of contacts had he wanted to order Matteo and Lola killed.

'Do we know who de Burgh has been representing of late?' Tom asked.

It was like Tom had handed Kennedy a birthday gift.

'I do,' Kennedy said, practically preening. 'Specifically, because it's a new gang and we've just started to notice them. There's a particularly nasty Albanian crew bringing in drugs and one of their runners was picked up in Dublin port, driving a van that had bags of coke stashed in among crates of cheap generic fabric conditioner.'

'I heard about that haul,' Tom said. 'Mainly contaminated.'

'Yep,' Kennedy said. 'De Burgh is representing the runner. Claims he was forced to do it, that they have his family at gunpoint back home. It's all rubbish. Interpol have images of the runner enjoying summer holidays with his bosses.'

'Why are you watching that gang, though?' Tom asked. 'They're drugs, not guns.'

'They're bringing in guns as well. Buying them on the Russian border and selling them here to the Dubs for a handsome markup. Drugs, guns, people, it's all import/export, as they say.'

'People? Any chance they're in the trafficked-sex-workers game? We're looking specifically at a brothel that just went up in flames.'

Kennedy jutted out his lower lip and considered for a moment.

'I don't know,' he said. 'Is this to do with the double murder?'

Tom nodded.

'It would be odd,' Kennedy said, 'for a gang to kill its own assets. The women earn more than the guns ever could. They're the crime that keeps paying. For the Albanians to do away with the pimp and one of the girls, they must have really caused a problem for them.'

'Caused a problem like upsetting a very popular and very useful solicitor?' Tom asked.

Kennedy held out his hands. Possibly, the gesture said.

'Do you have any names of the top guys in the Albanian gang?'

'No. Not the head honchos. But I'm working on it.'

Tom picked up his coffee and drank the dregs.

Well, this was all very strange.

Sharing coffee with Joe Kennedy and the latter actually being helpful.

It was one for the memory book.

CHAPTER 28

There were very few things that Linda McCarn and Emmet McDonagh were in full agreement on. But that their granddaughter was the most special, most wonderful, most brilliant little human being ever born had them singing from the same hymn sheet from the day they met her.

It had taken a while and almost never happened. Twenty-five years previously, Linda had reluctantly given up the baby she'd conceived during her affair with Emmet. When Paul, as an adult, had found his birth parents, he'd harboured a deep distrust and animosity towards Linda. He'd chosen instead to contact Emmet and bring him into his life, purely because Emmet could be forgiven. Emmet hadn't known of Paul's existence until that point.

After a lot of effort on everybody's part, an entente cordiale had been established. Relations were still strained between Linda and her son, but she was trying and so was he.

What they'd all agreed on, eventually, was that Hannah should have contact with both her paternal grandparents. Paul, matured a little, realised he didn't want his daughter to miss out the way he had.

So, every couple of weeks, he let Emmet and Linda spend time with their granddaughter, to the consternation of both

Linda's husband and Emmet's wife, who, quite vocally, did not enjoy the prospect of their spouses sharing such intimacy.

Emmet and Linda weren't for budging. They both knew they'd already sacrificed enough for their respective spouses. Neither had really wanted to end their affair all those years ago. Emmet had done it out of duty, because his wife was ill. And Linda had stayed in her practically loveless marriage because that was what people of her class and background did.

Nor had either of them gone on to have any other children.

So, this was the last chance saloon.

They chose Paul and Hannah.

And as Linda watched her granddaughter happily push Play-Doh through a plastic octopus's head, she thought there was nowhere she'd rather be, and nobody she'd rather be with. Enduring all Geoff's complaining was worth it, for these few hours of pure joy.

'More ice cream?' Hannah asked, grinning up at the pair of them.

They were seated at the tea rooms beside a large playground, full of children eking out the last of the afternoon's hot sun. The Play-Doh was a recent purchase from the nearby Smyths toy store. Both grandparents were unashamed to admit that what the little princess wanted, she got. They'd be the ruin of her, if Paul didn't keep an eye out.

'More ice cream? I don't see why not!' Emmet banged his hand on the table, decision made. 'You have to eat it all, though. I can't be finishing your ninety-nines. I'm watching my figure.'

Linda laughed at the puzzled expression on Hannah's face.

'Why don't you make us some more octopus cake, first,' Linda said, 'and then we'll get more ice cream?'

Hannah resumed playing, already distracted as the modelling clay squeezed through the plastic toy's holes.

'More coffee?' Emmet asked.

Linda nodded. A young woman ran past, her dark hair swishing from side to side, her denim shorts so tight they looked like they'd constrict the flow of blood. She scooped up a toddler from the bottom of a slide before the kid hit the dirt and said something to her in Russian.

She reminded Linda of Tyanna.

'She looks like that girl from the fire, doesn't she?' Emmet said, following Linda's gaze.

They did this, when they were together and Hannah wasn't the focus. Talked about work. They'd very little small talk to be going on with, otherwise.

'She does,' Linda said. 'I was just thinking of how terribly afraid Tyanna is. I'm no expert, but normally in these situations, the girl is frightened of their pimp. Not a client. The pimp is normally well able to sort out any troublesome customers. But Tyanna knows this Matteo chap is dead and she's still scared, of somebody or something. Tom met another girl from the house, earlier. Nina, she's called. She's frightened as well, he says. Who has such control over them that they're still afraid?'

Linda shook her head, unable to figure it out.

'This solicitor bloke you've told me about – are they frightened of him?' Emmet asked.

'I don't know.'

Linda looked over at Hannah, who was being pushed on the swing by a little boy, who'd forgone his turn just to see her smile.

'You know, all those girls started out like that,' Linda said. 'Just because they became something else, doesn't mean they aren't somebody's little girl. Somebody's darling. We should fight very hard for them.'

'Nobody in Tom's department would disagree with that,' Emmet said.

'No.' Linda nodded in agreement. 'But if they don't make progress, eventually – and you know this as well as I do – this case will go unsolved and nobody will be that worried about what happens to Tyanna or Nina or anybody else who went through that house. They'll worry about that baby, but the girls will be forgotten.'

Emmet didn't say anything for a moment.

Then he leaned forward, bringing himself closer to Linda, closer than they'd been in a very long time.

'Why is this affecting you so much?' he asked. 'You've seen a lot of terrible things in your life; you've sat in rooms with some very traumatised and very disturbed people. Why is this one getting under your skin?'

Linda hesitated. The proximity of Emmet was throwing her a little. She'd forgotten what he smelled like, up close. The same, as it happened. Turned out, he'd never updated his aftershave.

'You should have seen Tyanna, in that hospital,' she said. 'She had nothing. I brought her in a few bits. I'd guessed, because of what had happened, she might be stuck. But she'd no family to call, no friends to visit her. She really is utterly on her own. Maybe there's somebody back in Russia, but not here. She's the loneliest person I've ever met. When you're that much on your own, it must feel like nobody cares. I suppose it ... stirred something in me. I remember that feeling. I remember, after I gave birth to Paul and he was taken, how very, very alone I felt.'

Linda's voice caught on the last sentence.

It took her by surprise when Emmet reached out and squeezed her hand.

It wasn't entirely unpleasant, either.

'I'm going to ring Tom,' Linda said, and Emmet nodded. 'This doesn't add up to me, that those girls are still so scared. I'm going to tell him what I think. It's entirely possible there was somebody else monitoring the girls in that house. Somebody so dangerous, they're afraid to tell us about him.'

She'd no idea that Tom and Laura had already reached that very conclusion.

CHAPTER 29

The meeting with his Albanian bosses had been very productive.

Viggo was a much happier man that evening when he returned home to his wife and child.

He'd decided – or at least been helped to decide – to move.

Ireland was not a friendly place at the moment.

The Irish ones were starting to suspect what had happened to the baby from Shipping Row.

It was in Viggo's interest to get his own family out of Ireland.

'You must pack,' he roared at his terrified wife. She didn't like it when he raised his voice to her. It was a side effect of his job. He was used to shouting at women. But he had to remember not to shout at her. She was the love of his life. They had a lot to look forward to.

And she would love England. There was so much potential there.

Viggo just had to get everything in motion and leave before the Irish found out what he was doing.

He had a few loose ends to tie up.

The Russian girl, Tyanna, had been talking to the police. She'd had her warning and hopefully she'd heed it.

The Irish girl, however, was refusing to come out of hiding. For now. They knew where she was; they'd lure her back, eventually.

Viggo was worried about that.

The arm of the law was long and he didn't want it to reach him in England. He needed to be anonymous over there.

He also didn't want his Irish bosses to pursue him.

Tyanna and Nina knew too much.

Would it draw more or less heat on Viggo if he dealt with them before he left?

Even as he threw clothes into his suitcase, he was trying to work that out.

It might be better if he spoke to the Irish bosses himself. Got in first and planted his own seeds about the two girls.

Then maybe they'd be dealt with and he wouldn't have to lift a finger.

Yes. Now there was a plan.

Viggo smiled. Then he crossed the room and gave his wife a big kiss before she went upstairs to settle their kid to sleep.

All that mattered was protecting his own family.

CHAPTER 30

Orla Cusack was finding it extremely difficult to look her husband John in the eye.

The only way she could deal with him this evening was to work around him, doing everything she would normally do – preparing the dinner, sorting out laundry, preparing her clothes for the following work week, though she'd taken the week off sick and really, she didn't want to leave the house at all at the moment, so she didn't need to iron her blouses.

He knew he was in the doghouse. Normally, when Orla lugged the bag of potatoes into the kitchen and started to peel them, he was nowhere to be seen. He'd be in the sitting room watching telly or upstairs showering, or even out for a walk or a run. But this evening he chose to sit at the kitchen table, drinking a cup of tea and pretending not to watch her, while he watched her.

He'd taken the week off, too, and Orla desperately wished he hadn't. If she knew she was getting rid of him in the morning, she might be able to endure his company in the evening.

But, knowing they were stuck in the house together, Orla was becoming more and more irritated.

There was a little rap on the open back door, and Bob from next door stuck his head in.

'Hi John, hi Orla,' he said.

John signalled him in, causing Orla even more irritation.

Jesus, now he expected her to make small talk with their neighbour? How stupid was her husband? Orla had lots of time for Bob, of course, but not tonight. Not with all this going on. John was using him as body armour. He knew Orla wouldn't be rude in front of Bob.

'How's it going, Bob?' John said.

'Not bad, not bad. Just wanted to check in on ye. I was out at the grave today, visiting Irene. I was thinking it's such a shame she didn't last to see Nina back.'

Orla stopped peeling the potatoes. She looked over at Bob, her face filled with pity. Irene had died seven months ago, just before Christmas, and Bob had aged terribly in that time. He was only in his forties, like John and Orla, and his wife's heart attack had been sudden and unexpected.

And yet Orla had barely even noticed the deterioration in their lovely next-door neighbour, she'd been so caught up in her own problems.

Bob and Irene; at times they'd been more help to Orla in her search for her daughter than even John had. John, inexplicably, had given up early on. In her most charitable moments, Orla thought it was because all John's energy had been spent on helping Nina through her first detox and he couldn't live through another crisis.

But Orla had kept going, and she still remembered Bob and Irene using the printer at the wholesalers to run up hundreds of posters for her.

She'd gone to Irene's funeral, of course, and she'd noticed that Bob had gotten greyer over the last few months, his face more lined.

But the fact was that he'd still been calling in on her with little gifts; that he'd rushed out to get presents for Nina when he'd heard she was back – and the whole time Bob had been dealing with grief of his own. Orla had taken his kindness for granted. This was what the Cusacks' lives had become. A tiny universe, where Nina was the centre and they revolved around her. Whether she was with them or not.

Orla felt ashamed of herself.

'I'm sure Irene would have been so happy,' Orla said, her voice as warm as she could make it.

'Oh, of course she would have been,' Bob said. 'Listen, I won't keep you, I was only checking in and hoping to catch sight of herself. Is she all right, yeah?'

'Hiding upstairs,' John said, cocking his head up at the ceiling.

'I guess that's to be expected,' Bob said. 'I'm sure she'll come round. Won't you tell her we're all asking for her around here. She has nothing to be ashamed of or to be worried about. Everybody is just glad to have her home.'

'We will, Bob,' Orla said. She was struck by a sudden thought. 'Isn't it Irene's birthday next week? I mean – wouldn't it have been? She was around the same date as Nina, wasn't she?'

'Ah, you know, that's why I always remember the date . . .'

Bob trailed off, his face filled with sadness.

'Come and have dinner with us at the weekend,' Orla said. 'We'd love to have you. It's a celebration this year. Isn't that right, John?'

Her husband smiled thinly.

'Absolutely,' he said, and she could see he was irritated now. Well, good.

'That's fierce kind of you,' Bob said. He glanced warily at John, evidently aware the offer had been spontaneous and not previously discussed between the couple. 'If you're sure? I wouldn't want to intrude.'

John swallowed and smiled.

'No problem at all,' he said. 'We need to start getting back to normal. And look at it this way; it's a night out and you won't need to worry about drinking and driving home.'

Bob laughed.

'Fair enough,' he said. 'I'll chat to you about it again. Let me know what you need, Orla. You know I can get everything cheap.'

He bade them good evening and left.

As soon as the coast was clear, John spoke again.

'You should have cleared that with me first, Orla. It might be a bit much for Nina, having a birthday dinner with guests. We haven't even had our parents over yet. And she'll barely speak to us.'

'Don't you dare,' Orla snapped.

'What?'

'Don't you dare say that sentence to me – *you should have cleared that with me.* You lost the right to say that when you said what you did to Nina. Threatening to throw her out of her own home. What possessed you?'

She ran the peeler over the spuds fast, angrily, and with little care.

He stood up and came over to stand beside her.

'I just can't believe you did that,' she said, her voice shaking with anger. 'I can't believe you would take that risk.'

Nina had gone back upstairs when the police had left.

She'd been crying, but she wouldn't tell Orla why, or what had been said.

The bedroom door had slammed, then it was locked, and

Orla was left downstairs wondering if, at any moment, her daughter was going to descend with a bag and tell them she was leaving again.

'I called the police for her own good,' John said. 'She could be in danger, Orla. We couldn't . . . we didn't protect her before. We have to now.'

Orla dumped the second potato and reached for the next one.

'What do you mean, we didn't protect her? We did everything we could, John. It's not our job to stop her from doing what she does – it's our job to support her when she asks. Don't you remember anything from the counselling sessions? See, I *knew* you weren't listening. I knew you were just going because I made you. And now you've shown her that we're not on her side. She came to us asking for help, John. Oh, I know she didn't say it with words, but she said it with her actions, when she turned up. And you betrayed her. You— ouch!'

She'd done it, she'd sliced into her damn finger and now John would be gloating; he was bloody right about that, too.

Orla flung the peeler and the potato, which was fast absorbing the blood that dripped from her hand, into the sink and cried aloud with frustration.

John, rather than saying I told you so, turned on the tap and ran it gently over the wound.

He examined it, even as Orla tried to pull away.

'It's not too deep,' he said. 'I think we can avoid the seven-hour wait in A&E and sixteen stitches.'

Orla laughed, a sound somewhere between pain, irony, mirth and grief.

'Oh, John,' she said. The tears she'd been holding back all day burst forth and she let her husband, as angry as she was with him, pull her head into his chest.

'What if we lose her again?' she said.

'Why don't we go up and talk to her?' he said. 'Properly, honestly talk to her. She needs to know what her leaving did to us last time. This thing you're trying to do, where we walk on eggshells around her, it won't work, love. She needs to know we love her to bits and what she does impacts on us.'

'We said all that when we went to her group therapy sessions,' Orla protested. 'It had no effect then.'

'She was a kid,' John said. 'I don't think she's a kid any more.'

Orla knew he was right. She knew it. She just didn't want to admit it.

John knotted a sheet of kitchen towel around Orla's finger and, together, they went upstairs.

They knocked on Nina's door before trying to open it, but it was still locked.

'Nina, love,' John said. 'We need to talk to you. Open the door, please.'

Even then, the butterflies of dread were dancing in Orla's stomach.

There was a silence beyond that door. Not just the silence of a daughter who refused to talk to them.

It was the nothingness of an empty room.

'John,' Orla said, her voice low, wary. 'Break down the door.'

John looked at her, confused, a beat behind.

Then, realisation dawning, he went to the far side of the landing and ran at the door, shoulder first.

The lock gave on the first push. When they'd replaced the locks, years ago, it had been after several incidents of Nina locking herself in and taking drugs. John – and more importantly, his shoulder – had learned a lesson.

The door burst open, splintering at the frame.

The room was empty. The en suite door was open; she wasn't in there, either.

Nina was gone.

CHAPTER 31

The shelter was a bright, colourful affair which seemed to grow fuller and fuller every time Natasha McCarthy visited. On this balmy evening, it was practically bursting at the seams.

Natasha knew several such places across Dublin. This one was a halfway house for women and girls who'd been in particularly vulnerable situations, had somehow extricated themselves or been saved, and were now starting to venture out into the world again. Women who'd been trafficked, mainly.

The stats for Ireland weren't as high as those internationally – which also meant the supports in Ireland weren't as extensive.

And what made it worse was that Natasha wasn't sure if these trafficking stats were smaller because Ireland was less accessible and too small to live so hidden, or whether her force was just worse at identifying and infiltrating trafficking rings.

Natasha had made it her business in recent years to familiarise herself with all the international trafficking developments and legislation. She had no faith in her own government's ability to tackle it, not least because it was a crime that mainly affected women and those least likely to kick up a fuss. Her jaundiced view was borne out by the fact that not one conviction had been successfully achieved against a trafficking suspect since the new Irish legislation had been introduced four years ago, in 2013. A handful of people had been convicted of kidnapping and of organising a brothel, but their sentences were pathetic, in a word.

Yet, the victims Natasha's force did manage to access hinted at far more extensive trafficking activity. That was just in the sex trade. She was well aware that the majority of trafficking victims worldwide were used for forced labour. She'd even heard of cases of people trafficked for their organs, in international circles.

Natasha knew several women in the shelter – encountering them after they escaped their captors or had been freed, going on to become witnesses for the State. She'd held their hands as they gave videotaped evidence against the men who'd brought them into the country and then kept them in locked rooms. The women and girls were always offered a rest and reflection period – six months in which they could decide whether or not to testify against their tormentors.

Invariably, they didn't.

Natasha had met girls and women who'd been forced to have sex with up to thirty men a day in order to pay off their 'debts'.

Those debts were never paid off. They were inflated to begin with. The cost of travelling to the country, the alleged visas, 'paying off' officials, rent and board – most of the women were told they owed in the region of fifty thousand euro when they arrived.

They were never told how much their clients paid, and any tips they received were taken from them.

And a lot of the time, they were fed lies about money being sent back to their families, which meant their debts had either grown or remained static.

Violence, personal or against their families, was the big threat used to keep the women in line. When that failed, the traffickers got them hooked on drugs, anything that could keep them working but also under control. Some of the girls, particularly the ones coming from Nigeria, had been subjected to juju rituals, which put the fear of demonic possession in them and made it very difficult for them to break the cycle.

The juju girls were the ones Natasha and the organisations on the ground lost most frequently.

But it was one such girl, a survivor who'd come through the toughest of experiences, that the head of sex crimes was here to see today.

Ashanti had been found sleeping on the streets two years ago, after escaping her sex-traffickers. One of the first things Ashanti's jailers had done was pull her dreads out of her head, from the root, so nobody would recognise her.

This had all taken place in the back room of a small house on the outskirts of Dublin city centre. Not unlike the house Tom and Laura were currently investigating.

A place of torture, in plain sight.

Her traffickers – a woman who claimed Ashanti was a student renting from her and a man who claimed to be her uncle – had two houses on the go. One where they kept the new girls, with a gruelling, punishing system designed to break their spirits, and another where they sent them when they knew the girls were beyond the point of leaving.

They'd had twenty thousand euro in bank notes hidden in plastic bags in the main house, where they themselves had been living while Ashanti suffered under the same roof.

Natasha had read the initial interview notes on Ashanti, and when she'd seen that the interviewer had asked why it had taken Ashanti so long to leave, Natasha had wanted to scream with frustration.

They'd made a lot of progress in the force when it came to dealing with the victims of exploitation, but they still had a long way to go.

It was a miracle Ashanti had left at all.

Her escape spoke to the spirit of the girl, and Natasha knew that, more often than not, the people who came through trafficking rings weren't victims. They were survivors, tougher than most people could ever imagine themselves to be.

Natasha found Ashanti sitting in the art room of the shelter which, at first glance, felt welcoming.

Until you looked closer.

The walls were painted bright yellow and the curtains in the windows were a soft blue. Big vases of wild summer flowers adorned the tabletops that ran around the edges of the room.

But the pictures painted by the residents had been pinned on one of the walls, and they offered a chilling insight into the minds of the women who lived in the shelter.

Art as therapy, Ashanti had told Natasha, when she'd spotted her staring at the paintings, the large black swirls and splodges, the dark figures with red eyes and blood dripping from their lips and fingers.

Extract it from your head by putting it on the page.

Natasha had asked why they kept the pictures, why they didn't throw them away, like burning a letter after you'd spilled your inner thoughts.

Because we want people to know, Ashanti told her. *And we don't want to forget. We want to remember so it never happens to us again.*

Natasha understood it then.

The room still made her shiver.

Ashanti was washing brushes in the sink. She smiled when she saw Natasha.

Natasha smiled back, even though every time she saw the girl, she wanted to cry.

Ashanti was only twenty-one. But she looked closer to forty.

She kept her tight Afro natural, so proud to have her own hair back.

'My, you're busy here these days,' Natasha said. 'How are they coping with the bed space?'

Ashanti laughed.

'How you dey? They are not coping, o. Every meeting is about funding this and funding that.' She shrugged. 'I am helping them. They found a place for me – I will be sharing with two other girls in a flat and I can work here.'

'Oh, Ashanti, that's fantastic!' Natasha gave her a big hug, shocked anew at how insubstantial the girl felt. 'Did you get your papers?' she asked.

'Dey don butta my bread!' Ashanti said.

'Ashanti, you know my Pidgin is next to non-existent.'

'Oh yeah, girl. I forget. They butta my bread – they answered my prayers. I got my papers. I can stay here.'

Natasha clasped her breast. Part of the rest and reflection policy was that, in return for evidence, the victims were assisted in either returning home or claiming asylum. Most of them didn't want to return to where they'd come from. In many instances, they'd been tricked into going along with their traffickers, but in some cases their families had sold them. So, asylum was the goal.

'Wetin you . . . sorry, what are you here for, o?' Ashanti said. 'The big boss lady come here, it's no just because you want to see if I got my papers.'

'No,' Natasha said, shaking her head gently. 'I want to ask you about a girl. We think she was from Benin City and might have been forced into coming here.'

'There are a lot of people here from Benin City,' Ashanti said, frowning.

'I know. But not like this, Ashanti. She was working in a brothel in Shipping Row. The one that burned down.'

'I know it,' Ashanti whispered. 'Sad, very sad.'

'It is. I know your traffickers didn't keep any other girls in the room with you, Ashanti, but I wonder if you might have heard her name.'

One of the things Natasha had been amazed by was how much Ashanti had been able to tell them about her captors. She'd listened to their conversations whenever she could and when she'd agreed to make a statement against them, the amount of detail she'd provided about their business had been astonishing.

Once Tom had confirmed that Lola was Nigerian, Natasha knew Ashanti could help. While Nigerian women were in the higher numbers of trafficked victims coming into the State, there were still only a small number of gangs running them.

'She was calling herself Lola,' Natasha said. 'And we think her surname might have been Lowel or Lowal, something like that.'

Ashanti narrowed her eyes. She didn't even hesitate, just nodded.

'Lowal,' Ashanti said. 'Lola Lowal. But I don't think Lola is her real name.'

In another life, Ashanti would have made a fantastic detective or lawyer. Maybe she still would. Natasha knew if there was anything she could do to help this young woman, she would.

'Was she a victim of your traffickers?' she asked.

'Not the people who took me,' Ashanti said. She bit her lower lip. Natasha knew that was to stop it from trembling. Ashanti had worked extremely hard to be able to talk about what had happened to her in a casual, matter-of-fact way. It was still difficult, though, which was why Natasha only ever came here and asked questions when it was especially important.

Ashanti scrunched up her face, thinking.

'Sometimes they had other men over to the house where I was and they talked about deals, you know? Who they sell, who they keep. Maybe it was not her, but they had a girl, I think she was called Eniola? But her last name was Lowal. I know it. This other gang, they were trying to sell her to the people who kept me, but they did not want her. She was trouble, they said. She had run away; all the Nigerian gangs knew she was trouble. So, they decide to sell her to somebody else.'

'Eniola,' Natasha said. 'It could easily be shortened to Lola. Easier to say.'

Ashanti nodded.

'Thank you, Ashanti,' Natasha said. 'That might be her. Did they mention who they would sell her to?'

'Sometimes they sell the girls who cause problems to the Irish,' Ashanti said, shrugging. 'I remember . . .' She paused; a shiver seemed to run through her.

'Yes?' Natasha coaxed gently.

'I remember they laughed,' Ashanti said. 'They used to laugh about selling the problem girls to the idiots who would take them.'

An icy feeling ran through Natasha's shoulders and stomach and she was glad of it.

It meant, even after everything she'd seen and heard, she could still react with humanity to something so truly horrific.

It was all the girls were to these men.

Commodities.

Natasha had her phone to her ear before she'd even left the shelter.

When the person she was calling picked up, Natasha wasted no time with small talk.

'Let's catch up another time,' she told the man, with whom she'd once had a brief liaison. She hated ringing him. Each time she did, he thought it was to organise another weekend away.

Before he could protest her bluntness, Natasha was talking again. 'I need you to find out everything you can about Matteo Russo. I'm sending you what sketchy details I have, but you'll notice in there that he's lived in a few places. Don't be afraid to call in favours.'

Natasha's former lover sighed.

He was a high-ranking official in the Department of Justice; his section dealt with all interactions concerning external police jurisdictions and Interpol.

And, to her credit, Natasha had rarely called on his expertise like this, nor mentioned the fact she minded he had a wife and kids. But she was prepared to do whatever she had to, right now, to get the information she needed on this Russo character.

CHAPTER 32

It was late, but the incident room was still a hive of activity.

Nobody was saying it but everybody was thinking it.

There was a very real fear that Nina Cusack, like Lola's baby, was in serious danger.

There'd been two murders already and they knew somebody had got to Tyanna Volkov with that phone.

Tom and Laura sat with John and Orla Cusack in an office downstairs that had been hastily converted into a family liaison room.

Laura could tell from the mother's body language that she was blaming her husband for their daughter's disappearance.

She wanted to explain to Orla that the best-case scenario was that Nina *had* decided to leave of her own accord, in revenge for her father calling the police. The worst-case was she'd been lured somewhere and taken.

Nina's room had been locked when her parents realised she was gone, but the window was open. The back of the house had a small extension directly under her bedroom window, so it was easy for her to get out onto that and then drop again into the back garden.

Easy to get out.

Just as easy to get in?

Laura wanted to believe Nina would have screamed or alerted

her parents if somebody had appeared at her window or broken into her room.

But she also knew that Nina might have been terrified and just done what she was told.

Her parents had heard nothing, and bar chatting to a neighbour for a few minutes, they'd heard nobody in the house and there'd been no disturbances.

But, in her heart of hearts, Laura suspected that if Nina had wanted to teach her parents a lesson, she'd have had no problem storming out the front door, loudly and visibly making her point.

So, John Cusack mightn't be the reason his daughter had vanished.

But Laura couldn't say any of that to Orla, because what Laura was thinking was far worse than what Orla had settled on, which was to hate her husband for making this happen.

John, though, had already gone there in his head.

'Why did you call us in?' he asked. 'Last time, nobody cared that she'd gone missing. I'm sorry, you two seem like nice people and everything, but that's the truth of it. She was just some junkie runaway. You're worried about her, aren't you? You're worried because of what happened in that house she was living in.'

'They wouldn't have to worry about her if she was safe at home with us,' Orla snapped.

She shifted again, so her back was almost completely to her husband.

'We're worried because Nina is involved in an ongoing case,' Laura conceded, meeting John's eye. 'You're right, this is different to last time. But, until we know otherwise, we still have to treat this as though Nina left of her own free will. Especially because of the circumstances of her departure – through her own bedroom window. It's, um, unlikely somebody Nina's age and build could be snatched—'

'What?' Orla gasped. 'Are you serious? Of course she wasn't kidnapped. Jesus, she was upstairs, we didn't hear so much as a bang. She's always known how to get out of the house. She's been doing it since she was fifteen. She's gone now because her own father rang the police on her and told her she wasn't welcome in her family home.'

'That's not what happened.' John sighed.

Tom held his hands up, a diplomatic gesture, more in hope than expectation that he could soothe Orla's frayed nerves.

'Orla, tell us about the first time Nina left. Did she have any friends you thought she'd gone to at the time; anybody you didn't want her hanging around with that she might have gone to this time?'

Orla started to massage her temples. Laura noticed one of her fingers was covered with a large plaster, and some of the blood had seeped through. She would have to ask if that had happened when the Cusacks had broken down Nina's bedroom door. They'd need to know so they could rule out Orla's blood . . . if they found any other traces.

'She was seeing some older boy,' Orla said. 'He was the one getting her drugs. That's what happened at the start, anyhow. When we found out she was using. We got her into rehab but he kept turning up, like a bad penny. He used to wait for her at the school gates. I think he was in his late twenties.'

'He was thirty-two,' John said.

Orla gasped. She swung around in her chair, staring at her husband.

'How did you know . . . you never told me that! We never met him, how did you know what age he was? We only had her friends' accounts to go by.'

'I collared him outside the school on one of the days,' John said, his eyes fixed on the table.

Orla opened and closed her mouth, astonished.

'He was a smooth little shit,' John said. 'Just laughed at me. Told me his age, though, when I asked. Like it didn't matter. I tried to report him. Nina was sixteen at that stage but she was already getting into trouble. Stealing in shops, that sort of thing. It was like she didn't matter.'

His face had a greenish hue, while his wife's had lost all its colour.

'We think . . . I'm sure he helped her when she ran away two years ago,' John said. 'But he denied it. Do you think she might have gone back to him?'

'Why didn't she go back to him when the house she was staying in went on fire?' Orla said. 'Use your brain, John.'

'I am using it.'

It was the closest to snapping that Laura had heard from John.

She sighed inwardly. She could feel Tom tense beside her and knew he was thinking the same. It looked very much like the Cusacks' marriage had been through enough. She wasn't sure it could sustain any more of the pain being caused by their daughter.

'What was this man's name?' Laura asked.

'Matt,' John said. 'He's Italian or something. A foreign surname – Russo, I think. He was full of it. As my mother used to say, if he was an ice cream, he'd lick himself.'

CHAPTER 33

Laura was used to leading team meetings at this stage, but even she felt a little overwhelmed by the scale of the case she was now in charge of.

She tried to make eye contact with the large team of plain-clothes detectives and uniformed officers looking up at her, so she didn't appear nervous, but in reality she was quaking.

'Tyanna Volkov is still safe in hospital and, following the dis-appearance of Nina Cusack, has now been moved to a private room so we can keep a closer eye,' Laura said. 'Her wellbeing is of the utmost concern. That, and discovering the whereabouts of Nina and of Lola's baby. Now – you all know Natasha McCarthy from sexual crimes.'

Laura nodded in the senior officer's direction.

'Natasha has been good enough to lend her assistance in this case, given the nature of the crime and the victims. Natasha, you've managed to find out some information about Lola?'

Natasha nodded and stood up.

'We believe the female victim in three Shipping Row might be one Eniola Lowal. She entered the country on a false passport two years ago, seeking asylum. She was placed originally with the Child Protection Agency because she had no proof of age and was deemed to be under eighteen. If Moya Chambers has her aged sixteen at time of death, she was fourteen when she came here.'

A Mexican wave of deep breaths and sighing went around the room. Natasha visibly clenched her jaw to steel herself before continuing.

'The agency care home manager reported somebody hanging around – a man purporting to be a Nigerian national and a relative of Eniola's – but he was refused access to her. It didn't matter. Eniola ran away from the home and she wasn't heard of again – in our systems, anyhow. We still have her possessions from the care home in storage.

'Now, I think I know where she went. A contact of mine heard associates of the people who'd trafficked her discussing Eniola and trying to sell her. She was deemed too much trouble – apparently she had a history of running away – and my contact suspects she was sold elsewhere. She believes Eniola might have been sold to another gang – and that brings me to Matteo Russo. If it's okay with you, Laura, I have a bit of an update there?'

'Jesus, work away,' Laura said, forgetting for a moment she was in charge of the room and was meant to be the serious one. What Natasha had just told them was gold dust in their attempt to identify Lola.

Natasha consulted her files and looked up again.

'This is all I've been able to compile in the last couple of hours, so it's fairly skeletal, but it helped that Laura had already ascertained from Matteo's parents that he'd spent time in England. A contact in the Department of Justice contacted Scotland Yard and was put on to the Northumbria police service. Across England, as you know, there are specific units targeting trafficking gangs. They have far more resources than ours, as you're probably aware, but, of course, their problem is much bigger, too. Anyway, the long and the short of it. It transpires that an Italian national, by the name of Matteo Russo, came to the attention of Northumbria police five years ago.'

A collective sigh of anger and frustration rippled across the people in the room. Laura glanced over at Tom, who had his chin in his hand and was watching everything, deep in thought. She wondered if he was annoyed, if Matteo's stay in England was something Laura should have followed up on. But she knew if she'd put a request into Scotland Yard asking if they'd any information on Matteo, they'd be attending tea dances with their Zimmer frames before anybody deigned to respond. Whoever Natasha had been able to tap was far and above Laura's pay grade of contacts.

'Russo wasn't a big player,' Natasha continued. 'But he became a person of interest after anti-trafficking over there learned of a good-looking Italian who was the designated meet-and-greet at one of the airports where a lot of the girls were being brought in. Apparently, the North of England has a real issue at the moment. Russo came on the radar after a former victim described him. The English detectives were then able to pick him out on CCTV at Arrivals in Newcastle airport. Now, bear in mind how disparate the English police service is. They've around forty territorial police services and sometimes there's cooperation, but more often there's not. The point is – our contact is being really helpful here, but that doesn't mean he's getting everything entirely accurate.'

'But, Newcastle?' Laura asked. 'Why there and not London or . . . nearer the ports?'

'Newcastle is allegedly a popular route for one of the big trafficking gangs over there. The airport is quiet, so not crawling with security like the London ones. But it's still big enough for a passenger to retain anonymity. It's also – because of the

amount of hen and stag dos going through to spend week-
ends in the city – not uncommon to see good-looking girls
there. There's a strange twisted logic to the brains behind that
one. The southern ports are a real problem at the moment,
because of the amount of refugees trying to come across from
Europe, so they're more patrolled than ever. But most of these
girls aren't brought in like refugees. They travel with their own
passports; there's no need to hide them so much. Anyhow, the
traffickers bring them in; they spend some time in Newcastle
and then they move the girls where they want to. Apparently –
and this is something we're loosely aware of – this specific
gang brings some of the girls by land up to Scotland, across to
Belfast by boat and then down to Dublin – where they're for use
in the Irish market. That route goes two ways. When they can
get them in through Dublin ports, which aren't as patrolled as
Southampton, etc., they bring them up north and across for
sale in Britain. It's quite the trading route.'

'So, Matteo Russo was involved in that over there and then
he managed to walk out under their noses and start operating
here?' Laura said. 'How did that happen?'

'He just upped and left,' Natasha said, her jaw quite visibly
clenched. 'And I can tell you, we weren't informed he might
have arrived over here. But that's the problem with a police
force as big as England's – they're barely working with each
other, let alone with anybody else.'

'If Lola – sorry, Eniola – was fourteen,' Laura said, 'does that
mean these gangs are a paedophile ring?'

'They don't discern.' Natasha sighed. 'They'll line up the girls
at any age, from thirteen to thirty. Whoever they can force into
it. Sometimes they're specifically after kids to suit tastes, but
not always. It just happens that kids are easier to exploit and,

sometimes, the culture they come from is fine with girls of that age being sexually active.'

'This is a whole new line of inquiry,' Tom said. 'Our initial, and only, theory has been that Hugo de Burgh may have been involved. That he might have taken out a hit on two people who were causing him problems – Matteo and Lola. That doesn't quite explain why Tyanna and Nina are so frightened. If, in fact, Matteo was linked to more dangerous people, to a trafficking gang even, that explains why the girls won't talk to us. It also explains why Nina has vanished. But it also gives us a big headache.'

Laura nodded in agreement. The same thought had crossed her mind, along with an awful feeling about something else.

'You said that route goes two ways, Natasha,' she said. 'Is it possible Nina Cusack has been taken and sent over to England? I don't mean snatched from her room – she could have been coerced.'

'I would say that's a high probability,' Natasha said gravely. 'Tyanna could also be at risk. Sadly, I can't tell you any more about whoever Matteo was involved with. If I have more time, I can make contact with detectives on the ground in Newcastle and open a cross-border file, but we'd need some sort of proof she's travelled there and also – I'm just going to be straight with you – these officers are as run off their feet as we are. They're unlikely to pay too much attention to a girl who may or may not have been sent over from Ireland.'

'She's just gone, then?' Laura said, and she felt the weight of depression that settled on the whole room. Two murders, a missing baby and now a vanished girl who could meet a similar fate. The fact Laura and Tom had just sat with her parents and seen how distraught they were made it even worse.

Natasha shrugged sadly.

Laura looked at Tom. He was rubbing his jaw, deep in thought.

'Does it make sense, Natasha, that if Nina was Irish, they planned to send her abroad at some stage anyway? I'm guessing it's more difficult to keep victims in locations where the local police are aware of them, and when somebody they know could come in at any time.'

'It's something to think about,' Natasha said.

'And you're sure on the Newcastle link?'

'I'm not sure, no, but it's the best guess I can give you.'

'What are you thinking, Tom?' Laura asked.

'How quick do you think you can get somebody in Newcastle to talk to us?' Tom asked Natasha. 'I don't mean to go through the formal steps, to open files and so on. I mean, just to talk to one of us.'

'You're not thinking of going over, are you?' Natasha asked. 'That's a bit of a wing and a prayer, Tom, even for you.'

'I know that,' he said. 'But it's not just about Nina. If Matteo was linked to a gang over there, it might be that they're the ones who are involved in Shipping Row and Matteo was their Irish-based link. And it might be where the baby has gone.'

'I see what you're saying,' Natasha said. 'I mean, I could try to contact somebody over there, but I'll be lucky, considering the hour.'

Tom looked to Laura.

'What do you think?' he asked.

'I think you're meant to be on your holidays anyway and we've nothing to lose,' Laura said.

CHAPTER 34
Tuesday

'Champagne!' Louise exclaimed, as the Aer Lingus flight attendant poured her a glass. 'Oh my goodness. I didn't even know they served proper bubbles on short hops like this.'

The attendant smiled and winked at Tom.

Tom's nephew ran the Dublin trade union branch for the Aer Lingus flight crew. After a little greasing of the wheels, his nephew had been able to get the supervisor on board their flight to agree to Tom's plan to spoil his wife.

And spoiled she would be.

All the way to Newcastle.

Tom felt a little guilty.

No, he felt a lot guilty.

He'd arrived home the previous night and asked Louise if she was still up for an away trip.

The plans for Newcastle were already under way before he'd left work last night.

Tom was desperate to see if he could light a fire under the detectives over there. His very presence would probably mean they'd give the Irish case more attention than if they just received a memo requesting that they look out for a young blonde woman and a baby, possibly trafficked from Dublin.

The idea to bring Louise had occurred to Tom on the drive home.

He had figured that while he was working, she might enjoy a bit of shopping. They'd be in the same hotel room and they could have dinner together – he wouldn't be busy the whole time.

But before he'd been able to explain the purpose of the trip, Louise told him she was completely relieved; that she hadn't wanted to say anything, but if he'd worked straight through his two weeks of holiday leave, she'd have been really disappointed.

So Tom had panicked, gulped and adapted what he had to tell her, ever so slightly.

He'd told her that an opportunity had arisen for him to pass some sensitive information to do with the case to an English counterpart. It would be a quick meeting and, in gratitude, the force had offered him a couple of days in a Newcastle hotel.

A lovely one, in fact, right beside the old castle itself.

Louise had been very understanding about Tom's mission that would take, what, only a couple of hours, max? They were away for two days, right? It would be a lovely break.

Tom hoped she was right. Either that, or Louise's memories of the very expensive champagne would have to linger.

The taxi driver who took them to the Vermont Hotel was as friendly and entertaining as any Tom had ever encountered, giving them chapter and verse on every estate they passed, including – and especially – the so-called rough one.

'They look like lovely houses to me,' Louise said, sitting forward in the back of the cab. 'Jesus, you'd pay half a mil' for one of those over in Dublin.'

'Oh, aye, they're well built,' the taxi driver said in a sing-song Geordie accent. 'But I picked up a radgie there at the weekend – do you know what a radgie is, pet?'

Louise laughed, shaking her head.

'A toe-rag?' the taxi driver said. 'A flipping lunatic, like? Anyway, he has this big training bag over his shoulder, like a footie kit or something, but long. He has me drive him a few streets down and he gets out and hammers on some kid's door. Then he pulls a sword out of the bag, I'm not even kidding, like. Turns out, the lad owed him money.'

'Did you let him back in the cab?' Louise asked, her voice awed.

'Did I, heck. I did a one-eighty faster than Lewis Hamilton and got out of Dodge. Now, this road here is the main route into the city.'

He nodded straight ahead.

'They do the Great North Run along here,' he said. 'Sorry now, there are all these car parks coming up, built in the seventies. They take the look off the place, if you ask me. So, you know where you're eating tonight? I can give you some good reccies for down the Quayside, like?'

It continued in that vein, Tom listening, half enjoying the banter, but mainly panicking as Louise jotted down all the taxi driver's tips on what bars and restaurants to visit, the art galleries they should see, the streets they should walk.

She was going to kill him if he didn't get his business sorted quick smart.

They dropped Louise off to check in at the hotel. Tom had suggested he get his work over and done with before their mini-break began proper. The taxi driver, a little surprised at this turn of events, took Tom to the police station where he was due to meet Detective Inspector Alan Cummins.

'I didn't know you were a copper, like,' the driver said, as Tom paid and tipped him.

'Not over here, I'm not.' Tom smiled.

Natasha had struck lucky in establishing the contact. Cummins had Irish parents and retained some links to home. He'd spent a bit of time in London before moving back home to Newcastle to work in vice.

Natasha had been told he was good police, so he was the obvious connection for Tom to make, especially as DI Cummins was part of a new crew tasked to target traffickers using the ironically named Northern Run to move their victims.

The police station was a large, all-glass affair that Tom both admired and felt intimidated by. It screamed modern policing and ill-targeted resources, whereas Tom was used to the much older but certainly prettier and more private Garda headquarters in Dublin.

He wasn't sure what to expect of Cummins, but when the man himself approached, Tom gauged straight away that it had been a good call by Natasha.

Cummins appeared to be only a little younger than Tom, maybe in his late forties or early fifties. He was taller than Tom – and Tom was a pretty good height – with brownish hair and a warm, open face, matched by a strong handshake. When Cummins spoke, even though the Newcastle lilt was strong, Tom thought he could hear a hint of the old country in it.

'So, your folks were Irish,' Tom said, following Cummins towards the glass elevator to the side of the large reception area.

'Rebel County,' Cummins said. 'Cork. I think it near killed them coming over here, but they plumped for the North and aye, you know what they say. It's like home over here. People are similar; landscape, too.'

'They drink a lot as well, I hear,' Tom said.

Cummins laughed and pressed the number of their floor.

'Aye, that too,' he said. 'Good, hard-working people. Ant and Dec are good reps. Not Cheryl, though.'

'I won't hear a bad word said about her.' Tom smiled.

'Nah, she's forgotten her roots, man. Anyway, the dad came over looking for work and there seemed to be good industry here at the time. It all went tits up in the eighties, mind, with Thatcher. But my mum and dad were established here at that stage and, by all accounts, it weren't much better at home.'

'It certainly wasn't,' Tom said. 'My father had a decent job in the eighties and even he struggled to put me through college. I was a hair's breadth from emigrating myself. I think I would have picked somewhere a bit more exotic, though. London, maybe.'

'Ah, you don't want London. I've been down there. No proper Greggs in London.'

'No what?'

They exited the lift and Cummins brought Tom into a large open-plan office, not that dissimilar to the incident room at home, although, in this instance, the glass walls meant Tom could still see down to the reception area.

'Sausage rolls,' Cummins said, smiling. 'Greggs, the bakers. They do a great vegan, if you're man enough.'

'Aren't all sausage rolls vegan?' Tom said. 'I mean, it's not real meat they put in there, is it?'

Cummins laughed amiably.

They'd get along, Tom was sure of it.

Tom considered his new surroundings.

'Do you not feel a bit like a fish in a bowl up here?' he asked.

'Put it this way,' Cummins said, 'you wouldn't be scratching your arse while standing at one of the windows. My bosses argued for more personnel to take care of community policing. They got a shiny new building instead. Wonder which developer was speaking in which politician's ear there?'

'I already feel at home,' Tom said. 'Seems everything about Newcastle is like Ireland.'

Cummins led the chief superintendent over to a large board on which a number of profile pictures of various men had been pinned, along with a map dotted with multicoloured tacks, all connected by various strings.

'It's also nice to see you're not that far ahead of us with technology,' Tom said, eyeing the familiar-type board.

'Yes, but to more important things first,' Cummins said. 'How do you take your tea? Builder's or vicar's wife?'

'Middling,' Tom said.

He stood in front of the board and looked at the different faces, the names stuck underneath, black marker on white strips of paper.

'Angie,' Cummins called over to a woman who appeared to be a civilian worker. 'Two teas and I'll buy you a round in the pub at the weekend.'

'That's ten rounds you owe me and it's only Tuesday,' the aforementioned Angie called back.

'But you owe me fifteen for last week, so we're getting even,' Cummins said.

'So, I'm guessing from these names you're targeting an Albanian gang,' Tom said, looking back to the board. 'I'm not surprised. They seem to be our biggest trafficking gang as well, outside the Nigerians. The Brazilians take bronze. The homegrowns are getting in on the market but they seem to be relying on imports at the moment.'

'The Albanians are the largest on our radar up here,'

Cummins said, nodding gravely. 'And the most vicious. Not that we don't have our own gangs up to it as well but . . .'

'I'm looking at a brothel that seemed to operate like the United Nations. An Irish girl and a Russian. A Nigerian, we think. And a Polish one, though she's gone.'

Cummins inhaled deeply.

'Listen,' he said. 'I meant to say, I'm real sorry about the Russo boy. I wasn't in charge back then or I might have rung across and given your lot a warning. To be honest, I think my forerunner was probably glad to have one less reet worky ticket on their hands.'

'Reet what?' Tom said.

'Ha. Sorry, man. *Worky ticket*. Troublemaker. What would you call him in Dublin?'

'An arsehole,' Tom said, and Cummins laughed.

Tom smiled.

Angie reappeared and handed Tom a cup of tea. He looked at it – it was barely a shade lighter than black.

'Haway, man,' she said. 'You'd fit right in doon here with that mouth on you. Who do you follow?'

'The underdog,' he said.

'We all like to see an underdog win,' Cummins said. 'Especially around here. And on that note, do you want the good news or the good news?'

'Can we start with the good news?'

'We're raiding a brothel today run by the gang we're monitoring. We've been working with the hotels and some landlord organisations, helping them read the signs, because normally the girls are moved around. But sometimes, if we're lucky, the gang'll set up shop, especially if some of the girls are addicts and unlikely to run. The drugs squad suspects the girls in this house aren't there of their own free will. An undercover detective bought a baggie there and one of the girls said she hadn't been allowed to phone home for a year.'

'And the other good news?' Tom asked.

Cummins chewed his lip. Tom knew whatever he had to say, Cummins wasn't sure if it would help his cause, but that his colleague really hoped it did.

'There's been a new arrival,' Cummins said. 'And she's not Eastern European. Look, I'm nervous about getting your hopes up, but we know Russo worked with the Albanians over here and this is an Albanian den. The surveillance team spotted her. They've been watching this place for two weeks, mind, and this one just turned up late last night. Now, she might be English, but she might also be Irish. All we got in the description was blonde hair, pale and very, very scared-looking. They got some pics, but it's just her from the back.'

Cummins pulled out his mobile phone and showed Tom some images taken with a long-lens camera.

Tom zoomed in with his finger and thumb.

'I don't know,' he said, concentrating hard. 'It could be her. She'd her hair in a ponytail when I met her, so I can't tell you what length it is. Looked that shade, though. Would they not have dyed it or something?'

'Why?' Cummins asked. 'Who looks for these girls? You're the exception, man. Not the rule.'

Tom sighed.

Of course, Cummins was right.

'I guess, if they'd moved her only last night, they wouldn't have even had time,' Tom said.

'Exactly,' his new colleague said. 'So, you want to go see if this is your girl?'

Tom glanced over at the clock he'd spotted on the wall.

Louise would have found the spa, he reckoned.

He'd a few hours.

He hoped.

CHAPTER 35

The email in Laura's inbox was a polite 'go to hell' from the solicitor representing his fellow solicitor, Hugo de Burgh.

No, it said, Mr de Burgh would not be volunteering for a second interview and it would be appreciated if the police would desist this campaign of harassment against said solicitor's client.

'Campaign of harassment,' Laura muttered to herself. Then, aloud and to the amusement of the uniformed officer at the desk next to her: 'I haven't even started.'

Out of the corner of her eye, she spotted Natasha McCarthy and Linda McCarn.

Laura held up her hand to indicate she'd be with them in five.

She dialled Moya Chambers and waited patiently for the pathologist to pick up.

When she did, it was accompanied by the strains of Stevie Wonder singing 'Happy Birthday'.

'Party central,' Moya said.

'There was I, thinking I was dialling the morgue,' Laura said.

'What, we pathologists can't celebrate each other's birthdays?' Moya retorted. 'We're human, too.'

'Very special humans,' Laura said. 'Among the best in the world, I'd say. I'm not going to pass any judgement on one of you having a birthday party that starts at 3 p.m. on a Tuesday afternoon.'

'Well, we're all in bed early tonight so it seemed like the sooner we started drinking, the better. I suppose you're ringing for the DNA results?'

'The very ones,' Laura said.

'I can confirm the victim is Eniola Lowal, if that's even her real name. The care home she stayed in when she arrived in Ireland gave us her hairbrush and some other personal items that had been bagged up. I was able to make a match from that.'

'At least we've cleared that one up,' Laura said. 'Thanks, Moya. Have a slice of cake for me.'

Laura pushed her chair in and joined Natasha and Linda at the door.

Linda had a large paper bag with her.

'I'll bet you haven't eaten all day, darling,' she said. 'Sandwich in the car?'

'You're an angel,' Laura said. She could have fainted with the hunger. Tom had been away one day and already she was missing meal times.

She really did need minding.

When they arrived at the hospital, the senior nurse informed them that Tyanna had become very distressed that afternoon.

'She says she wants to discharge herself,' the nurse told them. 'Between us, if the consultant thought she had somewhere stable and safe to go, he'd let her. Beds, not to mention private rooms, are in short supply around here. But while Tyanna's burns are minor, the dressings still need to be changed in a clean environment.'

Laura furrowed her eyebrows in concern.

'We'll try to sort out somewhere,' she said, and Natasha nodded in agreement. 'Whatever happens, don't let her walk out of here on her own. We're concerned for her safety and we want to keep an eye on her.'

The nurse's eyes widened.

'Yes, well, I've a whole floor of patients to worry about,' she said, and turned on her heel.

'They should put the nuns back in charge.' Linda sniffed. 'At least they had a sense of responsibility towards their patients. These agency nurses are all about the pay cheques. Right, what do you want to do here – are there too many of us to land in on top of her? Will we take turns?'

Laura shook her head.

'We don't have time,' she said. 'Tom wants to find out if she knows any of Matteo's associates and I don't want to talk to her without Natasha's expertise in the room. She seems to have connected with you, Linda, as well. Come on. It's a big room.'

'Actually, I like this.' Linda grinned. 'The three amigas. Who needs men?'

Laura and Natasha strode ahead as Linda brought up the rear, carrying a tray of styrofoam cups and smiling cheerfully to herself.

When they opened the door to Tyanna's private room, the young woman was pacing the floor.

'And now *you* come,' she said, throwing her arms out in frustration. 'Did they send for you? I want to leave. I am going.'

'Going where?' Natasha asked gently. 'Why don't you get back into bed, Tyanna? It's not good for you to be up like this. You're still recovering. We brought tea, look.'

Tyanna flashed a suspicious glance at the cardboard container in Linda's hands.

'Nobody sent for us,' Laura said. 'We came to talk to you about how we can help you leave here and where you'd like to go. But we all have to wait for the doctors to agree, Tyanna. You do not want those burns to get infected. It will be worse for you in the long run.'

Tyanna collapsed onto the bed, deflated.

Natasha reached behind her and plumped up the pillows. Then Linda handed Tyanna a cup.

'Black with sugar,' Linda said. 'As you like it.'

Tyanna sipped from it, quieter now.

Her hair was pulled back into a tidy ponytail and Laura thought – though it might have been the pacing that brought it on – that the colour was starting to return to Tyanna's face.

'Why are you so anxious to leave today, Tyanna?' Laura asked. 'Did something happen?'

Tyanna shook her head.

She looked from one to the other, suspiciously.

'Why did you all come? You cannot all be here to talk to me about where I can go from here.'

She frowned.

'You want to ask me things.'

The three women exchanged guilty glances.

'We all just want to take care of you,' Laura added. 'But we do have to ask you questions, Tyanna. I need you to know, first, that in this country, trafficking women into the sex trade is considered a crime. Any woman who legitimately reports trafficking to us is given temporary visa status and gets all the help we can give her. Do you know what trafficking is, Tyanna?'

Tyanna stared down at the plastic lid on her cup.

'I am not stupid,' she said.

There was a pregnant pause.

Laura watched as what could only be described as a film of pain descended on the young woman's face. Then the cup tipped in her hands and the liquid spilled onto the blue cellular blanket that was draped over the bed's pristine white sheets.

Linda jumped up and grabbed the cup, not worried about the bed but desperate to make sure the hot tea didn't land on Tyanna.

She started to cry. Silent tears at first, then great big gulping sobs.

Natasha placed her hand gently on the young woman's arm, barely there, but wanting her to know she had support.

Laura stayed where she was. Her heart ached for Tyanna as she broke down, but Laura also knew this required proper expertise that she wasn't trained in.

'I am dirty,' Tyanna said.

'You are not dirty,' Natasha said.

'I am. I have done things. I am bad.'

'You are not dirty,' Natasha repeated. 'You are not bad. You are a survivor. What happened to you, very few people could survive. You are very, very strong, Tyanna.'

She looked up, but her eyes still couldn't quite meet Natasha's.

'I did not want to be there,' she whispered. 'My boyfriend, I come with him and he leave me in that house. Он оставил меня там. He leave me there.'

Laura sat forward.

'Was Matteo your boyfriend?'

'No. Another boy. From home.'

'But Matteo,' Laura said. 'You told us he was good to you.'

Tyanna nodded. Her nose was running and she looked at her hands despairingly. Linda produced a Kleenex from somewhere and wiped up the leakage, like a mother taking care of a toddler.

'Matteo was kind,' Tyanna said. 'I wanted to leave but I had nowhere else to go. I didn't know what to do. I owed so much money and I had no way of going home. I was afraid – the boy who had brought me here, he said he'd return for my two sisters if I tried to run. Matteo told me I wasn't to get upset – that things would get better and he'd make them easier for me. And it wasn't too bad there. Not like the first house my boyfriend brought me to. I wasn't allowed to leave my room in the first house. I had to ... when I had to go to the toilet, I was not allowed to leave the room.'

Tyanna swallowed.

'But you didn't want to be in Matteo's house either,' Linda said gently. Both she and Laura looked to Natasha, prompting her to take up the baton.

'Did Matteo ever hurt you?' Natasha asked.

Tyanna shook her head, then shrugged.

'He did what he had to,' she said, and it came out as a long, sad sigh. 'He wouldn't hurt us if we did our job and saw to the customers. That was all. We just had to do our job.'

'Were there others in charge, along with Matteo?' Laura asked. 'I don't mean the men who came to see the girls – I mean, were there other bosses?'

Tyanna's eyes flicked sideways, enough of a tell for all of them to spot, but Laura could practically see Linda's antennae shoot up.

'Tyanna,' Linda said, her voice low and soft. 'Why do you want to leave the hospital? Don't you feel safe here?'

Tyanna hung her head.

'Has somebody given you another phone?'

'No!'

It came out too fast. Laura's heart sank. They couldn't go rooting through Tyanna's possessions. She hadn't resisted them taking the first phone, but they'd been chancing their arm when they did that. They had no right to take it from her, unless she was in custody.

'If somebody has come here and said something to frighten you, you must tell us,' Linda said. 'That's what we're here for. What Natasha and Laura have told you is true – we will protect you.'

'You don't understand,' Tyanna said.

'What don't we understand?' Laura asked.

'They are so dangerous.'

They barely heard it, the whisper was so low.

'Who's so dangerous?' Laura repeated. 'Do you know their names?'

Tyanna glanced up at Laura, and for a moment, the detective chief inspector thought she was going to reveal the names of Matteo's associates.

But Tyanna's mouth set in a thin, clamped line.

She was too scared to speak.

It was time to push things.

'Tyanna, we think the person or people who killed Lola took her baby. Are we right?'

Tyanna whimpered, but said nothing.

'They killed Matteo, too, even though he worked for them,' Laura continued. 'He worked *with* them, even. You are right, they are dangerous. But you can't protect yourself by not naming them. They won't take the risk of you changing your mind. They won't hesitate to kill you, too. The very best you can hope for is that they decide you're more valuable alive and they move you to another house. We might never find you again. What you were forced to do – that could be your life for years to come. Forever.'

Tyanna stared at her, aghast.

'And . . .' Laura hesitated. 'You need to know that Nina, the other girl in the house? The Irish girl? She has gone missing. Do you understand? She's disappeared from her parents' home. We don't know where she's gone, Tyanna, but we're working on the assumption she was taken.'

Tyanna started to tremble.

'So, anything you know, you need to tell us,' Laura said. 'You need to tell us now.'

Nothing happened for a few moments.

Then, Tyanna began to talk.

CHAPTER 36

DI Cummins had organised for Tom to tag along on the brothel/drug-den raid, though he wouldn't take part in the actual operation.

Instead, they sat in Cummins' car, parked up the street with a perfect view of the target house.

Tom had one eye on the clock on the dashboard and another on the red-brick house they were watching.

Every other home on the street was perfectly respectable – tidy lawns and well-kept flower beds, all in bloom.

The end house, with a high hedge separating it from its neighbours and plasterboard shoved up behind broken panes in the windows, looked like it had been transported from another estate altogether.

A rental, Cummins had told Tom. It had been vacant for months and then the Albanian gang had taken the lease.

'They send in some lad in a suit to pay up the first three months' rent,' Cummins said. 'We see the same thing over and over. He says he works in finance and he looks slick – nice car, nice tie, briefcase. He's never seen again.'

'Interesting you say that,' Tom said. 'Russo got a job in Dublin's financial centre for a while. Used it to get his rental leases.'

'Very common. Less common that he stayed but maybe he was settling down. If there is such a thing. Anyway, soon the neighbours are complaining to the landlord, but when the landlord comes to check out what's happening, he's met at the door by a couple of bulky lads who claim they can't speak English.

'The boards go up, the house becomes no-go except for clients. It looks like a drug den, so who'd go near it anyway? And the girls are made to work there without anybody who'd ever care knocking on the door. Though, of course, in this instance, it is a drug den as well.'

Tom nodded. He recognised the pattern.

'What I don't know is whether Matteo Russo was just a minder over in Dublin for this gang or if he set up shop himself. A franchise, if you like.'

'It's possible,' Cummins said. 'They don't get to leave, the ones who work for the gang. They can branch out, like, if they're paying their dues. But you should be warned, more of our gangs are moving over to your patch. As soon as that Brexit referendum passed, Ireland became the land of a thousand welcomes, and all that.'

'Don't depress me,' Tom said. 'We want your industry and your banks, not your bloody crims.'

'Then don't take our banks,' Cummins snorted. 'Anyhow, I should have some IDs for you later as to who's over on your turf and who else might have been working with Russo. If he was still working for the Albanians, it's likely somebody was there keeping an eye, on and off. Aye, aye, we have movement.'

They both watched as two police vans rolled silently onto the street.

Tom's phone buzzed silently in his pocket.

He was going to be in so much trouble with his wife.

But now was not the time to answer it. He was desperate to

see if he'd won the lotto and this blonde girl was Nina Cusack. What if this raid even led to the baby? Then, armed with his victory, he could explain everything to Louise and apologise. Profusely.

It was all over before Tom realised it had even begun. Two loud thumps sounded across the street as the raid unit rammed the door, then it was a matter of mere seconds before four men were being dragged from the house, arms behind their backs, already in cuffs.

'Just a few minutes more,' Cummins said.

They watched another man being brought out, this one sweating, blood running from the side of his head.

'Must have tried to do one,' Cummins said.

More officers streamed out, carrying bags of what Tom could only imagine was the narcotics haul.

'Good day at the office,' Cummins said.

One of the men in full body gear and a helmet nodded down at Cummins' car.

'Alree,' he said. 'Let's do this.'

As Tom opened his door, three more detectives got out of the car behind theirs.

He walked to the house with them but waited outside while they went in. Tom had no jurisdiction here and Cummins' hospitality didn't stretch to causing any potential difficulties for a prosecution case.

He tried to keep his expression neutral as the girls were brought out.

They were dressed in their work clothes. Tiny skirts and bratops, stiletto heels. They all had little purses and each was heavily made up. They could have been heading to a night out in a club, aged up so they could get in.

And yet, outside in the warm light of the July day, they looked confused and frightened. Their real ages weren't hard to guess.

They were just kids. All of them. Late teens at most.

Tom wondered what the men who paid for sex with these girls told themselves. Did they really believe they were willing participants? How did they compartmentalise so well, afterwards, when they went home to their own daughters? Did they know they were as much monsters as the men they tutted at on the news, the ones arrested for abusing children?

He waited, anger coursing through him, until DI Cummins emerged with a female detective. A blonde girl walked between them and before Cummins had even shaken his head, Tom's heart sank.

It wasn't Nina Cusack.

It had been a very long shot, he'd known that, but he'd still allowed the hope to build. It had seemed surreal and yet entirely plausible that Nina could have been transported to Newcastle. The truth was, she was just one young woman in a very big world, and if the gang had her, she could be anywhere.

The female detective led the girl to a car and Cummins indicated to Tom to step inside the house.

'I knew as soon as she opened her mouth,' Cummins said to Tom, his voice apologetic. 'She's a runaway from London. They had her in a place around Leeds and moved her up here yesterday because the family got wind.'

'It would have been too good to be true,' Tom said.

'You want to see where they were keeping them?' Cummins asked.

Tom didn't.

But he nodded, reluctantly.

'You notice they all had little bags?' Cummins asked.

'I did.'

'Grab bags,' Cummins said. 'We raided a farm last month – they'd been keeping five lads from Somalia for slave labour and a couple of girls for everything else. When we opened the caravan they lived in, they all had little backpacks with their passports, clothes, a few pounds. It's to make it look like they're there of their own free will but all that stuff is kept from them normally. It's just flung at them when the raid takes place – I think they actually do preparation drills.'

Tom shook his head, unable to find the words to respond.

He followed his counterpart upstairs and stood behind him on the landing as Cummins pointed in at a small bedroom.

Tom stepped into the door frame, his heart beating faster and bile rising up the back of his throat.

The room, designed to fit an average-sized double bed and the necessary bedroom furniture, had been stripped of anything resembling home comforts. Three bunk beds had been installed, one against each wall. They were heaped with the girls' clothes and make-up, the detritus spilling onto the floor.

Tom looked over to the window. It was covered on the outside with thick steel bars. Barely any of the summer sun soaked through.

He looked back to the door that was open against the inside wall. It had various locks and bolts screwed onto it; their matching slots were on the side of the wooden door frame where Tom was standing.

Had there been a fire in *this* house, those girls, all of them, would have died. There was no way out.

It made the brothel in Dublin look practically idyllic.

His phone buzzed again in his pocket, insistent, angry.

'Sorry, do you mind?' Tom asked.

'Do what you have to.'

Tom took it out. Four missed calls from Louise.

He dialled her number. She picked up after one ring.

'Where on earth are you?' she snapped.

'Eh, that's a difficult one,' Tom said, looking back into the girls' bedroom.

'You'd better explain fast,' Louise said, and her voice brooked no room for quarrel.

'Technically, I'm in a brothel,' Tom said.

There was dumbstruck silence for a few seconds.

Cummins mouthed, *Who is it?*

The wife, Tom mouthed back.

'Say that again,' Louise said.

'I'm at a house where a number of trafficked girls were being held.'

Louise said nothing.

'You two should join us for dinner later,' Cummins whispered.

'Who's that?' Louise said, her voice low and angry.

'Eh . . . DI Cummins and he's invited us to meet up tonight,' Tom said. 'He's the local I had to meet. Sorry, love, I got held up and then there was this opportunity—'

'Come back to the hotel, now,' Louise said.

She hung up.

'Shit,' Tom said.

'I'll get in plenty of wine for the table, so,' Cummins said, eyebrows raised.

Tom, still looking at his phone, realised one of his notifications was a text message from Laura. He read it quickly, seeing the NB she'd marked at the top.

'Alan,' he said, glancing up, 'does the name Viggo Datcu mean anything to you?'

Cummins frowned.

'It's familiar,' he said. 'Definitely ringing a bell.'

'He's just cropped up in my investigation in Dublin,' Tom told him. 'Our only remaining witness named him. Any chance he was part of your gang here?'

'It's the only way I'd be aware of the name,' Cummins answered. 'But I'll have to check the files.'

It was all starting to come together.

CHAPTER 37

The second time Ray turned up with Joe Kennedy in tow, Laura really thought he was taking the piss.

She was standing looking at the picture of Viggo Datcu that they'd managed to get hold of on social media.

Shaven head, heavy-set, not pleasant-looking, he smiled into the camera from over the handlebars of a motorbike, wearing full leathers. He seemed to be at some rally and was definitely enjoying himself.

Tyanna hadn't been able to tell them much – just his name, what he looked like, and how scared everybody in the house had been of him. Matteo included.

'He is the boss,' Tyanna said. 'Matteo minds us but when Viggo comes, we all know. He is a horrible man. Big, ugly. He sweats a lot. He dresses like he is a kid, yeah, in stupid skinny tracksuit bottoms that make his legs look fat and like a woman's.'

'You're sure Viggo is the boss?' Laura said. 'Is he the one who brought you to the house?'

Tyanna had closed her eyes, her cheeks flushed.

'He was my boyfriend's friend,' she said. 'He was the one who kept me in the room the first time. Then, when I moved to the house I did not see him so much. It was just Matteo. And I was glad.'

'Was he violent?' Linda had asked.

Tyanna had shuddered.

'He is not a nice man. But he did not pick me. He picked the other girls. Wendy, he liked her. A lot. I hear he has a family. Wife, child, but he doesn't act like it.'

'Was he ever with Lola?' Laura asked, hopefully.

But Tyanna had shaken her head. Viggo Datcu had not made a favourite of Lola, it seemed.

'Tyanna, was it Viggo who attacked Lola and Matteo?' Laura asked.

'I didn't see anybody attack them,' Tyanna insisted. 'I tell you, I just saw the fire start.'

Laura didn't believe it. She couldn't believe that Tyanna had been in the house and not witnessed the attack on her pimp and another girl. But she was clearly too afraid to tell them any more.

'Did he take Lola's baby?'

'I don't know who took Lola's baby!'

Back in the office, Laura was about to ask Brian if they'd made any progress finding Datcu in their files when she spotted Ray walking in with Kennedy.

They'd had words after the stunt at the restaurant. The importance of Kennedy's info on Hugo de Burgh hadn't been lost on Laura, but the fact Ray hadn't warned her he was coming irritated her.

She didn't want to pull the rank thing, and she was nervous that every time she had a go at Ray he'd perceive it as such, but her temper had got the better of her and she knew it wasn't a senior/junior thing. It was a husband/wife, colleague/colleague thing.

Ray was still coming to grips with it, but the reason Laura had been promoted over him wasn't because she was a superior detective. Ray could match her case for case when it came to collecting evidence and spotting clues.

It was those moments when he displayed an absolute lack of sense that had done for him.

And now he'd done it again, this time bringing Joe Kennedy into her incident room. The last time Kennedy had frequented this space was when he'd been their chief superintendent and was making all their lives hell.

'A word,' Laura snapped at her husband.

Ray followed her over to the corner, while Brian Cullinane stared open-mouthed at Kennedy and Michael Geoghegan eyed him with barely concealed contempt.

'Before you say anything,' Ray started, 'he's found a link between Viggo Datcu and Hugo de Burgh.'

Laura's anger evaporated as quickly as it had surged.

'You're joking?'

'You want to give me a talking-to, now?'

'No, but seriously, Ray, will you stop bloody springing him on me? You know I can't stand him.'

'I'm only bringing him to you because he can help, Laura; I'm not doing it to annoy you.'

Laura frowned.

'Well, you've a reprieve for now.'

They walked back over to where Kennedy was waiting.

Laura didn't bother with the small talk.

'You've established a link?' she said.

If Kennedy was taken aback by how abrupt she was, he didn't show it.

Instead, he rested back on a desk and folded his arms across his suit jacket.

'You're probably going to turn this up in your search anyway, but last year Viggo Datcu was arrested and charged with threatening bodily harm and subsequently assaulting a bouncer at a club in the city centre. The case fell apart before the DPP could prosecute. The bouncer and three witnesses all withdrew their statements, which was quite a feat on the bouncer's part – his jaw had been broken in three places and he was laid up in hospital with two fractured arms, yet he still managed to write a note to express how he couldn't remember who'd attacked him and wouldn't be seeking a prosecution if the police identified his assailant.'

'And Hugo de Burgh was Datcu's solicitor?' Laura asked.

'Yep. We have Datcu on file as a suspected member of an inner-city Albanian gang that's involved in weapons deals, drugs and prostitution. The gang have international links, including to England.'

'Viggo's a busy boy,' Ray added. 'And extremely nasty. That wasn't the first time we tried to bring him to book, but every time the case fails to make it to court. I'm not sure he would have turned up in your searches because he's never been prosecuted. Joe only knows about him because he's doing his research on de Burgh.'

'Okay,' Laura said. 'Let's put out an APB and see if we can get a chat with Mr Datcu. And I think I'll bring in Mr de Burgh and see if he can tell us anything about his little friend.'

'I can sit in on that with you, if you like,' Kennedy volunteered. 'I feel like the filing cabinet in his office at this stage, I have so much background on his former cases.'

Laura hesitated. She tried to guess quickly what Tom would do in this scenario.

In all likelihood, he'd be less reactive to Kennedy, even though he'd have more cause to be.

Tom was good like that; magnanimously waiting in the long grass.

'Sure,' Laura said, slowly. 'We appreciate the help.'

CHAPTER 38

Louise wasn't in a forgiving mood and the additional bottle of champagne that Tom had ordered up to the room had only served to annoy her even more.

'Jesus Christ,' she snapped, when she emerged from the shower. 'How do you think I spent the afternoon while I waited for you, Tom? I'm already hung over from the two glasses of wine I had at the hotel bar. And you want to ply me with more booze before we go out? This plan of yours to keep me inebriated and off your back for the next thirty-six hours only works if I'm not absolutely hammered and in need of being carried places.'

'I'm just trying to make it up to you,' he said contritely. 'I genuinely didn't think I'd be with Alan for so long.'

'That's not the point,' Louise said. 'The point is you made me believe the work element of this trip was secondary to the holiday bit and, as it transpires, it's the other way round.'

'It got away from me,' Tom said.

'The truth?'

'You were so excited when I mentioned travelling . . .'

Louise held her hand up and Tom trailed off.

'So help me, Tom,' she said. 'If this couple tonight aren't the most entertaining people I've ever met, I will get plastered and make an absolute show of you. You have my word. Now, zip me up.'

Louise had stepped into a black, sleeveless dress. Tom was instantly distracted.

'We're early,' he said, a hint of something in his voice.

'Zip. Me. Up.'

Tom did what he was told.

He needn't have worried about Louise not enjoying the company.

She'd been cool with him when they'd taken the lift down to the hotel reception. But when they saw the cocktails Alan had ordered in the hotel bar and his wife Jess embraced Louise with the affection of somebody they'd known their whole lives, Louise instantly warmed to the couple.

'Aye, I hear these lads were right buggers today, pet,' Jess said. 'Leaving you on your own when we only live round the doors. Bloody hell, I'd have given you a walk through the whole toon, like.'

Jess's accent was thicker Geordie than her husband's and she smiled through every word, her face open and expressive and her hands constantly gesturing.

Louise laughed and slid onto the bar stool that Alan had pulled out for her so she could sit beside Jess.

'Oh, I didn't mind,' she said, and Tom pocketed that one for later.

'I hope you're wearing comfortable shoes, like,' Alan said. 'I thought we'd walk down to the restaurant, it's just a few flights of steps. Best grub round here and you can see the bridge lit up later on. It looks best at night.'

'Of course she's wearing good shoes,' Jess said. 'We're not in our twenties now, lad. Car-to-bar days are behind us, am I reet, Louise? I used to walk this town in me stilettos, but I'll tell you, it's been block heels for a good few years now. You're the same, reet?'

'You're reet, Jess.'

The women erupted in laughter.

'Aye, she has it an' all.' Jess giggled. 'Wait until I impress you with my Dublin. I *love* Cillian Murphy in *Peaky Blinders*.'

'He's speaking in a Brummie accent and I keep telling you he's from Cork!' Alan exclaimed.

'Aye, well, it's a real pity his looks don't run in your family, if that's what they look like in Cork,' his wife retorted.

By the time they reached the restaurant, Louise and Jess were the best of friends. Louise hooked her arm under Tom's as they entered through the small lobby area of the grand building that housed their venue.

'Such a lovely couple,' she said.

Tom breathed a sigh of relief.

Still, he and Alan were on their best behaviour. They waited until their wives had ordered and gone to the ladies' before Tom even dared to mention Viggo Datcu again.

'I'd a quick look when I got back to the station,' Alan said, hurriedly.

Their server arrived with two Newcastle Brown Ales and two glasses of Prosecco.

Tom and Alan clinked glasses and each took a gulp.

'Anyhow, Viggo is a known associate of the gang we're watching over here. Word is, he was sent over to keep an eye on the goods in transit through Dublin port. In case that helps your lot at all, we know for a fact you have more of a shipping problem than an airport issue. Your air security is actually quite good.'

'So, you know more about our illegal points of entry than we do,' Tom said. 'I suppose that wouldn't be the first time a Brit had more intel on something happening in Ireland.'

'You're welcome. I checked and there hasn't been sight nor sound of Datcu back on our side, so it would appear he's still your problem, unless he's travelled somewhere else.'

'Tell me something,' Tom said, one eye on the bathroom – he didn't know what they were doing in there to cause such a delay, but he was grateful for it. 'I've been eyeing a possible suspect for my homicide in Dublin, a solicitor who might be a lot nastier than he makes out and has gangland connections. But if the pimp and one or two of the girls had upset Viggo, or somebody like him, would Viggo have killed them?'

Cummins frowned.

'To be honest, Viggo would want to be some hothead to murder paid-for girls,' he said. 'And yes, he definitely has form for violence over here. But not murder; not that we know of.'

'What about a baby?'

'I hate to say this, but babies are extremely valuable, Tom.'

The server was back with baskets of bread.

Tom's stomach lurched.

What sort of world did they live in where selling the baby of a raped woman was not abnormal conversation?

The door leading to the bathrooms opened and the ladies emerged, smiling broadly.

'By the way, there's something else I want to talk to you about.' Alan stopped and smiled a welcome to the two returning wives. 'But it can wait until tomorrow.'

Tom nodded.

CHAPTER 39

Looking at Hugo de Burgh's smug face was not how Laura had wanted to spend her Tuesday night.

In fact, she wanted to lean over the interview table and slap him, if she was entirely honest.

But she would not be doing that.

Instead, she sat calmly on her side of the table, Joe Kennedy to her right, and asked de Burgh a series of questions designed to out the man as a complete and utter scumbag.

'And this case,' Laura said, glancing down at the note Kennedy had just pointed to, 'where you helped in the defence of a man after he assaulted his teenage babysitter because she wouldn't let him have sex with her – would you say that was a case you were driven to take on out of a compassion to see justice done, or was it just about the money?'

De Burgh sighed heavily. He'd arrived flanked by his solicitor, the angry man from the emails, who refused to sit still and kept jumping up and down to answer Laura's questions first. He was sweating now, the flabby white of his neck breaking out in red blotches.

De Burgh, on the other hand, was much cooler than his solicitor.

'Look,' de Burgh said. 'We can do this all night. I'm a criminal law solicitor, Inspector. You're going to find a whole lot of mud to rake through if we go over all my previous cases. I don't decide who's worthy of being represented in the justice system; I just ensure that everybody is treated fairly by having representation when they need it. You know the game as well as I do.'

'I'm not disputing what criminal law solicitors do,' Laura said. 'You just seem to have a weighted number of cases linked to some of the most notorious gangsters in the State. Why's that? Are they passing your number around? Are you finding dodgy pubs and sticking flyers on the tables? "For all your scumbag needs, de Burgh can do the deed".'

'Very funny, Inspector.' De Burgh smiled benignly.

Laura bit back her frustration.

'Viggo Datcu. Have you stayed in touch with him?'

De Burgh narrowed his eyes.

'Albanian national?' he said.

Laura nodded.

'No. I can't say I have.'

'Right. He has a connection to that brothel you were using on Shipping Row, we believe. He was certainly a likely associate of Matteo Russo's. They were both involved with a trafficking gang based in England; quite a nasty one.'

As soon as she said it, Laura realised Datcu was another face they'd have to start searching through the CCTV for. They'd only that evening spotted Nina Cusack arriving in the vicinity of Shipping Row on the morning of the fire, as she'd told them. The same camera had picked her up running in the opposite direction a very short time later.

The team were going to cry when Laura told them she'd need the footage scanned yet again for Datcu.

'It's just a coincidence that I visited that particular massage parlour,' de Burgh said.

Laura and Kennedy snorted.

'Is that what you're calling it now?' she said.

'I'm not denying what I did in there,' de Burgh continued. 'And I know you guys don't like coincidences, or believe in them even, but I can assure you, Viggo Datcu didn't leave me with a business card for Shipping Row. The people I represent know I'm straight up, that I don't involve myself in any criminality.'

'Straight as the Leaning Tower of Pisa, you are,' Laura said. 'You don't involve yourself, but you will help defend it.'

'Inspector!' The solicitor, the other one, was up on his feet again.

'Do you have piles?' Laura asked, staring at him. 'Can't you sit down for any length of time?'

'Maybe you'd like to get your boss in,' he snapped back, 'leave the grown-ups to do the talking.'

'She is the boss,' Joe Kennedy snarled.

The solicitor sat down, taken aback at Kennedy's tone.

Laura took a deep breath. De Burgh was still smiling in that cooperative, infuriating way he had.

'Can you give us the last known address for Viggo Datcu?' she said.

'Absolutely,' de Burgh answered. 'Anything I can do to assist the guards.'

'You could give us a DNA sample so we can check it against what we found in the house.'

That was a complete bluff. They'd picked up no useful DNA in the house post the fire. But Laura wanted to have de Burgh's on file, so if they found Lola's baby they could establish if he was the father.

De Burgh flushed red. His solicitor was about to hurl a

protest at Laura, but de Burgh silenced him with a hand on the man's arm.

'You know what, Inspector, if it will clear my name, then fine. Take one. I know what you're thinking. You're wondering if I'm the father of that poor girl's baby, but I can categorically tell you I'm not. I believe the taking of a sample violates my rights to privacy and I suspect you aren't going around looking for other visitors to that place, but, if you insist . . .'

De Burgh held his hands out in defeat.

Laura felt a momentary flash of victory but it was quickly replaced with anxiety.

There was no way de Burgh would offer up his DNA if he had anything to do with Lola's baby.

Absolutely no way.

Over an extremely early breakfast with Ray the next morning, which consisted of a slice of toast, a double shot of espresso and a printed-out email that had arrived after midnight from Hugo de Burgh, Laura mulled on Joe Kennedy's apparent efforts to be helpful.

'I thought he was going to jump down de Burgh's solicitor's throat,' she told Ray, through a mouthful of bread.

She read the street address on the email sent by de Burgh late last night. It was situated in an expensive residential area of North County Dublin, not far from the sea. Was that really where Viggo Datcu was living?

'I, more than anybody, appreciate what Kennedy did to Tom,' Ray said, putting more toast on Laura's plate.

She ignored it.

'Laura, it's not even seven yet, you're hardly banging on Datcu's door this early, are you?'

'If he's even there,' Laura said. 'He's a suspect in a double murder, Ray; I'm not waiting for office hours.'

Ray shrugged.

'Anyway, as I was saying, I think Joe is really trying. He's very committed to the new unit and he's doing a lot of good work identifying possible customs leaks that are allowing the weapons in, not to mention vessels landing illegally. He's got a whole map of potential anchoring spots drawn up.'

Laura hesitated. Against all the odds, the anti-gun crime unit seemed to have got off to a good start and she realised she hadn't once checked in with Ray to see how he was doing, even while she knew he was working really hard.

'Tell me more,' Laura said. 'The amount of guns out on the streets, I'm starting to wonder if they're bringing them in by the containerload.'

'Kennedy seems to have stumbled onto something,' he said. 'Outside the customs fraud and illegal boats. It looks like some of the gangs are sending what appear to be family units over on the larger ferries. Father, mother, kid, sometimes a dog, in people carriers. They buy tickets to France, book into family campsites, then the man drives down east or south and meets his contact. The weapons are sealed into the interior of the seven-seater and then the family comes home, two weeks later, sailing through the port checks, excuse the pun. Because customs officials are way more likely to stop the artics and vans than a people carrier with a kid in it.'

Laura shook her head.

'I suppose two weeks in a Eurocamp is a small price to pay for a cache of firearms.'

'You know what else Joe was telling me?' Ray said. 'That a lot of the younger gang members rent the guns. Apparently it's 200 euro for an unloaded weapon, 500 for a loaded one with limited bullets. They don't want to risk having a weapon in the house, especially as most of them live with their mammies.'

'Kennedy told you all this?' Laura said.

'He's a real gold mine of info,' Ray said. 'I don't know where he's getting it all from, but wherever it is, he's working hard for it.'

Laura pursed her lips.

She still didn't trust Kennedy. But she couldn't deny she was impressed.

Datcu, because of his involvement in multiple incidents involving violent crime, was considered enough of a threat for Laura to bring back-up when she went looking for him.

She, Brian and two uniformed officers pulled up on the quiet, salubrious residential road, just as various members of the local community began heading out to their cars to join the morning slog to work.

'Do you reckon they know who they're living next door to?' Brian asked.

'Do any of us?' Laura replied.

'Fair point.'

'He's stocky,' she said. 'Has a bit of power in him. We need to be prepared for him to make a run for it. Look at this.'

Laura pulled up a video they'd downloaded from Datcu's Facebook page.

She and Brian watched as Datcu jostled with two men who looked so similar, they had to be brothers. The camera panned out, shakily, to reveal the three men in a large back garden, somewhere rural if the surrounding trees were to be believed. A stone shed with a patched-up aluminium roof was in the foreground, and on a small wall beside it, a selection of glass bottles had been lined up.

The men were taking potshots at them with a pistol, laughing and speaking in Albanian as they took turns.

The youngest was clearly the best shot, and as he gloated, Viggo pushed him. It took little effort on Viggo's part, but almost floored the other man.

'So, he's a shit shot but has lots of muscles,' Brian said.

'Exactly,' Laura said.

They got out of the car and walked up the garden of the well-kept, two-storey detached home. They reached the expensive oak front door and rang the bell.

A minute passed, then the door was opened by a vision in pink silk pyjamas.

'Um, we're looking for Viggo?' Laura asked the model-esque blonde, whose bed-tousled hair only added to the general air of sensuality she exuded.

'He not here,' she answered, accented. 'Maybe his club?'

She stared over Laura's shoulder at the two uniformed guards.

'Is he in trouble?'

'Who are you?' Laura asked.

'His wife.'

Laura chewed the inside of her cheek.

'Where's his club?' she asked. 'Does he own it, or is he a member?'

'He owns it,' the wife said, as if it was the most obvious thing in the world.

They walked back to the cars with the name of the night club that Laura suspected wasn't a night club at all already typed into their search engines.

'Viggo's wife nearly turned me,' Brian said, opening the driver's door.

'She nearly turned me,' Laura said. 'If I ever offer up a threesome to Ray, I'll be calling her to check availability.'

'Saucy.' Brian laughed.

'Do you think she looked nervous?' Laura asked.

'A little,' Brian said. 'I did spot the bag on the floor behind her.'

'Me too. The good news is, if the bag is still there, he hasn't run. The bad news is, he wants to. Phone in and get a car put on the house; we can leave his name with the airports and ports as well.'

Three hours, one dodgy club, a bar and another house later, they were no closer to putting their hands on Viggo Datcu.

Brian had pulled into the forecourt of a garage to load up for lunch and use the facilities.

Laura took the opportunity to phone Moya Chambers.

'Laura,' Moya said. 'I'm starting to feel like we're best pals.'

'If you give me some good news now, you can be godmother to my first child,' Laura answered.

'Are you expecting?'

'No, I'm not expecting. Why is everybody waiting for me to announce I'm pregnant? It's just a . . . saying.'

'You're married a couple of years, now. That's also a saying.'

'Have I jumped back a few decades? It is okay for me not to be determined to get pregnant as early on in my marriage as possible, isn't it?'

'I guess when you're in my line of work, you know it doesn't pay to delay things,' Moya said.

Whatever Laura was about to retort, she didn't bother. It was only natural Moya would be of that opinion.

'Anyhow,' Moya said, 'I'm afraid I have bad news for you.'

'Bollocks,' Laura said.

'But not Hugo de Burgh's bollocks, it turns out. I got his DNA sample along with a little note from his solicitor – a copy of the file from his doctor recording de Burgh's sterilisation after the birth of his last child a good number of years ago. Same doctor did my husband. Isn't that a mad coincidence? If we find that baby, I can tell you already de Burgh is not its father.'

'He knew,' Laura said.

'Of course he did.'

'Can you imagine how many men she'd been with?' Laura said, despairingly. 'We'll probably never know who fathered that child.'

Neither woman spoke for a few moments.

Laura hung up, both sad and frustrated.

She could see Brian through the garage shop window, his arms full of crisps and sweets.

Her stomach rumbled. She should have had more toast this morning, then she wouldn't be about to binge on a pile of empty calories.

She dialled Ray.

It went to answer machine.

'Damn it!'

Brian had dumped his haul on the counter and gone over to the drinks fridge. He had his phone to his ear.

Laura looked back at her phone.

To hell with it.

She rang Joe Kennedy. He picked up after a few rings.

'Inspector Lennon, what can I do for you?' he said.

'I'm trying to get hold of Ray,' she said. 'You haven't seen him, have you?'

'Have you not heard?'

'Heard what? I'm on the Viggo Datcu hunt. He wasn't at his house or any of his allegedly legal places of ownership and employment.'

'Right. Well, there was another shooting last night. A field at the back of IKEA. Locals reported something that sounded like a car backfiring. The body was found this morning by a dog walker. Ray's out there now. We think it might have been retaliation for that bloke in the van the other day.'

'Oh,' Laura said. 'I see.'

In her head, Laura swore. She had already begun to regret assigning Ray to the new unit. The bigger this case got, the more she realised she needed him with her. They worked well together as a team. Whatever she'd thought when she'd offered him to the new unit, it hadn't been that he'd be bounced from one shooting to the next. There had probably been a part of her that assumed the unit would just be a box-ticking exercise and Ray would still be on hand to assist her.

Brian was back at the car and struggling to open his door.

Laura stuck Kennedy on hands-free and leaned over to pop the lock.

Brian got in and immediately offered her a Kit Kat.

'I'll put the word out for Datcu,' Kennedy said. 'And I'll let Ray know you're looking for him.'

'Thanks,' Laura said, through a mouthful of chocolate. 'I'm sending you through a video of Datcu from his FB page. He's distinctively ugly, shouldn't be hard to locate. You'd think.'

She pressed Call End and angled herself in the seat so she was facing Brian.

'No deli counter in there, no?'

'Did you want a roll?' Brian asked.

'I've heard tell they're legendary. But this feast of cheap chocolate and crisps will do. Who were you on the phone to?'

'Michael,' Brian said. 'He's found Viggo.'

'Seriously?' Laura felt her heart soar.

'Sorry. I mean, he's found him on CCTV. The day before the fire, he was definitely in the vicinity of that Spar near Shipping Row.'

'But where the hell is he now?' Laura exclaimed, frustrated. 'He must know we're looking for him. If he's legged it back to Newcastle, we're screwed.'

Brian shrugged.

'There's something else,' he said. 'The phone you got from Tyanna Volkov? IT were able to salvage deleted texts from it. Two numbers came up. One is a pay-as-you-go mobile. The other is a bill phone.'

'In whose name?'

'That's what we're trying to find out. Phone company is slow; it's one of those new outfits, not Vodafone or anything handy.'

Laura finished the chocolate bar.

'Home, James,' she said, banging on the dashboard. 'To HQ.'

Outside, the sun beamed.

CHAPTER 41

Ray was standing just outside the tent that had been erected early that morning to protect the latest victim of gangland violence from the sun and the long-lens cameras of the media.

The scene would make a stunning front-page photograph, even Ray knew that.

The area that stretched across acres at the rear of the giant blue-cubed IKEA was as desolate as any modern-day landscape and the parched earth had the feel of a spaghetti western movie.

To their right, cars flew up and down the M50 motorway. To their left, the houses stood open and exposed, not even a lone tree to interrupt the view of the soulless motorway.

The paramedics were about to remove the body. The victim was well dead by the time anybody had arrived. Gunshots to the chest and the head. Most likely a Glock, if the wounds were anything to go by, but Emmet McDonagh would make sure the bullets were retrieved – either from the victim or the surrounding area. A professional hit. Whatever had lured him out there, Ray bet barely any time had passed before the victim was regretting his decision to turn up.

Kennedy arrived at Ray's side as the stretcher was brought into the tent.

'Didn't expect to see you here,' Ray said, his eyes on the activity unfolding before them.

'The inspector was looking for you,' Kennedy said. 'And I think she needs all hands on deck to find this Viggo Datcu bloke. I suspect she's missing you from her team right now.'

Ray took out his phone, saw the missed call.

'I'll buzz her on the way back from here.'

'They have an ID for this one yet?' Kennedy asked.

Ray shook his head.

'Nobody reported missing yet but it's been less than twenty-four hours. If he was involved in a gang, the families will be ringing around one another right now, trying to work out who went for a drink and didn't come home.'

'And the public will just be hoping it was a gang member and not somebody caught in the crossfire,' Kennedy said.

He was right. Ray knew what ordinary Dublin residents would be thinking as the news broke of another shooting.

He deserved it. You live by the sword.

Ordinary people were a little more engaged these days because of the sheer volume of shootings, but even so, it happened at a remove.

But in every case, a station somewhere had to take a call from a mother or a sibling or a wife or a girlfriend reporting that their loved one hadn't come home the previous night.

That's when the victims weren't being gunned down in front of their families.

'Are we comparing his picture to the ones on our watch lists?' Kennedy asked. 'The local cops can't just tell, no?'

The police had taken to issuing warnings to gang members who they knew had a contract out on their lives, for all the difference it made. These guys thought they knew death, but they still lived like it would never touch them.

'We can go have a look at him,' Ray said. 'See if we recognise him. Crime scene are about done with the body, I think.'

He and Kennedy walked into the tent just as the victim was lifted into the body bag on the stretcher.

Adidas tracksuit bottoms, a Chelsea jersey.

He'd probably been bundled into a car.

Ray hoped it had been quick.

This one, at least, didn't look particularly young.

He turned to say it to Kennedy, but Kennedy was shaking his head, a look of incredulity on his face.

'You know him?' Ray asked instinctively.

'It's Viggo Datcu,' Kennedy said.

CHAPTER 42

The local detectives covering the Viggo Datcu hit were more than happy to have the head of the murder squad sit in on their incident room gathering that afternoon.

Ray had been expected, but when DCI Laura Lennon and Detective Joe Kennedy came with him, Detective Jackie McCallion was visibly relieved to welcome what looked like the cavalry. She'd worked with Ray and Laura a couple of years previously and remembered them as efficient and professional.

Her patch of Dublin had been particularly blighted by gangland crime in recent times and her on-site detectives were consistently having to draw on the support of adjacent stations, not to mention the assistance of the national murder squad.

McCallion stood at the top of the latest incident room, straightened her skirt and patted the ends of her dark, bobbed hair. She'd just informed her crew of the most recent plea for resources and the formula with which they'd try to solve Datcu's murder, with the cooperation of both the newly established anti-gun crime unit and their representative from the murder squad, Ray Lennon.

'The victim has been identified as Viggo Datcu,' McCallion said. 'Thirty-seven years of age, Albanian national, resident in Ireland for the past two years. A patrol car has been dispatched to inform his family at his recorded permanent residence. Our colleague here, head of the murder squad, DCI Laura Lennon, has some further information on Datcu for us.'

Laura nodded gratefully and stood up.

'Our very recent intelligence from England informs us that Viggo Datcu was a member of an Albanian gang engaged in the transport and sale of weapons, drugs and trafficked women. We suspect Datcu was situated in Dublin to monitor the city as an entry point for deliveries to and from England. We believe he was involved in the operation of at least one brothel using trafficked victims, possibly more.'

She took a breath.

'Viggo is currently of specific interest in relation to the arson attack in Shipping Row last Friday, which we believe was carried out to destroy evidence after a double murder. A woman, who had been resident in the house, is in hospital receiving treatment for burn injuries. Another woman has gone missing. And of course, most worrying of all, a baby has been taken.

'My colleague here, Joe Kennedy, has been looking over Datcu's illustrious career since he landed on our shores. Our deceased has been involved in several violent incidents, all of which have failed to make it to court thanks to the sudden vows of silence taken by his victims. The long and the short of it is, Datcu most likely made a lot of enemies who wanted him dead. But my interest in him is focused on whether he was involved in the deaths of two other people before he met his own demise.'

Laura looked around the room, seeing the solemn faces staring up at her.

Until now, the majority of the gang victims that this squad had dealt with were white and Irish.

The introduction of an international element to this latest contract killing chilled them all.

They looked overwhelmed.

Laura understood. She felt that way herself.

Jackie McCallion stood up again.

'I'm going to take the lead on this one, with the assistance of Detectives Ray Lennon and Joe Kennedy. DCI Lennon will need updates on our progress. It's highly likely, given the nature of these attacks to date, that Datcu fell foul of a local gang; perhaps he infringed on their patch.'

Laura nodded encouragingly. She'd known Jackie when she'd been based out in the Little Leaf station and was involved in the mistaken arrest of Natasha McCarthy's nephew, Daniel. But she'd also played a role in subsequently vindicating his name and, by all accounts, had done a lot of other good work since. Laura was aware that Jackie had requested the transfer to this station, knowing it was among the busiest in the State.

'Datcu was seen by quite a few people last night,' Jackie said. 'There's already talk on the vine. Up until roughly midnight he's believed to have been in the company of our pal, Johnny Cowell.'

'Cowell?' Ray interrupted, as an audible groan went around the room.

Jackie nodded.

'As in, of the Cowells? One of BLT's nephews?'

'The very same. The youngest. This was their home turf when they were top dogs. You know this guy as Johnny Fleming.'

Laura saw the recognition dawn on Ray's face. Even she knew that name – another member of the one-to-watch list, a rising star of the criminal underworld.

'He uses his mother's maiden name, publicly,' Jackie continued, 'to try and stay off the radar. We know him round here as Cowell and that's how his associates and enemies know him, too. All our touts tell us that while the Cowell enterprise went quiet for a while, it was only because Johnny was laying the groundwork to take over and run his uncle's operation. He has a number of clubs – which we and the Criminal Assets Bureau believe are just fronts for laundering cash – and Datcu was spotted going into one last night, before leaving with Johnny. We're seizing CCTV but eyewitness reports have them getting into the same car. Apparently, Datcu was acting drunk. And descriptions have him in an Adidas tracksuit at the time.'

'He'd no ID when he was found,' Ray said.

'If he was drunk,' Kennedy mused, 'Cowell could have bundled him into the car. Datcu may have found himself in that field without even realising what was happening.'

'Your informants, Jackie,' Laura asked. 'Any chance of them knowing what Cowell's beef might have been with Datcu or if he was involved with the Shipping Row fire?'

She tried to keep her voice calm but Laura couldn't help the excited feeling she had in the pit of her stomach.

The Cowell name kept surfacing and when she and Tom had spoken briefly last night, Tom had suggested that perhaps Viggo and Matteo had forged some Irish links.

'We've the feelers out,' Jackie answered. 'The big problem for Johnny is that he's just not as intimidating as his uncle. He's cleaner than his brothers, which the Cowells must have seen as an advantage. And he's ambitious. But he's also a good family man. Got a few young kids and he dotes on them, by all accounts. The speculation is that Johnny has ordered a couple of hits but not actively involved himself in anything. His uncle used to torture people and had everyone absolutely terrified of him; Johnny is at a remove from his killings. Whereas that makes him less likely to be caught out by us, he looks weak to others because he's never served real time and doesn't have proper blood on his hands. It took us years to build a case against Patrick Cowell because people were so scared. Johnny's gang leaks like a sieve because they aren't.'

'Lucky for us,' Laura said. 'Listen, I have to head, but see if you can track anything back to a Matteo Russo, or to Shipping Row. I'll look at Viggo from our end. And when you bring Cowell in, let me know.'

'We have him coming in in an hour,' Jackie said. 'He's already volunteered. He's smart.'

'Well, when you've done with him, let us have a go,' Laura said.

Laura caught Ray's eye on the way out.

Sure, he was technically taking orders from multiple bosses now, but she hoped that look told him she needed him to prioritise tracking Viggo and Cowell back to the arson attack.

CHAPTER 43

Laura had returned to HQ and was now sitting in her office, her head in her hands, a fan blowing cold air onto her face. Were it not for the possibility of somebody popping their head in at any moment, she suspected she'd be weeping.

What had started as a mystery surrounding a naked girl on a city street had exploded into something far more all-encompassing.

Laura had just watched the CCTV footage of Nina Cusack that they'd lifted from the cameras near Shipping Row.

Nina had been returning to the house with a large bag on her back, indicating she had told them the truth about being away with a client.

Gerry Reid from the fire department had sent an email confirming that his final incident report would state, as verified by the arson inspectors, that the fire had started before eleven on Friday morning and spread at an accelerated rate. Petrol had been poured upstairs and downstairs – ordinary petrol, which could be sourced from any garage forecourt in Ireland.

Laura had also studied Viggo Datcu's face on camera – picked up a day before the fire in Shipping Row. He'd been crossing the road, heading in the direction of the house, and looked up at the camera, face on, like he knew it was there. They hadn't picked him up leaving.

She'd emailed Tom what they knew and was now concentrating on reducing her heart rate to a normal number of beats per minute.

This was the biggest case she'd been in charge of since taking over as head of the squad.

And, if she was honest, she was starting to doubt if Tom had made the right choice.

It had been fine for the last two years. Nothing had occurred that she hadn't been able to cope with. They'd helped with several gang murders and she'd handled a couple of domestic violence-related deaths. They'd all been individual cases with straightforward investigative routes, even where they hadn't succeeded in securing prosecutions.

She'd known that she couldn't expect to keep cruising without running into a significant challenge. God knows, there'd been plenty of them when Tom had been in charge.

Shipping Row was it.

But now, she wanted the grown-ups to take over. For Tom and Sean McGuinness and Linda McCarn and Emmet McDonagh, all of them, even Ray, to tell her what to do. To give her just one task and let her concentrate on that, not try to juggle everything at the same time.

Her hand kept hovering over her phone.

The email she'd sent to Tom was professional and efficient.

But she'd wanted to text him, in capital letters: PLEASE COME BACK.

The phone buzzed with a text, and Laura jumped.

It was Ray, telling her they'd brought Johnny Cowell over from Jackie's station.

Here. Here was her one task.

She could watch this interview and focus on that and that alone.

Kennedy brought her a coffee before heading into the interview room with Ray.

Jackie McCallion had already been through the preliminaries with Cowell but, while he admitted he'd been with Datcu the night before, he claimed that he had dropped the man off near his house before midnight and then returned home, alone. His entire family would back up his version of events – his wife, a brother who lived there and all his kids were his alibi. Even his youngest son, aged four, had been up at midnight, apparently.

Laura took the coffee from Kennedy without the astonishment that would have previously greeted such a thoughtful gesture.

Tom would have her head examined if she admitted it, but Joe Kennedy was starting to grow on Laura.

Perhaps Ray was right and the former chief superintendent was a changed man.

She looked into the monitor that captured the angle of the interview room best, and studied Cowell.

Buzz-cut hair, a handsome if skinny face, tattoos up his neck and all the labels. A Ralph Lauren polo, Armani jeans – new season, none of your TK Maxx cast-offs here.

Cowell glanced up at the camera, just as Datcu had done with the CCTV.

It was like a trademark move for these guys.

I'm not afraid of you, I don't care if you're watching.

Laura sighed.

Apparently, Johnny Cowell had studied engineering in college.

However this case panned out, she knew he'd be – best-case – in prison within a few years, if not before.

Worst-case, he'd wind up dead any day now.

They were all immortal until they weren't.

This one hadn't even asked for his solicitor.

Laura would bet a million quid that when he did ask for his solicitor, it would be Hugo de Burgh who turned up.

Ray had started talking.

Laura sat closer to the monitor and turned up the volume.

'. . . kind of circles you mixed in to come across Viggo Datcu. With you a respectable businessman and everything.'

'He owned a club,' Cowell said, with a hint of a smirk. 'We'd meet the odd time and talk business. I'm appalled at what's happened. But I did always suspect Viggo ran with the wrong sort. Dangerous men. I don't think he was all that enamoured of the entertainment business.'

'Dangerous men like your uncle?' Ray asked.

'My uncle hasn't been dangerous in a very long time,' Cowell answered. 'The family has moved on. It would be nice if you could stop tarring us all with the same brush. For example, you keep referring to me as Mr Cowell, when you all know I use my mother's maiden name.'

'We're well aware,' Ray said. 'And isn't it tarring, if you're still living off the proceeds of your uncle's criminal activities? You hardly bought all those clubs off a – what did you do after college? You worked in a bar for a while, didn't you? Your own father owned a pub before he died; that was also bought and paid for by your uncle.'

'I was just learning the trade, working in bars. I knew I'd follow the old man and go into the drinks business one day. All of my holdings are above board. You can check. I've an excellent accountant.'

'Why didn't you put the engineering to good use?' Ray asked. 'What was the point of that degree? You wanted to become an expert at pipe-bomb-making, did you?'

'I'm pretty sure that's slanderous. Do *you* think that's slanderous?'

Cowell turned in his chair so he was directly facing Kennedy.

Laura watched Kennedy's reaction – he looked distinctly uncomfortable. It was the first time she'd seen him in an interview situation where he seemed out of his comfort zone. She tried not to judge. The guards knew that these gang members would think nothing of following them home and making threats; even carrying them out. It wasn't stupid to be afraid of them. It was smart.

These were not ordinary members of the public.

Kennedy shifted in his seat and looked at Ray.

Ray took charge again.

'That was uncalled for,' Ray said. 'I'm not implying you're in any way involved in bomb-making. I apologise.'

'Accepted,' Cowell said, leaning forward. 'Who put those good manners on you? Your wife, was it? What's her name again ... Laura, isn't it?'

Laura's stomach clenched.

Not because she felt intimidated – but because she feared Ray was going to lean over and thump Cowell in the face.

There was a moment of tension, then Ray sat back and laughed.

'My mammy's responsible for all my manners,' he said. 'I was caught fighting one too many times in school. The last time, she dragged me by the ear up to the lad's door and made me apologise. I learned my lesson then. Don't ever get caught by my ma.' He smiled. 'I was a terrible scrapper. My parents always said the worst job I could have landed was one where I was allowed to carry a gun.'

Ray touched the firearm at his side.

'A fucking loose cannon.' He laughed. 'I bet your mammy thought the same.'

Cowell smiled, like they were all friends, but Laura studied him closely.

Ray had pretty much just threatened to shoot Cowell if Cowell mentioned Laura again.

And from Cowell's eyes, Laura could see he knew it.

Cowell had access to weapons.

Ray carried one all the time, legally.

Cowell stared over at Kennedy again, the one man in the room he seemed to be able to intimidate.

'Anyway, like I said, I only knew Viggo through being a fellow club owner. We wouldn't have had any interaction beyond that. I can't help you any further. I dropped him off last night; he was fine. Drunk, but fine.'

'Detective McCallion explained that we're following up on the movements of your car on CCTV,' Ray said.

'She did indeed,' Cowell said. 'Lovely woman. Course, as I said to her, if I was the sort of person who intended to harm somebody, I wouldn't use my own car to take them to the spot said harm would occur. And I would also be careful to take routes that weren't lined with cameras, you know. And then, when Detective McCallion asked for my mobile phone details, I added that in all likelihood, if I had planned to commit a wrongful deed, I would have turned off my phone to avoid any calls being triangulated by local masts.'

'Wow,' Ray said. 'That's an impressive amount of knowledge to have about how to stage a crime scene.'

'I'm a huge fan of crime shows on TV.' Cowell smiled. 'Do you watch *Line of Duty*? I love it. All those corrupt-as-fuck coppers. It seems so real, doesn't it?'

'Have you heard of number three Shipping Row?'

'No.'

'Do you know a girl called Lola?'

'No.'

'Matteo Russo?'

'Is this the phone book you're reading from?'

Laura massaged the bridge of her nose.

They were all so bloody clever.

And they'd still end up, as she predicted, dead or in prison.

She was dragged from her reverie of despair by Brian, who knocked and then stuck his head around the door.

'Sorry,' he said, 'I thought this was important.'

'Distract me,' Laura said. 'Actually, do you have any headache tablets? I'm on a sugar comedown.'

Brian reached into his trouser pocket and pulled out a foil strip of Nurofen.

Laura didn't want to ask how or why he had them so close to hand, and she didn't even mind that they were warm and had possibly been sitting next to his groin for days.

She just wanted one.

'Do you remember the friendly taxi driver who was only too delighted to tell us that he reckoned number three Shipping Row was a brothel?' Brian said.

'Oh, I remember him well,' Laura said, knocking back the painkiller with a sip of cold coffee.

'So, I was reading the papers. I know the press office is under pressure at the moment, but you might want to have a word about them missing this. The neighbour's been shooting his mouth off to one of the tabloids. He's full of tales about how he's been living up the road from immigrant-slash-prostitution hell. I think the only reason this particular piece hasn't been picked up by the wider media is because the paper's a bit of a rag. But it will travel, no doubt about it.'

Brian held out the paper to Laura that he'd been carrying in his hand.

Laura scanned the article – noted the sensational headline, the lack of fact-checking, the speculation passing as news – until she got to what Brian wanted her to see.

Mr Paul Carroll had purchased his house for quite a tidy sum when it had been built, coming as he did from the local area and wanting to stay in the vicinity for family reasons, the article stated.

That'll be his mammy, Laura thought.

As it turned out, Paul Carroll had been badly deceived into thinking that rising house prices would mean a safer neighbourhood and a nicer community. Shipping Row had been bought up by investors looking to rent and they'd had no qualms about who they were willing to let move in, so long as the rent was paid. The road was hopping with foreigners working up in the IFSC, which was bad enough, but it also had quite a few of the wrong sort, apparently. Number three had been a brothel and Mr Carroll had been complaining about it to the police for quite some time.

'Any complaints on file?' Laura asked.

'Not a single one,' Brian answered.

Laura read on.

She read the sentence she knew had grabbed Brian's attention, then she read it again.

'We haven't released that information,' she said, looking up at him.

'Exactly,' Brian said.

And that was when the bottom fell out of the case Laura thought she was building.

CHAPTER 44

They brought Paul Carroll into headquarters to impress upon him just how seriously they were taking him as a suspect.

Laura's stomach turned when she saw the taxi driver being walked downstairs to the interview rooms.

Only days earlier, she'd stood on his front doorstep while he preached at them about the young women who'd lived in the brothel.

She'd considered him then to be an unpleasant piece of work, who might very well have been inside number three, availing himself of its services, even while he lectured the police from the moral high ground.

But she hadn't thought he was involved in the murders.

Moreover, since then, everything had taken off in an entirely different direction.

Once the trafficking aspect had been introduced, the inquiry followed its own complex path.

The thought that the whole time it might have been so much simpler, and Paul Carroll could have been involved, made Laura want to stuff her fist in her own mouth.

Like de Burgh, they didn't have enough to arrest Carroll yet, so they'd have to build a case against him before they could ascertain if he was the father of Lola's baby.

'It's not against the law to speak to the papers,' he said, the second Laura sat down. 'Half my neighbours are doing it. I'm not the only one. And you don't get paid for it, in case you're wondering. I just offered the information. I thought it might be of use.'

'It's of use, all right,' Laura said.

'I also want it recorded that I don't want this interview to go ahead until I have my solicitor here. I don't appreciate being brought in here at night, my busiest working hours, by the way.'

'You haven't been arrested yet,' Laura said. 'I presume, like the rest of them, your solicitor charges by the hour, so unless you think you're going to need one . . .?'

'Arrested?' Carroll nearly leaped out of his chair. 'What would I be arrested for? Talking to a reporter?'

Laura picked up the newspaper.

'Is this a direct quote from you?' she said. She cleared her throat and began to read:

'*When they found those people inside, it was absolutely terrible, but especially that young one in the suitcase in the attic.*'

Laura looked up at Carroll.

'This was today's paper. Those are your words, am I right?'

'Well, more or less. I mean, I might have said it was awful, not terrible, but you know what those reporters are like. They dress it up, don't they?'

'But you definitely said that the second victim was found in a suitcase in the attic.'

'Yeah.'

Carroll was still making good eye contact but Laura could see the twitch.

'You're saying that you weren't paid for that interview?' Laura said. 'Who contacted who? Did the journalist ring you or did you get in touch with her?'

Laura already knew Carroll had emailed the journalist. She also knew he'd been paid three hundred euro for his information.

This was merely getting to the heart of how far Carroll was willing to go with his lies.

'She, eh, she'd been hanging around the road,' Carroll said.

Very far, it seemed.

Laura flung the newspaper down on the table and sat forward.

'The thing is, Mr Carroll, the Garda press office never released the information about how and where the second victim was found. Deliberately so. It's one of those things we do so the killer can trip him or herself up, by revealing the information only they and we know. So you'd better tell me how you discovered that victim was found where she was, because right now, I can only assume you know because it was you who put her there.'

Carroll's eyes expanded to the size of small saucers. He started to swallow repeatedly and his face broke out in angry red blotches.

'I didn't kill anybody!' he shouted, to all intents and purposes absolutely horrified.

The really irritating thing was, sitting in front of him now, Laura was inclined to believe him. He was either convincingly acting stupid, or actually stupid, and she was leaning towards the latter.

But he'd had the information, so where the hell had he got it from?

'Then it's in your interests to answer my questions or I'm going to be forced to treat you as the number one suspect and arrest you,' Laura said. 'And I'm already thinking about a charge of wasting police time and interfering in an ongoing investigation.'

Carroll swallowed again. Laura knew instinctively she was not going to have to drag this information from him.

Carroll would throw his own granny under a bus to protect his skin.

'It was one of the firemen,' he said. 'I was driving him home from a night out and we were just making small talk. He was well oiled. I told him I lived beside the house that burned down and he said he'd been at the scene. He'd found the woman in the suitcase.'

Laura puffed out her cheeks in utter frustration.

What a waste of an evening.

She stood up abruptly and walked out, followed by Brian.

'Get on to Gerry Reid,' Laura said. 'Have him read that fireman the riot act. I was there when he found Lola and he was utterly traumatised, so I hold some of the blame for not reminding him of his responsibilities. I'm not bringing him in for being stupid but he needs a talking-to.'

When Brian left, Laura slumped in her chair.

One step forward, two steps back.

CHAPTER 45

Tom's second day in Newcastle had been devoted to his wife. Even when the news came in earlier that day about the discovery of Viggo Datcu's dead body, Tom had just communicated it to Cummins by text, after asking Louise if it was okay to even do that much.

Louise was currently upstairs going through all the stuff she'd bought, which would require the purchase of a full-size suitcase to get through the airport, and Tom had been given an hour to catch up with Alan Cummins downstairs in the hotel bar.

'You see much of the toon today, then?' Cummins asked.

'There's nothing left to see,' Tom said. 'Lovely city you have here. Though Louise dragged me through some modern art building across the river and I felt like I'd gone on a weird acid trip. Nice bar on the top floor, mind.'

'Not one for the modern art myself.' Cummins laughed. 'Haway, that's some turn-up on the Viggo lad, eh? I bet that's sent ripples right up his organisation over here. We'll be keeping an eye. I figured the Albanians had found themselves some Irish colleagues. You can't run an inter-country trade route without some locals involved.'

'My DCI at home is starting to feel the pressure, I suspect,' Tom said. 'I picked a great time to abandon her.'

'They got any idea who killed Datcu?'

'We have a mob, the Cowells, they would have had control of drugs and brothels in whole swathes of the city up until the last few years. We'd nobbled them, or so we thought. The head man has been in jail the past number of years – but they seem to have grown a new head. I didn't think they'd any involvement in trafficking, and maybe they don't. Maybe Datcu and Matteo just got up their noses. I don't know. My DCI is doing her best but any information I can bring home from here will be well received.'

Cummins lifted his pint and took a large gulp.

'The Cowells,' he said. 'You're sure on that?'

Tom nodded, his eyebrows furrowed in question.

'You know them?'

'I've heard of them.'

Cummins fell silent again.

Tom could see Alan was struggling with whatever he had to say. Unfortunately, Tom didn't have the luxury of time.

'I don't have long,' he said, to get things moving. 'We're having a romantic room-service night in. Even Louise's legs are too tired to go out anywhere, and that's some feat, I tell you.'

'Oh aye,' Cummins said. 'I'll let you get back up soon as. It was just the one thing I wanted to put you wise on. Especially seeing as you're wondering about Irish gangs getting into trafficking. Look ... I think you might have a bit of a problem. I mean, internally.'

Tom frowned.

'What's this now?'

'You've been suffering a bit on the gun-supply front, am I right?'

'We've set up a new unit to tackle it,' Tom said. 'Or to be seen to be tackling it. You know yourself.'

'I do, aye. Anyway, one of your officers has accessed quite a high-level grass over there.'

'Okay?' Tom frowned. 'That doesn't surprise me. I'm surprised you know about it, but I guess you're going to tell me how.'

Cummins took another sup of his pint. Tom watched him, intrigued and concerned in equal measure.

'Listen,' Cummins said. 'I shouldn't be really telling you this, but it's your backyard and you seem like a man who'd do me a favour if you could.'

Tom sat back, puzzled. He still didn't know where this was going.

'You have a problem,' Cummins said. 'Your cop has agreed to turn a blind eye to this gang's main business in exchange for information. In fact, more than a blind eye. He's assured them eyes will be kept off their new venture if they cooperate with him. They're passing him info on guns being smuggled into the country. It's all for that new unit you set up.'

'Okay. And what's the gang's main business?'

'Trafficking women.'

'What?'

Tom felt the colour drain from his face. He picked up his own pint.

'Say that to me again,' he said, after taking a gulp. 'You're telling me that an officer in my force is accepting information on how guns are being smuggled into the country, on the promise that he'll keep eyes off a human-trafficking operation?'

Cummins nodded.

'How do you know this?' Tom asked.

'Your cop's informer is somebody we're watching.'

Cummins looked uncomfortable – and bloody right he should, Tom thought.

'Much and all as I'm grateful for this rather unorthodox information,' he said, 'what the hell, Alan? You'll have to slow this down for me. You have eyes on an informer in my jurisdiction? Again, for what reason?'

'It's in relation to trafficking, man. That's what I do. And his gang – a Dublin gang – is starting to dip its toe into it. So far they've been very successful and very under your radar. Hence why this informer is probably happy to be seen to be helping on the weapons front, where your focus is. Because – and I'm not kidding, Tom – the real money is in the trafficking. The weapons are only a sideshow and they can be got anywhere, at any time. You're never going to stop them. Not now there are so many in circulation. But trafficking, it's the new cocaine. It makes even more money and, the best part is, when you do catch these guys, it's almost impossible to get a prosecution. And long sentences for it are virtually unheard of.'

Tom brought his hand to his jaw and rubbed it. He was clenching his teeth so hard, he risked lockjaw.

'Who's the informer?' he said.

'You know who he is,' Cummins said. 'You have him under lock and key. Patrick Cowell. Maybe he isn't as active as he was, but it's his people who've launched themselves into trafficking. We're sure of that. His visiting orders are full of people involved with the supply side. If you look, you'll probably find he was visited by Viggo Datcu. His is the gang we think are involved with our Albanians. Cowell only came to our attention because we have our own grasses in the Albanian gang. And these informants are telling us Cowell is boasting that he's got the police sorted on the trafficking side and all he's had to do is throw a few rival, smaller criminals under the bus. Presumably his rivals are more heavily involved in bringing in weapons.'

'And you're sharing this with me now?'

'I wouldn't have known who to contact about this before meeting you,' Cummins said. 'No offence, mate, but strong and all as our relations are with your force, you have an awfully leaky pot over there.'

'And your system is a stunning example of modern-day policing,' Tom said, knowing his words were petulant before they even left his mouth.

'Aye, right enough,' Cummins said. 'I'm nae gonna pretend like we don't have problems, man. But we're getting on top of this trafficking issue a lot quicker than ye lads.'

Tom sighed. There was no point in keeping the argument going. Cummins was in all likelihood entirely correct. Partly because the problem was newer to Ireland than England, partly because they just didn't have as big a problem. But prior to the arson attack, the brothel in Shipping Row had operated entirely under the radar, and who knew how long it would have continued in that vein?

'So, Cowell is leaking to somebody in the new unit,' Tom said.

Cummins nodded.

'Who?'

'That I can only partially help with,' Cummins said. 'Cowell hasn't been so stupid as to fully name his contact. I know it's somebody very senior, male and involved in the anti-gun unit. And it's possible he goes by the name . . .'

'Joe,' Tom said.

Cummins' eyes widened. He was impressed.

'That's the one,' he said.

'Ah, Christ,' Tom said.

He signalled to the barman.

'Two whiskeys,' he said, then turned back to Cummins.

'You're positive you have this right?' he said. 'That the cop said he'd keep the focus off trafficking?'

Cummins shrugged.

'Touts don't tout for no reason, Tom. Especially when they've nothing you can threaten them with. Cowell is in prison. The only reason he's telling this Joe bloke anything is because he's had assurances. That's what my source has told us, anyway.'

The whiskey arrived.

Tom knocked his back in one.

Kennedy was the gift that just kept giving.

'The Cowell organisation is back up and running and its new racket is trafficking women,' Tom said when he arrived in Laura's office just before midday.

He'd come straight from the airport and had been bursting to tell her.

He'd only barely managed to hold off ringing her the previous night. But the additional information about how he'd learned of Cowell's involvement meant it really was a conversation that Tom preferred to have in person.

Right up until an hour or so ago, he was still undecided as to what to do about Joe Kennedy, but then the absolutely perfect solution had come to him.

Laura sat back and processed what he'd just told her.

'I know,' she said. 'Johnny Cowell is who we're looking at for Viggo's murder. And quite possibly, he's involved in Shipping Row. We had him in yesterday.'

'You're kidding me.'

Tom dropped into the chair on the other side of the desk he used to sit behind.

'It's all starting to link up now, isn't it?' he said. 'Matteo working for Datcu, Datcu doing business with the Cowells.'

'How did you find out about the Cowells being involved with trafficking?' Laura asked.

And so Tom told her what he'd discovered about Kennedy.

When he'd finished, Laura sat quietly.

She pulled open her drawer and reached for the remainder of Brian's supply of Nurofen, popped one in her mouth.

'I knew it,' she said. 'I knew Kennedy hadn't had a Damascene conversion. You know ...' She frowned, remembering, 'he didn't look right in that interview with Johnny Cowell. I just thought he was intimidated but now I think there's more. Patrick must have told Johnny who he had in his pocket. He made some jibe about corrupt policing.'

'Bloody right, Kennedy was intimidated,' Tom said. 'Tell me, what's your plan now?'

'Well, we have to get to the bottom of the Cowells' interactions with Shipping Row and how Viggo ended up dead. There's no doubt Johnny Cowell was involved in that, but why? Why bring all this down on himself? It's one thing to take out Lola – even Matteo – but why your business colleague? When Johnny decided to murder Viggo, he made things very complicated for himself. And which one of them took the baby?'

'Is there somebody talking inside Cowell's gang?'

'Jackie McCallion is dealing with that end,' Laura said. 'Is this what we've come to, though? Relying on unreliables? Hoping somebody will tell us what happened?'

'That's what always gets them, Laura,' Tom said. 'They're too good at evading the rest of our policing. Everything we usually rely on – the CCTV, the phones – the top-level guys in these gangs have all that sussed.'

'You should have heard Johnny Cowell telling us how, theoretically, he'd avoid being caught for Datcu's murder. It was all about how he'd change cars and avoid cameras and keep his phone off.'

'Let's hope Jackie's team turn up something,' Tom said. 'How's she doing, anyway? She enjoying being in gun central?'

'She's on her A game,' Laura said.

Tom smiled thinly. About that, at least, he could be pleased.

'Let's talk to Cowell ourselves,' Tom said. 'Put the shits up him. There's nothing these wannabes dislike more than thinking you know more than they do. And by the sounds of things, he's not as smart as his uncle. He might be hotheaded enough to give something away if we apply the pressure.'

'Let's go,' Laura said.

They caught up with Johnny Cowell in one of his clubs. It was a shame going inside when the day was so warm and bright outside; even more of a shame when they saw the state of the place.

Tom imagined the club looked half decent at night-time, when the lights were low and the place was hopping. But in daylight hours, it was like any other dive: sticky floors, grubby paintwork, the sounds and smells of the industrial dishwashers churning, and hot; very, very hot. The only people present were a lone bartender cleaning optics and the owner himself.

Cowell was sitting at the counter, nursing an orange juice brimming with ice, that might or might not have had an added ingredient.

He certainly looked worried enough to be drinking, but that fell off his face when the detectives sat on either side of him, making their presence known.

'Having a slow day, are yis?' he asked, smiling. 'What'll ye have? I bet neither of you mind a drink on the job.'

'I'm DCI Lennon,' Laura said. 'We've never met but you know me, by all accounts. At least, you indicated you did to my husband.'

'Just being polite.' Cowell smirked. 'And you're the famous one.' He nodded in Tom's direction. 'You used to be on the news all the time. My sympathies.'

'What's your coffee like?' Tom asked.

'Don't have much call for coffee in here,' Cowell said. 'Even for the espresso martinis we just lob some Nescafé in.'

'It's that attention to detail that must have this place thriving,' Tom said.

Cowell laughed.

'What can I help you with?' he said. 'You still trying to save the world and jail all the bad guys?'

'Just a couple will do,' Laura said. 'Tell us something, do you visit your uncle often?'

'Family is family. My dad would have wanted me to stay in touch with his brother.'

'Naturally. And is there anywhere or anyone else you'd visit out of loyalty to the family? For example, have you been helping with your uncle's new business, bringing women into the country? Does three Shipping Row ring a bell?'

Cowell considered for a moment.

'There's that address again. It means nothing to me.'

'It's real easy to disprove a lie,' Tom said. 'Unless you and Viggo were thinking of setting up a new club together, the only place I can imagine you had in common was Shipping Row.'

Cowell shrugged, but he looked angry.

'I'm not a fan of forcing women to do things they don't like,' he said.

Tom frowned, watching the other man.

A little unhappiness in the ranks there, perhaps?

'Is your uncle a fan of forcing women to do things they don't want to?'

Cowell said nothing.

Tom cocked his head sideways.

'I've heard you have kids, Johnny. That you're good with them. That right?'

'Love my kids, I do.'

'Would you hurt a kid? A baby?'

'I'm not a fucking animal,' Cowell sneered.

'There's a baby missing from Shipping Row,' Tom said.

Cowell tensed.

Tom studied him closely.

Cowell knew. He knew about Lola's baby. Tom felt it in his gut.

'Where's the baby?' he asked.

'I don't know anything about a baby.'

'Bullshit. Where's the baby?'

Cowell ran his tongue over dry lips.

'I don't fucking know!'

Anger. Distress.

Tom could hear it. Laura, too.

'Right,' Tom said. He hesitated. 'So if I said to you that one of the girls in there had a baby and it's missing, and we think it's been trafficked for God knows what, what would you say? How would you feel about that?'

'I'd feel fucking sick,' Cowell snapped. 'You don't touch babies. Young kids. No. That's not right.'

Cowell stared into his orange juice.

'What would you do to a man who'd put a baby in harm's way?' Tom asked.

Cowell met his eye.

Without blinking, he said:

'I'd put a bullet in him.'

Tom took a sharp breath.

Laura spoke next, quietly.

'Johnny,' she said. 'Did you ever visit Shipping Row and sleep with any of the girls there?'

Cowell raised the glass of orange juice to his lips.

He said nothing.

'Would you leave a baby in a brothel?' Laura asked. 'Do you think a good father would do that?'

Cowell looked like he might say something.

'Boss, the kegs.' The barman had come down to their end of the counter.

'I'm coming now,' Cowell said.

He walked off.

Outside, Tom looked up at the sky and let the sun warm his face.

Inside, he felt chilled.

'Viggo took that baby,' Laura said. 'To sell it.'

Tom nodded.

'He had a family himself,' Laura said. 'I don't understand.'

'Don't try to,' Tom said. 'It's beyond our comprehension.'

'Is Cowell the baby's father?'

Tom held out his hands.

'I don't know,' he said. 'But if I had to guess, I'd say yes. He could have been sent to that brothel to keep an eye, make sure the Albanians and Matteo were doing their jobs right. He might have been ordered to sample the goods.'

Laura shook her head.

'I don't know where to go with this goddamn case,' she said. 'If Viggo killed Lola and Matteo, unless Tyanna or Nina offer themselves up as witnesses, we'll never prove it now. And to think the bloody Cowells are all involved in this. By the way, we need to let Ray know that Kennedy is as much a liability as ever. What are you going to do about him?'

'I'm not going to do anything,' Tom said. 'I extracted a promise from our Newcastle contact. He's going to get a memo sent over to Bronwyn Maher outlining the suspicion. Let her deal with it. Everybody knows I've a problem with Kennedy, so I'd rather not be the one to raise it.'

'Clever,' Laura said. She made to get into the car, but noticed Tom wasn't doing the same.

'Where are *you* going?' she said.

'The Cusacks' house isn't far from here,' Tom said. 'I'm going to use the walk to steady my nerves and think about how to break it to them that they're unlikely to be getting their daughter back.'

CHAPTER 47

John Cusack was home alone.

Orla, he told Tom, was doing what she'd done the first time Nina had vanished: dropping leaflets all over the city in the hope that somebody would report seeing her, or that Nina herself would see them and call.

Tom took John up on the offer of a cuppa. He hadn't stopped since flying home earlier that day and the fatigue was catching up on him.

'You didn't want to go out with your wife?' he asked John, hoping it didn't come across as judgemental.

John shook his head.

'It's no use,' he said. 'I don't . . . I'm not entirely sure myself and Orla are on the same page on this one. Anyhow, our next-door neighbour has gone out with her. We were making plans for a dinner this weekend. Her twentieth birthday.'

Tom sat at one of the kitchen chairs while John poured the hot water from the kettle into two mugs.

'Orla still blames me, for involving you lot,' John said. 'I don't know what else I could have done.'

'There was nothing else,' Tom said. 'And if Nina is involved with the people we think she's involved with, John, I have to tell you, it's unlikely she had a choice about going, which also means she'll have no choice about coming back. The fire was an opportunity for her to escape them. It's unlikely that will happen again.'

John paused in squeezing the hot water out of the teabags.

'I never thought it would come to this,' he said. 'Can I tell you something?'

Tom nodded.

John sat down. He'd left the half-made tea on the counter.

'In a way, I'm used to Nina not being here,' he said. 'When she started on the drugs, it was horrendous. She was ... she was like an insane person. Do you know she broke Orla's fingers?'

Tom shook his head.

'She did. She slammed the door on them so hard she broke four of her mother's fingers.'

John rubbed his hands together nervously, distressed at the memory.

'It was okay for a while, after we got her through rehab, but then ... I knew she was using before Orla did. Maybe Orla was pretending not to see it, but I could. One night ...'

John flushed bright red and Tom knew that whatever was coming was awful.

'One night, she came in, off her face. She offered to ... she offered to do something, if I gave her money. Me, her own father. When I ran her out of it, she started claiming the reason she used drugs was because she'd been abused as a kid. I swear on my life I never laid a hand on her.'

'Addicts say things,' Tom said. He could see the man was telling the truth. It was nearly killing John to relay what his daughter had said, lest there be a hint of suspicion.

But that didn't mean Nina hadn't been abused by somebody else.

'When she came back this time, I was waiting, you know.

I was waiting for something to kick off. And it will always be like that. Nina hasn't been my little girl since she turned fifteen. She never will be again. She's done too much.'

Tom placed a hand on the man's arm. His heart went out to him.

He didn't know what was worse.

Not knowing where your daughter was.

Or hoping it stayed that way.

CHAPTER 48

Despite the case being ongoing for six days, the energy in the incident room hadn't diminished.

Laura was proud of her team and the fact they were still generating results.

The only problem was, for all the information they were compiling, they were no closer to getting anything confirmed. What had happened in Shipping Row was all still speculation.

'Boss, Viggo Datcu's number is the bill-phone number on Tyanna Volkov's phone,' Brian said, when he spotted Laura making her way through the room.

'Excellent,' Laura said. 'Have we run CCTV in the hospital to see if Datcu visited Tyanna?'

Michael glanced over from his desk.

'I'm doing that so moany bastard Brian over there doesn't get any more headaches. I've spotted Viggo already, hanging around outside near the car park.'

'Excellent work,' Laura said. 'Right, has anybody seen . . .'

She didn't need to finish the sentence. Jackie McCallion had just arrived, along with Joe Kennedy.

'DCI Lennon,' McCallion said. 'I have some information.'

'Okay,' Laura said. 'We can do this in my office.'

She glanced at Kennedy, who looked set to follow them.

'Detective Kennedy, I don't need you for this. Thanks.'

Kennedy nodded, but he looked taken aback.

Laura didn't hang around. She led Jackie at speed out of the incident room and upstairs.

'So,' Laura said, when she closed the door to her office. 'What have you got for me?'

'Something decent,' Jackie said. 'But I need a favour in return.'

'For a tout?' Laura said.

'It's not a big one. He's low down the ladder and he's done nothing – yet.'

'Tell me,' Laura said.

'My informer is a driver for Johnny Cowell. And Cowell instructed him to take out *the Italian*, which I can only assume is Matteo Russo.'

Laura sat back, agog.

They'd presumed Viggo had killed Matteo and Lola.

Why the hell would Cowell have wanted them murdered?

'Jackie, we can't show this tout any leniency,' she said. 'Not if he stabbed Russo and Lola to death.'

'No,' Jackie said. 'Let me finish. He was told to do one job, just the Italian. But he didn't do it.'

'How do we know he didn't do it?'

'He was to take him out last weekend. But Matteo was already dead. And my tout would have used a gun. Not a knife. That's not a gang hit. You know yourself, knives are up close and personal.'

Laura threw her head back and looked up at the ceiling. It needed a lick of paint. Tom Reynolds used to smoke cigars. Laura wondered if he'd indulged in his office, which might explain the yellow tinge to the ceiling.

The idea, when it landed, came entirely from her subconscious.

That's where they'd gone wrong.

Assuming it had been one killer.

The case was more complex than that.

The presence of both Albanians and Irish had made it so.

She picked up the phone and dialled Tom.

CHAPTER 49

Laura hadn't expected Tom to visit the hospital with her that evening. She knew he hadn't even been home since he'd landed at Dublin airport, but as soon as she voiced her theory, Tom had agreed.

What if Viggo had killed Lola so he could take her baby? And then Cowell had killed Matteo, and then Viggo, to find out where the baby was? Or it could be more complicated than that – and Viggo had killed Matteo before Matteo could rat him out to Cowell.

The only person they could put those theories to was Tyanna.

She would know if Viggo had killed Lola when she refused to hand over her baby and she might have witnessed Cowell in the house.

It was time to go hard on Tyanna. They needed her to talk or they'd be stuck in this limbo, filled with questions and half-answers, when they had a witness who'd actually been in the house and had quite possibly seen what had happened.

'Tyanna, we wanted to ask you a few more questions about Lola,' she said, when they were sitting at the girl's bedside. 'How well did you know her?'

Tyanna shrugged.

'Matteo did not like us to talk to each other too much.'

'But you lived there together,' Tom said. 'Surely you talked sometimes.'

'I know I would,' Laura added. 'I'd need to talk to somebody. I would feel very alone, otherwise.'

'We were supposed to be alone,' Tyanna said. 'I talk more to the other girls, from Russia and Poland. Nina talked to Lola more.'

'But you talked to her sometimes,' Laura said.

Tyanna shrugged.

Laura sat forward, her phone in her hand. She'd pulled up a photograph.

'Tyanna, this man here, do you recognise him?'

Tyanna stared at the photograph of Johnny Cowell.

'I have seen him in the house,' she said.

'With Lola?'

'Yes.'

'What about with Nina?'

'No.'

'Was he with you, or ... what was the Polish girl called? Wendy?'

'No—'

She paused.

'Viggo preferred the blondes.'

Laura caught Tom's eye and nodded. She'd met Viggo's wife – a blonde.

And Nina was blonde.

Laura sat back, chewing the inside of her cheek. If Viggo had taken Nina, where was she now?

'Why did Nina stay at the brothel?' Tom asked. 'She wasn't like you girls. She's from here. She would know who to talk to. How to get help.'

Tyanna shrugged.

'Nina was angry. About what happened to her. To all of us. But she felt for herself that she deserved it. I don't know. Something happened to her when she was young. I think a man touch her. She hates men but she hates herself more.'

Tom shook his head.

'Who took Lola's baby?' Laura asked.

'I do not know, I see nothing.'

'You saw something,' Laura said. 'And you should know, Tyanna, Viggo Datcu – he's dead. If that's who you were afraid of, you can talk to us now. We need you to talk to us.'

'I don't know who took the baby. You say Viggo is dead. But there are more. There are always more.'

Laura glanced over at Tom, her eyes narrowed with whatever thought had crossed her mind. Tom nodded at her. Whatever strategy Laura had, she should run with it.

'Tyanna, did you attack Lola?' Laura asked.

'What? I . . .'

Tyanna stopped. She stared straight ahead at the wall, refusing to look at either of them.

'I go to bed on Thursday night. I go early. I am tired. I have customers the night before and during the day. I need to rest. When I wake on Friday, I see no one. Then the fire starts and I run.'

She was lying.

'Tyanna,' Tom said. 'Two people were stabbed to death in that house and I don't for a moment believe you don't know anything about it. We know you're not being truthful with us. What we don't know is why. Unless you're trying to protect yourself.'

'It was you, wasn't it?' Laura insisted. 'That's why you keep saying you saw nothing. You're protecting yourself.'

Panic filled Tyanna's eyes.

'If you won't cooperate with us, I'm going to have to arrest you for obstruction,' Laura said, her voice grave.

'She means it,' Tom said. 'There are two people dead. We have a baby and now Nina missing. We can't protect you if you're lying. And the only person we know for sure was in that house when the murders happened is you. You haven't denied it.'

'You can't deny it,' Laura added. 'You did it.'

'I didn't. I swear it. I swear.'

As they walked back through the quiet car park, Laura asked Tom if he thought Tyanna was still in danger.

'Why do you ask?' Tom said.

'She wants to leave the hospital. The doctors are fine with it as long as she has somewhere safe to go and I think Natasha McCarthy can help with that. There's a shelter for girls who've been through what Tyanna has. And if she's there, we can keep an eye on her.'

'She's right to be scared,' Tom said. 'We know about Viggo. We know about the Cowells. But we don't know about the gang behind Viggo. Didn't you say you've footage of him in the vicinity of Shipping Row the day before the fire?'

Laura nodded.

'Then let's try to track his movements. If he did away with Matteo and Lola, it's likely he'd have told somebody. We need his phone records and we can talk to his wife. I'll ask my contact in Newcastle if anything is being whispered over there. And just to be sure, let's go through that CCTV again, but this time, let's bring in somebody like Jackie McCallion, see if she can spot any known associates of Cowell's, because it's entirely possible he's caught up in all this, somehow.'

They'd arrived at their car.

'You could have a real problem solving this in a manner that leads to prosecutions,' Tom said. 'You know what they got Patrick Cowell on in the end?'

'Yeah,' Laura said. She opened the driver's door. 'Money laundering.'

She sighed. Then she stopped short.

Tom looked back at her.

'What?'

'I'm wondering about that Polish girl, Wendy,' she said.

'What's on your mind?' Tom asked.

Laura shrugged.

'Just a hunch,' she said. 'I'd like to know where she ended up. It's out there, but I think I might have an idea.'

CHAPTER 50

Friday

Natasha had brought in clothes for Tyanna provided by the shelter.

There were more in the room that awaited her arrival and Ashanti had also organised a care package of hygiene products and the bits and bobs that Tyanna would need.

Natasha helped her into the T-shirt, as she held her hands nervously in the air.

'You will like the girls you meet at the shelter,' Natasha said. 'I have a friend there. Ashanti. She's been through a similar experience to you. They all have. Some of them are more troubled but I think you're strong, Tyanna. I think you'll be okay.'

The T-shirt slipped onto the other woman's body.

'I do not think anybody is like me,' Tyanna said.

She sounded so miserable, Natasha stopped what she was doing.

'What do you mean?' she said.

'I . . .'

Tyanna closed her eyes.

'I need to tell you something,' she said.

Natasha frowned.

She sat on the edge of the bed beside Tyanna, her body angled towards her so she could see her face.

'I do not deserve you to be sorry for me,' she said.

'Why do you say that?'

'I am a bad person.'

'I don't think you're a bad person, Tyanna,' Natasha said.

'But I am. You are so nice to me but I do not deserve it. I have done bad things.'

'Doing bad things does not mean you are bad inside.'

'I am bad inside.' Tyanna hesitated. 'When I was in my home, in Russia, I sleep with men. I sleep with men for money. I tell myself that is not what I am doing, but it is what I am doing. And when I come to Ireland I think I will also sleep with men for money.'

She turned to Natasha.

'So I am not good.'

Natasha took a deep breath.

'When you were in Russia, did you ever have enough money? Did you have a happy home life and parents who loved you, and financial security?'

Tyanna shook her head, almost smiling in surprise.

'I had none of those things,' she said. 'Nobody had, where I lived. Even most of the people who have jobs.'

'Okay,' Natasha said. 'So you made a choice. You were young and you were foolish and you did some things. Like many, many people have to do. You thought when you came to Ireland you would do the same things, yes?'

'Yes.'

'Were you allowed to leave that house?'

'No. Only when Matteo was with me.'

'Did you choose who you had sex with?'

'No.'

'Did you get to keep the money you earned?'

'No.'

'Did anybody have a right to do that to you?'

Tyanna opened her mouth and closed it.

'No, Tyanna,' Natasha said. 'Nobody had the right to do that to you. If you felt that you could say no, that you could stop what was happening to you, then you would have to come to terms with the choices *you* made. But what you did before, that was not the reason you ended up in this situation. The men who do this to women, they prey on people. They made you think you were responsible for what happened to you. But you were *not*. You did nothing wrong. *You* are good.'

Tyanna hung her head.

Natasha put her arm around the girl and felt her shoulders heave as she sobbed.

Tyanna would need a lot of help.

But she would get there.

Natasha hugged Tyana until the doctor arrived.

'Now, Tyanna,' she said. 'I'm going to talk you through your burns care. I'm just going to bring you down to the nurses' station and we'll go through the packs we'll be sending home with you, okay?'

Natasha took a tissue from the side locker and dabbed Tyanna's eyes with it.

The doctor waited until she was ready, then led her from the room.

'I'll be here,' Natasha called.

She sat there for a moment, then decided to make herself useful.

The bag Linda had brought in was in Tyanna's locker and Natasha started to pack up the girl's belongings, what little of them there were.

She pulled up the blanket on the hospital bed and then,

because she was bored and she knew the nurses would do it anyway, she stripped the pillows.

If she was honest, there was a part of her that had been looking for it.

Who strips bloody hospital pillows? she'd thought to herself, even as she was doing it.

The phone fell out onto the bed.

The text message that had just been received but had yet to be opened was visible on the screen.

A nine-digit number over a single word and an emoji.

Shh.

Then, a smiley face.

CHAPTER 51

Viggo's wife did not look like she was in mourning.

She greeted Laura at the door in a different pair of silk pyjamas, her hair knotted in a messy bun this time, and welcomed her in.

The house smelled fresh and clean.

The bag that had been in the hall was gone.

'You're, um, feeling okay?' Laura said, as she followed the woman through to the kitchen.

In the corner, a playpen was strewn with toys. A monitor sat on the kitchen counter, the light set to green. A steriliser stood beside it, and baby bottles waiting to be filled.

Laura blinked rapidly.

She had to take this slowly.

If she was right . . .

The kitchen oozed money – a Meneghini refrigerator, a Victoria Arduino espresso machine and a selection of wines that Laura knew hadn't been purchased in the local Tesco.

'Mrs Datcu,' she said, sitting on the breakfast bar stool she'd just been directed to, 'I wanted to say I am so sorry—'

'Alicja,' the woman said. 'I am not Mrs any more.'

'Oh. Um, right.'

Laura watched as the woman moved seamlessly around the

kitchen preparing coffee, her every movement as graceful as a dancer's.

But when she lifted her hand to reach up for more ground coffee from the cupboard, the sleeve of her top slipped down and Laura spotted the fading trace marks of bruises along her forearm.

Alicja was aware her arm was on display but she didn't react. She didn't try to cover it up.

'Black?' she asked Laura.

'Please,' Laura said.

She waited for the other woman to sit back down with the two cups.

'How are you coping with your husband's death?' Laura asked.

Alicja shrugged.

'I am fine,' she said, with absolutely no hint of sadness.

'Right,' Laura said. She was growing more certain of her theory by the second. 'How long were you married?'

Alicja blinked.

'Not long.'

Laura looked around the kitchen that resembled a showroom in an extremely expensive house for sale. She thought about the hall on the way in, the glimpse she'd caught of the living room.

Not a single photograph on display.

This woman looked like a model but she seemingly hadn't posed in any photographs in the recent past.

'Are you living here long?' Laura asked.

'Viggo had the house before,' Alicja answered.

Laura stared at her.

'Was your husband violent with you, Alicja?'

Another shrug.

'He is a man. Sometimes, he gets carried away.'

'And where are you from? Originally, I mean. It's not Albania, is it?'

'No. Poland.'

Laura had guessed right.

'Alicja, were you married to Viggo Datcu or just living here with him?'

Alicja blinked.

'This is my house,' she said.

Laura touched the side of the china coffee cup – direct from Brown Thomas, she reckoned.

'It will only be your house if you have a marriage certificate to prove it,' Laura said. 'You won't be able to stay living here without people finding out. I imagine Viggo has friends, family. They'll want to know about his assets. And I mean, all his assets.'

Laura glanced over at the baby monitor.

The other woman's cool demeanour was gone, replaced with something Laura was far more familiar with.

Alicja looked panicked.

'But they cannot throw me out. He said he would marry me. Look.'

She held up her hand, the engagement ring on her third finger. It was so large, Laura hadn't noticed the absence of a wedding band when she'd called in the first time.

'What was your other name?' she asked. 'When you worked in the house? Was it . . . Wendy?'

Alicja glared at Laura.

Then she lowered her eyes, pink spots dancing across her collarbones and up her neck.

Another mystery solved.

'Alicja, it might not be safe for you to stay here,' Laura said. 'Men will come. They won't let you live this life you want. They've only stayed away because they know the police are watching. And I need to see your baby.'

Alicja nodded. She walked upstairs, leaving the kitchen door open.

When she arrived back downstairs, she was carrying a baby in her arms. She hesitated for a moment before she handed the child over to Laura. Something had kicked in, some maternal instinct that had formed over the last few days.

But, in the end, it was easy. Alicja had too many scars of her own to care for another person.

The infant's skin was darker than Alicja's. It wouldn't have been hard to figure out had they seen the kid when Laura had called in the first time.

It had taken the realisation that Alicja was actually Wendy to work out that the child Viggo had in his home couldn't be his.

'We were meant to travel together as a family,' Alicja said. 'Viggo was not the smartest tack in the box.'

Laura almost laughed.

'I think he thought he loved me,' Alicja said. 'I was happy to take whatever I could get, after . . . it was better than being in that house.'

'I understand,' Laura said.

'What will I do?' Alicja asked, terrified.

Laura pursed her lips.

'First, you tell me everything you know about Viggo Datcu,' she said. 'Especially what he was doing last Thursday and Friday. Then, I'm going leave with this baby. I'm not saying what you should do next. All I am going to say is that I imagine there are things in this house that would fetch a lot of money. Do you have your passport?'

'Viggo got me a new one.'

Laura said nothing.

The two women looked at each other.

Then Laura nodded at the other woman's arm.

'That looks like the after-effects of some rather nasty bruising,' she said. 'I think you're owed.'

Alicja blinked again.

Laura looked down at the baby. Her features were fixed in a little smile.

'We've been looking everywhere for you,' Laura said softly.

She wasn't mistaken.

There was a tiny fluttering of wistfulness somewhere inside Laura.

The baby felt very natural in her arms.

Bloody hell, she thought.

CHAPTER 52

Tom and Jackie had got the IT department to compile all the relevant CCTV files on the one desktop and the two of them were now sitting in an empty office going through them together.

When his phone rang, he was glad of the distraction.

'I'll bring back tea,' he told Jackie and stepped outside.

The call was from Laura.

'Any joy?' Tom asked her.

'Viggo's *wife* Alicja is Wendy,' Laura said.

'Seriously? Good work, Laura. How did you make that connection?'

'It was Tyanna saying Viggo had a thing for blondes. That's not all I have.'

'Spill.'

'I'm holding Lola's baby.'

Tom slumped against the wall beside him.

'Are you . . ? Laura, I could kiss you.'

'We can never let Louise and Ray know.'

Laura laughed, a sound light and full of joy. Tom's return laugh sounded the same.

Michael Geoghegan was approaching.

Tom was about to tell him the news about the baby when he stopped himself. Michael smiled and walked on.

'Boss?' Laura said.

'Just hang on,' Tom said.

Michael was gone.

'What's happening with the baby now?' Tom said.

'I've a good person in child protection,' Laura said, then, 'I mean, the baby's mother is dead and we have no idea who the father is.'

Tom let it hang there.

If they declared to all and sundry that the baby had been found, its father could come forward to claim her.

That could mean handing the baby over to Johnny Cowell. And while he might have a soft spot when it came to kids, he was still a criminal of the highest order and a potential murderer to boot.

'I think that's the right course of action,' Tom said. 'We'll selectively inform the team members.'

'I'm glad you agree,' Laura said. 'This baby will end up with a good family. I'm sure of it.'

'What's the story with Wendy – Alicja, I mean?' Tom asked.

'I left her salvaging what she could from the not-so-family home. She was hoping she could keep up the pretence and live there. You wouldn't believe how Viggo treated her. But can you imagine what his bosses would do if they found her living there like a princess? A former employee?'

'Does she have a passport?'

'Yep. I offered to find her a place in a shelter but she wants to go home. She'll be going back a wealthy woman, too, I think. Hopefully she stays off their radar this time. Before you ask, I spent a little while wondering if she was in on any of this, but she's just a victim. And she's been minding that baby like she's her own. She cried when I had to take her out of the house – I think the baby was the only thing keeping her sane. I advised her to move fast. It wouldn't be beyond the Albanians to swoop her up.'

'Did she give you any new information?'

'All she knows about last Thursday is that Viggo came home that evening with the baby and he was angry. He never told her anything about his business and she didn't ask. But she said he was very bad-tempered on Thursday and he was, eh, extremely rough with her as well. Has Jackie spotted Cowell or anyone linked to him on the CCTV?'

'Nothing yet. We saw the footage of Viggo heading down towards Shipping Row but there's nothing to indicate when he left. What time did Alicja say he got home?'

'Six. A couple of things,' Laura said. 'She says he didn't leave the house on Friday. In fact, he made a point of staying in and making her stay there with him. She was allowed out to the shops on normal days, things like that, but he insisted she was with him all day Friday. He ordered baby supplies from Tesco and told her to take care of the infant.'

'He was hiding from Cowell.'

'Sounds like it. I thought so, anyway. She says when he found out about the fire, he was furious. Like, properly furious. And scared. She said on the night he went to meet Cowell, he was frightened, too.'

'Okay. So, we're back to your idea. Viggo killed Lola and Matteo. But who set the fire? A soldier of Viggo's?'

'I don't know. Maybe it was Cowell. Maybe he saw what had happened in the house and was trying to cover it up. Of interest – Alicja said Viggo didn't drink alcohol when he was out. He only ever ordered water. He drank at home, from his own bottles. So, when he met Cowell, he would have been on water.'

Tom nodded, thinking. Cowell must have drugged Viggo.

His phone beeped to tell him another call was coming in. He moved it away from his ear to check who was trying to get hold of him.

'Natasha McCarthy is calling,' he said. 'I'll get it but, just to let you know, the phone company sent through Viggo's phone records. He was making calls to a couple of unknown numbers in the last few days. Brian is about to start making his way through them. They might be Tyanna's and Nina's phones.'

'It makes sense,' Laura said.

They said their goodbyes and hung up.

Tom caught Natasha the second time she rang.

'Tom,' she said, her voice low and urgent. 'Somebody is still threatening Tyanna Volkov.'

Tom, who'd arrived at the canteen and had been about to get the teas, ground to a halt.

'What are you talking about?' he asked Natasha. 'We reckon Viggo Datcu gave her the phone, and he's dead.'

He listened as Natasha explained what she'd found in Tyanna's room.

And out of the corner of his eye, he spotted Bronwyn Maher, walking in the direction of the stairs and her office.

Behind her, Joe Kennedy trailed, his head hanging.

CHAPTER 53

Bronwyn Maher considered herself a fair woman.

Years ago, when Sean McGuinness had first indicated he'd be retiring from the chief superintendent's job at the NBCI, Bronwyn had asked if he had any personal preferences for his replacement. She'd been hoping he'd say Tom Reynolds, and of course, Sean had.

But Tom had resisted the promotion.

So, when Joe Kennedy had been chosen by the internal panel assembled by Bronwyn's boss at the time, comprising other department heads and senior officers, Bronwyn had rallied behind him.

She did so even though he would not have been her choice. Joe's father had been a member of a notorious group of police officers that had abused their powers liberally in the 1980s. When police corruption began to come under the microscope, several of the group's cases had come in for a lot of scrutiny, resulting in many convictions being overturned. It transpired that this particular group of officers had an MO that involved riding roughshod over most acceptable policing procedures. Their trademarks included violent interview techniques, fudged evidence and downright lies to secure prosecutions.

Kennedy wasn't judged on his father's reputation and was well regarded as a good communicator and an efficient administrator.

But it had always struck Bronwyn that the son had made very little effort to distance himself from the father. It had worried her.

And in the end, Kennedy had proved a disaster. In the top job, he'd nowhere to hide and it became apparent, very quickly, that he was more spin than substance.

Over a short period, he'd caused more than a little discord in the murder squad and other departments within the NBCI. She hadn't needed Sean McGuinness ringing her weekly to tell her that; she could see it.

She just hadn't been sure what to do about it, because Kennedy was slippery. He made a convincing case, each time he was confronted, that he didn't mean to upset anybody, that he was doing his best.

But when the head of the press office had discovered that Kennedy had formed alliances with certain journalists, behind the back of the communications unit, and was selectively leaking material to his pals, things had taken a turn.

Especially when it transpired he was passing over personal details about senior officers.

Tom Reynolds had been the most high-profile victim of Kennedy's malicious regime, but he hadn't been the only one.

In time-honoured fashion, when his treachery was unearthed, Kennedy had been moved sideways. Bronwyn would have sacked him, but her boss was old school and didn't believe in hanging your own out to dry. He'd known Kennedy's father, and while he had lot to say about the carry-on of the notorious 80s gang, Bronwyn had always suspected that, in private, her boss thought that was the way to get policing done.

Bronwyn was not like her boss.

She didn't believe in protecting officers at any cost.

She was slowly but surely rooting out the parasitic weeds from the police force.

The only problem was, she had to have solid evidence to do it.

The communication she'd received from the British police was worrying but it wasn't compelling. 'Joe' could be one of any number of officers, if they were even correct about the name.

But Bronwyn knew that wasn't the case. She knew the man sitting in front of her was the idiot who'd been dealing with Cowell. She'd even seen his visiting orders to Mountjoy Prison.

But unless Kennedy admitted to offering Cowell a deal in exchange for information, she couldn't prove it.

And so far, he was being very clever – confessing to a half-truth that covered the whole truth.

'I visited Cowell a few times,' Kennedy said, pushing his glasses up his nose. 'He had very useful information about the movement of firearms through the docks and I was hoping – I'm still hoping – it will help our new unit. My colleague Ray Lennon has been in to visit him as well, at the suggestion of DCI Lennon, I believe.'

'And Cowell told him nothing, by all accounts,' Bronwyn said. 'So why did Cowell agree to tell you anything? He knows you can't promise him any time off his sentence. Cowell will serve the full term, we're all sure of that.'

'I suppose he's trying to show that he's a reformed character,' Kennedy said, deadpan. 'Maybe he's found God, I don't know.'

Bronwyn stared at him. He met her eyes, unblinking, in return.

'So, he wasn't filling you in on gun shipments because you told him you'd ensure a blind eye was turned to his other activities? Like certain people-trafficking ventures?'

'Absolutely not,' Kennedy said, indignantly. 'I wouldn't even dream of making such an offer.'

Bronwyn placed both her elbows on the desk.

'The problem is,' she said, 'if you thought you could lie to extract information, you must be aware that Cowell is a phenomenally dangerous individual. He would want payback for being tricked. We know that the gangs in this State do not see police as untouchable, Joe. Things are not like they used to be.'

'Of course, I'm well aware of that. And I wouldn't take any risks with Patrick Cowell. If he's under the impression the information he gave me was tit for tat, then he's jumping to conclusions of his own making. It's nothing I've said.'

Bronwyn sat back.

'I can't prove whether or not you deliberately misled Patrick Cowell, Joe. If you weren't misleading him, then we have a far more serious issue, because it is implicitly accepting the commission of one crime in order to tackle another. That's not how we do things.'

'I would never, ever make such a careless move,' Kennedy said. 'It would be putting my whole career at risk. I know I've done stupid, naïve things, but I've never broken the law.'

'No. But you think you're cleverer than you are.'

Kennedy opened his mouth to interrupt but Bronwyn silenced him by raising her hand.

'That aside, my concern is that you are now at risk, Joe. Whether you intended to put yourself there or not. So, to that end, I've decided to move you to a less high-profile role. The anti-gun crime unit is just too much in the public eye.'

Kennedy's face fell.

'You have put yourself on Patrick Cowell's radar,' Bronwyn said. 'What matters now is taking you off it.'

'But I've added value to the new unit,' Kennedy protested. 'I've worked hard. I'm shaping it; I'm helping to make progress.'

'I appreciate that,' Bronwyn said. And she did. It was how Kennedy had been getting his information that was the problem.

'This is not a demotion,' she said.

She could see from his expression that he knew full well it was; he just didn't think he had any grounds to fight it on.

Which meant she had him bang to rights on what he'd offered Cowell.

Inwardly, she sighed.

He probably had no intention of honouring his deal with Cowell. Bronwyn knew Kennedy was more stupid than bent.

But he was still a problem.

'Where are you moving me?' Kennedy asked, in a resigned tone.

'Sex crimes,' Bronwyn said.

She'd spoken to Natasha McCarthy only hours ago. Natasha didn't want Kennedy in her department but when Bronwyn told her she didn't care what assignment he got and that it would be a huge favour, Natasha had agreed. On the condition he undertake an extensive training course first.

'Sex crimes?' Kennedy repeated.

Bronwyn nodded.

They looked at each other, Kennedy silent in his defeat.

CHAPTER 54

Tom was still trawling the CCTV with Jackie. They'd moved on to Friday's footage.

On the other side of the desk, Brian was dialling numbers from Viggo Datcu's phone. Alicja had given them Viggo's passcode – something she'd managed to spot, as opposed to him telling her what it was – and they were now ringing all the numbers on it that they couldn't identify, to see who Viggo had called in the days around the Shipping Row murders and after.

Most of the numbers were ringing out or going straight to voicemail.

His gang colleagues would know of his death. They wouldn't be answering calls from his phone and no doubt they'd have changed their own numbers by now anyway.

Laura arrived and Brian put Viggo's phone on the desk, set to loudspeaker.

Laura was busy texting and Tom knew she was keeping an eye on Alicja's progress to the airport. The police weren't actually driving her there; Bronwyn Maher might have something to say about that. Alicja had booked her own taxi, but Laura was having her followed to ensure her safe passage. And Alicja, after giving her sworn statement, had committed to being on the end of the phone for Laura if the Irish police needed anything more from her.

Tom watched as Nina appeared on the CCTV screen, a large bag on her back. She was highlighted in red marker, something the wizards in the IT department had come up with. It made it look like they were watching a football match and a football pundit had just circled a player on the pitch.

Brian dialled another number.

This time it was answered.

'Who is this?'

Brian looked up at Tom.

'Is that you, Natasha?' Tom asked.

'It's me,' Natasha said. 'But I'm on Tyanna's phone. We're at the shelter.'

'We're ringing from Viggo's phone,' Tom said. 'Right, well, that confirms that number. Brian's going to check the next number. Thanks, Natasha.'

'Tom—'

But Brian had already hung up. He looked up at Tom to see what he should do.

'I'll call her back,' Tom said. 'Just dial that next one.'

As Brian rang the next number, Tom's phone beeped with a text.

It was from Natasha.

He read it, unable to make sense of it for a moment.

Brian's final number rang out.

Laura was off the phone, so Tom showed her Natasha's text.

She frowned as she read the message.

The number sending threatening texts to Tyanna is not the one you rang me from.

'Hang on – if Viggo wasn't threatening Tyanna, who is?' Laura asked.

Tom was already phoning Natasha.

'Natasha,' he said, when she answered. 'Sorry, hang on, I'll put you on speaker. We didn't mean to cut you off there, I thought you were finished. Will you read out that number that sent the texts to Tyanna's phone so we can check it off Viggo's phone logs to see if it's anybody he was in contact with?'

Natasha read out a nine-digit number.

'Brian?' Tom asked.

Brian scrolled through Viggo's phone.

'Viggo rang that number a couple of times this week,' he said. 'But I dialled it a while ago and it just rang out. When he dialled it, the call was logged both times – it was answered, I mean.'

'Is it Cowell's number, by any chance?'

'I've been checking all the numbers Viggo dialled with the phone companies,' Brian said. 'Loads of them are pay-as-you-go, so we can't find out who was using them. That number you called out is a pay-as-you-go. Tyanna's is too.'

He showed Tom the highlighted numbers he'd marked.

Tom sat back.

It was just there, almost within reach.

'Laura,' he said. 'What's Alicja's number?'

Laura pulled out her phone and read it out.

They all looked at Brian, who consulted his notes.

'That's pay-as-you-go,' he said. 'Viggo dialled it every day, a few times a day. It looks like he liked to give pay-as-you-goes to the girls in the brothel. Probably because they needed prepaid credit to dial out.'

Tom looked up at the CCTV footage on screen again.

It felt like if he just concentrated hard enough, he'd get it.

What was he not seeing?

He strongly suspected Laura was onto something with her theory about two possible murderers.

He just couldn't join up the pieces.

He looked away from the screen, out at the clear blue sky.

For a few seconds, he allowed his brain to rest completely.

Lola didn't want to give up her baby.

Somebody wanted her baby.

Viggo had taken her baby.

Lola had fought to keep it.

She'd been killed.

Then Matteo was killed.

Lola, Viggo, Matteo, Cowell.

What was it?

Was there another layer?

Or was it even simpler?

And then he realised.

'Oh, shit,' he said.

Laura and Brian stared at him.

'Shit, shit, shit.'

'What is it?' Laura said.

'Look.'

Tom turned the screen around to show Laura the CCTV footage, frozen where they'd caught Nina on camera heading to Shipping Row last Friday.

'I know,' she said. 'What am I missing?'

'No, look,' Tom said. 'What do you see?'

It took a moment.

And then she got it.

'No,' she said.

'Yes,' Tom said.

'I don't get it.' Brian was completely lost.

'And she would have had a pay-as-you-go, too,' Tom said.

'What will we do?' Laura asked, her eyes on Tom.

'Is Alicja at the airport?' he asked.

Laura nodded.

Tom considered for a moment.

There was an obvious way of doing this. If they could pull it off.

'Okay,' he said. 'I think I have a plan. Natasha, are you still there?'

CHAPTER 55

The food in the shelter was so much better than the hospital fare.

The woman who served Tyanna told her she could take it to her room but Tyanna was enjoying sitting in the company of the other girls, even though she wasn't ready to talk to any of them.

She'd felt a little bereft when Natasha left. Natasha had become a friendly face, and here Tyanna knew nobody.

But she sensed that they were nice people and, if it was even possible, Tyanna thought she might actually feel safe here.

When she asked the woman at the desk if it was okay to go outside and have a cigarette, the woman had told her to stay in the shelter's garden.

Tyanna didn't usually smoke, but she needed to do something on her own, something to calm her nerves, and one of the other girls had offered her a cigarette not long after she'd arrived.

She shivered a little in the garden, despite the warm breeze and the sun shining brightly overhead. She'd been indoors for the past week and just being outdoors felt strange.

It felt liberating. Like she could go anywhere.

But where could she go?

Tyanna wondered if she would ever return to Russia.

What was there for her?

Nothing.

But were her siblings safe, now that she had disappeared?

Tyanna couldn't think about that now. She needed some time to recover from what had happened to her. From what she'd witnessed.

A car rolled past the multicoloured railings on the far side of the garden, just slowly enough that Tyanna noticed it.

It stood out because the housing estate the garden faced onto was deathly quiet.

She stiffened, and watched as it crawled past.

An elderly woman was in the driver's seat, phone to her ear.

She didn't look at Tyanna.

Tyanna realised that the woman was just driving cautiously because she was on the phone, probably ringing whoever she was visiting to ask for their house number.

She dropped the cigarette on the ground and stubbed it out.

Then, because the garden was so pretty, she leaned down and picked it up with the tips of her still-tender fingers.

'I'll take that for you.'

Tyanna jumped, but it was only Ashanti, the girl Natasha had introduced her to, the one who'd given her the cigarette.

'You have a visitor,' Ashanti said.

If it had been Natasha, Ashanti would have said. It must be one of the other two, the man or the woman.

'Where?' Tyanna sighed. She was tired of talking to the police. She just wanted it all to be over. She wanted them to leave her alone.

'Inside. I'll show you.'

Ashanti led Tyanna back indoors, pausing to toss the cigarette butt in a bin by the door.

When they arrived at the lounge, Ashanti held the door open for her but didn't follow her in.

She smiled at her, though, sympathetically.

Maybe she'd seen the footage of her walking naked down the street.

Tyanna walked inside, ready for a new round of questions.

She didn't even see who it was until the door closed behind her.

'What are you doing here?' she asked, staring at Nina.

'You texted me and told me to come,' Nina snapped.

She was sitting on the couch. Tyanna could see she was angry. Her face was covered in the red blotches that Nina always got when her temper flared.

'What were you thinking?' she hissed at Tyanna. 'Telling the police everything? You think they'll protect you? Do you think they'll let you shack up here or help you go back to Russia after what we did? All you had to do was keep your bloody mouth shut.'

'Nina, I did not tell them everything.'

'It was us or him,' Nina cried, then lowered her voice.

'I know!'

'Well, what's your plan, then? Because I didn't come here to help you wrestle with your conscience. I'm trying to stay low. Come on, you said you knew what we should do. So, what?'

'I did not text you. I do not have my phone. The policewoman took it.'

Nina stared at her.

Tyanna stared back.

In the same instant, they both realised what had happened.

Nina jumped off the couch.

She opened the door to see the woman from the front desk

standing outside, blocking her exit. Behind her, Tyanna spotted the two detectives who had been questioning her, along with Natasha.

The girls backed into the room, as all three detectives and the woman from the desk came in.

'Nina, Tyanna, this is a colleague of ours, Detective Sergeant Jackie McCallion,' the man Tyanna knew as Tom said. 'And Nina, you haven't met Natasha McCarthy yet, our head of sexual crimes. Now, how about we all sit down and you tell us exactly what happened in Shipping Row last week.'

CHAPTER 56

Nina, to her credit, didn't try to protest her innocence.

She met Tom's eye as he sat across from her and did most of the talking.

Tyanna sat nervously beside her, biting her bottom lip, her hair hanging in her face.

'How did you know?' Nina said.

'There were a couple of things,' Tom said. 'First, it had been niggling at me that the fire started downstairs. Tyanna had said she was in her room at the time. The fire spread rapidly but she had very few burns. She should have been more severely injured, if she'd had to come downstairs and force her way through the flames.'

Tyanna's cheeks flushed as Tom spoke.

'Then, Tyanna told my colleague that she wasn't allowed to go anywhere without Matteo. It didn't make sense to us from the start that you, Nina, would have been sent out with a client. But when we spotted you on the CCTV with a bag on your back, it looked like you were returning to the house. We couldn't spot you on the CCTV leaving, though. You obviously walked in the opposite direction and then circled back on yourself, looking for a garage. But then it dawned on me. You had a huge bag on your back. But all you returned to your parents with was a small handbag. Where did the big bag go? And what was in it?

We realised then – it wasn't your belongings from being away for a few nights. You'd have kept them; you'd have brought that bag back to your parents' house. There was something else in that bag. It was the petrol to start the fire.'

Nina blinked, but she didn't even try to deny it.

'It was the way Matteo and Lola were killed, as well,' Laura said. 'The men we were looking at, they use guns, not knives. They don't stab their victims. Too much DNA when you stab somebody. You were clever, though, to start the fire. It destroyed most of it and obscured Matteo's injuries to the point that we couldn't identify if his wounds were different to Lola's.'

Nina nodded.

'I think I saw that on TV,' she said.

'But who killed Lola?' Laura said. 'Was it Viggo or you two?'

'Seriously?' Nina snapped, horrified. 'I wouldn't have harmed a hair on Lola's head. And it wasn't that Viggo shit. It was fucking Matteo.'

'Tell us what happened,' Tom said. 'You know there's no point in lying any longer, so tell us everything.'

'She wanted to keep her baby,' Tyanna whispered. 'Matteo held her back when Viggo took it away.'

Tyanna started to cry.

Nina stared at the floor.

'Matteo, he was good, most of the time,' Tyanna said. 'But when Viggo took the baby, Lola went crazy. She flew at him and they are having the fight and then he—' Tyanna raised her arm. 'She was like a mad woman. He picks up the knife in the kitchen and he stab her with it. We are screaming but he does not stop.'

'When was this, Tyanna?'

'On Thursday morning.'

'And then what happened?'

Tyanna's face paled.

'Matteo is very scared. He rings Viggo and Viggo is angry. I think Viggo says he has destroyed something valuable and asks him why and Matteo says he had to do it, that Lola was crazy.'

'He knew what he was doing,' Nina hissed. 'Lola wanted her baby back. Viggo said they had to hide the baby, that the baby's father hadn't wanted her to have it. But Lola wouldn't stop talking about the baby. She would never have stopped. She knew what would happen to that baby. She knew Viggo would sell it.'

Nina's breathing had quickened.

Tyanna still had that dead-eyed stare. She was blanking it all out, Tom realised. What these two girls had witnessed had been beyond what he could even conceive of.

'When he was finished, even though we were crying and sick, he made us clean up,' Nina said. 'There was so much blood. I've never seen so much blood.'

She looked away, over Tom's shoulder, out the window. Then she blinked back tears and swallowed. When she spoke again, it was quieter.

'Viggo phoned back. He was angry that Matteo had killed Lola and even angrier that we'd seen it. He told Matteo that they had no choice now, that they had to get rid of us before we told anybody what had happened.'

Tom frowned, but he said nothing, indicating instead that Nina should continue.

'We knew then that Matteo was going to kill us. Didn't we, Tyanna?' Nina looked at the other young woman.

Tyanna nodded.

'We knew it was us or him,' Nina said. 'So we . . . we waited until he was asleep, and then we – we did what we had to.'

'You stabbed him?' Tom said. 'On Thursday night?'

Nina nodded.

'On Friday, I went and got the petrol. We knew we had to burn the evidence. It was like you said. I couldn't find a garage but then I thought, I'd better walk far anyway because otherwise people would know I'd bought it. We poured it all over downstairs and then we ran. Didn't we?'

Another glance at Tyanna.

'But you went back in, Tyanna,' Tom said, his voice gentle but firm.

Tyanna looked up. She nodded, a little more strenuously this time.

'Why?' Tom asked.

'I ... I wanted to see if I could get Matteo's phone,' she said, but lowered her eyes. 'I thought if I could get his phone I could give it to you and then you could find out where Lola's baby was.'

'You could have told us, anyway,' Tom said. 'Why did you really go back in?'

Tyanna glanced at Nina.

'I had to make sure he was dead. We stabbed him but I needed to make sure. But I couldn't get up the stairs and my dress caught fire and I panicked. I pulled everything off and I started to run. I forgot my bag and my things. I didn't know what I was doing.'

'Why?'

Nina shifted nervously beside her. Tom kept his gaze locked on Tyanna.

'You wanted to save him,' he said. 'Why? After what he'd done to Lola? After what he planned to do to you?'

'I ...'

Tom felt it, the invisible pull of Nina. Tyanna was desperately trying not to turn and look at the other girl.

'I do not know why I went back in,' she said. Then her shoulders slumped.

Tom sighed.

'Is it because you weren't convinced Matteo was going to kill you and Nina?' he said.

'He was!' Nina interrupted.

Tom held his hand up.

'Did you think he regretted killing Lola, Tyanna?'

'He didn't care about us!' Nina shouted.

Tom looked at her.

'It strikes me as odd, Nina, that Viggo would get so angry at Matteo for killing one of his assets and yet he then told him to kill you and Tyanna. How did you even hear that side of the phone call? Because it seems far more likely to me that you two girls would have just been moved. The gang Viggo was involved with has houses all over England. You could have been sent there.'

Tom looked back to Tyanna.

'Did you hear Viggo tell Matteo to kill you?'

Tyanna shook her head.

'Who told you he'd said that?'

Tyanna turned and looked at Nina.

Nina's face filled with panic.

'I just wanted to protect us,' she said. 'You were there, Ty. You saw what Matteo did. He stabbed Lola to death.'

'It was wrong,' Tyanna whispered. 'It was wrong what he did. But he did not mean to do it. Lola was trying to kill him. You remember, he'd even told her to get rid of the baby. Early on, he said. He said he'd help her. She knew what would happen if she kept it. And Matteo was good to me. He was better to me than my boyfriend.'

'He forced you to stay there!'

'But it wasn't as bad as before.'

'Jesus, you're an idiot.'

'It was okay for us to defend ourselves,' Tyanna continued. 'But only if our lives were at risk. Were they, Nina? Tell me.'

She stared at Nina.

Nina broke first.

She looked at the floor.

'We were defending ourselves,' she said. 'Matteo or one of them would have killed us eventually. They would have. And I didn't want to live that life any more. It was enough. I'm sorry, Tyanna. I did it for both of us. I just wanted to get away.'

Tyanna stared at Nina, aghast.

Then she brought her bandaged hand to cover her mouth as she started to cry.

CHAPTER 57

Laura had brought the two young women to the station to take official statements.

Before she left, she approached Tom.

'I should have figured it out,' she said. There was real doubt in her eyes – the fact that Tom had managed to spot what she hadn't.

Tom shook his head.

'You realised who Viggo's wife was. You found that baby before something bad happened to it. It's teamwork, Laura, it always is. You realised that during the Sleeping Beauties case. You got to that killer before any of us but we'd all pulled in the same direction. If another member of your team guesses at something quicker than you, that shouldn't mean you start to doubt your own abilities.'

Laura nodded, a little uncertainly, but Tom knew she'd taken it on board.

Natasha McCarthy drove him home.

They sat at the lights in silence, reflecting on what they'd heard.

'What will the charges be?' Natasha asked, eventually.

'You tell me,' Tom said. 'Laura will have to decide. They've both admitted to stabbing Matteo. Two stabs each. Though, in Tyanna's case, she thought she was acting in self-defence. And while Nina might have been more cunning – she definitely needed Tyanna's help, in case Matteo woke up and fought back – we can hardly argue with the fact both girls were being held captive against their will. There's no happy ending here, for them or for us. What do you advise?'

'I'd advise the DPP to go as easy as possible and I'd definitely recommend psychiatric care for them both. You can't put either of them into the general prison population. Not after what they've been through.'

'Nina was abused when she was a kid,' Tom said. 'I'm sure of it. And Tyanna didn't have it easy, either.'

'Of course not,' Natasha said. She sighed heavily. 'I wonder what I'd do in that situation, Tom. I'd like to think I'd bloody well fight back, that I'd stab and shoot and do anything in my power to defend myself and get away.'

'I'd like to think I'd do the same,' Tom said. 'If Nina had gone and done it all on her own, we would be having a different conversation. Where she's concerned, it's roping Tyanna into it that's problematic. Not only did she need her help, but she was obviously worried that Tyanna would spill the beans unless she thought she was keeping her own secret, too. And even then, sending her those texts – that was intended to remind Tyanna to keep her mouth shut. It's calculated.'

They pulled up outside his house.

'Thanks for all your help with this, Natasha,' he said, unclasping his seatbelt. 'You know, whatever debt you think you owe me is well repaid at this stage.'

Natasha smiled.

'Yeah, I think the tables have turned a little,' she said.

'How so?'

'Joe Kennedy has been dumped on me.'

'Ah,' Tom said. 'That Bronwyn. She's a hoot, isn't she?'

'Absolutely hilarious. Sex crimes. He's in for an interesting few years.'

'Not as interesting as you're in for,' Tom said.

Louise was watching the news when Tom arrived in.

She smiled at him and let her legs fall on to the floor so he could sit beside her.

'All done?' she asked.

'More or less,' he said. 'I've handed over the messy bit.'

'Tom.' Her voice grew serious. 'What's going to happen to that baby?'

Tom smiled, thinking of the pictures Laura had shown him. They'd told people they trusted that the baby had been found, but they didn't make a huge announcement of it. Just to be on the safe side.

'She's going to be fine. Absolutely fine.'

'Oh, thank God for that. I couldn't bear thinking of anything more happening to the poor child. What's your plan for tomorrow?'

'Well, the question is, what's your plan?'

'Nothing, actually. I have to do some grocery shopping and I thought maybe we could go for a drive or something afterwards?'

'I've one better,' Tom said.

He took out his phone and pulled up the confirmation email he'd been sent in the car.

The past week had been so traumatic, Tom needed this as much as his wife.

He showed her the email from the airline.

She looked at him.

'Tom Reynolds, this isn't another stunt, is it? I don't fancy walking around Paris on my own for five days while you sit in with the Sûreté, or whoever else you're going over there to hang out with.'

'No work, just five days of summer holidays,' he said. 'The flights were last minute so I haven't got a hotel yet, but I reckon we'll find some deal or other. It'll cost a bomb this time of year but, hey, the department paid for Newcastle.'

Louise laughed.

'You are a clever, clever husband,' she said.

She jumped off the couch.

'Where are you going?' Tom said. 'I thought you'd be thanking me all night long.'

'Tom, I haven't even emptied the suitcases from Newcastle yet. I'm going to put a wash on and then I'm going to cut the labels off my new clothes and get them ready for packing.'

Tom smiled.

'You can thank me tomorrow night, then,' he said.

'If we're not sleeping on a park bench,' she countered.

He laughed.

On the television, a news bulletin flashed an image of the charred house on Shipping Row.

The strapline read that two suspects had been arrested in connection with the case.

It was Laura's biggest solve to date.

And even if she had her inner doubts, she had led the investigation and she'd overseen the case being solved.

Tom had made the right decision promoting her. He could rest easy with the squad in her hands.

He just needed to learn how to let go.

CHAPTER 58
Saturday

Chief Superintendent Reynolds called around to the Cusacks' house early that morning and explained what had happened. He told them he was due to fly out that afternoon but had wanted to tell them in person how they'd found Nina and why she'd done what she'd done.

John had listened wordlessly.

Orla had taken it stoically.

John knew she was overwhelmed with relief, just knowing that their daughter was alive and well, but eventually it would all sink in.

John, if he was honest, was in shock.

They were sitting in the reception of the police station now, waiting to see their daughter.

It wasn't that Nina had fought her way out of the situation she'd been trapped in that had distressed John the most.

It was what Tom Reynolds had told him before he'd left that had hit him hardest.

John had walked Tom out to his car, listening to the man make small talk about Paris and the trip he was heading off on.

Just at the gate, Tom had turned and looked up at the neighbour's house.

'Nina hasn't said this to me,' he said. 'But her solicitor informed us. She's working with your daughter to build a decent defence case, which in all likelihood will result in a plea of diminished responsibility. As part of that, Nina has told her solicitor that she was abused by somebody when she was younger.'

John had flinched, but Tom placed his hand on his arm.

'She says it was a neighbour,' he said. 'I don't think you're the sort of man who just reacts, and that is the only reason I'm telling you, John. But I suggest you talk to your daughter and get her to tell you the truth. For her, and for you, to make sure there's justice. But also because it will help with her case, do you understand?'

John nodded dumbly.

He'd walked back inside without even a glance at Bob Laird's house, even though it nearly killed him.

There'd be time enough for that later.

And he'd said nothing to Orla, just held her hand silently all the way to the police station.

An officer arrived and the two of them were led to a small room, where Nina was sitting.

Orla grabbed her daughter and hugged her tightly.

John watched with a lump in his throat.

It was Nina's birthday today, not that this was the time to celebrate it.

Nina started to cry.

John walked around the table and put his arms around her.

Nina was stiff, unresponsive for a few seconds. Then she relaxed and let him embrace her.

When they sat down across from each other, ignoring the officer in the corner of the room, Orla held on to Nina's hands.

But it was John who had her attention.

'Nina,' he said. 'Tell me what Bob Laird did to you.'

Orla's head whipped around. She stared at her husband and then back at her daughter.

'What?' she said.

Nina's eyes were fixed on her father's. They were filling with tears.

'Don't be so stupid, John,' Orla said. 'What does Bob from next door have to do with any of this? All he's done is try to help us.'

'Nina,' John said gently, ignoring his wife. 'Tell me.'

Nina nodded.

'It started when I was thirteen,' she said.

John felt his wife crumple beside him.

CHAPTER 59

Joe Kennedy didn't usually drink during the day.

But he'd taken a week off work to get to grips with his punishment.

He'd start to think about how to deal with the mess on Monday, but today he just wanted to drown his sorrows.

Tomorrow, he'd visit his mother and have Sunday dinner. They'd reminisce about Joe's father, something his mother did more and more these days, now the dementia was setting in properly.

Joe knew his father was a great man, but the way his mother told it, he was a latter-day saint.

Perhaps if Joe was still married, he'd have been able to deal in a more proactive way with the shit that kept being flung at him at work.

Instead, he was left to mull on it alone and even Joe knew this probably wasn't entirely healthy.

When the press office stuff had come to light, Joe hadn't been happy. But he'd been man enough to accept that not all his leaks had been entirely professional.

In his defence, Tom Reynolds, after turning down the chief's job, had been under the impression that he could undermine Kennedy with impunity. Joe had tried to get on with him, but

Reynolds, damned egomaniac that he was, had disrespected Joe from the off.

And his handling of the Sleeping Beauties case had been disgraceful. During that, Reynolds had pulled in a fellow officer for questioning without so much as notifying a union rep. The officer had turned out to be innocent, too.

Reynolds had no respect for his colleagues, so what matter if Joe, over a pint, had let some of the details of that case slip out.

But he shouldn't have revealed Reynolds' home address. Kennedy could admit that. It wasn't his proudest moment.

The Cowell stuff was different. It was stupid.

Of course Joe had no intention whatsoever of turning a blind eye to Cowell's trafficking activities. It was just what he'd told him to extract information, and that information had been good.

Police did it all the time.

Kennedy had got a handle on Cowell when he'd been moved from the chief superintendent job into white-collar crime. Cowell's had been used as a sample case of criminals being nailed though tax evasion and money laundering in schemes sophisticated enough they could have been designed by top bankers.

Kennedy's interest had been piqued. Then he learned money was still flowing in the Cowell empire – just from a different source in a different direction – to his nephew.

Kennedy knew Cowell was smart enough to still be in charge and he also knew the gangster would be careful enough to avoid getting caught this time.

It didn't take long to reach the conclusion that trafficking was the new A game for gangs. It was a safer bet than drugs and generated more income.

It was Cowell's new business and also the Achilles heel that Kennedy could use to target him.

It wasn't lost on Kennedy what Bronwyn Maher was trying to teach him by exiling him to sex crimes – like Joe had some blind spot when it came to women being harmed.

Well, he would show her. He'd be the best bloody detective in that department.

He'd end up running it one day.

Because there was no way he was taking any more sideways demotions.

Kennedy finished his drink and stood up.

He'd had three whiskeys; he'd better stop there if he wanted to drive home.

The fresh air outside helped to sober him up a little bit.

Joe didn't know how, but he had a feeling that Tom Reynolds had played some part in Bronwyn Maher finding out about the deal that had been struck with Cowell.

He knew that Tom's former lackey, Ray Lennon, had been in to see Cowell. Maybe Cowell had double-crossed Joe and told Ray, who had fed it back to God Almighty.

Either way, Joe just knew Reynolds was involved.

And he also knew that the first chance he was presented with, when he knew Tom wasn't expecting it and he could get away with it, he'd serve Reynolds up his own arse.

Joe was as sure of it as he was sure that he wasn't going to be caught out again.

He'd wait in the long grass for as long as necessary.

He pulled out his car keys.

Joe didn't see the motorbike that had pulled on to the road.

He didn't hear it, as he stepped out onto the pavement.

He didn't notice it slow as he opened the driver's door.

But he did hear the voice when the teenager on the back of the bike raised his visor and shouted: 'BLT says hello!'

The shot was straight to the side of the head.

It blew Joe Kennedy's glasses off, along with the left part of his cranium, and sent him flying into the driver's side of the car, half his body still hanging out onto the road.

The teenager jumped off the back of the bike, fired two more shots into the already dead detective's chest, then jumped back on.

It sped off.

There were no CCTV cameras on the road.

No witnesses.

Nobody to see Kennedy's blood form a small puddle on the tarmac and a larger one on the driver's seat of his own car.

Joe Kennedy died alone on a bright summer's day.

ACKNOWLEDGEMENTS

As always, thank you to my fantastic team at Quercus – Stef, Rachel, Milly, Hannah, David, Bethan, Jon and Cassie for unending support and generally just being the best. Also, three cheers for the cover design team for these phenomenal jackets and for my copy-editor Sharona, for being the repository of all things Tom Reynolds.

Thank you Nicola Barr, agent and friend.

A huge dept of gratitude to the German Jo (you know who you are) for reading and giving me the best guidance and critical direction.

Martin Spain, who makes my English ... eh, English. I wouldn't swap you for any other editor. I mean husband, obviously, husband.

Thank you Izzy for reading over my shoulder and enjoying; and Liam, Sophia and Dominic for wanting to read mammy's books but being too young. Soon, I promise. You'd better like them, too.

Thank you to all my family and friends who will make sure this sells, oooh, at least twenty-odd copies. At least! And thank you to the lovely reviewers, bloggers, booksellers and readers who have championed Tom Reynolds from DCI to Chief Superintendent. He might be about to have a little sabbatical, but I've no doubt he'll be back!

And finally – this book is dedicated to the memory of a dear friend, recently departed and who I know would have loved the contemporary backdrop. You're sorely missed, Larry.

If I could have had two more dedications, however, I would have also mentioned Liam and Grace Doyle. The warrior and the princess, remembered every day.

All my love to their mammy Nina.

Read on for an exclusive extract
from Jo Spain's thrilling new novel,
The Perfect Lie

THE
PERFECT
LIE

Erin

THEN

JULY 2019

The day your life changes can begin in the most ordinary way.

Danny's arm is draped across my body and I wake to the feel of him stirring.

His hand cups my face. I sense he's actually been awake a while; that he might, in fact, have been watching me.

'You had a nightmare,' he says.

I crawl into the space of his body and inhale him.

I had a nightmare, again.

I never have to pretend with Danny.

My husband knows my history, all the things that haunt me.

The bad dreams are frequent, even after all this time. The feeling of being suffocated, of screaming but no sound coming out. The feeling that there's nobody there to help.

Danny, too, has seen evil. I guess it's what drew me to him.

My parents might struggle to forgive me for emigrating to this side of the pond but I made a decent dent in hostilities when I married a cop.

Danny kisses away the residue of the dream and then we make love, slowly, at his insistence.

He's intense, quiet; there's meaning in all his movements and his eyes never leave mine. Danny's had a lot on his mind recently. Work, long hours, late nights. There's ongoing trouble in his job but we don't talk about it. Our promise to each other is to keep his work and our home life separate. But I've barely seen him these last few weeks and last night we exchanged only a few words. I guess both of us are due a reminder that it's us against the world, even if the world keeps intruding.

When we're done, he rests up on one arm and tickles my nose with his. His forehead is damp; his eyelashes long enough to make any woman jealous.

I laugh – a giddy release.

'Hey!' he says.

'I'm laughing with you, not at you, Detective,' I say.

'Mm-hm. How do you want your eggs?' He jumps up, an athlete's recovery time, asking for my breakfast order but, I can tell, already distracted by the day ahead.

'From a chicken,' I say.

'Duck, you sucker,' he shoots back. Then, hesitantly, 'Sorry.'

'For not giving me an orgasm?'

He smiles, but his eyes don't play ball. Danny is drowning. He needs time off; I know he does.

'For having to leave you,' he says. 'I love you.'

'The bed's not the same without you, but I'll forgive you if you get the coffee going.'

Danny heads for the kitchen and I lie there, listening to him tinkering with the temperamental coffee pot, then padding towards the bathroom down the hall. I hear the sound of the shower being turned on. It needs a full three minutes before it reaches any temperature above freezing.

The bedroom is already awash with sunlight, even though it's barely 7 a.m. I ordered the drapes online and their blackout ability was oversold. It bothers Danny more than me; he's a light, restless sleeper. I love waking to sun, I love waking to rain. Let it all in. Be happy to be alive.

It feels like a good day. Hell, I might go on that run I keep threatening. On the beach, before the tourists hit. Then I'll read through some manuscript submissions and check in with the office – the joy of working from home and making my own hours. When we first moved here, I commuted daily to the city and the publishing house I work for. Three hours a day on a train to and from paradise. I'd planned to go freelance but my boss offered option C and I've never looked back.

I force myself to sit up and search the floor for clothing, find Danny's T-shirt and a pair of leggings.

In the large, open-plan area that comprises the main living space of our top-floor apartment in Newport, Suffolk County, I'm faced with the detritus of last night's takeout. White cartons and plates congealed with chow mein and egg fried rice. I glance at the sink, already overflowing with crockery, and then at our faulty dishwasher and sigh.

Part of the lease's selling point was all mod cons included.

I turn the dial on our old-fashioned radio to listen to the local morning news programme, then make a start.

What our apartment lacks in efficiency, it makes up for in location. Our pretty white-painted building, with its black Georgian-esque ornamental window shutters, has an unimpeded view of Bellport Bay, right over to Fire Island. We're a minute's walk from the beach, its miles of grassy dunes and white sand; two minutes away from McNally's, our regular bar; and we've a host of restaurants and stores at our disposal.

This town is a picture-perfect diorama of a Long Island seaside port and our apartment is slap bang in the middle of it.

I open the floor-to-ceiling French windows to admit some of the already hot summer's day and let the salty sea air hit my lungs.

The news programme is hosting a panel discussion and I listen as a contributor, who's also running for office, gets stuck into Newport PD. They discuss the latest hot controversy – the failure of the local PD to deal with an increase in drug dealing, a problem that's spilled over from Nassau County. The locals in these parts get quite agitated about tourism-impacting headlines and this issue is definitely a vote-getter. Another of the panellists is shrieking about ineptitude and corruption in law enforcement when I turn off the radio.

Danny works in homicide, not drugs, so the latest furore doesn't have direct relevance for him. But attacks such as these put a dent in the morale of every police department. It's hard enough doing an often thankless, frequently dangerous job on low pay without enduring unfounded and ignorant accusations about competence.

I've done a decent surface clean by the time the coffee is in the cups and the shower has stopped running. I wonder if I can talk

Danny out of a quick scrambled eggs and into stopping by the new diner on Maple Street before he leaves for work. We can discuss the long-awaited weekend we have planned. Danny has vowed to take next Saturday through Monday off. We're going to drive up to Hartford, stay somewhere quaint, eat and drink our way through New England.

And then: a cop's knock on the door. Quelle surprise.

They have a special sound, those fists the police learn to make.

I mutter under my breath. It's not even 7.15 on a Tuesday morning and already Danny's being summoned for work. Bang goes the dream of us sharing pancakes.

Another rap on the door, seconds after the first.

Fuckity fuck, I'm coming.

I can hand over my detective husband for the rest of the week, I remind myself, because then he's all mine for a good seventy-two hours.

I ignore my inner warning system, reminding me of all the other times in the last two years when I forgot I was with a cop and made plans.

I open the door and see Ben Mitchell, Danny's partner, standing there.

Danny told me that when they were first paired, back in homicide in Manhattan, the boys on the force used to hum 'Ebony and Ivory' every time the two of them entered the office together. Ben's blond and his skin is practically translucent. Danny is as black as night. There wasn't a whole lot of woke thinking behind that one.

The two men work well together, but Ben and I don't. I got the sense, early, that he didn't like me. I think it's down to the fact that Danny used to follow Ben around like a little puppy. In fact, Ben's the reason Danny works and lives in Suffolk County. Then I came along and inserted myself in the middle of the bromance.

There are two other uniformed officers in our hallway and Ben has a look on his face that tells me, for the love of all that is holy, something big has happened and the forthcoming weekend is now a non-runner.

I never learn.

Behind me, Danny enters the living space and I know he's seen Ben's face too. He's probably already planning how to make it up to me.

'Erin,' Ben says, his voice grave, 'I'm afraid I have bad news.'

The day your life changes can begin in the most ordinary way.

I've experienced it once before. Just like this, the knock on the door.

I wait for it, my stomach tight, the battle response of a war-weary soldier.

Who's dead?

Ben's expression changes – his attention is drawn over my shoulder, to Danny.

I turn, thinking Danny has caught Ben's tone, recognises it, and is probably readying himself to comfort me. I might be far from my family, but he'll get me to them, ASAP. He'll take care of everything.

But Danny's not looking at me.

He's staring at Ben, utter defeat on his face.

Then my husband walks to the French windows and out on to the small balcony.

I watch him, confused.

He turns, I catch his eye.

Danny doesn't look like Danny at all.

His expression is indescribable. A mixture of pain and apology. He opens his mouth as if to say something, but instead, just swallows. He looks away, like just the sight of me is causing him pain.

He lifts one leg over the balcony.

What the fuck are you doing, I think, but am too confused to say.

Then he raises the other leg so he's sitting on the iron grille.

He uses his hands to push himself off.

He's gone.

Sudden movement at the door as Ben and the others rush into our apartment.

I'm paralysed.

Four floors down, there's a thud.

That's my husband's body.

It's all over in seconds.

Erin

NOW

DECEMBER 2020

Somebody has tried to make the bowels of Suffolk County Court seasonal. A mini Christmas tree looped with cheap tinsel scents the guards' office with pine and a small portable radio is dialled to a station that's playing festive tunes on loop.

Feliz Navidad.

It's incongruously cheery.

I think of Christmas three years ago, the first in our then new apartment. Danny and I had only been married a couple of weeks. I'd picked up a plug-in, artificial, cheap white tree in a thrift store, just to tick a box. I wasn't a fan of the season. I'd fallen out of love with it back in Ireland, right about the time the world had reminded me there's no Santa Claus, no magic, no innocence at all.

Danny, though, was the Christmas fairy incarnate. Six feet of rugged hunk who liked nothing more than watching *Home Alone* while munching on candy canes.

I heard him before I saw him, outside our front door, struggling to get his key in the lock, cursing as he tried to turn it just the right way, jiggling and pushing it at the same time. That door, he was fond of saying, expects you to whisper to it like a lover before it'll open up.

He'd dragged in a six-foot Fraser fir and laughed at the look of surprise mingled with horror on my face.

'We don't have enough decorations,' I'd said. 'And how the hell did you get that thing in the lift?'

'I took the stairs,' he'd replied.

Then he'd wrapped his arms around me.

'She'd want you to enjoy our first Christmas here,' he'd whispered in my ear.

That Christmas, Danny reminded me there was no guilt in living.

He made cinnamon toast, along with eggs, his expert culinary turn, and handed me a beautifully wrapped box. He'd bought me a green cashmere scarf from Barney's, one that would suit my black hair and emerald eyes perfectly. By eleven, we'd had a whole bottle of champagne. Lunch in McNally's with its owner and our friend, Bud, an experience made edible by our inebriation. A heady mix of seasonal cocktails back in the apartment, then some fooling around on the rug beneath the Fraser, during which we discovered exactly what people mean when they say those pine needles get everywhere.

All happy memories.

They make me wince.

Karla arrives and sits down beside me, a billow of ridiculously shiny black hair and expensive material she wouldn't usually wear, smelling of red apples and cold air.

'The blouse looks good on you,' she says, teasing a button closed and tucking my hair behind my ear. Convent girl; that's the look she's going for. She visited yesterday to drop off a new outfit, told me to scrub up so I look like I actually give a fuck about living. She also tried to press a holy medal into my hand but I refused to take it. She can pray to the God she believes in. I'm trusting to the justice system. I'm not sure which one of us is more deluded.

When I first walked into Karla Delgado's office in Patchogue, I had no idea how things would end up. But, within an hour of meeting her, I knew that if I was ever in a corner she was somebody I'd want on my side. At thirty-five, she's only three years older than I, but she's the person I've come to depend on.

I can't lean on my family.

They expect what we got before.

Justice.

They don't understand what it's like over here. They don't understand how flawed the system is.

'Are you ready?' Karla asks.

'No,' I answer, honestly.

She watches me for a moment, knows that I'll stand and walk into court when I'm told.

I've been saying no for the last seventeen months while still putting one foot in front of the other.

She leaves, tells me she'll see me in there.

When I enter the courtroom, I'm taken aback by its size.

It's small – tiny – with wood panelling on the walls, church-like pews, a witness box, the judge's bench, the defence and prosecution tables.

Out of the corner of my eye, I spot some of Danny's former colleagues to the rear of the court. I recognise them, even in civvies. Colleagues and friends, allegedly.

One of them glances in my direction and the others follow his gaze.

The look on their faces.

I turn my head away, heat in my cheeks.

Everybody here wants the truth.

Not all of us agree on what that means.

There's a flutter of activity.

The sheriff appears, announcing Judge James C. Palmer. A native of Sag Harbor, Karla tells me. Yale law and renowned prosecutor in his day. Experienced, conservative, but fair.

Karla crooks her arm under mine to help me stand.

It's time.

I'm about to be tried for murdering my husband.